Born and bred in Yo  of *Ravenswyke, The Homeward Hae, The Years of Change* as well as *Kibbutz, The Long Day's Dying* and *The Long Summer.*

By the same author

Ravenswyke
The Homeward Tide
Kibbutz
The Long Day's Dying
The Long Summer
The Years of Change

A. L. WHITE

The Vanishing Land

PANTHER
Granada Publishing

Panther Books
Granada Publishing Ltd
8 Grafton Street, London W1X 3LA

Published by Panther Books 1983
Reprinted 1983, 1985

First published in Great Britain by
Granada Publishing 1982

Copyright © A. L. White 1982

ISBN 0-583-13408-4

Printed and bound in Great Britain by
Collins, Glasgow

Set in Times

AUTHOR'S NOTE

In the years that have elapsed since the Industrial Revolution changed the lives of the people of Yorkshire, styles of dress, of manners, morals and speech have changed radically.

Since I am writing these volumes in order to give the present-day reader some knowledge of the lives of the people involved in my story, there will inevitably be problems of communication if I try to reconstruct the language and speech of the day or use names of common objects that no longer have m'eaning. I shall not, therefore, attempt to reproduce eighteenth-century rural speech other than by indication; nor shall I use outdated terms for everyday objects.

In this way, I hope there will be no barrier between the reader and an understanding of the stories I am trying to tell.

Book One

Despite his years, John Aysgill strode up the hill that ran alongside the common. He'd always favoured this time of day above all others, before the village had stirred into life, before the sun had risen above the tops of the trees which bordered the common land to the east. 'Nay, lass, come on,' he said, pulling gently on the plaited sisal with which he was leading the cow, with sheep, goat and bull-calf tied behind in a string, like pack mules. He took a fierce pride in turning his beasts onto the common before the others; the night dew freshened the grass though some said it brought the risk of belly-bloat. He knew from experience that belly-bloat comes only to beasts left empty; he always fed his a couple of handfuls of oats or corn before leading them from the byre; that way they had something in their insides to soak the moisture from the grass.

He turned the cow loose, the sheep and the goat, then stood there coiling the ropes in his hand. The goat went springing away, as usual, released from its tether, freed after a night in the byre. The sheep moved quickly away, the cow stayed placidly where she was, mooing lustily, opening her lungs to the cold morning air. 'Don't tell me th'art in love again,' John Aysgill chuckled. The cow had been well covered by Sam Weighton's bull but she'd take a week or two to settle down in her pregnancy.

John looked out over the village from the knoll, seeing sights familiar to him all his life, feeling a strong sense of order in all God's works. He caught the flash of a rabbit moving across the common, heading for the acorns in the woods; he heard the morning cackle of pheasants in the chestnut stake coverts, the whirr of plovers, the quiet murmur of bedded grouse in the long grass before the tree line began. Doubtless, Lord Barthwick would give them two days to set traps, to shoot their arrows, to provide meat for the table. A liberal squire, he always permitted the villagers a couple of days during which they could take anything they might catch, except for the pheasants. They would still be able to take pheasants if that greedy devil Sam hadn't disobeyed the unspoken rule of not culling hens. He watched the smoke from his own chimney curling upwards in the still air, elevated by its own heat. One of the lasses, Gertrude most likely, would have lit the sticks to start the breakfast pot on its way. Lie-a-bed Dodie would be curled up still, awaiting Gertrude's warning that their father was coming back. The three lads, as was their right, would stay sleeping until he called them out for work. One by one he watched the cottage chimneys begin to smoke, saw the first figures come from the cottages to urinate in the yards. He turned his head and saw the big chimney on the Manor start to smoke and steam; Polly had told him how his Lordship liked a big fire to come down to these days and needed a couple of pots of mulled ale before he came properly alive.

'Aye,' John thought, 'it would be a fair treat to start your days with a pot of spiced ale!'

There was no envy in his thought; more than any other man in the village he was happy in the rightful order of things, content with his strips of land, the few beasts he could graze on the common, his family of five. Of course he missed his wife, dead many a year, and by rights should have taken somebody in to mother his bairns but he couldn't be bothered putting himself about to accommodate another in his bed. He counted himself lucky to have survived in fitness and health to his eightieth year; few men achieved that many, and never a woman. He knew his years gave him a stature in the village – even Lord Barthwick himself always spoke civilly to John Aysgill and referred to his opinion on matters that concerned the demesne.

10

Aye, he was John Aysgill of Barthwick, right enough.

The thought pleased him as he set off down the slope, heading back to his cottage, the rope clutched in his hand, his step firm, his eyes clear, his senses alert to what another day would bring.

Lord Barthwick sat firmly in the centre of the seat of his coach with his knees spread despite the obvious discomfort of his wife and daughter on the padded bench opposite, forced to crouch in the corners by his girth, by the thickness of his knees in the heavy satin of his laced suit.

'You've both cost me a pretty penny this day,' he growled fiercely at them. 'I can only pray it will all be of some avail.' His face softened a little as he looked at them. Certainly they'd make as fine a pair of ladies as any at the ball that night and he could take an enormous pride in them. But his look was grim as he remembered. Flanders lace for heads and ruffs at thirty-nine pounds – damask for eighteen pounds – cambric for heads and ruffles for eight pounds – what the devil was the world coming to when the gentry had to ape the fashions of the folk of London, when a simple squire could no longer dress himself as he pleased for fear of being thought fusty, old-fashioned, out of touch.

Who could have thought, forty years ago at the turn of the eighteenth century, when he inherited the title from his father, that he'd be riding in his coach dressed like some Court fancy, with his pink satin suit, his silver-buckled leather shoes, his head covered by a powdered flaxen periwig which already was beginning to itch like the very devil. Once he'd safely deposited the ladies, he and a few like-minded cronies would go down into the gun-room, sit and yarn with their wigs off and their feet up over a pot of ale. They had much to yarn about: 1740 was turning out to be a most curious year with many strange new ideas abroad. Though George II seemed more in touch with the English than his father, George I, had been, seeds of discord were still being sown in the Government; and the effects of the uncertainty in the capital were being felt throughout the land, even, let it be said, up here in Yorkshire.

He glanced idly through the square apertures of the coach side, seeing his land rolling by. The Barthwicks had been Lords of the Manor for four hundred years – absolute rulers of this terrain, everything and everybody that moved upon it. He loved the swell of the folds of the hills, the rolling heather, the plentiful trees. The day was comfortably cool for September and the rain of two days ago had laid the dust of the track. It was a day to be on horseback, not dressed like some Court jester on his way to a ball in Stonebridge Castle, twenty miles away. Stonebridge was his nearest neighbour, a simple country man like himself. His son and heir, Rupert, was thirty, had sown his wild oats in York and London, and now was ready to be settled into matrimony. Stonebridge and Barthwick had mentioned it years before – it would be logical to unite the two estates into one very substantial fief.

Barthwick glanced at his wife. Too damned bad she hadn't given *him* a son, when the Stonebridge girl would have been carted over to Barthwick Manor instead of the other way around; the barony would have been vested in the Barthwick instead of the Stonebridge line, and he could have spent this night free from care, in his slippers by his fire with a pot of mulled claret by his side and Ellie to minister to his carnal requirements.

'Rupert is catching himself a fine prize this night,' he said softly, turning back to look into the coach's tapestry-covered interior. Clarissa blushed modestly as he tapped her knee affectionately. 'Mind you care for him,' he said. 'He's a good lad and needs only the steadying hand of a woman. You must learn to tweak the reins, not pull them the way you saw the mouth of yon stallion I gave you.'

'Clarissa knows her duties and responsibilities,' Lady Barthwick said primly. 'She has not lacked instruction.'

'I'm not speaking of the bedchamber, ma'am,' he said

curtly. 'The lad's a taste for the tables he picked up along with a few other bad London habits. It'll be a hard task for Clarissa to wean him from them.'

Clarissa's face coloured again and she lowered her eyes modestly. 'I'll do my best, Father,' she said quietly.

'Aye, that's all we can expect,' he said abruptly, ending the conversation.

They had reached the edge of Barthwick Forest, and he could never ride beneath the shelter of the great trees without a feeling of composure settling upon him like a comfortable old nightgown. As they rode along through the vaulted gloom of the forest track his eyes were everywhere. He saw the nests of the grouse in the undergrowth, the fresh cut of the axe where they'd felled the great oak the previous week, the stacked cordage he'd give to the villagers at Michaelmas as a token of his benevolence. The great trunk would be seasoned for a year or two before being dragged to the pit for sawing into beams. The beams would be stacked and wedged, left a further twenty years to mature. Happen Clarissa's first-born would be a grown man before that oak took its place among the beams of Barthwick Manor.

'Stop the coach, Simms,' he suddenly roared, banging on the underside of the roof. The coach halted as Simms reined in the four horses.

Tonkin and Pearce, the footmen, leaped from their stands and one of them flung open the door while the other placed the matting-covered box ready for his Lordship's feet. Lord Barthwick stepped down and, disregarding the moist loam of the forest which clung to his fine shoes, he hurried across the glade to where the freshly cut stakes of a chestnut clump showed bare.

'Who the devil has been here?' he roared in anger. It would be safe to say that Lord Barthwick knew every tree in his forest, every clump of hazel and chestnut.

'I do not know, your Lordship,' Tonkin, the senior footman, said hurriedly.

'Whoever it is,' Lord Barthwick roared, 'I'll have his

13

head for this.' He examined the clump as if hoping to see some clue in the manner of the cutting. It was apparent that the axe used had lacked the sharp fine edge of a woodman's instrument since several of the chestnut stakes had been half torn from the clump and left in splinters.

He dusted the loam from the knee of his breeches and hurried back to the coach, fuming with anger. 'Drive on, Simms,' he said, once he was ensconced inside.

Neither of the ladies spoke since both knew to do so would precipitate another explosion of wrath. Lord Barthwick guarded his woodlands with a father's eye and would brook no interference with them. They both remembered Will Forsyth, who had been hanged for cutting a beech and his family dispossessed from their cottage which his Lordship, in his rage, had ordered burned to the ground.

They had proceeded only a few minutes through the wood when suddenly they heard the sound of horses' hooves approaching from the rear of the coach and from the side. They heard Simms' voice as he whipped up the horses; Tonkin's cry, 'Head down, My Lord – highwaymen.'

They saw the shadowy figures approaching through the trees, trying to cut them off.

'Highwaymen, by God,' Lord Barthwick shouted, reaching for the loaded piece that sat in the leather boot beside his seat. It was as long as a man's arm, with twin barrels and twin flintlocks. He capped both barrels of it, rested the swivel on the window ledge. 'Keep your heads down, my dears,' he called.

The women needed no telling since already they were cowering in their corners.

The horses were racing through the woods now, swerving wildly, pulling along the woodland track. Simms kept a tight rein on them, giving their heads just sufficient leather for the jerk of the gallop. The highwaymen were around the coach now but keeping their distance since they knew the two footmen would have loaded pieces apart from any that might be within the coach. They were jolting wildly now as they bounced over roots and large stones, tossing from side to side in the wildness of the gallop. The sunlight penetrated the overhead branches infrequently, dappling the leering faces of the highwaymen in half shadows that added to the terror of the two ladies.

Lord Barthwick rested the piece on the seat beside him, took the other piece from its boot, and carefully loaded it with heavy ball and a full charge. He checked the fit of the flint, saw it was in good condition, then placed it on the seat between his wife and daughter. 'Cover that with your skirts,' he commanded and, terrified, they did so, trembling even more violently at the thought of its explosive potential.

The highwaymen came swiftly in, one to each side, and caught the snaffles of the lead horses, pulling back on their own reins to brake them. One footman – Lord Barthwick couldn't tell who – discharged his piece and the bang rang through the forest glade. All in the coach heard the savage yell, the scream, but couldn't know the other had been caught full in the chest by a cleaver as the coach slowly drew to a halt, the horses coughing and wheezing with the effort of the chase.

The face of one of the highwaymen appeared in the window and then the door was flung open.

'Greetings to you, Lord Bar'ick,' the highwayman said. 'Pleased to make your acquaintance.'

'Get from me, you blackguard,' Lord Barthwick said with a show of strength that only caused the highwayman to laugh.

'That I'd like to do, your Lordship,' the highwayman said, 'and will do, once I feel the weight of your ladies' jewels and your purse in my hand! I've a mind you'll be going to Stonebridge Castle where there'll be high festivities this night. A few jewels less, a few pieces of gold less to weigh down your belt, will do you no harm. And think of the story you'll have to tell, that you've been the temporary guests of Jack Overton this day. Now, if you'll

15

oblige me by getting out, for I know you have the custom of carrying your finery in a box beneath your seat.'

He moved back courteously to let the ladies descend, using the box the trembling footman had placed on the ground. Simms sat still with a knife at his throat. Lord Barthwick looked about him rapidly. The man at the door was not Jack Overton, by God. Overton was sitting his horse, a black stallion, a short distance away.

'Go stand by the heads of the horses,' Lord Barthwick commanded his womenfolk. He could see several of the men eyeing the women in an obvious manner and that made his blood colder, his mind sharper than ever. He went to descend from the coach, turning his back on the highwaymen. As he turned round and came upright, the piece was in his hand, the flint cocked, the barrel thrust forward. At that range, he couldn't miss.

'Stay where you are,' he bellowed, and the highwaymen, taken by surprise, did as he commanded.

'Quick, man,' he commanded Tonkin. 'The other pistol, on the seat.'

Tonkin reached in quickly and grabbed the piece over which Lady Barthwick had draped her cloak before she stepped from the coach, hiding it from view. Tonkin came out with it, holding it menacingly before him.

'Get off yon horse,' Lord Barthwick said.

Jack Overton did as he commanded.

Lord Barthwick didn't hesitate. 'All off your horses,' he bellowed.

The man who'd opened the coach door made the error of kicking in his heels. The horse he was sitting on reared. Lord Barthwick waited until its feet touched the ground again and then calmly shot its rider neatly through the head, his face exploding in a mass of blood and bone as the heavy shot charge took him.

The other men jumped quickly down and stood in a small knot. Four left, Barthwick noted. Pearce gone. Damned fools, discharging the pistol too soon.

'Come down here, Simms,' Lord Barthwick called, 'and

16

you ladies get back into the coach.' They climbed in quickly and closed the door behind them.

'Tie these rascals' hands, Simms, but keep out of the way of this charge.' Simms took thongs from the trunk of the coach and, circling warily behind the men, he tied the feet and wrists of each one brutally together.

When he had finished, Lord Barthwick went to the coach and took the whip from the shaft pouch. 'Right, Simms, take the ladies up the track a piece,' he said. The men with Jack Overton had dropped to their knees, their faces raised in supplication. He saw the one on the left, no more than a lad, was blubbering with fear. Jack Overton's eyes were glistening hate at him.

'You will be sorry for this day's work, Lord Bar'ick,' he said in his coarse local voice.

'You won't have time to be sorry,' Lord Barthwick said, testing the weight of the whip as he watched the coach jingle away up the track. 'You have time to say a prayer, to ask for a higher forgiveness than is mine to grant.'

The whip whistled among them and drew blood across one man's face at the first crack. It whistled again, and drew blood again. The men tried to shamble away but Simms had tied the thongs to each other and they tripped and fell.

Lord Barthwick worked efficiently and swiftly, cutting them about the face and shoulders, driving the thong of the whip through the coarse calico of their shirts, drawing blood with every stroke. Three of the men were crying and screeching with each cut – Overton said nothing, held his face closed against the onslaught, trying to stay on his feet, to keep his balance, to gather the last vestiges of dignity about himself amidst the howling terror of his cohorts. The whipping became a contest between him and the Lord Barthwick as to who would break first; when Lord Barthwick's arm tired and he threw the whip down, Jack Overton was still on his feet, though one of his eyes stared sightlessly and one ear had almost been severed from his head.

'I curse thee, Bar'ick,' he said. 'I curse thee for a dog and a cur, for a pox-raddled whore's whelp.' He sank to his knees, his bodily strength exhausted but his spirit still strong.

Barthwick snapped his fingers at Tonkin, who gave him the length of rope they'd taken from the coach trunk. He tied a loop expertly at one end and cast the other over a bough of the great beech beneath which they stood. He hung the loop round Jack Overton's neck, then seized the other end.

'Give me a hand, man,' he said to Tonkin, and together they heaved at the end of the rope, dragging Jack Overton upright, then heaving him until his feet were clear of the ground. When his feet swung clear, Lord Barthwick made the end of the rope fast around a nub on the tree trunk.

The other three men were huddled beneath Jack Overton, already dead.

'Leave them,' Lord Barthwick said. 'The vermin will clean them away for us.'

Without a backward look, he stalked away along the woodland path. Tonkin cast one glance behind him as he followed his master, seeing Jack Overton's feet swinging clear, his tongue already protruding from his mouth.

He shuddered, but knew better than to say anything.

John Aysgill walked slowly along the rutted track that led the short distance from the village to the fields where he could see his family already at work despite the earliness of the hour. The Aysgill family possessed three of the many strips contained by the barrows of earth, yard-high banks that separated one man's holdings from the next. Even Gertrude and Dodie had come to help with hoeing the young turnip crop, and he paused and watched them for a few moments, thinking, as he always did on such occasions, of the differences between them. Gertrude took after her dear departed mother, Emmeline, who had died in childbirth in 1720. Now twenty-three years of age, Gertrude was shy and retiring, with rarely a word to say for herself and no suitor among the young men of the village. Dodie, twenty-two, was like John himself in his youth, a quick, lively, interested and interesting person who had a nose for every mischief, for every possibility of adventure. Dodie had suitors in abundance but so far none in whose hands John would trust his daughter.

The morning was cold for September but the moisture in the air was welcome to the crops. He bent and, despite his near eighty years, scooped a handful of loam from beside the track. When he squeezed it into the great ball of his fist it held together like baked bread and he grunted in satisfaction. Simon, Matthew and Peter had finished clearing the potato haulms from their second strip and despite their protests Simon had yoked Matthew and Peter, as the two youngest, to the wooden shafts of the plough. John rested on his stick by the barrow mound, watching the lads at work. He saw that once again Simon had taken the easy task for himself, and was gripping the plough's handles while the other two strained to pull the wooden blade through the soil.

'Keep a straight furrow, lad,' John growled, seeing how slovenly Simon, as usual, was in the handling of a task. The lad was feckless, that was certain, and would need to learn more care and attention if he was to make his way in life. As John's heir he would one day own the three strips and would have the responsibility of looking after the others. The blade bit, turning the top four inches of soil below which the earth was hard and barren. The potato crop had helped to break it down and John knew the pulling would be easy. The hard time with the plough was in spring, when the frost lay heavy and clods were indistinguishable from stones. He glanced up at the sky; with luck they'd still get the onions in on this patch.

The third strip would lie fallow the next year after they'd gleaned the corn. Half of that crop would go to Lord Barthwick, of course, but they'd had a good year of catch crops and were well provided for the long winter ahead. It'd be a hard winter for Jenny Pearce, he thought, with her man killed in yesterday's outing with his Lordship, slain by the damned highwaymen who seemed to be everywhere these days. Nobody had asked Billy Fogg what *he'd* been doing in Lord Barthwick's forest, to see the coach halted, the highwayman flogged and hanged, Pearce killed with a blow from the cleaver that was the usual weapon of Jack Overton's men. They'd all gone out and carried the body of Pearce home on a withy trestle. Dodie had been late to bed from comforting the widow and her family of eight children. Now they'd be turned out of the cottage when Lord Barthwick took a new footman and would have to fend for themselves in Bradford or Leeds. Doubtless Pearce's widow and the other children would find some kind of employment there in the new mills that were being started, or in the coal mines.

'Put your weight on it, lad,' John called to Simon, who was letting the plough ride high, the lazy devil. 'Put your weight on it and dig it deeper.'

Matthew and Peter, drawing the plough, looked back at him and groaned. Damn it, he thought, a man needs to look out for everything these days.

He put down the leather bottle of water he'd brought, and the bag of oatcakes. 'When you've been to the far end and back you can break your fast.' he said. 'But not before!'

The girls had finished hoeing and walked along the top of the mound to flounce down on the earth beside him. 'It's grand to be out, Father,' Dodie said, 'instead of being cooped up back there with the spinning.'

'And how would we last the winter, missie, if I let you out here all the time?' he asked, though there was affection in his voice. Throughout the long winter's days and nights, the two girls spun the wool and wove the cloth the boys took into town to sell. Simon and Matthew wove wicker baskets for bottles, and hampers tied together with the hemp that John and Peter worked. Peter had proved best of all at selling their products – the lad had a head for figures better than any other in the family, John had to

20

own, better even than John himself. The lad could strike a bargain and stood in awe of no man, however high born, in his dealings. Many times John had been afraid that Peter was rising above his station in the way he spoke to his betters. He'd even given his father a blistering when John had let one gross of bottle' wandings go for eight shillings. Peter had said that if they'd held on, they could have demanded at least eight shillings and threepence and had then had the cheek to say that, if his father hadn't been with him, he could have asked nine shillings the gross, since he'd seen the wine merchant was eager to stay with the new fashion. John was worried about his youngest son, Peter. Now twenty, the lad had developed in strange ways, seeming to have none of the Aysgills' characteristics. They'd always been known as a close-knit family, taking their line from John, who'd tried to be affable, amiable, generous-hearted. He'd prided himself on the fact that no-one had ever been turned hungry from the door. Peter seemed to have none of this generosity of spirit and John had been astounded one day to hear him belabouring a vagrant who came to the cottage seeking a bite to eat.

The lads finished their ploughing and flopped down beside the girls, while John passed round the leather bottle and Gertrude dug into the bag for the oat-cakes, still warm from the hearth.

'That's a bad business with Pearce,' Matthew said slowly. At twenty-one he had become very thoughtful and withdrawn and often asked questions the more simple-minded John couldn't answer. Only the other night, he'd asked his father, why does the sun come up and go down, why does the moon change shape?

All his father could find to say was, that's the natural order of the heavens and the seasons, as much God's will as the natural order of sowing the seed and growing the plants.

'It's God's will,' John said.

'God might have thought about the widow and the children,' Matthew said. There was a shocked silence, then

21

Gertrude crossed herself.

'We'll have none of that heathen talk when we're eating,' John said sternly. 'And we'll have none of your Jacobite nonsense, missie.' Twice recently Gertrude had walked the four miles to the church where the new cleric, some said, had strange teachings to offer. The Aysgills had always been firmly Protestant and shared the general mistrust of Catholics and Jacobites; they worshipped each Sunday in the chapel of Barthwick Manor and left God to look after them for the remaining days of the week.

'We should think about her – perhaps we could send her on her way with something to tide her over . . .' Matthew insisted.

'Our hard-earned money,' Peter said instantly. 'Pearce ought to have put something by. It's not our fault he was improvident.'

'Happen we'll do something,' John said, more to provoke Peter than to suggest a real commitment. He saw the boy's face close in despair. 'Any road, we'll talk no more of that.'

They sat in silence, each preoccupied with his own thoughts as the day lengthened into morning and the sun started to burn off the light night haze. The odour of burning brushwood came to them from the smoking chimneys of the cottages of the village as fires were lighted to boil the pots of food for the midday meal. Dodie watched as Fanny Colborn came out of her cottage staggering under the weight of clothing in her wicker basket. Fanny had been left a widow a few years back, but when Lord Barthwick turned her out the villagers set to and built her a one-night cottage, taking advantage of the old law that said that any cottage built in a night, with a door and a roof, could be kept. The irony was that they'd built Fanny's cottage on the site of one that Lord Barthwick had ordered burned down when he'd caught a man poaching in his woods. Lord Barthwick personally had come to inspect their work at first cockcrow. Fanny had opened the door and had invited him in; inside he'd

22

seen the hearth they'd built for her in which a log blazed. He'd had the good grace to smile then, knowing they'd bested him, and mutter, 'Tha'll have to pay me a rent, mistress.'

Fanny earned her rent, and her living, by spinning and weaving, by washing for some of the outside workers of the Manor and, Dodie remembered with a faint smile, by gaining a coin or two from restless men on their way home from the tavern and coaching house on the road that ran half a mile from the village along the bottom of the dale beside the trout-stocked stream. Dodie had spent many a stolen hour talking with Fanny and they were firm friends. Fanny had a worldly knowledge that extended miles beyond the village in which they lived. She'd talked with men who'd travelled to York and to London, even across the waters into France, and she had many an eye-brightening story to tell Dodie of the way people behaved in far parts. She'd also talked with Dodie about men, about their interests and their requirements. In so many ways she'd been like the mother Dodie had never known, since she'd died when Dodie was only two, or like an older sister. Though no-one, not even Dodie, could have known, it was Fanny, with her deliciously wicked talk of men and what a woman must do to secure a good husband for herself or, even better, a wealthy lover, who had given Dodie an unconscious air of coquetry that ensured she would never lack for suitors.

Gertrude followed the direction of Dodie's eyes, but when she saw Fanny Colborn her lips closed tight in disapproval. How could she know she was consumed with envy of Fanny and her own sister Dodie? She envied them their freedom of expression, their laughter and gaiety, their self-confidence. She knew she was plainer than either Dodie or Fanny and already, at twenty-three, felt that life had passed her by. So many of the village girls managed to capture a husband by the time they were eighteen; but no-one, she knew, had ever approached her father to ask for her. There had been adventures, of course; in the rough

23

and tumble of harvest suppers she'd been kissed and Silas Prentis had even grasped her breasts that one time, but then he'd been drunk of beer and had taken his hand away to go and vomit. Many times Dodie had asked her to come to sit with Fanny, but each time Gertrude had pleaded other things 'more important' to do. Two minutes after Dodie had left each time, she'd wanted to change her mind, run after her sister, sit there and listen to their deliciously wicked conversations, but could not bring herself to admit her interest, not even to herself.

'Perhaps we could build Mistress Pearce a cottage like the one we built for Mistress Colborn,' Dodie suggested, her eyes glinting.

'I think not,' her father said sternly. 'She'd better take herself away where she'll have the better chance of finding a new husband. Anyway, one young widow in the village is enough.' He was looking at Simon as he spoke; knowing the lad had been seen coming out of the back of Fanny Colborn's cottage a couple of nights did nothing for his humour. All right, a lad should sow a few wild oats, but experiment with the lasses rather than widows who took a man's coin for favours given.

Simon said nothing, unwilling to be provoked. Anyway, he had other things on his mind. 'Colley was telling me he heard from Pearce the other day that this Enclosure is coming. We mun happen think about that.'

John waved his hand airily over the open fields. 'It'll do nowt but good,' he said, 'if we can get all our land together. Think of the extra land we'll take between the strips when we can bring down the barrows. Every man has his entitlement – they'll not be able to take that away from him no matter how many laws they pass in London. This has always been Aysgill land and always will be. Ten bold steps by forty in each of the three sections, that's our entitlement. If they put it all together, as I've heard they're going to do and already have in other places, why, we'll have three times ten plus two times two in the width. How much is that, Peter?'

'Thirty-four . . .'

'We shall gain a strip four bold paces by forty, and that's as much as some folk have to live on.'

'But the enclosing?' Simon persisted.

'The will of God will prevail,' John said stubbornly. 'We have our land, and no man will take it from us, nor even try. Now, yoke yourself to the front of yon plough and let's see thee do a bit of work for a change. And you lasses get back home and start the spinning. The winter will be on us afore we know and you'll be asking for candles to see by.'

As John walked back from the fields his face wore a worried expression he had been careful to hide from his family. He was a simple rural man, unused to change, and the events of 1740 were proving too much for him. This new Act of Enclosure was worrying. Some said they'd been hearing about new methods of tilling the land – there was talk of a man, Jethro Tull, who'd travelled about the countryside explaining some new-found method that meant going ever deeper into the ground. They were mating new animals, brought from afar, with each other to create new strains of cows and sheep. It all went against nature, it seemed to the unsophisticated mind of John Aysgill, and was bound to provoke the wrath of God in some particular. If man dug deeper into the ground with his plough, wouldn't he disturb the earth that had lain there untouched, releasing the Lord knows what malevolent forces? If the Lord had meant man to dig deeper into the soil, he wouldn't have put the stones there, would he? Many strange and ununderstandable forces were at work – only the previous day he'd seen his Lordship setting out in his coach, doubtless for the social occasion in Stonebridge Castle, and wearing finery such as John Aysgill had never seen before. Whoever thought to see his Lordship doff his fine cloth coat and his breeches and boots for a silk satin suit and silver-buckled shoes? And settling like a lady in the coach instead of climbing like a man on the back of his horse. No wonder the highwaymen had thought him fair game!

He walked into the village and crossed the step of their cottage, which was divided into two rooms by a hessian curtain on a pole. The two girls were behind the curtain and he could hear Dodie chattering to Gertrude, and the short replies she was getting. Gertrude had never been one much for talk, that was certain.

'Hold thy tongue, missie, and get on with thy work,' he growled. He sat on the bench that ran beside the hearth beneath the chimney, a giant of a man seeming even bigger tucked into the small space of the inglenook. He took a clay pipe from the shelf above the hearth, stuffed it with the herb mixture that always served to relax him, and lit it with a spill from the embers of the fire. Soon the girls would feed the flames with brushwood and set the pot on the hook to cook slowly.

Dodie came from behind the curtain; she'd changed from her outside clothes and was wearing her cambric dress, with the ribboned sleeves and the touch of coarse lace at the neck. She was a handsome girl and no mistake with a ripe and swelling figure, a sweet face, well managed hair tied into a plait behind her head. John looked at Gertrude when she came through. Plain Jane, and a face sour as apples, looking down her nose as if the world was beneath her contempt and all mortals in it were sinful creatures to be despised. Dodie sat herself at the spinning wheel, and soon her deft hands were following the bobbin, gently combing and teasing the wool into long fibres on the cop. Gertrude sat on the loom bench clacking the shuttle backwards and forwards, pressing the pedals with her feet to make the pattern they'd always used for their fine homespuns. He'd thought many a time of getting a bigger loom; they had one now that would shoot the bobbin across and even return it at the pull of a handle. That way, they could weave cloth anything up to two yards in width whereas at present they were limited by the extent of Gertrude's arms spread wide. But it all meant digging farther into his pocket and that was the trouble. Though John Aysgill didn't own himself an extravagant man, somehow the groats always seemed to slip through his fingers and he never managed to have anything put by. He knew, for example, that he'd give the Pearce widow a few coins to start her on her new life. He knew Peter would criticize him for it, but that was John Aysgill's way and always had been. The folk of the village always came to him first in case of need and he always provided, whether it was a handful of corn, a few potatoes, a handful of giblets, a peck of seeds to get them started. His pipe finished, he knocked it out gently into the embers of the morning fire, stood and stretched himself outside the inglenook. He looked at the weaving loom, noting the neat way Gertrude was binding in the ends of the woollen yarn, running his hand over the nap of the woven cloth.

'Odd to think yon piece of stuff will finish, most probably, on the back of some foreigner in distant parts,' he said.

Dodie smiled cheekily at him. 'It would make a warm cloak for me,' she said. 'Winter will soon be here, and I've nowt warm to wear.'

'Tha's more shifts and chemises, gowns and cloaks, than thy mother ever owned,' he said. 'Happen a husband will be the next one to provide for you.'

'Then what'll you do for the spinning?'

If she'd been of a mind to it, he'd have let her be married a couple of years back despite the loss her absence would cause. None of the others could spin so fast as she, he knew, and her departure from the family home would mean a real financial sacrifice. She seemed to be happy in her single state, in no hurry to tie herself to one suitor, to settle down into a home of her own with bairns about her feet. He couldn't blame her. The life of a wife and mother was still hard, even though there was much prosperity about these days despite the war that Sir Robert Walpole had called the previous year against Spain. A couple of lads had gone from the village, but they'd been a pair of rapscallions always out for adventure.

He left the cottage in a strange heavy mood he couldn't

understand. More and more these days, in his eightieth year, he seemed to be at odds with himself. Of course, he told himself, he'd never settled since his dear wife Emmeline had died. He'd married her late in life as was the local habit; she'd been a bright lass of twenty-two and he a mature man of fifty, with his own land he'd got from his father. One by one they'd had their children, each a year apart as was fitting until Peter, a difficult birth, had killed his mother in the delivery. They'd had good fortune and mercy that all their five had survived, a miracle of God's understanding. Life had held its unchanging pattern for him all his life, the same cottage, the same fields, the same seasonal tasks. He'd taken time to improve himself and could even read and write, an achievement not many village men could boast. He had a sense of belonging – John Aysgill of Barthwick, he was called, and he accepted what amounted to the title with pride. He *was* proud, he knew, but had a reason to be so. He'd never raised his fist to a man in anger save that it was warranted. He knew his place in the village, touched his forehead to his Lordship with respect, paid his tithe without complaint, had even paid the levies when his Lordship contributed to raising a regiment. He went to worship regularly, said his prayers every night, brought up his bairns in godly ways. Why, then, did this feeling of gloom and despair settle over him these days, as heavy as an overfull belly after a Manor house feast, or an ale-house head?

His walk took him to the common where the beasts were grazing under the watchful eye of Simple Tom. Some said Tom had been dropped on the hearth after his birth, and certainly his head had a flat top and his eyes were crossed.

'Now then, Tom, you keeping alert?'

'Aye, maister, that I am,' the lad said. He held in his hand the big stick that he would use to rattle the tinned bucket should anything befall the beasts grazing the common land of the village. Foxes had been known to creep slyly in and suckle at the teats of the cows, or tear out a sheep's throat. John had heard that a band of men had come to the common land at Betlaby, the nearest village, beaten the minder, a young girl, to death, and driven away most of the beasts.

John's cow was grazing at the far end of the common, swishing her head from side to side as she ate the lush September grass to keep the other beasts away from her chosen patch. He could see his sheep, telling them instantly from the other sheep though he couldn't see the distinguishing colour mark on their necks. His bull-calf was butting the side of a cow playfully – come the next year he'd be ready to sire cálves of his own and already was feeling playful. A cow and a bull-calf, six sheep, two of them rams in the growing, and one goat – life had never been so good. The girls had thirty-five yards of good worsted ready for the market. The barn behind the cottage was half full of corn, he had a sow ready for farrowing, two dozen of chickens and a bantam cock, three geese, half a ton or more of potatoes, a stall of turnips and another of beets, and two bags of seeds. So, why did he feel so saddened? Why was every step before the other a burden to him?

Walt Smith came up the track that led to the common, saw John, and came over to greet him. Walt was a good archer and often accompanied Lord Barthwick on a hunt – last time out he'd brought in five rabbits and a hare his Lordship had given him as payment for his labours. Lord Barthwick was freed from the Royal Prerogative by decree and could hunt all the deer on his land without Royal Favour or Consent – that day they'd shot three buck and his Lordship had also given him the hocks. He'd given one to John for the pot.

'That hock went down right well, Walt,' John said. 'I owe you my thanks for that.'

'Nay, tha's given me enough in thy time,' Walt said, embarrassed by the thanks. 'It'd take more than a hock or two to get me out of thy debt!'

The men stood companionably together each looking at his animals. Soon the lasses would be up for the milking, and then the lads would come by to take the beasts down into their stalls. His Lordship always liked the beasts off the common by nightfall and his beadle often came by to make sure his wishes had been carried out. Nobody minded – it was bad husbandry to leave the beasts out after nightfall to attract the foxes and the weasels, as well as the human predators.

'So, all this is going to go,' Walt said softly.

'All what . . .?'

'Haven't you heard? When they bring in Enclosure, the common is included.'

'Nay,' John said heatedly. 'They can't do that?'

'It's true. The common is included with all the other land for the calculation.'

'Nay! Never!'

'I heard them talking about it on the hunt. *All* the land is included for the calculation, then it's parcelled out according.'

'And where are we to run the beasts henceforth?'

'On our own land – such land as is granted to us. It's up to us what we do with the land. Put it for grass to feed the beasts. Plough and sow it according to season. Perhaps divide it, half and half. They say it's been worked out that if you divide your land into five, you can move the animals from piece to piece.'

John listened to Walt's words in amazement. Divide the common and enclose it? Make a man have beasts on the fields where since time began he'd grown his crops? What, indeed, was the world coming to?

'They'll never agree,' he said, indicating the village with a sweep of his hand. Fifty souls lived there, not counting the young ones living in their fathers' cottages. Half of them had strips of land in the open fields. The rest were in the direct service of his Lordship, either in the Manor or out. They even had their own farrier, and their own tinker, both of whom went for miles around when his Lordship didn't require their services. They had two carpenters and two masons all permanently employed at the Manor, building and rebuilding, and even their own smithy, a recent innovation now that iron was increasingly being used for brackets and hinges. The Manor even boasted an ironwork gate, and protective grilles to the embrasures. Many of the embrasures had been closed with spun glass to keep out the weather – Lord Barthwick was a modern man who liked to have everything that was new.

The grounds of Barthwick Manor were among the last in the district to be farmed by the old method of open field strips. Ever since the present Lord Barthwick had succeeded to the estate he'd longed to change the system. The old laws wouldn't permit him; he'd have needed to get all the villages into agreement and that no man could ever hope to do.

Now the laws were being changed, and petitions were being successfully presented in Parliament. Now, if the Lord of the Manor took the agreement of a *majority* of the strip-holders, he could push the petition through. Some had said Lord Barthwick had used pressure, and rumours ran rife through the village that this man or that had gone over to the other side. John Aysgill had held out against it – he wasn't a curmudgeon and served his Lordship loyally, but he didn't see why they should have change just for change's sake.

Walt Smith was looking embarrassed, he could see, and a sudden suspicion came to John Aysgill.

'Tha's not gone to the other side, Walt?' he asked softly.

He didn't need Walt's reply. Man and boy they'd known each other. Walt was twenty years younger than John. John had taught him to bend his first bow, to fletch his first arrow, and had watched him rise in the May Fair to be the top archer for miles around. John himself could bend a big bow but his pupil had soon outmatched him, snatching the May Fair prizes from him year after year. John had put Walt to bed in his straw the night of his wedding feast, had watched Walt's bairns grow, and even bought elm for two of Walt's bairns to lie in when they were buried. Walt had only two sons left, both married and gone south somewhere, seeking their fortunes. Walt owned a strip, and that gave him a vote in the enclosing. The *majority* was in people, not in size of land, and a man with ten paces by two was counted. When Walt's wife had died, John had sat with him in the ale-house, and then had carried him home.

'Yon strip yields me nowt,' Walt mumbled. 'It's as much as I can do to work it on my own.'

'I've told thee times over never to plant wheat on bad clover. That's why tha's overrun with quick tha'll never get rid of. My lads will give thee a hand to get it out and tha can plant turnips.'

'I'm too old, John, and my chest is that bad that some mornings it's as much as I can do to climb from my bed.'

'But tha can still see to take the eye of a buck at three hundred paces.'

'Aye, and that's the only thing about me that stays. His Lordship is offering me wages, letting me keep my cottage in my lifetime. I've nobody else, John; my lads'll never come back. His Lordship will give me what's left from my land after the tithe.'

'You'll throw your lot in with his?'

'It's the only thing left to me, John,' Walt said, the misery showing plain on his face. 'I had to come and tell you, man to man. I owed you that . . . for the past.'

'Aye, Walt, I reckon you owed me that,' John said. He didn't want to be angry with Walt. He could *understand*. But it didn't make his heart any lighter to know what Walt had done. Or to learn at first hand what his Lordship was doing to secure his wishes. It seemed somehow underhand and sly, the sort of thing a lesser man would have done, to buy the support of people by offering them advantage to betray their way of life. He turned abruptly and began to walk away. He heard Walt call after him. 'John . . .?' but he hadn't the heart to turn again. His mind was busy. Very well, if his Lordship was behaving in that way surely he forfeited his rights in the matter. Surely he forfeited the absolute loyalty of the man who'd respected him. John would call a meeting of the men of the village with a right to vote, and see what their mood was. His mind ran through the ones he knew would never surrender their right to the common land, the men who'd help him *oppose* Enclosure.

This was the first time the idea of active *opposition* had come to him, and he found himself stimulated by it. Why *should* things change, just because a group of men in London, who knew nothing about local life or conditions, chose to behave the way *they* thought fit. The idea of opposition, of resistance to the words and deeds of men like Lord Barthwick, to whom he'd always touched a symbolic forelock, was new and daring, and immediately dispelled the gloom that had lain heavy on him all day. Now he knew what had ailed him. He'd come to think of himself as powerless to resist the changes that seemed to be all about him, but he wasn't powerless, was he? He had rights, hadn't he? He was John Aysgill of Barthwick, wasn't he, a man in his own right. These weren't the dark ages when men were serfs; these were modern times and men were becoming independent, were beginning to enjoy their hard-earned liberty and prosperity. He had three sons and two daughters, and they were worth – yes, that was the word – *fighting* for . . .

'You're a brave man, John Aysgill,' Job Hirst said; 'but then you always were.'

The men of the village had been uneasy about meeting in John's cottage, especially by firelight. 'Nay, John,' Billy Fogg had said, 'they'll take us for Catholics or Jacobites, meeting in t'dark like this.'

The men had come round the backs one by one – all were strip holders, and all, John hoped, were against the enclosure. The two lasses were safe behind the curtain but the lads sat around, taking it all in. Matthew sat by the fire in the corner of the inglenook, thumbing a book in its calf leather binding. 'Tha looks like a preacher,' Charles Cryer had said, 'wi' that in thy hands.' In common with many of the village men, Charles had never learned to read or write, even though the preacher had offered to teach anyone in the village to scan the Bible. Charles Cryer was a big bluff man whose holding was as big as John Aysgill's. He was strongly against enclosure, John knew, and he hoped the two of them might be able to influence the others to hold fast.

When John had told his sons about the meeting, Matthew had given John a good idea, though Peter had grumbled that they were going in the face of nature to oppose enclosure. 'It's going to come, Father,' he'd said. 'You mark my words.'

'And you mark mine,' John had snapped back though he's right enough,' Thomas Clay growled. 'It'll be short intention to fight it with every bone in my body!'

The men had settled on the floor round the fire, squatting on their hunkers, on anything they could find to rest their backsides. 'His Lordship is trying to unite the ones in favour of enclosure by offering them advantage,' John said, starting the meeting in his blunt way. 'I think we should do the same. My lad Matthew has stepped forward wi' a suggestion I think merits our attention. He says we all know good times and bad, and he's right.'

'If by bad times he means the blight in my wheat, then he's right enough,' Thomas Clay growled. 'It'll be short commons for us this winter, and no mistake.'

'Aye, that's what he *does* mean,' John said. 'But why should it be like that? There's twelve stripholders in this room. A bit from each one to tide you over the winter wouldn't do us any harm. Matthew is of the opinion we ought to divide what we get from our labours, sharing it equally amongst ourselves.'

The room was silent – the men had never *heard* such a suggestion.

'Share what we get?' James Waterton said. 'Share it?'

'Aye. Then, if we have good times, we all have good times. If we have bad times, it's bad for us all by equal measure. If one man has bad times while the rest of us has good, then we help him over the bad time.'

'I had five lambs last year,' Samuel Weighton said. 'Jonathan Phillips here, well, his old ewe went barren. How do you have a mind to work that out?'

'I haven't thought about the details,' John said desperately. 'I was just thinking about the principles involved.'

'Aye, well . . .' Samuel was notoriously mean; they said his wife had died of starvation when he had plenty in his barn, and certainly his daughters were all sickly and no man could be found to take them on. He was known to hoard his coin and some said he had a bag of nobles sewn into the straw of his mattress.

'You're asking a lot, John Aysgill,' Job Hirst said. Though not mean, Job was a careful man. His clothes were well patched, even his boots. He fed his folks well, but it was mostly brewis of oats sprinkled on a broth that was more potato and turnip than bones. His daughters wore his wife's cast-offs and they'd mostly come from his mother. They said unkindly that his family of nine could live off a chicken for a week, soaked up in barley. 'Man looks forward to the good times to get ahead and put a bit by for the lean ones. It'll make men careless and improvident, if they know they'll be carried through the bad times – often it's the only thing as keeps a man active, to know how he'll suffer when the bad times come.'

'It's not good for a man to have things too easy,' Samuel said primly. 'We were all brought on this earth to suffer out our time. Some of us is careful – we don't all have your open easy hand.'

'Aye, and more's the pity to that,' John Aysgill said. The bailiff had been that afternoon and had turned the Pearce widow out after her husband had been buried. John had given her a purse with a few groats in it as she'd set off with her cart and her children, pushing them down the road that wound out of the dales towards the city of Leeds. Samuel had watched her go, his hands folded over his waistcoat, the only one present who hadn't offered her

35

something to ease her path. When Jessica, her fifteen-year-old daughter, had called cheekily to him, 'How about a coin, then, Samuel, for all the pleasures your eyes have taken from us?' he'd turned on his heel and stomped away. The older Pearce girls all had plump ripe figures – and the Weighton cottage overlooked the Pearce backyard, where the girls had washed themselves until they'd realized Samuel made good use of his vantage point to observe them. The Weighton girls were all thin as wheat stalks.

More and more as the meeting progressed, John realized he had been in error to introduce Matthew's proposal at the start. The idea of sharing was too new for them to grasp. Traditionally they'd all believed in good times and bad being the Will of the Lord – good times the reward for industry and diligence, bad times the punishment of the Lord for some transgression. It was going against the will of the Lord to try to affect the balance as well as encouraging men to sloth and idleness.

John recognized his task was hopeless, and the meeting disintegrated by ten o'clock, when the men started to drift away to go to bed in preparation for the long day ahead.

As soon as the men had gone, the girls, who'd been too excited by the meeting to sleep, came from behind the curtain.

'Do you think enclosure is coming, then?' Dodie asked.

'It has to come,' Peter said, 'and a good thing, too. It'll make for a much better use of the land and a more efficient working.'

'Hold your tongue, lad,' John said, plainly troubled. 'And you, missie, get back to your bed and cease your meddling in what doesn't concern you.'

The two girls went through behind the curtain and Gertrude plumped the straw in her mattress bag. 'It seems to me that it's a lot of fuss about nothing,' she said as she settled down and drew the cover over herself. 'Everybody's getting excited, all over nothing.'

Dodie was not so sure and lay on her pallet with her eyes wide open, staring at the roof beams. Though she couldn't know it and couldn't have said why, she shared her father's discomposure, his feeling of certainty that with the enclosing of the open fields and the common, they'd be setting out on a new and troubled journey.

When Lord Barthwick came back from Stonebridge Castle after a couple of days spent riding with his friend, hawking and coursing through the extensive grounds of Stonebridge's estate while the ladies sat around gossiping and drinking their tisanes, discussing the latest London styles and examining the stuffs the agents were sending up for their approval, he plunged immediately into the matter of the enclosure. 'I'll see Sam Weighton first,' he said to his bailiff. 'Bring him up at midday.'

When Sam Weighton arrived he was astounded to see a table laid in the game room, carrying a brace of pheasants, a mutton pie, a haunch of venison ready for carving. His eyes nearly dropped from his head when Polly came in, carrying a jug of beer which she set on the side table. Her large fulsome breasts were almost dropping out of the top of her gown, bound together at the sides so that they met in a chasm in the centre, down which his eye was inexorably drawn. Lord Barthwick grunted when he saw the expression on Sam Weighton's face at the sight of the food and the maidservant – so the stories he'd heard were correct.

'Polly's a good lass to have around, and very obliging,' he said.

Sam Weighton was stunned by surprise. Being invited to sit at table in the Manor! More food being offered than he'd see in a month at his own frugal board! And Polly, in her Manor House finery that would have done her credit if he, Sam Weighton, had been King George himself!

'Help yourself to anything you fancy, Sam,' Lord Barthwick said graciously. Polly's bright eyes were cast down as was only fitting, but she raised her head and shot Sam a wink that stirred his breeches.

'You set a fine table, my Lord,' Sam said, remembering

37

his manners in time. 'I'll not say no . . .'

Polly poured him a pot of the ale he knew his Lordship bought in Tadcaster in barrels. Many people in the village brewed their own home beer, but none of it derived the benefit of Tadcaster water and skill. The beer was rich and strong tasting and Sam couldn't bring himself to set the pot down until he'd drained it, when Polly immediately refilled it.

'I thought it was time that you and me sat down together,' Lord Barthwick said as he settled himself to table. 'Times are changing, and we have to learn to change with them. It's time to end the old feudal ways, and recognize each other as what we are, both men of property.'

'Aye, if you say so, my Lord,' Sam said, quite mystified by this direct approach. Of course, Lord Barthwick had always been a *country* squire, not like some of the ones who resided in London and rarely visited their estates. He knew every man in the village, aye, and the names of most of the kinder.

'This Act of Enclosure is very much a part of the new ways,' Lord Barthwick said smoothly, 'part of the new advantage we shall all derive. Just think of being able to walk your land in one piece, to work it in one go, to guard your own animals against the problems that beset them when they feed from common ground, sickened by common ailments that, as we both know, can strike an animal down by infection. They're not all as careful as you are, Sam, in the guarding of their beasts, in the tilling of their soil, in the husbandry of the land their fathers have left to them. I want you by my side, Sam, in this matter. I think you're a man who knows best how to look after his own. You're a careful man, not like some we could name who'd give away their last groat for a night of ale-house pleasure.'

'You can say amen to that,' Sam said, the beer working in him and making him bold to speak his mind to his Lordship.

'I want you by my side,' Lord Barthwick reiterated. 'Together we shall carry this Act of Enclosure through. Rely on me, I'll see you right in all particulars. I've been noticing that roof of yours. You'll be needing a few reeds and some withies to thatch that roof before the winter sets in. I'd be obliged if you'd cut what you need from the banks of the river by the mill, for the reeds there are growing that thick and high . . .'

'I was thinking to put a door on my store room,' Sam said, recognizing that they had passed into the bargaining time.

'And you shall have it,' Lord Barthwick said, 'though many a man would look at his oak and set a high price to it. Jebediah shall come and span it for you and set to and make you as fine a door as any here in the manor.'

'Framed . . .?'

'If you so desire . . .'

'*And* braced?'

There was a pause in which both knew the bargaining was coming to an end.

'Bracing makes a sturdy door,' Lord Barthwick said.

'As befits a man who wants no more than to safeguard his property from marauders the better to serve you, my Lord.'

'Then, framed and braced it shall be,' his Lordship said. 'Now, Sam, I must take my leave of you. The estate is a constant and demanding mistress and I have much to do. I'd be obliged if you'll kindly help yourself to anything you may choose while you are under my roof. We must seal a bargain of agreement this day, and agreement without advantage is never assured. Polly, you'll oblige me by looking after Maister Weighton's requirements to the best of your ability,' he said before he went out of the door.

Polly bobbed and curtsied low. Sam Weighton, who'd had the grace to stand when his Lordship left the room, found himself looking down upon her.

'What's your wish, Maister Weighton?' Polly asked. 'For I'm an obedient girl as befits my station. What can I get you from the sideboard?'

'Come, sit on my knee,' Sam said, his voice hoarse. 'The sideboard can wait for I've other needs in mind.'

After his abortive meeting, John Aysgill did nothing to try to win the men to his side, recognizing that any association would have to scale the mountain of self interest and prejudice. Talk of the Enclosures was everywhere in the air until everyone became heartily sick of it. One by one, each of the men was invited to the Manor but all came away tight lipped. When it was Aysgill's turn, he found his Lordship standing by his hearth, carved from a solid piece of stone, they said, with two gargoyles' heads holding the slab of York stone that served as a mantel. The room was vast and lined with old wood that gleamed with the polish of a thousand hands. The chairs were solid, covered in hide, with brass pinnings and relief patterns stamped on them. The table was one gigantic slab of beech sanded smooth, set on wrought iron legs with brass covered decorated filigree bearers.

The windows of the room, some eight feet tall, were of spun glass, much of it coloured and cut in patterns. With the sun shining upon it, the light glinted and glittered at him, reddening Lord Barthwick's already ruddy features. His Lordship was wearing a coat of some heavy cream coloured material, dark green breeches, and brown boots with lighter fawn edgings at the top. His shirt was fine lawn, clean as snow. In every respect he looked what he was, a wealthy man of position and privilege, a man to be obeyed, not opposed.

As John came in, wearing his oatmeal coloured homespun outer smock over his black leather scuffed boots, Lord Barthwick was talking with his bailiff while one of his agents stood respectfully by. 'Right, here's Maister Aysgill, so you mun set about it quickly,' he said, dismissing them. They touched their forelocks and withdrew, not turning their backs.

John could hardly know they'd been rehearsed in this

procedure until they had it step perfect.

'What's this I hear, Maister Aysgill, about you meeting together at dead of night like a pack of Quakers doing the devil's work?' his Lordship demanded, though the twinkle in his eye took away any suggestion of severity.

'Aye, a few of us had occasion to talk together,' John said, in no way put out by his Lordship's display of strength. 'Though I reckon there'd be no recruits signing on for the Quaker cause among us.'

'This share and share alike idea of your lad, Matthew. Did that come from the Quakers? It sounds the sort of rubbish they do talk.'

'It came from the lad's conviction, your Lordship, that the God we all serve would like to see all men being more brotherly, one with the other, like it says in the Bible.'

'Aye, Maister Aysgill, I'd quite forgotten you were a reading man, and doubtless have passed all that on to your kith, though I say fairly I can't see how it would avail them in maintaining the land and paying the tithe.'

It was a bold reminder that above all Aysgill and his decendants bore the responsibility of finding the annual tithe – in default they could be turned from the cottage and the land confiscated. Most kindly patrons set the tithe at a third of the man's corn crop, and even forgot the tithe in bad years, but the kindness of the patron could be ended at will.

'Perhaps you could quote the Bible at the bailiff when he came,' Lord Barthwick said, smiling hugely.

John took his line from the humour. 'There's no way one could say, your Lordship, that the bailiff would understand.'

'Aye, maister, that's right,' Lord Barthwick said. 'Now, tell me man to man, are you with us, or against us, in this matter of the enclosure?'

'I have to say, your Lordship, that I can find no wrong in a system that was right for both our grandfathers.'

'Then tha's a stick-in-the-mud, John Aysgill,' his Lordship said vehemently, 'and should heed the advice of your own lad, Peter, and the knowledge of your betters who've gone deeper into the matter than you have. The ground will yield more and there'll be more of it. The crops will be bigger. We shall all improve our situations. We can breed better animals more resistant to diseases of all kinds, standing higher on the hock, with more meat and less fat and thicker pelts, longer threads. It'll mean more prosperity for us all, thee included. I want thee by my side in this, Maister, but if tha won't come, then tha won't and that's all there is to it.'

John Aysgill was saddened by his own convictions. He would dearly have liked to believe what his Lordship was saying, but something inside his being was resistant to change. He knew that in previous generations he wouldn't have been given the option and he could respect Lord Barthwick for that. There'd be no enmity, no reprisals, that he knew for certain.

'I'd welcome a while to think about it, Lord Barthwick,' he said hesitantly. 'I'd not like it believed I was being stubborn for nowt, without giving the matter a lot of thought.'

'Tha's too late, Maister Aysgill,' Lord Barthwick said brusquely. 'The petition's prepared and signed, ready to go. Being that you're a writing man, I thought to give thee the chance to pen thy name to it, at the bottom, right above my own. But, if tha won't, tha won't, and I bear thee no malice. Mister Wilberforce sets off with it at first light to present it to Parliament. I can tell thee now, it'll be granted since we have the majority with us. I would have liked thee on it, but it makes no never mind whether thy name is there or not. We're going to enclose the village, and there's an end of it.'

Slowly the September of warm harvest days drew to a close; all thoughts of enclosure were set aside for the Harvest Fayre that would be held by tradition on the village green, directly before the Aysgill cottage holding. As if knowing it would be the end of an era, Lord

42

Barthwick donated two sterile cows to the festival, to be roasted over fires set in deep pits dug for the occasion. The village was in a frenzy of preparation as the day of the festivity neared – the ladies twined garlands of leaves and herbs and thought about their clothing. Dodie talked her father out of one of their lengths of cloth to make a fine cloak she embroidered with scraps of silk and ribbons procured for her from the sewing boxes of the Manor by her crony, Sal, Lady Barthwick's chief seamstress.

Even Gertrude, normally staid, permitted Dodie to persuade her to a ruched shift which set off her fine neck and gathered what small bosom she had into a delicate display though, try as she might, she couldn't get a cleavage in any way to compare with Dodie's over-generous endowment.

John Aysgill's green coat was repaired and pressed with a stone heated in the fire until the nap shone. 'You'll be the smartest man there, Father,' Dodie promised as she trimmed his hair and cut his whiskers close to his face.

On the morning of the Harvest Fayre folks from miles around streamed into the village with their baskets of moor-gathered cranberries, wild strawberries, flowers of all descriptions. The tinker came with his cart, and set it up by the village green, not to work but hopefully to sell a few new pots. The fires had been lighted before dawn and now the ash had settled thick in the bottom of the pits, generating heat that sent the air swirling over the green. The beasts had been spitted and set on the trellises; boys vied with each other to turn the handles that constantly exposed different parts of the animals to the heat of the flame, while the fat ran slowly out like sweat, dripping into the fire, exploding in smoky flame with each drop. Lanthorns of grease with rush wicks had been set among the trees to await the dusk, and everyone streamed about visiting, borrowing threads here, a bodkin there. Men sat before their doors smearing tallow into their boots, spitting on them and rubbing them, while inside mothers and sisters worked on each other's hair, brushing and

43

combing, teasing out the knots, washing, drying, setting in coils, pressing in curls with iron tongs heated in the fires on which the breakfast had been quickly cooked and impatiently eaten. The Gods had conspired that day to provide a clear sky over which the sun shone and a gentle breeze blew; it was a grand day with the air an elixir of happiness. All the previous weeks the lads and the girls had laboured over straw dollies, fashioning the wheat stems into elaborate effigies of animals, birds, loaves of bread, even a tree.

The fiddlers arrived at twelve o'clock – that they'd been in the ale-house beside the road some distance from the village was obvious in their demeanour and conduct; as they walked along one of them played a fast jig the others couldn't keep up with; he danced on his toes, pirouetting around them, dressed in the Continental fashion in what once had been black velvet but now was rusted at the seams, sunbleached, the survivor of a hundred drunken exhausted nights on tavern floors. They sat beside the village green watching the bustling ladies, making an acceptably coarse joke, reaching out to grab a passing skirt. One of them had carried a small barrel which they passed from hand to hand, tipping it and drinking from the bung-hole. The pungent odour suggested some foreign liquor, or perhaps a powerful gin distillation. One of them held a lute and his fingers idly plucked at it as he sat, waiting for the celebrations to come. Matthew came and sat beside him, awed by the delicate tracery of music the man's coarse fingers were making despite their work-worn thickness. Gradually the swirl between the cottages concentrated itself on the village green itself, as the girls, finally dressed, their faces scrubbed and sparkling, their hair combed and coiffed, came gaily out onto the grass. The boys were there before them and had been awaiting this moment to come forward and stand nearby, ogling favourites, timidly at first, then increasingly more boldly as the smiles they'd hoped for but hadn't dared expect were bestowed. Trestle tables borrowed from the Manor had been set across the side of the green. Now the loaves arrived in wicker baskets, the cobs, the rolls, the bread twists, the cottage loaves, the patterned shapes of twisted dough decorated and glazed with egg-white and hard seeds.

With the bread came the mounds of peas and beans, the turnip mash leavened with egg and butter from the churn, the mounds of home-made cheese of cow's, ewe's and goat's milk. Then came the pies of rabbit and hare, the mounds of bone stock jelly sprinkled with herbs, the liver, kidneys baked with onions and leeks into a cake ready for slicing. The fiddlers came to their feet and cheered when Thomas Clay and Jonathan Phillips staggered from the Clay cottage carrying the large cauldron in which had simmered cuts of beef and bone, potatoes and turnips, enriched with pork offal and blood, thickened with oatmeal to the consistency of a porridge. The cauldron was the signal for which they'd all waited – each had brought his plate, his pot, his mug, his tin, and the scoop flew in and out while the fiddlers played and the barrels of beer were tapped into pots and tankards.

When Dodie, holding her stew cup in one hand, her beer pot in the other, paused by the bread table, Mark Ottershaw stepped briskly forward. 'I mun help thee to a piece of bread, since thy hands is full,' he said.

She glanced up at him, smiling. 'Bold, are we today, Mark Ottershaw?' she asked. 'I'd have thought you'd have been busy helping Emmie Hirst to her fill of bread.'

He blushed. 'Emmie and me, we're like brother and sister,' he said.

'That'll be why you seem so fond of holding her hand, I suppose?' she said, still smiling.

'Aye, well . . .'

'Don't explain,' she said. 'I can see it'd be an attractive hand to hold, if a man's mind were set that way. Though I'd have thought a man of taste and discrimination would have preferred a cleaner person.'

'My what long words we're using, Dodie Aysgill,' he said. 'And how sharp our tongue today . . .'

45

'Happen you'd be better fetching bread for that simpleton, Mistress Cryer,' she said. 'I'm certain she doesn't use long words and her tongue is far too long and waggles too frequent to be sharp.'

He squirmed under her piercing look. 'Oh, Dodie,' he pleaded. 'Let's not fight, today of all days. I've been so looking forward . . . I made you a token, if you've a mind to accept it.'

He went to fumble in the deep pocket of his skirted jacket, but dropped the cob he'd been holding for her in his hand. She laughed at his discomfiture, put her cup and pot on a nearby cut tree trunk and picked up the bread, dusting it fastidiously with the hem of her pinafore.

He managed to get what he was seeking out of his pocket and held it in his hand. 'I made it, specially for you,' he said as he opened his hands. It was shaped like a heart, of wheat straw, about the size of an ear. One wing of the heart was somewhat larger than the other, destroying the symmetry. 'Look,' he said, 'it opens.'

It *did* open, but the wheat straw acting as a hinge came apart in the process. Inside it, nestling on grey moss from the bark of a tree, was a stone from the river bed, of a reddish hue, with a gold pyrites stripe running across it.

'Sorry it broke,' he said gruffly. 'I'm not much of a hand for fashioning things . . .'

'Why, Mark Ottershaw, it's beautiful,' she said. 'It's simply beautiful.'

She linked her arm in his in a public display of affection and ownership. 'It's the nicest thing anybody's ever given me,' she said. 'The nicest ever!'

His heart glowed with happiness as they sat down together by the cut tree trunk, their food before them. What a Harvest Fayre it promised to be, with Dodie Aysgill by his side!

The festivities of the Harvest Fayre traditionally reached a peak with the introduction of the Wassail Dolly, who, for some reason no one could recall, was always called Sall o'

Bob. No-one could remember a man called Bob in Barthwick who'd had a daughter called Sall, but the name stuck. Sall o' Bob was a woman figure built onto a broom handle, using wheat straw wrapped around tightly packed grass. Her head, decorated with bright yellow flax, was always a turnip and her eyes two bright shining coals. Her bosom was always of the most generous dimensions and often, depending on the skill of the manufacture, revealed two pig's bladders tied and inflated, peeping from beneath the wheat straw in a most suggestive manner. Her nethers were hidden modestly, at least at the start of the festivities, beneath folds of scraps of cloth stitched together in a patchwork pattern. Invariably, the patches had not been too tightly joined, and pieces would fall off, or be snatched provocatively by daring youths – if any were seen at this nefarious task he would be called out and belaboured with Sall o' Bob's 'protector', another broom handle tightly wound with wheat straw over dried grass to the shape of a long sausage called the flog.

Sall o' Bob was always carried from the cottage in which she had been made in great ceremony, while people called, 'Make way for Sall, make way for Sall', while the musicians played vigorously any dashing jig that came to mind. On this occasion, however, the fiddlers played the recently popular song, 'The Roast Beef of Olde England', as Hettie Fogg advanced from their cottage. The youngsters danced round her and the fiddlers, already pretending to snatch at Sall o' Bob's multi-hued petticoat. Everyone exclaimed when they saw Sall, saying it was the best one ever. Certainly, Billy Fogg had used much breath in blowing up the pig bladders beneath the wheat straw, and the flaxen hair was long and shone with wax and polish. Everyone was in a lather of excitement as Hettie proceeded to the green, Billy Fogg behind her carrying the flog, the musicians dancing round them in an endless spiral, tripping over youngsters trying to dart in to snatch at the petticoats.

The youths of the village and many of the grown-ups, too,

were formed on the green in two concentric rings, the ladies on the outside, the men on the inside. Billy walked solemnly to the inside and took up his position, the flog held ready in his brawny arms. Hettie held the effigy of Sall o' Bob high; the musicians were silent, and then began to play furiously. The dance began at once with each circle revolving counterclockwise to the other. Sall danced round in the arms of Hettie, with Simple Tom and Emmie Hirst twirling round as a ring within a ring. Simple Tom leaped up and tried to snatch at Sall, but Hettie whirled the effigy away in time, passing it to Emmie. Emmie whirled about, carrying Sall o' Bob in *her* arms to confront Gertrude Aysgill, with young Tom Phillips the assailant this time. The three of them twirled and cavorted in their own tight ring while all the others swirled and clapped in time to the music, the men exhorting Tom to 'go you in, lad, and snatch a bit for me', while the girls were screaming, 'watch him, Emmie, watch him, Gertrude, or he'll have the skirts off you . . .'

Tom decided it was time to try, to be the first. He ducked and weaved through, keeping time with the music in the rustic dance, bowed his waist, bobbed his body in with his hand held high. It was no accident, of course, that his hand clutching for Sall o' Bob's skirt should brush against Emmie's side.

There was an immense shout from the girls — 'he's touched Sall o' Bob, he's touched . . .' but Tom sheepishly held up his hand, empty. The outer ring broke and several of the girls clasped Tom and pushed him into the centre where Billy Fogg began to belabour him with the flog, beating him over his head and ears. The flog, of course, was soft and did little damage except to Tom's honour at having tried, and lost.

When it was considered Tom had been flogged sufficiently, the dance resumed its bright excited round, with voices already beginning to sound hoarse as each side tried to drown the sound of the other.

The first to come out with a snatch of Sall o' Bob's skirt,

surprisingly, was Matthew Aysgill, who'd managed it by accidentally tripping at the last minute of his roundels, and clutching forward without aim. There was a roar of approval from the men when Matthew, more astounded than triumphant, held aloft his prize, a small square of blue cotton. The competition was not aimless – by tradition the one who gained the most squares of cloth by the time Sall o' Bob was destroyed was given a fulsome kiss by the last girl to hold the effigy.

John Aysgill was sitting on a log before his door watching the festivities, chuckling as he remembered the adventures he'd had with the Sall o' Bob nigh on sixty-five years ago, when his blood had run high as a lad of fifteen and many a village lass had tried to catch his eye. His eyes clouded as he remembered the Harvest Fayre he'd proposed to his wife, by then a mature man of fifty, but still capable of ripping off more squares of cloth than any of the hasty impatient lads.

He made to rise when he felt the hand of Lord Barthwick on his shoulder.

'Nay, John Aysgill, keep your seat. I've a mind to sit with ye for a while.'

His Lordship came round the log as John made more room for him and sat down without ceremony. The day was going and already one or two of the rushes set in the trees around the green had been lighted. It had been a gorgeous September sunset, with colours not elsewhere seen splashing themselves with abandon across the pale azure sky – browns and mauves, primroses and the reds and ambers that tinged men's faces with a ruddy health.

Lord Barthwick was holding a pewter pot half full of ale; he put it to his lips and drank deeply. When he had drained the pot he set it on the grass beside him. John caught his son Peter's eye and beckoned to the pot. Peter went to the barrel and loaded a tin jug from which he filled both his Lordship's pot and his father's. 'I'm obliged to you, Peter Aysgill,' Lord Barthwick said.

The two men sat side by side in old trusted companionship. Though Barthwick was twenty years his junior, John felt a sense of belonging sitting beside him, as if, in some curious way, they were not man and master but two long-serving members of the same regiment.

'These are halcyon days, John,' his Lordship finally said. 'But they're passing from us, falling out of our grasp. Don't worry, I'm not about to bring up the matter of enclosure again – but the world is changing as it passes us by, and I can see it all about me.'

'Memory is an unkind taskmaster, my Lord,' John said, 'that serves us ill more often than good. We've seen a few scores of Harvest Fayres together. I can remember when it was a feat of great daring to catch a fold of Sall o' Bob's. With every lass defending her as if she were defending her own honour and virtue. Now it often seems to me the lasses are at one with the lads, offering Sall o' Bob rather than defending her. It'll be a sad world if lasses surrender their virtue so quickly to any snatching Tom, Dick, or Harry.'

'That'll never happen, John, so long as there are men of good heart to defend them. You've raised your two lasses well, aye and the three lads. I could nobbut wish fate had given me the opportunity to have lads of my own, to teach them to your example.'

'There's a world of difference in the three lads, my Lord. Almost as if I were being stopped from being prideful. Simon, my first born, is all heart and head but no intention. Matthew, the second, he's all heart without head *or* intention. And Peter, the third, well, he's all head and intention, wi' no heart. And I'm sorely afeard, he's the one who'll go the farthest.'

'You've had heart, John,' Lord Barthwick softly said, 'all your life.'

'Aye, and here am I, with the curtain ready to be drawn over my face, and not a coin in my pocket save what the next harvest will bring. I've lived ten more than my three-score years and ten from harvest to harvest, from hand to mouth. Aye, and when there's nowt i' the hand, there's nowt i' the belly either without a purse to dip into, to tide us over.'

'You know, John, you'll never want, so long as I'm master.'

'Yes, my Lord, I know that . . . and I thank thee for that! Any road, tonight is Harvest Fayre once again, so what say we join the throng and see if the pair of us can't snatch a cloth or two?'

Lord Barthwick had laid his hand on John Aysgill's knee. 'Never forget what I've said this e'en, John Aysgill. So long as I'm master, tha'll want for nowt.' He rubbed his hands together as he stood up and they surveyed the scene together.

'What about yon Aunt Sallies,' Lord Barthwick said. 'I'll wager I can knock down a sight more than thee.'

The Aunt Sallies had been carved into weird shapes of men and women, dwarfs, gargoyles, upright beasts, and were resting on a flat plank about two feet from the ground. Each person trying was given a handfull of balls made by stretching wool through a ring and then fluffing it out. At the centre of the ball was a nut which added little force. It required a throw of great violence, correctly aimed, to knock one of the figures off the plank. The side-show was only one of several being run by itinerants, who travelled the country attending fairs, usually with a cart on which their side-show was carried. There had always been travelling people, John Aysgill thought. The musicians, the man who came with the dancing bear, the Italian with the monkey, even the black man with two thumbs on each hand. They'd always been well received, fed and housed, given a sack of food, a coin or two, and had gone on their way. Now it seemed that people had started to make a living at it, charging money or kind to entertain folks who, John reflected, had always entertained themselves.

'I've no stomach for these fancies,' John said. 'But I'll wager at yon knurr and spell.'

They crossed the green to the edge of the pond, where the knurr and spell contest was being savagely fought.

Each competitor had carved a number of pieces of wood about the width of a hand, so that when laid on the ground each end rose an inch. The player held a stick in his right hand and with it struck the end of the wood so that it rose into the air. While the wood was flying, the player attempted to hit it squarely as it whirled in the air, driving it with great force across the pond. Each good hit was acclaimed as it rose through the air. 'It's a go-er, it's a go-er . . .'

The Cryer lad was standing at the far side of the pond with a handful of withies, poking one into the ground where each knurr landed. Sam Weighton, of big belly and broad shoulders, had been village champion for many a year. John Aysgill had never been in the running, but each year had jestingly challenged the champion. 'What's it to be this year, John?' Sam Weighton asked.

'Same as ever . . .'

'Four eggs. I hoped this year you might make it five.'

'Aye, and cocks might crow a tune, happen.'

James Waterton gave John his spell and three knurrs. John examined them then hefted them; they were well balanced in the cutting. He put one on the ground, noting how it ached him to bend so deep. Sam Weighton stood by, a broad grin on his face as if the contest had a foregone conclusion. John didn't know whence it came, but suddenly he felt himself to be a champion. Sam Weighton represented to him, at that moment, the evil forces of change he felt all about him. Sam, he knew, had sold out to his Lordship, had given his agreement for an advantage like many others in the village. John had held out against them all. It had been a futile gesture; Lord Barthwick's man had gone to London with the Petition and none doubted it would be granted, unless the Parliament met in time and stopped it with the Tory amendment. Though John knew nothing of what happened in London he was wise enough to realize the Petition would not have been sent unless his Lordship had reason to believe it would go through. 'What's it to be John? Best of three, or best to count?'

'Best to count,' John said. He knew he'd have little chance if all three were counted, since it'd take him two to get the stiffness out of his bones. His first was a poor lob, ill-seen in the gathering gloom, ill-struck so that it whirled up in the air, spending its force without achieving any distance, falling in the near part of the pond with great ignominy.

'Nay, John, tha'll need to do better than that,' Sam said as lightly he tapped the end of the knurr to lift it just above waist height, then drove it straight as an arrow on a low trajectory clear across the pond. The Cryer lad marked it. 'Best so far,' he shouted.

The other lads realized a contest was on, and raced around the sides of the pond to assist with the marking.

John overhit his knurr; it rose shoulder high but forward and when he slammed it with the spell it drove downwards and forwards, not even reaching the pond's edge. The assembled crowd which had swelled when John came to the stand, groaned but Sam chortled. He was still laughing as he indolently flicked the knurr for his second shot, suspecting that the first had already won the contest for him. He banged it with the spell; the knurr spun viciously around and curved in a higher arc than his first shot, landing about two paces shorter.

The cheering, though Sam didn't realize it, was for the shortness of the stroke rather than the length.

'Make your mark, Sam,' John said, tight-lipped.

Sam, still grinning, drew a line on the hard ground of the stand and both stood three paces from it, each with a pebble in his hand. Sam tossed his pebble; it fell to the earth a hand span from the line. John tossed his pebble – it bounced twice before it rested on the line itself.

'Tha can go first, Sam,' he said, 'and may the Lord tha doesn't believe in take mercy on thee and give strength to thy arm!'

Sam sensed the atmosphere that had thickened between them, recognizing that this was no longer the annual friendly match, with four eggs at stake. He looked round the crowd of spectators and could even sense their antagonism as they pressed in. 'Nay, give us room,' he growled, the over-confident grin wiped from his face. He rubbed his forehead with the sleeve of his jerkin, pulled his breeches clear of his crotch and set down his knurr with great care, rubbing the patch of earth where it lay to flatten it as it pointed down the course and over the pond. He wiped his sweating hand on his breeches and clasped his spell tight. He stepped back, measuring the stroke, reaching out a fraction since the knurr would be nearer to his body when he came to drive it. He took a couple of practice taps in the total silence that attended his effort. Then he tapped. He started to smile as the knurr came up beautifully from the ground, a perfect straight ride. He drew the spell quickly back watching the knurr turn, waiting for the exact second when it would be at right angles to the course. He tensed the great muscles of his arm then flicked in using all his weight, all his force, all his skill. The knurr flew with its trajectory slightly high but a good one, a damned good one. Despite their antagonism, the crowd sighed in appreciation as they watched the knurr fly over the heads of the waiting lads who were trying to run backwards, to keep their eyes on it.

It fell to the ground and stayed at least four paces beyond Sam's first stroke.

'That'll do,' he grunted. 'Beat yon bugger, John Aysgill,' he said.

The crowd groaned – they'd never seen a shot like that one, and knew John had never hit one that far all his life.

John put his knurr down with a sinking heart, a feeling that life was repeating itself. He'd been beaten over the matter of enclosure – was he now to be humiliated in a mere *game*. He chided himself for once again taking on the impossible, reproaching himself for what he knew had always been a failing. He had never learned to recognize the impossible, to accept that some forces of movement are as inevitable as the seasons. He straightened up, feeling again the age in his bones. He looked round at the crowd, sensing that they were willing him to do the impossible. He looked down at the knurr, concentrating all his efforts and thoughts on it. Tap the knurr a finger's width from its end and it would stay straight, rising vertically without spinning. And then hit with all the might of his still powerful arm and shoulder.

He tapped.

The knurr rose in slow motion, vertical, the length of its side exposed to him. He'd brought the spell back and now he brought it in straight armed, all his force behind it, whirling on the ball of his left foot to add the weight of his body to the strength of his arm. When the spell hit, the click told everyone that it was a good one. John didn't hear it. As the spell came forward, and just before the moment of impact, he felt a surge of blood in his head and a pain in his temple that drove the sight from his eyes.

The onlookers saw the knurr fly on a perfect arc, not wasting its energy by twisting, curling slightly along that trajectory like the perfect far bow shot. Over the pond it flew with the crowd silent, over the heads of the lads tripping backwards from the edge of the pond, from the first landings, through Sam Weighton's first flight, up to and past his second. The Cryer lad, withy in his hand, watched the knurr strike the ground and triumphantly dug the withy in.

Two hand spans beyond Sam Weighton's.

'Two whole hand spans,' the Cryer lad shouted triumphantly.

The crowd turned as one to congratulate John, but found him lying on the ground. 'You've won, John,' they were calling as they pressed round, but then something awkward in his lying silenced them. Many a man fell over as the energy he put into the spell overbalanced him, but John was lying face down on the ground. Lord Barthwick reached in and turned John over. John's face was white and his eyes were open and sightless.

Lord Barthwick reached inside John's jerkin and shirt.

55

'His heart is beating,' he said. 'Fetch a truckle and let's get him back to his cottage.'

John stirred and his eyes blinked, coming back into focus. He tried to sit up, but Lord Barthwick held him down. 'Stay where you are, John,' he said, but John struggled to get up and Lord Barthwick realized it might harm him more to hold him down.

'Nay, I must have fainted like a lass,' John said.

'Aye, I reckon you mun . . . Any road, tha's had enough for this night.'

'What happened to my knurr . . .'

'I don't know,' Lord Barthwick said seriously. 'I think tha knocked it somewhere into't Pennines . . .'

'You won,' the crowd shouted. 'You beat Sam Weighton.'

Despite the pain he could still feel in his head, John smiled. 'Them'll be the first eggs I've taken off thee, Sam Weighton . . .'

'Aye, ye devil, and the last,' Sam grunted as he turned and stomped away from the scene of his defeat.

The fiddlers played no more; the fires gave off slow spirals of acrid fat-laden smoke visible only in the dull red glow from the roasting pits. All around the green the sated and exhausted villagers sat in small groups talking in quiet voices, or snoring in drunken sleep, stirring, bellies grumbling with the surfeit of beer and food, the frenzied dancing, the singing and handclapping that had led, finally, to exhaustion.

The darkest fringes of the edge of the green hid small knots of couples who lay side by side, whispering, stroking, risking and daring. 'Tha's a grand lass, Gertrude,' Willie Waterton said, one hand round her neck plunged into the bodice of her dress, the other beneath her shift, stroking the calico of her underdrawers. Three times he'd tried to untie the string of her drawers at the waist; three times she'd refused him though she was aching with desire for him, and her nipples were hard enough to burst. Everyone knew

Willie Waterton wasn't constant in his affections: May blossom lasted longer than Willie's ardour.

'Do you love me, then, Willie?' she asked.

'Aye, lass, that I do,' he said, anxious to swear to anything that would improve his chances. They'd always said Gertrude Aysgill was as cold as yesterday's mutton but it had been his proud boast there wasn't a pair of knees he couldn't open wide, once he set his mind to it. It looked as if he'd failed this night.

'I'd love thee a lot more if I could get closer to thee,' he said desperately, 'but tha's wearing that much clothes I might as well be stroking the buttocks of a ewe.'

'That's hardly complimentary, Willie,' she chided him.

'Well, I'm not one much for fancy talking. Come on, Gertrude, take off your drawers. No-one shall ever know we've pleasured each other! Harvest Fayre's only once a year, after all.'

'So I can be carrying your bairn in my arms by the next Fayre, is that it.'

'I'll not give thee a bairn.'

'I know you won't because my drawers are stopping where they are . . .'

'Nay, Gertrude,' he groaned, 'I'm dying of love for thee.'

'Then, you'll have to die, won't you.'

Mark Ottershaw couldn't believe his good fortune. 'Don't give me a baby, now, will you,' Dodie said.

'No, I won't,' he replied, hardly hearing what she said as she moved beneath him. By heck, fancy him, Mark Ottershaw, with Dodie Aysgill! It was hardly credible.

'Oh, Dodie, I love you that much,' he said, carried away in the euphoria of ecstasy.

'That's as may be,' she said. 'But be careful, don't give me a bairn . . .'

'I won't, Dodie,' he promised fervently, thrusting himself ever deeper inside her. 'I won't. I won't. I won't. I won't.' Suddenly there was a press of limbs, a heave, and he found himself on his side on the ground, with the dew-damp grass chilly against his bare buttocks, his ankles entangled in his breeches, his precious manhood spurting from him over the grass. Dodie was lying by his side with her knees closed, her eyes smiling at him.

'It's a good job one of us kept her senses, Mark, else you'd have been giving me twins wi' that lot . . .'

'I got carried away,' he mumbled as he fell back, exhausted and replete.

'I know you did,' she said. He looked so vulnerable, so ridiculous, lying there on his back in the pale moon-glow that she felt compelled to reach out her hand and stroke his face. 'I reckon you're feeling better, now, Mark,' she said.

'That I am,' he said faintly, his eyes closed as his head lolled back on the damp grass that served to cool him.

'Do you love me, then, Mark?' she asked.

'That I do. You know I do.'

'Enough to marry me?'

'If that's what you want?'

'Not now. But I might, one day.'

'You'll find me ready, and willing.'

'Aye, I reckon I will, at that!'

Lord Bristow looked at the sallow face of the man who sat uneasily in the leather armchair in his study. 'Really,' he thought, 'one has to seek allies where one may find them these days.'

Giles shifted in his chair. 'Of course I am in no hurry to inherit,' he said unconvincingly. 'I trust my uncle, Lord Barthwick, will enjoy many years of healthy life on his estate . . . but one must always think of the future.'

'Aye, th'art a lying upstart,' Lord Bristow thought. He could see that Giles had a passionate lust to succeed to his uncle's estate and become a landed country squire. God help his tenants when Giles takes command of them. 'Of *course* one must, my dear Giles,' he said smoothly. 'That is why I thought to discuss the Acts of Enclosure with you, since it is a matter of direct concern to you.'

Giles sat in Parliament; his father had bought him a

Rotten Borough to give the lad something to do, to acquire a status he knew the lad would never find by his own endeavours.

Their conversation was interrupted by a timid knock on the door, and Lord Bristow called out, 'Come in!' The door opened to admit his two daughters, shyly holding hands, each clutching a sewing frame.

'Ah, there you are, my dears,' he said, smiling across the room at them. 'Come in, come in; this gentleman will not eat you!'

'Mama said we might come,' the older of the two girls said, 'to show you our sewing.'

'And so you shall,' Lord Bristow said. Though it grieved him that so far his wife had not given him a son and heir, he could be delighted by the two daughters he thought uncommonly pretty in their seventh and eighth years. He didn't miss the other two girls, both of whom had died of the plague a couple of years before, nor the latest born, again a girl, who'd died of colic. Lady Moira would have to move quickly if she was to give him the lusty son he so craved. She was pregnant again, and this time, surely . . .

'I trust I do not disturb you, my dear Giles, by spending a few moments of domesticity with my family. The girls are most able with their needles, and soon will be taught an instrument. Nothing, I feel, more delights an assembly than a modest maid at the keyboard.'

''Tis a pleasure no man should deny himself,' Giles said, licking his thin lips nervously.

'You, alas, have never married?' Lord Bristow enquired.

'Alas, I've never been blessed with that happy union,' Giles said.

Lord Bristow clutched his daughters to his knee and looked at their sewing.

'I have a notion a stitch or two has gone awry here, Rosalind,' he said severely. 'You must pay more attention to the details. As you grow older you will learn that the grand pattern of life is nothing more than a compilation and mastery of small details, will she not, my dear Giles?'

'Aye, that she will,' Giles Barthwick said.

'If that weren't true,' Lord Bristow thought, 'you'd not be sitting here in my study. I'd have no truck with thee, nor any of thy sort.'

'There, Rosalind, listen to the words of Mister Barthwick, for he is grown wise in many things. And you, Marietta, must learn to proceed more quickly, for you have only covered the half of your frame. We must learn to be diligent and expeditious in all we do. As Mister Shakespeare teaches us, "if it were done, t'were well it were done quickly." Though you are, as yet, too young to profit by Mister Shakespeare's wisdom.'

'Or to be sullied by his bawdiness, I'll be bound,' Giles said.

Lord Bristow looked up at him. 'Aye, I can see you'd find the plays bawdy,' he said smoothly, 'though I've a feeling they truthfully reflect the desires of *honest* men. Now my maids, you may run along to the nursery and I will see you again on the morrow at this time hoping to find some improvement in your needlework. Attention to detail, Rosalind, and more diligence, Marietta. You may each give me a kiss.'

Each did so. 'And now,' he said, his eyes glinting mischievously, 'you may give Mister Barthwick a kiss, for, in his unmarried deprivation, he must surely take a fancy to feel the lips of a maid upon his cheek!'

When the girls had left, Lord Bristow rose to his feet, indicating that the interview was over. Giles Barthwick also rose.

'So, my dear Giles,' Lord Bristow said, 'we are of a mind? If we can get the Acts of Enclosure you will greatly benefit on your succession to your Uncle's title and estate. I can count on you in the House, in all matters?'

'You can count on me, my Lord.'

'Good. And you, my dear Giles, can count on my support in the other matters of which we have spoken so confidentially and frankly. And now, alas, I must bid you good-day.'

60

He put his arm round the shoulders of the younger man and escorted him to the door. 'I think it might be better if you were to let yourself out by the back.' He chuckled and couldn't resist a parting sally. 'You are, of course, familiar with the back way.'

Lord Bristow had taken his house in the newly developed Grosvenor Square in London from his friend the Earl of Scarborough. Situated on the north side it was solid but elegant, with an imposing entrance hall that soared for two storeys round a wide staircase. The ground-floor rooms, which had been built sufficiently higher than the pavement outside to maintain the privacy of those within, were paved in marble brought from Italy, furnished in the elegant French style then much in vogue.

Lord Bristow was the descendant of a merchant family; his grandfather had been active in the coal trade from the north coast of Yorkshire and Cleveland, and had devoted his newly acquired fortune to the East India Trading Company and other overseas financial enterprises. One of the few men to get out of the South Sea Bubble with a vast profit, he wisely bought a title and a Parliamentary seat for his son and heir. By astute personal management at a time when one had to declare oneself either a staunch Whig or a staunch Tory, Sir Carodin Bristow had managed to please both political factions, and his son had obtained, at no small expense, a peerage and a seat in the House of Lords.

Throughout his life, Lord Bristow had been interested not only by London, by the bustling commercial and political life of the capital, but also by his extensive country estate on the moors of North Yorkshire. A progressive landlord, he had long ago divided his estates into individual farm holdings, let at suitable rents to tenant farmers to whom he'd given agricultural autonomy. His estate now supported many tens of thousands of sheep and was a major provider of the prosperous wool trade. He himself owned a large mill near Huddersfield where much of the wool was processed, travelling from his estate farms to the mill and thence to the merchants in Leeds and Bradford by pack mule train, and even by water along the river Aire and its tributaries.

When the Acts of Enclosure were first mooted, Lord Bristow, ever a progressive thinker, had seen this as a way to free the poverty-stricken strip holders – if they could have their strips combined and properly enclosed, they could develop a more intensive husbandry that would greatly increase their annual income.

Of course, there had been many opponents to his Bill. Many saw the dangers of giving that much freedom to the lower classes. It would set a dangerous precedent to permit them to enclose their land, as if they had the first right to it. The land, they argued, belonged to the estates and to the ancient rights of landlords. If peasants could enclose portions of it and deny access to his Lordship, what would the world come to?

In vain Lord Bristow had pointed to the increased yields the estate owners themselves would obtain. As it was, the estate owner couldn't turn a peasant off the land except for a malfeasance, or a failure to pay tithes. It would be infinitely better for the estate owners to surrender that small portion of their land in order to acquire a proportion of the common and have space in which to work the ground left to them more efficiently and more effectively.

In all of this he had been greatly helped by the publication of Jethro Tull's book on *Horse-hoeing Husbandry*, which in principle showed the advantages of a metal plough drawn by a horse over an ineffectual wooden one pulled by human labour. If the soil could be tilled twice as deeply, Tull had argued and then proven to Lord Bristow's satisfaction, the yield from it would be twice as heavy.

Lord Bristow was sitting in his study in Grosvenor Square when his steward announced the arrival of a messenger – 'bearing the seals of Lord Barthwick of Barthwick, my Lord. He seems a middling gentleman, much stained by travel, but of a peaceful disposition, my

Lord. He says his name is Holroyd.'

'Then show him in, Bates, show him in! Tobias Holroyd is well known to us.'

The man Bates showed into the study was, indeed, much stained by travel since he had ridden down from Yorkshire along the Great North Road, stopping only three times on the way to change horses and refresh himself. 'His Lordship impressed upon me the need for all speed, your Lordship,' he said as he took the rolled document from the large pouch he carried, slung across his shoulders by a leather strap. Lord Bristow unrolled the document and held down its corners with paperweights of finely etched glass.

'Yon's a fine hand,' he said, his voice thickened by his northern antecedents. He looked at the flush on Holroyd's tired features. 'I'll be bound you had a part in the scribing of it?'

'I was permitted that favour, my Lord,' Holroyd said. If asked he would have admitted his greater pleasure at sitting beside an inkwell, rather than cocking his leg over a fast steed to brave the footpads and highwaymen along the Great North Road.

'Aye, you were always a bookish man, Holroyd. If you weren't so firmly in the service of my dear friend, Lord Barthwick, I'd bring you here to take a hand with my library, for there's many a page needs setting to rights by a hand such as yours.' As he spoke he was scanning the petition, checking points of detail. It seemed to be complete and in the form in which he had dictated it to Lord Barthwick's attention. Three pages in length, it bore, on the last folio, the signatures of the villagers or their attested marks, with Lord Barthwick's signature at the bottom and his embossed family seal. Attached to the document by a ribbon passed through a hole that pierced each page was a four-page map composed on a thicker parchment, which showed the Barthwick Estate in general, then in larger scale the centre of the village. On the third page the strips were marked with numbers, which corresponded to the names of their holders. Some strips were delicately shaded, and bore no number.

The fourth page showed the names of all the inhabitants of the village in two columns, those for the Petition, those against it.

Seventy-six per cent, by calculation, were for the Petition.

Lord Bristow grunted in satisfaction when he saw the figure. 'Aye, we'll have no difficulty with that,' he said. 'I'll place it before the Lords myself, this very day.'

'Lord Barthwick was afeared the amendment would already have been raised?'

Lord Bristow laughed. 'And would have been, for sure, had I not blocked it time and time again. Nay, Tobias Holroyd, you can assure your Master there'll be no talk of amendment until this has gone through. There've been too many men walking into this house with favours to ask for that amendment to see the light of day until we're ready. The Tories can push and push all they've a mind, but we'll hold them back until we're ready, and then we'll let them raise all the amendments they desire, and knock them down one by one like Aunt Sallys at a Fayre, believe me!'

'You're a man of great power, my Lord,' Tobias Holroyd said. 'You must see many opportunities each day to reward those who serve you loyally. And what man could refuse you his loyalty, if bidden to your service?'

'You're a rascal,' Lord Bristow said, laughing. 'When my friend, Lord Barthwick, no longer has use for your services, then come to me and I'll see what can be found. But I'll take no man from the service of a friend, you can be certain of that. Now, tell the Steward to feed you and give you a bed, for I imagine you'll be in no condition to ride home to Yorkshire this day. But watch yourself in the ale-houses this evening. There are too many scoundrels down here in London for you to be safe in any tavern.' He pulled the tasselled cord that hung by his painted desk and after a few minutes the Steward reappeared and was given instructions. 'I shall be leaving in an hour,' he said. 'I shall wear full dress – please arrange that with my valet. Also the Ceremonial Carriage. Wilkins is to accompany me with this document. I shall be returning with a dozen or so gentlemen around five o'clock. Please see a suitable meal is prepared. This evening we shall have gaming in the upper drawing-room. There will be no ladies but the girls can say goodnight before we sit to table. Tell them to bring some token of their industry for me to admire – a painting, a sketch, a piece of embroidery. I will say goodbye to her Ladyship before I leave. By the way,' he added as an afterthought, 'see Holroyd here is looked after.'

An hour later Lord Bristow descended the staircase from his dressing-room on the second floor, wearing a suit of greyish gold laced with silver. The pleats of the skirt of his jacket were set fashionably back, revealing his shortened waistcoat and his breeches gathered just below the knee. His white silk stockings showed a well formed, even muscular leg, and his half-pointed black kid shoes were fastened with a silver buckle.

His tie wig, considered the most fashionable full dress wear in 1740, had the curls drawn back and was tied in a single tail with a bow of black ribbon. He had dispensed with what he considered the foppish habit of enclosing the end of the wig in a bag.

A diamond sparkled in his elegant frilled cravat and he wore a ring on each little finger, matching diamonds set in gold and surrounded by emeralds. Under his arm he carried a cocked hat of stiffened black material, edged with silver lace. The impression he gave was exactly as he had calculated it – he had the look of a rich titled gentleman in touch with the fashionable world of the day, but neither eccentric nor foppish. He was a serious minded modish man, a man to be taken seriously, a force to be reckoned with.

Wilkins, who awaited him by the coach which had been brought from the mews with its two horses champing and pawing, steam blowing from their nostrils in the cool morning air, was dressed in black as befitted a secretary, and carried a leather deed case.

The coach made its way north to Tyburn Road, then turned east to join Oxford Street, one of the main east-west arteries that connected the newly fashionable west with the City of London. Oxford Street was a quagmire filled with horse-drawn carts and small carriages, flys and dog-carts. Occasionally another imposing sprung carriage similar to Lord Bristow's would come by carrying some gentleman he knew and each would doff his hat to the other. The mornings were the times for calling, when men of position waited on other men of position to solicit or give influence and favours. The government of the country would have been impossible if these meetings had not constantly taken place – the Houses of Parliament were only the showcase, the theatre playing out a script which had been written in the studies, the drawing-rooms, the gaming rooms, the whore-houses of gentlemen of rank and privilege. Alliances made in the powerful houses of the new squares of the western part of London were sealed by the social occasions, the elaborate dinners, the elegant balls.

The Lord Chancellor kept his house further east than was considered fashionable, but it was convenient to the courts if not to Court, and he liked its spaciousness. Sturdily built of stone with a plain almost humble façade, it sat in its own courtyard surrounded by stables, by accommodation for the hundred or so servants in the Lord Chancellor's employ, by all his panoply of scriveners, officers of the seals, keepers of the libraries and collections of documents.

Lord Bristow's steward had taken the precaution of sending round a servant with a hand-engraved card bearing the advice that *Lord Bristow presented his compliments to the Lord Chancellor, and would be obliged to wait upon his Lordship on a matter of urgent business at eleven of the clock.*

Gentlemen didn't ask permission to call upon gentlemen. Gentlemen didn't try to call upon gentlemen at an hour that would not be convenient.

'Bristow, dear friend, come ye in . . .'

'Chancellor, how kind . . .'

'Do ye take a cordial?'

'I'd be obliged, Chancellor, to leave it stand, for I've no thirst on me for these modish ways.'

The Chancellor laughed. 'You'd not say the same if it was a pot of your own Yorkshire ale, I'll be bound. I can offer you French wine . . . Spanish sherry . . .'

Laughing, Lord Bristow shook his head. 'I'll wait until I'm in Yorkshire with my home brew,' he said. At the wave of the Lord Chancellor's hand he flung the unpadded skirts of his coat wide and sat on the plain wooden chair beside the desk at which the Lord Chancellor had been seated when he was shown in. Rumour had it the Chancellor was eighty-five years of age, though he didn't look it. He was dressed in a fashionable but simple brown working suit with slit cuffs, a working cravat of plain linen wound scarf-like round his throat. His eyes were bright and piercing, set beneath bushy snow-white eyebrows. Only the backs of his hands gave a hint of his age; the skin was wrinkled and his knuckles twisted by rheumatism.

'If I can't supply a drink,' he said, 'I can at least give you my attention. May I hazard a guess you want to discuss your pet subject, Enclosure?'

Lord Bristow nodded. 'My man Wilkins is without,' he said. 'He carries a petition from Lord Barthwick and seventy-six per cent of the strip holders of his estate for a Deed of Enclosure.'

'And you'd like the Deed to be pushed through before the amendment is tabled?' the Lord Chancellor asked.

'If it were convenient . . .'

'Of course it's convenient, Bristow. You know that as well as I,' the Chancellor said testily. 'But I don't like it. It cuts across Parliamentary procedure, as you also know, and if we're ever going to get that beleaguered institution to work we're going to have to learn to observe its procedures, not only in Whitehall, but in those mansions you're all building. Tell me, why can't this Petition of

Barthwick's wait its turn like the rest?' The Chancellor's keen eyes were on Bristow's face, but his mind was working smoothly along the paths of political expediency. 'Nay, don't tell me,' he said. 'Young Barthwick, nephew to his Lordship, in the Commons. I'll be bound he wants Enclosure since he succeeds to the estate unless his Lordship belatedly gets himself a son and heir. You want young Barthwick's vote on the Customs and Excise Act that would cripple your family's Newcastle connection. You've offered your influence with the Enclosure of his uncle's land, in exchange . . .

Bristow bowed his head in mock supplication. 'Guilty, m'Lud,' he said, 'but I plead extenuating circumstances. The Customs and Excise Act is a bad act, restricting trade, injuring many men and property. Dare I say, Lord Chancellor, that your family interests in Bristol and Spain are not immune from such a crippling policy. Though I'm certain,' he added hastily, 'that such consideration would not influence *you* were *you* called upon to vote.'

'Damned right you are,' the Lord Chancellor said grumpily. Damn it all. Young fellows coming in here, peddling influence like damned tinkers, asking for favours to further their schemes, all of which had but one thing in common — self-interest. Bristow here didn't give a damn about the Lord Chancellor's family interests in Bristol. He was thinking about his damned coals, his Newcastle trade. Damned tinker. 'I'm getting too old for these games,' he thought. The Law should be the Law; the Lord Chancellor should be able to form the bridge between Parliament and the Law, without having these tinkers come to him to peddle their damned influence. 'Have my man send in the Petition,' he said. 'I'll see it goes through today.'

'I knew we'd see things the same way, Lord Chancellor,' Bristow said smoothly. 'We haven't seen you in Grosvenor Square recently and Lady Bristow was asking about you and your health.'

'I don't get out much these days with my damned rheumatism,' the Lord Chancellor said. 'I've taken a place

68

in Bath to get away in October.'

'Then we must be certain to see you in Grosvenor Square before then,' Lord Bristow said. 'I'll get madam to send you an invitation.'

'Be sure to do that,' the Lord Chancellor said, his humour somewhat restored. Bristow's parties in Grosvenor Square were fast becoming the acme of the London social scene, frequently attended by no less a personage than the King. It would do the Lord Chancellor no harm to hob-nob with his Majesty, even though, privately, he considered him an uncouth Hanoverian upstart.

When Lord Bristow left the Lord Chancellor, he ordered his coachman to make his way to St James's Street, passing by Long Acre and Leicester Fields to Piccadilly. Though the streets were thronged as ever by sedan chairs and carriages, by the infamous gin carts and beer drays, while tradespeople of both sexes and all descriptions carried their wares most often in creels above their heads, the journey was uneventful. The autumn rains had not yet come and the streets, though foul smelling of urine and dung, were not yet choked by the mud that would follow the deluge. Lord Bristow glanced at his pocket watch; he was in good time still.

The scene outside White's Chocolate House compared with that inside the mad house of Bedlam as the elegant St James's Street, with St James's Palace at its southern end, filled with the midday crowd. Before Lord Bristow descended from his coach he saw several bailiffs hanging about at the side of White's, doubtless there on information that a wanted debtor was inside. White's Chocolate House had become the centre of the profligate social scene of fashionable London, with many fortunes wagered and lost by the inveterate gambling of the aristocracy. Lord Bristow's footmen cleared a path for him between the door of his elegant coach and the entrance, pushing the beggars and pedlars brusquely aside with their staves. He shuddered as he saw the pock-marked face of one of the beggars, a man without legs strapped into a tub, holding leather pads in his hands with which he contrived to swing himself and the tub along. He swung beneath the legs of the footmen and placed his tub in Lord Bristow's path. A footman raised his foot, pushed the tub over, and sent it rolling along the pavement to the laughter and jeers of all present. 'Give him a coin,' Lord Bristow said in his cultured London voice, from which all traces of the Yorkshire brogue he'd revealed when speaking to Holroyd had been removed. The crowd cheered and hands were raised in supplication, but his Lordship passed quickly through the throng and made the entrance unscathed.

The turmoil abated somewhat within the walls, though many fashionable men were strolling around between the widely spaced tables, and servants in waistcoats and breeches were running everywhere with mugs and fashionable trays of porcelain cups of chocolate. It was the custom for ladies to be admitted at the noon hour; later they would leave to return home and the men would have the exclusive use of the place until the late hour, when the courtesans and kept-ladies would put in an appearance, soliciting companionship and patronage.

Lord Bristow wrinkled his nose in some disgust though he was careful to keep an affable smile on his face as he passed through the outer rooms to where he knew he would find the people he was looking for. Lord Pendleton was seated at the gaming table, a hand of cards on the table before him. His opponent would instantly be recognized by anyone who liked a gamble – Jack Wokingham had earned a considerable competence at play and was the rock against which every young rake who wished to make a splash in London felt he must dash himself. To have taken a few pounds from Wokingham was a subject of interest in every fashionable drawing-room in the metropolis. Jack carefully guarded his reputation, permitting some to win, taking his pleasure and his wealth only from fools and bucks of no social importance, word of whose losses would do him no harm.

Lord Bristow greeted Pendleton with affectionate enthusiasm, nodded to Wokingham, and sat at the table. 'Don't tell me you've come to hazard your hand, my Lord,' Wokingham said provocatively.

'I'd as soon ride alone to Epping,' Lord Bristow said smoothly, 'though there I might *see* the fist that took my purse.'

Wokingham bowed his head. He had no wish to engage Lord Bristow in badinage, knowing that if ever Bristow should speak against him his days at the table would be numbered. He rose, bowed to Lord Pendleton, and started away from the table. 'Dammit, man,' Pendleton said petulantly, 'ye can't leave now with my notes in your pocket and no chance for me to retrieve them!'

'I shall return, my Lord,' Wokingham said. 'It is my custom to refresh myself at this hour with a stroll through the rooms.'

Pendleton slouched in his seat as he watched Wokingham go. 'I'm into the devil far too much for him to leave now,' he grumbled. 'Can you oblige me with a couple of thousand, Bristow? The devil left just when my luck was on the turn.'

'I seem to remember . . .' Bristow said quietly.

'Dammit, don't tell me you're to remind me of the five I already owe you, Bristow. I thought better of you than that.'

'I was about to say, my dear Pendleton, that I seem to remember your accepting an invitation to dine with me this day. Or perhaps you were too far gone at the time to make a note of the engagement . . .'

'Me, too far gone! Dammit, Bristow, are you suggesting I was in my cups, like some common ale-house fellow?'

'Not at all. You leap too quickly at conclusion, my dear Pendleton. I seem to remember that on the last occasion we met you were suffering a high fever.'

'Aye, Bristow, now I recall it. Just as I recall your

71

invitation to dine, which I remember accepting.'

'Good. Shall we leave together?'

'Aye,' Pendleton said, 'there's but one problem. The trollop across the room there was kind enough to tell me the bailiffs were waiting outside for me, front and back. My tailor, damn him to all hell, has set them on me for a trifling sum. Since I've but scant wish to spend the night in Newgate, I'm obliged to tilt my lance against Wokingham at least until I can win enough to secure my safe conduct out of here . . .'

'My dear fellow,' Lord Bristow said, 'you must leave the bailiffs to me and I will quickly send them packing.'

'Could you, dear friend, could you? I'd be eternally in your debt . . .'

'So you would, my dear Pendleton, so you would,' Lord Bristow said as he helped the youthful and far from sober Lord Pendleton to his feet and escorted him from the room.

When he'd despatched Lord Pendleton in his own coach, with strict instructions to the coachman they were not to stop on the way and that the coach was to return immediately for him, Lord Bristow returned inside White's.

The Earl of Chesterton had watched his progress across the room with amusement. 'Always the good Samaritan, Bristow,' he said. 'Though I don't doubt Pendleton's gratitude will serve your cause.'

Bristow knew the Earl for an old campaigner who was now inactive in politics since he'd fallen out with Walpole and with George II. He still kept a wary eye on the Palace of Westminster, and was reputed to be better informed than many within the House.

'The Tories will try their damnedest to destroy your Act of Enclosure, you know,' he said affably. 'This amendment they're trying to foist on you is only the first. That's their way, so to amend an Act that it ceases to have any value or merit.'

'So what would you recommend?'

72

'I think you need no recommendations from me,' the Earl said, looking shrewdly at Bristow. 'You've prepared your big guns; now I see that with the lesser fry, like Pendleton, you're preparing for a skirmish at your flanks. When the amendment is tabled, you must be ready for it, and defeat it soundly at the first contest or the Tories will worry you like the pack of self-interested dogs they are.'

'I see it as a matter of timing,' Bristow said.

'And you're damned right!' The Earl took a pinch of snuff from his jewelled box which he offered to Bristow, who refused it with a smile. He waited until the Earl had finished flourishing his lace-trimmed handkerchief, trumpeting from his nostrils and sneezing like a man with the ague. 'Sorry about that,' the Earl said, 'but there's nothing like a touch of the Araby for clearing one's head. Timing will be all, my dear Bristow,' he said. 'But make damned certain you have all your troops on the battlefield when the time comes. You'll need no champion – you've a silver tongue you can use like a rapier when you've a mind, and against Walpole's broadsword and cutlass, you'll draw blood, I'll be bound. But if you'll permit a word of advice . . .'

'I know of no-one whose advice I hold in greater esteem.'

'Aye, Bristow, that's as may be. You'll need to look carefully into your own heart in this matter. No man can plead a cause to full effect unless he himself is convinced by it. We live in cynical times, Bristow, and I can smell radicalism strong as May blossom. I'm too old now to do anything but offer advice to young bloods like you. Give conviction a place in your heart, Bristow, along with ambition and determination. Give it a place in there, I implore you.'

The dining-room on the first floor of Lord Bristow's house was separated from the ante-room by a great arch supported on marble pillars whose capitals had been carved by the mason after a design of Michelangelo, the Italian.

The archway itself was faced with curved oak panels into which had been inset Cleveland Pottery plaques of sprays of roses, each coloured differently. The elegant dining-room was lined with pictures hawked from France and Italy, most set too high for anyone to examine the detail. The space between the pictures was lined with a rose-coloured damask cloth specially woven for the room; six massive chandeliers each held thirty candles though the light that streamed in through the tall windows prevented the necessity of lighting them by five o'clock when the gentlemen sat down to table. The plates of food had been set out already, and Lord Bristow's servants went round the guests with jugs of claret wine from France which the guests drank from the new lead crystal glasses brought from Bohemia.

Lord Bristow sat at the head of the table and looked at his guests. Pendleton appeared to have improved with a couple of hours' sleep on a sofa in Bristow's dressing-room and was engaging his neighbour, Sir Walton Dempster, in spirited conversation about his experiences at the Southwark Fair a few weeks previously. Bristow let his eyes wander across the table as he saw them pluck voraciously at the plates of beef, the pheasants and grouse, the plovers' eggs, capons, meat pies, all set out on the latest delicate porcelain from France. Lord Northam, at the far end, would vote against the amendment when Bristow fanned the flames of his hatred of Sir Robert Walpole. Giles Barthwick was already in Bristow's pocket. Sir Humphrey Lockart would vote against it in exchange for a seat in the Lords, his burning ambition. The other two, Jonas Pickles and Ephraim Stanbury, could be bought by self-interest. Pickles' daughter, Nellie, was a pretty thing and came well endowed. Pendleton was in debt over his head and rumour had it he'd pledged half of Pendleton Hall to the Jews of the City of London to keep himself from Newgate, disgrace, and ruin. Pickles, though a miserly curmudgeon, would like to see his daughter take on a peerage – the association would also stand him in good stead in the House of Commons, where he sat as Member for the Westlake Hundreds, a seat he'd bought with his Hull timber shipping profits. Stanbury, the pompous fool, wanted a title. Any title. Thank God he had the money to pay for one, though, observing him at table and the uncouth style of his dress, Bristow could see he'd need more than a few lessons in deportment if he was to be accepted within the closed ranks of the aristocracy or the ruling classes. It would be easier now, with George II on the throne. Since the House of Hanover brought its dull pedantic style to the glittering Palace of Westminster life at Court had reached a low ebb of decorum and elegance; and many more uncouth fellows, with their plain dowdy wives, were being permitted than would have been possible before.

The rest of the men at table were firmly against the amendment, and would offer a leavening of conversation to any of the special guests who might turn so foolish, in wine, as to dissent from Bristow's well-known and oft-stated opinion. The Act of Enclosure must go through – Bristow must get it through if eventually he was to hope to climb high in office, if his dream of one day becoming Prime Minster were ever to become a reality.

'I've been watching your eye,' Sir Walton said, 'and following its flight, seeing where it settles. I'm reminded of words of our dear great Prime Minister this last year when he spoke to those who have high expectations of place. "They have a *lively* sense of *future* favours," I believe he said.'

'He also said, I'm led to believe, "all those men have their price." '

'And my price, my Lord, what is my price?'

Lord Bristow laughed gently. 'My dear Sir Walton,' he said gaily, 'how could I know that? You are a gentleman of the utmost probity, of that we can all be certain. Nor gaming, ale, nor whore-houses have ever known your patronage. You have a gracious and loving wife who sits by her easel when not enchanting you on the spinet, or giving you progeny in, might one say, profusion. Your estates are managed to the acme of perfection, every furrow straight, every copse well stocked, every weir cleaned to perfection. As if that were not sufficient, you are also a Freeman of the City of London, a Member of the Court of Clothworkers, a Magistrate. What more could any man desire?'

'What more indeed,' Sir Walton said sourly, not amused by the bantering tone with which Bristow listed his attainments.

'Perhaps there is a small wish one might have?'

'A small wish . . .'

'I know nothing of these things myself, you understand,' Lord Bristow said, 'but I suspect a man whose wife had harboured Jacobites on his country estate during his absence, a man whose wife's sweet voice and artistic talents hid a Papist's heart, might not want that fact bruited abroad, lest it should damage his reputation. What was it Lucretius said – since you've a turn of tongue for the apt quotation even from such a doubtful source as our little respected Prime Minister. *Tantum religio potuit suadere malorum.* Such evil deeds could religion prompt . . . especially, the wrong religion . . .'

'You devil. How did you learn that?'

'I have learned *nothing*, alas, my dear Sir Walton. *Nothing*. Only to hope piously that when the time comes to vote for or against the amendment to the Act of Enclosure, friends who have supped at my table will take the same passionate delight in opposing the amendment as I myself shall.'

'I'd have your word . . .?'

'My dear Sir Walton – my word upon what? I'll give you my word, but I heard it only yesterday, that Bath is reckoned a soothing place these days and the waters are reputed to cure the ladies of all manner of ailments and disquietudes, humours and fancies. The social scene, I'm

76

told, is most elegant and appealing to any lady of artistic inclinations.'

'I'll rent a house and she'll occupy it until the waters have cooled her wayward fancies,' Sir Walton vowed. 'I'm obliged to you, my Lord.'

'You're a good fellow, Sir Walton. Here's my hand, shake it like a brother.' The two men solemnly stood and shook hands.

Lord Northam watched the exchange. 'Another lamb being led to the slaughter,' he thought, though wisely he said nothing.

The strip-holders assembled in the Great Hall of Barthwick Manor, where his Lordship, to mark the occasion, had caused his servants to place a couple of barrels of beer and to fill the long sidetables with cold meats, poultry, pies and sweetmeats.

The Great Hall was cold despite the enormous log fires that burned along one side, their spit-roasting machinery for once idle.

John Aysgill had worn his leather jacket with the fur inside; wisely he kept it on his back and was glad of its warmth since he knew how cold the Hall could be in February. All his family kept close about him and he noticed that Mark Ottershaw left his father to come and stand beside Dodie. He looked at his lass, seeking signs and symptoms. She looked healthy as ever and as indifferent as always to a man's attentions. Happen she still wasn't ready to be wed though it was apparent from a glance at Mark Ottershaw's moonstruck face that he was in a lather of hope and expectation. John saw the lad start to frown when Dodie, helping herself to a piece of the roast pork, exchanged a few words with Cryer's lad. Poor young devil; Dodie'd show him the fires of hell afore he'd wait for her in the chapel. She sat herself at the bench, the slab of meat delicately set on her trench of bread to catch the gravy. Immediately, John saw, she had three lads about her and Mark Ottershaw, glowering with suppressed rage, stood and talked with Gertrude.

It was three o'clock when his Lordship appeared with Tobias Holroyd trailing behind him carrying a long leather tube from which he extracted a number of large papers. A piece of timber had been erected on a stand between two of the fireplaces; Holroyd hung the papers on the protruding nails and smoothed them down; they were best linen-backed stuff and took quite a bit of straightening before he got them to his satisfaction.

Polly, who'd been giving a hand with the beer and taking away empty wooden trays, left the room when Lord Barthwick waved his hand. Tobias Holroyd banged on the timber-mounted brass gong, and the villagers were silent, shuffling forward to form a ring round his Lordship, who'd stationed himself beside one of the legs of the stand.

'You all know why we are here,' he said. 'It's my duty to inform you all that a Petition of Enclosure has been granted to the village of Barthwick and is hereby declared legal and binding. Any who want to examine the Petition may do so by application to Tobias Holroyd; at the moment it's being worked and bound and will form part of the archive of this village, to be preserved for ever more in the library of the Manor. The main provisions of the Petition are simple and clear. As of this day, all land in and around this village is forfeit to the common weal. The land, as you all know, will be assessed by the County Surveyor who arrives in the morn with his assistants, and each man's holding will be put to his name in the Common Book of Deeds. As soon as the surveyor has completed his task, the land will be divided again in shares, with each man receiving his exact entitlement in one suitable apportionment.'

'What's meant by suitable, your Lordship?' Sam Weighton asked.

'Suitable, Maister Weighton, means, taking into account the terrain. Obviously we're not going to give any man, not even thee who has a taste for liquids, any land at the bottom of the pond.'

There was general laughter which lightened the tone of the meeting considerably.

'What about the Scars?' James Waterton asked.

'No man will be given land which cannot be worked to advantage. Anyway, if we give away the Scars, where will the courting couples go of an evening?' The Scars, a jagged outcrop of rock to the north of the common, was a well-known courting spot, despite the legend that said one of Lord Barthwick's ancestors, jilted in love, had thrown himself from the top. His body, the legend continued, had jammed in a cleft which no man could reach and had been obliged to rest, lodged there, until only the skeleton remained. On stormy nights wind howled through the cleft and some said they could hear a human voice calling *beloved*.

'And the common, my Lord?' John asked quietly.

'According to the Petition, which was drawn in London according to the provisions of the Parliamentary Act of Enclosure, the common land is to be included in the division,' Lord Barthwick said flatly. The division of the common had caused the most dissension, but the Act was quite clear and quite specific on that point, since it was on the question of retention of the commons that the Tories had tried to fight their unsuccessful amendment.

'This is how it will work,' Lord Barthwick said. 'The surveyor will be the final arbitrator. He will look over all the land and divide it into entitlements. Any man who is not satisfied with his entitlement will have the right to appeal to a committee composed of *all* the land holders, including me. That way, I pray we shall see justice done. Once the land has been divided, we shall enact a Deed of Title in which each man will be given the holding of that land, as of right. I have agreed to waive all my rights in this matter and to make a Gift of Tenure to each of you, by legal document, drawn up for the purpose by a lawyer who'll come from York. The Deeds of Holding, the Deeds of Gift of Tenure, the Deeds of Title, will all be registered and held in York for public perusal. That is to say, copies will be held there. The originals will be kept here, as part of the record of life in our village. Now, when all that has been done, and so that the ploughing and sowing will not be unmindfully delayed, the lands will all be adequately fenced.'

'At whose expense, my Lord?' Sam Weighton asked.

'Why, at the expense of the land holder, of course. Common boundaries will be fenced at the joint expense of the holders sharing the boundary.'

'And if a man fails to fence his boundary?'

'Then the land shall be forfeit. The land must be fenced. It's in the Act and the Petition. *The land must be enclosed!*'

There were mutterings throughout the room. Everyone knew the cost of even the cheapest form of fencing, chestnut stakes tied together. They lacked the stones locally for dry stone walling.

'We could grow hawthorn, my Lord?'

'It would take many a year to grow a thick hawthorn hedge, you all know that. Nay, the allocations must be fenced within a month as the Act says, and any man who cannot, or will not, fence it will be obliged to quit. I'll stretch the Petition's provisions a bit. Any man who can't or won't fence his land will be permitted to sell his entitlement to anyone willing to buy it.'

Now the mutterings were loud and Lord Barthwick knew this would be the major bone of contention. The Act was quite specific – dammit, it was called the Act of *Enclosure* – it held no meaning if the lands weren't divided and *enclosed*. The whole new business of farming and agriculture depended on people segregating the land so that each could work it in his own way or choose, if he preferred, to run animals on it. What would happen to one man's crop of rape if another man chose to run sheep, without a fence to keep the sheep away from the crop? What quarrels would they have over the ownership of strips of land at the boundaries if they weren't clearly delineated by a fence?

'This plan of the village will stay here,' he said, 'until the matter is settled. The surveyor will draw everything clearly on this map, so that each man will see exactly what the other man is entitled to, and is getting. Tobias Holroyd will be the clerk of the map – any disputes can originally be brought to him for consideration by the surveyor. Now, I'd be obliged if you'd help yourself from the tables – I regret that business calls me away. One final word – the door of the Manor is, as always, open. We'll have no Leet Court, nor Star Chamber, here in Barthwick. We're embarking on days of prosperity such as we've not yet known. With the help of God, piety, industry, and respect for the common weal, you should all see better days ahead. You all have my best wishes in our common endeavour.'

His Lordship was so obviously sincere that all could only respect him. He moved forward through them all until he stood before John Aysgill, to whom he offered his hand. John held out his and the two men shook solemnly, reconciled to whatever the future might bring. Lord Barthwick saw John wince at the handshake.

'Thy back no better, John?'

'A touch of winter's ague, my Lord,' John said. His back had been paining him since the Harvest Fayre but he'd said nothing about it. 'It's nowt a hot poultice won't cure – or a touch of spring sun after this o'erlong winter.'

'I'll send down some mustard and tar,' Lord Barthwick promised. 'They say in London it does wonders for rheumatism.'

When his Lordship had gone, wisely absenting himself so that they could discuss the matter of the enclosure without his stifling presence, John seated himself at one of the benches, his back towards one of the fires. Gertrude saw him sit down and came to him with a pot of ale. 'Are you all right, Father?' she asked solicitously.

'Aye, lass, I'm grand . . .'

'You don't look grand, Father,' she said. 'Shall I fetch you owt?'

'Nay, lass, I've no appetite.'

Matthew came and sat across from them. 'You all right, Father?' he asked, gnawing hungrily at half a chicken.

'Nay, lad, don't thee start. I'm all right.'

'I wonder what bit of land we'll get. I hope it's up yon by the Scars. That soil passes through your hand like sugar.'

Peter brought his food and sat. 'Nay, tha's never going to eat all that,' John said. 'Tha moan't be greedy, times like this . . .'

'Eat it while we have chance, that's my belief.'

'Cheeky whelp. Has tha never heard of the sin of gluttony?'

Simon came to the table with a portion of beef. 'Nay, Peter,' he said when he saw his brother's hand, 'tha's not going to eat all that?'

'Of course I'm not,' Peter said. 'But tomorrow's another day, isn't it, and we don't get Petitions every day, and invitations to t'Manor. Aye, it'd be right grand to live in a place like this!'

'Don't talk with thy mouth full,' John said automatically. Dodie came and sat, and John looked at each of them with great pride, knowing they belonged together, knowing that soon he'd own his own land with a Deed of Gift from his Lordship. He ought to be happy with his family about him, even if he did have to act the Father with them.

'Don't mind me, lad,' he said, rumpling Peter's hair then slipping his hand affectionately round the lad's shoulders. 'Eat all you've a mind to. Like you say, we don't get Petitions every day, nor invitations to sup at the Manor. Fetch us another pot of ale, Gertrude. I've a mind to sup a few, afore we go down home.'

'Aye, Father, sup a few,' Gertrude said. 'Happen it'll make you feel a bit better.'

It took the surveyor, a well-fleshed lugubrious man in his fifties who kept his own counsel and spoke but rarely, fifteen days to assess the land and to apportion it. So skilled was he that each man had good land and bad, soft ground and stony. Since it was most conveniently placed to the Manor holdings, the common was given to his Lordship so that all his fields were contiguous. He hired a group of itinerants, most of whom seemed to have come from Ireland seeking employment, and work began immediately on his fences, using chestnut rails on chestnut stakes driven deep into the ground. At the same time he hired masons and their labourers, had stone carted from the quarry fifteen miles distant, and started to build a more substantial wall that would eventually encompass all his property.

Sam Weighton was delighted. One side of his new land ran along his Lordship's; Sam negotiated a tithe payment for each of the next five years as his share of the fencing cost. At the same time he shared boundaries with Job Hirst, James Waterton and Thomas Clay. They bought chestnut from his Lordship's forest, cut and hauled it in unison, and soon had the makings of excellent enclosures.

The Aysgill lads were delighted with the land they'd been given. It was the nearest to the village and, to their eyes, accustomed only to seeing their land in small strips far from each other, it seemed a vast field. 'We'll not plough that in a day,' Matthew said, excited by the thought of the crops the land would yield.

'We mun be businesslike,' Peter said. 'One section for animals in one year, so that the dung will fertilize the soil next year for crops.'

John's heart sank when he saw the land, which had only one common side, and that shared with Fred Ottershaw. The other three sides were exposed to the village itself and would need to be fenced entirely at John's own expense since there was no-one to share the cost of a common border.

He was standing, looking over his land, when Fred Ottershaw walked over to him. 'Aye, it's grand to have our own land,' Fred said. 'Now we're free men and can do what we like, eh, John?'

'Aye, I reckon we can.'

'I was wondering,' Fred said, 'about the fencing. Happen I had a bad year, last, and we're short of pobbies as it is without buying fencing. You know his Lordship won't let us take more than a mite from his forest so us'll have to go further afield and it's going to cost a sight more. Could you see your way to putting up our common fence, and taking my share back over the next year or two?'

'I'll see what I can do,' John said, his heart sinking. He'd been hoping to ask Fred Ottershaw the same favour. With three fences to put up with no help from neighbours, he'd be hard pressed to find the money.

As always when he was troubled he waited until they sat down for their meal before asking the opinions of his sons. 'Peter, tha'd better do the reckoning,' he said, 'since tha's the only one good at it.' Peter got out his slate, sponged it clean, took up his piece of chalk stone.

'I reckon we're going to need a stake at every pace,' John said.

'Nay, Father,' Simon said. 'They're putting them two stakes to every three paces, with three rails across.'

Peter was scratching on the slate.

'Nay, give it a lick,' Dodie said. 'That screeching sends shivers up my back.'

Peter licked the end of the chalk stone and silenced it as he started on his calculation.

'I reckon his Lordship will allow us forty posts and a hundred paces of rail, though we'll have to cut it and drag it ourselves,' John said.

'We'll have to find fifteen pounds for that,' Peter said after his first calculation. He bent over the slate again and scratched more figures. 'And we'll have to find ten pounds for the rest and cart it from Betlaby. I reckon the carting will come to at least a pound.'

They looked silently at each other, knowing there was no way they could find a total of twenty-six pounds. Peter started scratching again and in frustration Dodie took the chalk stone from him and licked it herself.

'Aye, tha always had more spit than me,' he said

mischievously. He was adding their assets, calculating what he'd get for the cloth they'd woven this winter, what they had in the box, what their animals would fetch, what was their total wealth.

Seven pounds . . .

'Nay, Father, we can't do it,' he said as he put the slate down.

They were all silent. It was true. They simply couldn't fence their land, couldn't enclose it. 'Dear Lord,' Gertrude said with a sob in her voice, 'the land will be forfeit!' She expressed the fears of them all. Lord Barthwick had stretched a point in offering to let any man sell his land if he couldn't enclose it, but how much would they get for it . . .? The whole field wasn't worth, wouldn't even fetch the price of enclosing it!

John rose to his feet, and reached for his leather jacket which he put on over his smock. He covered his head with his felt hat. Without telling, they knew where he was going.

Only Lord Barthwick could help them now.

Tobias Holroyd was fussing with the papers when John Aysgill arrived at the Manor. 'So much to be done,' he said petulantly. 'You people have no idea.'

John was too worried in himself to banter with Tobias Holroyd, who sought only to aggrandize himself in the eyes of other folks. 'I'd be obliged if I could see his Lordship,' he said baldly.

'You can talk to me,' Holroyd said in his hectoring manner. 'We can't go bothering his Lordship for every small problem.'

'I've no desire to talk to thee in this matter,' John said stubbornly. 'His Lordship and I were talking together long before tha was born, long before tha stuck thy nose in college books.'

'You can't see his Lordship. Not today,' Holroyd snapped. 'For he's away to Stonebridge. I'd have thought you'd have known, if you're as *familiar* with his

Lordship's affairs as you claim, that today he's bound for Stonebridge to formalize the engagement of his daughter to the Stonebridge heir. Tomorrow she's to be dowered and there'll be celebrations. You'll have to wait until his Lordship returns, for I swear he's already upon the way.'

His Lordship was, indeed, on the way and in pain. These last few days he'd been suffering mightily from the same sort of rheumatism that John Aysgill had, and was at that very moment thinking of John, wondering if the tar and mustard had done Aysgill any more good than it had done him. So painful was his back he couldn't sit a horse and had to ride amidst goose-down-stuffed cushions in the coach, though every stone, every ripple in the road sent stabs of pain through him. 'Drive more slowly, more carefully, Simms,' he kept growling in his ill-humour, knowing the roads were so bad the coachman could do no better.

They had reached the forest and were driving slowly through it, hearing on all sides the sound of axes chopping the stands of chestnut and hazel for the fencing. Here beneath the trees the fallen leaves had rotted into a carpet which eased the path of the coach considerably. He leaned back, comfortable for the first time on this journey and took a sip from his silver flask into which Polly had poured French cognac.

'Tell me, Clarissa, with what feelings you approach your marriage?' he asked.

She was surprised to hear him express such a question to her. The wedding was arranged, the amount of the dowry decided. What mattered her *feelings*?

'I approach it with humility, Father,' she said demurely. 'I would like to be a good wife. With the help of God, perhaps I shall succeed.'

'Aye, lass, you'll need the hand of God for there's much restlessness in Rupert, your husband to be. It's my intention to entail your dowry – at least, the part that is in land, so that Rupert shall not have the spending of it. For your part, ye'll have to learn to be warm and loving to him – nothing drives a man to London and the tables faster than a cold wife in his bed and a sour face across his dinner board.'

'The girl has much to learn, my Lord,' Lady Barthwick said, 'but I mind myself of when you were young and full of impatience.'

'You go too far, my Lady,' he growled, but they caught the humour in his eyes. He'd been a notorious hell-raiser when he was young though York and not London had drawn him.

'Drive slowly and carefully, dammit, Simms,' he shouted.

They'd left the forest behind and were rolling over the wide expanse of moorland that separated the two great estates and the track was stony again, and rutted with potholes. Lord Barthwick recalled the time he'd driven a favourite mare hard over these moors and she'd broken a leg in one of those damned holes. 'Take care for the horses,' he shouted.

'Aye, my Lord, that I will.'

Lord Barthwick normally liked being out here on the heather where herds of deer sported, and rabbits and hares ran. He recalled the days of his youth when they'd come out with the archers and taken as many as four or five deer, culling the herds of young males. He remembered being chased by a wild boar until his father had made him turn to face it, knife in hand, and he'd watched its wild progress with fear in his heart. He hadn't known at the time that Old Smithers had been standing with the cross-bow, loaded with a bolt, ready to fire should the boar seize the advantage of him. He'd stood and waited for it, seeing its fearsome red eyes staring wickedly at him, seeing its dreadful snout and the horn damaged by some previous contest, possibly with the antlers of a deer. When it had charged, he'd side-stepped at the last minute as he'd been taught a hundred times, and had slashed in and upwards quickly, ripping its throat, hearing it squeal in its death-throes when he knelt on it and stuck his knife into its heart for the killer thrust.

When they heard the shot they thought someone was using his gun on deer.

'Stop, Simms, for God's sake stop,' Lord Barthwick bellowed. But the coach was already stopped by the fall of the lead horse, which had taken the blast full in its face and was falling in the traces, the shafts of the coach dipping and plunging with it as the other two horses fell in a maelstrom of swirling legs and tails.

'Keep down, my Lord,' they heard Tonkin yell, but the carriage was already tilting to the left and Lord Barthwick had been thrown across the seat space and was sprawled across the laps of the two ladies.

They heard the agonized neighing of the horses; the trace horse had snapped the nearside shaft with the force of its plunge; the weight of the coach plunged the broken raw ends of the shaft into the horse's side, gouging out its stomach. As it kicked, the support of the box smashed away and Simms the coachman fell down into the writhing mass of horse flesh, rapidly kicked to death by the flailing hooves of the demented animals. The other horse reared in fear and agony and the off-side shaft lifted, tilting the coach onto its side. The horse, imprisoned by the tackle and the kicking pounding animals, smashed back its feet wildly, kicking in the front of the coach below the seat on which the three passengers sprawled. Lord Barthwick felt his wife rear beneath him and scream as he tried to extricate himself, to climb up to force a way out of the door. He pushed Clarissa upwards through the space and she struggled out.

When he tried to pull his wife up she screamed in his arms with pain and fell; he could see where the horse's hoof, smashing through the thin wood of the coach panel, had smashed into her lower spine. He turned her back tenderly – she was already dead. Cursing and sobbing with rage and frustration, he lifted himself up, reaching out at the arms which pulled him, realizing too late that the sleeves of the jackets were rough buckskin and not the velvet of his footmen's uniforms. 'Aye, come ye out, my Lord,' coarse voices said.

He looked about him; the coach pistols were lost in the wreckage – he was unarmed. He climbed from the coach and saw his footmen lying beside the road with their throats cut. Simms, his coachman, and all three coach horses were also dead. Clarissa was being held by each arm by two ruffians, and a third was holding a pistol on him, with the flint cocked.

Another man was sitting on the dry stone wall beside the road; he doffed his cap when he had Lord Barthwick's attention.

'You don't know me, my Lord,' he said mockingly. 'We have never met in person. Though I believe you had the pleasure of meeting my brother.'

'I know nor kith nor kin of thine!' Lord Barthwick said, fuming with anger.

'You stand corrected, my Lord,' the man said. 'You met my brother, exchanged a few strokes with him, and then hanged him. Jack Overton.'

'I recall the blackguard,' Lord Barthwick said. 'I predict the same fate will befall you afore long.'

'Not at your hands, my Lord, if I may make so bold.'

Overton walked to the wreckage of the coach and freed the coachman's whip from the traces. 'Not at your hands, my Lord,' he said softly as he hefted the handle. 'Tie his arms behind him.'

The two men came behind his Lordship and, despite his powerful struggles, held his hands behind him and tied his wrists together with pigskin thongs. One of them tripped him deftly, and bound his ankles together. Then they picked him up again, and tied his wrists behind him to one of the spinning carriage wheels. The pain in his back and wrists was excruciating, but he made no complaint.

Clarissa was watching these preparations with mounting horror; when she finally realized what they were about to do she ran forward. One of the men caught her arm and dragged her back. She fought him bravely, her tiny fists pounding against the broadcloth of his tunic. She raised her hand to try to scratch his face. 'A lively whelp we have here, Percival,' he said, laughing. 'I've a notion to take her in yon heather and calm her down!'

'Tie his Lordship's feet to the bottom wheel,' Percival Overton commanded the other man, who grabbed the end of the pigskin thong and secured it firmly round a wheel spoke. Now Lord Barthwick was imprisoned between the wheels and the top one was free to revolve. He had no stability as the ruffian spun the wheel to its limit, dragging him sideways, then pushed the wheel to bring him upright again.

'You've no need of going far into the heather,' Percival Overton drawled. 'I'm certain his Lordship would dearly like to be present at his daughter's inauguration.'

The man he was addressing effortlessly picked Clarissa from the ground and set her down on the grassy bank beside the road. Lord Barthwick went berserk trying to tear his hands from the bindings, but the second ruffian kept spinning the wheel in each direction, robbing his efforts of power.

The man slowly and methodically pulled the finery from Clarissa's body, his hand tearing the delicate fabrics, ripping the lace and the ribbons, until she lay sobbing in a torn heap of what had been her fine costume. The second ruffian ceased twirling the wheel and went to his partner's side. Together they forced Clarissa down; first one and then the other took down his breeches and forced himself upon her. At first Clarissa screamed, and Lord Barthwick roared and shouted like a bull, but it was to no avail. Clarissa's screams faded and became agonized sobs as each of the men started on her again. Lord Barthwick couldn't watch any more and hung his head but suddenly Overton was by his side, grabbing his chin, lifting his face.

'You flogged my brother to death, my Lord,' his evilly quiet voice said. 'You should be happy I'm permitting your daughter to be pleasured to death instead of flaying the skin from that lovely white body. Believe me, my Lord, my men are beasts at the sight of a woman's soft belly and they've been under constraint for many a day, waiting for your coach to pass this way for my revenge. And revenge I'll have, my fine Lord.'

He stepped back, measuring his distance, his back turned to Clarissa and his men. He raised his arm and the lash curled then flicked forward. Lord Barthwick felt the first bite down the side of his cheek and started to pray . . .

The village waited in stunned shocked silence as the Stonebridge carriage arrived, carrying the bodies of Lord and Lady Barthwick and their daughter Clarissa. Rupert Stonebridge had taken the humour to ride out and meet his bride-to-be on the way, and had come upon the terrible scene by the roadside minutes after the outlaws must have left, since the blood was still running from Lord Barthwick's corpse.

The footmen and Simms the coachman had already been returned on the backs of pack mules and their families had taken charge of them. Already, men were at work digging holes in the ground outside the chapel where the dead of Barthwick were traditionally laid to rest.

His Lordship, his wife and daughter would be interred inside the mausoleum attached to the chapel itself.

Rupert's face was full of grief as he escorted the coach with its macabre burden. He'd been genuinely fond of Clarissa and had looked forward greatly to their marriage. Lord Barthwick had been a favourite uncle to him all his life and had always welcomed him at Barthwick Manor, even if he had disapproved of the young man's increasing rakishness. A messenger had already been despatched to London to bring the tragic news to Giles Barthwick, Lord Barthwick's true nephew and nominated heir, who would inherit the title and the estate. The doctor had been sent for – he'd given instructions to the embalmer coming from Leeds, who, with his team of men and women, would take care of the mortal remains of this noble family. The master mason had been sent for; he'd work with the Barthwick masons to prepare the tomb.

Tobias Holroyd had brought out his Lordship's Last Will and Testament and had laid them on the study desk, ready for Rupert Stonebridge to peruse. He knew the provisions of the Will quite well. It made a few small bequests to the staff of Barthwick Manor. Bates, the Steward, and he, Tobias Holroyd, were to receive ten guineas each; both were commended to the next Lord Barthwick as being loyal and industrious servants. Holroyd had privately decided to seek his fame in London – he imagined that Lord Bristow would honour his promise of finding something for him and the thought of working in Grosvenor Square, so close to a man at the centre of politics, excited him beyond measure. Bates on the other hand had built all his life around Barthwick Manor, in which he had his own quarters – Bates would be content to stay in service here in the house he knew and loved so well. Holroyd's lip curled with contempt when he thought of the stick-in-the-mud Bates.

The bodies were laid on trestles in the Great Hall, still wrapped in the sheets Rupert had requested from Stonebridge Castle. The main door of the Hall was bolted and barred – body-snatchers were everywhere and such a wonderful prize would be bound to attract them.

A footman was stationed before the door with a pike, and strict instructions to let no-one in. He'd be relieved each four hours of the long night ahead and luckily he did not believe in ghosts.

Only when all these preparations had been made did Rupert Stonebridge settle himself down in one of the guest-rooms, to try to sleep. He'd drunk deeply of his Lordship's claret in an attempt to drown the thoughts that came surging into his mind; the meal the cooks had made for him sat heavily on his stomach, and half an hour elapsed before finally he dropped into slumber. They let him sleep the following morning while the doctor and the embalmer proceeded with their grim tasks of draining the blood from the bodies and replacing it with fluid, of removing the entrails and organs, of composing the features of the dead ones and, in his Lordship's case, of sticking flesh-coloured calico strips over the visible wounds that disfigured his features and making up the cheeks with rouge and powder, the lips with red dye. They dressed what was left of each body in fine robes, stockings and shoes before laying them side by side on a catafalque, hands crossed across their breasts in the case of the two ladies, across his stomach in the case of his Lordship.

At the head and foot of the catafalque, a hemp string standing in a bowl of wax was lighted; the flickering smoky flames sent shadows scurrying across the giant beams of the Great Hall and voices were hushed as footsteps echoed across the flagstones. At midday Tobias Holroyd, who'd always fancied himself in Holy Orders and often said prayers before the family, read from the book of Common Prayer to the villagers who thronged the chapel. He would dearly have loved to conduct a Service for the Dead, but even he acknowledged that would be sacrilegious. The Chaplain would come the following day from York to conduct the funeral ceremony. Only when these arrangements had been completed did Rupert return to Stonebridge.

For John Aysgill as for many other men in the chapel that day, it was the end of an era. All remembered Lord Barthwick's many humanitarian acts, his friendliness and understanding. All would have agreed, had they discussed the matter, that he'd been a severe man and a hard taskmaster, vigorous and ruthless in his condemnation of evil-doing, but generous in dealing with those of his villagers who behaved well and tried their best.

Many also wondered how Giles, Lord Barthwick, would match up to the standards his uncle had set. On that subject there was much speculation. Giles had come infrequently to the village and one could see at once that he was unskilled in country ways, lacking knowledge of country life. He could ride a horse but as a city-bred gentleman who does it for the sport, rather than a countryman who sees an animal as a means of transport as well as a good companion. He had no knowledge of archery, of the hunt and the chase, though he was said to dance very prettily whenever his uncle held a ball in the Great Hall, with musicians brought from London playing all manner of foreign style dances.

Lord Barthwick knew the name of every man and woman, every boy and girl, in the village. Giles, Lord Barthwick, called everyone *my man, my good woman* whenever he bothered to speak at all, which wasn't often and only when he had a need.

The style of his dress, of course, had caused the most comment. He was a dandy and obviously greatly in fashion. Little did he know that he came already nick-named, or that the name would stay all his life in the village.

'When's Dandy Jim due?' Sam Weighton asked John Aysgill as they left the chapel.

'He couldn't be here before the morn.'

Jonathan Phillips had just returned from Betlaby with a load of timber for his fencing. 'The flyer were spattered wi' mud when it passed us,' he said. 'I reckon the rains have started further south.'

Winter rains often made the Great North Road virtually impassable; they doubted Dandy Jim would make the journey on horseback. 'He'll be a-coach,' Sam said, 'if only to make a good impression and keep his finery. I'm reet glad Holroyd had time to inscribe the agreement I struck with his Lordship over the fencing else I doubt Dandy Jim would honour it. But I got his Lordship's signature below my mark, and there's an end of that.'

John turned away, sickened by Sam Weighton's speech; he hadn't heard him express one word of sympathy for the murdered man or his despoiled daughter, seeking only to explore his own present and possible future advantage. He also had to confess to himself, however, that he was envious Sam Weighton's agreement had been signed while he himself had failed to speak to Lord Barthwick, who, he felt certain, would have accommodated him over the matter of the fencing, the cost of which remained such an insupportable burden on his household. He followed the other villagers inside the Great Hall, the door of which had been flung open to bring in as much light as possible. He approached the bier with dread, all too conscious of his own mortality. Who could have thought the Barthwicks would go before he did? And in such a tragic way. His age lay heavy on him as he looked down at the features of the man who'd been his master but, he also thought, remembering the many words they'd spoken companionably together, his friend. The features were no longer those of Lord Barthwick as he knew and remembered them, with the tanned leather look of ruddy health. He hated the work of the embalmer who'd tricked up his Lordship like a young lass, a Court pimp with his white skin, his over-red lips and cheeks, his powdered full wig. John shuddered and turned away – this effigy in no way reminded him of the man he'd known and respected.

'You turn your head, my man,' the sharp voice sounded behind him and he turned quickly. Sam Weighton had been wrong; Giles, Lord Barthwick, had obviously ridden a horse, and fast at that, since his coat was flecked not only by mud but also with a galloped horse's spittle foam. 'Is there something in my uncle's countenance that displeases you? Or are you one of the villains who gave him trouble in life and now come to gloat over him in death? I warrant you'll not find me so lenient as my saintly uncle with his easy-going ways.'

'My name is John Aysgill, my Lord,' John said, mustering his dignity, trying to understand how emotion must have been working in the young man on his mad gallop from London. He wasn't to know that the messenger had found Giles on his way north, and that the new Lord Barthwick had spent the night in a coaching house not thirty miles from Barthwick. The foam which flecked his jacket was caused by the unskilled manner in which he'd sawn at the horse's mouth with the inexpertly held reins, not by the efficiency of a full tilt gallop. 'I have served your father's family man and boy these eighty years. No man has ever termed me villain before this day. Be that as it may, because of the proud name you bear, my Lord, I shall pledge my allegiance to you, in your turn.'

'Stuff and nonsense,' Giles, Lord Barthwick, said. 'Now get out of my way.'

John held himself tall and proud as he walked from the Great Hall though his heart was heavy within him, wounded by the unnecessary discourtesy. 'The boy is troubled by his uncle's death,' he told himself, 'and by the terrible manner of his dear cousin's defilement.'

He tried to hold to this opinion, even to defend the young inheritor despite the village outrage at what happened subsequent to Giles, Lord Barthwick's, arrival.

When he had removed the stains of travel from his person, he immediately ordered the door of the Great Hall closed. The three bodies were removed by the back stairs into the mausoleum attached to the chapel and there, without ceremony or grace of prayers, were entombed. The mason stood beside the tomb while his assistants put the last touch to the marble slab that covered the vault.

'It was his Lordship's intention to have a figure carved in that marble,' the mason said. 'He even helped in the selection of the piece. I'd be pleased to put the carving in hand immediately, or perhaps your Lordship will be bringing someone from London?'

'There will be no carving,' Giles, Lord Barthwick, said. 'Now you can get about your business. We need detain you no longer since these local men can do all that I require.'

Bates was the first to speak out. As steward to the former Lord Barthwick he had been a man of consequence, of some authority.

Giles, Lord Barthwick, was sitting in the study, his feet on a footstool, a glass of cognac beside his hand when Bates went in.

'Yes, Bates, what is it?' he asked without ceremony.

'May I have permission to address your Lordship?' Bates asked.

'Yes, man, what is it?'

'It's a matter of tradition and custom, my Lord,' Bates said, rubbing his hands nervously together.

'Can't it wait until morn, Bates? I'm deuced tired . . .'

'With your Lordship's permission,' Bates persisted. He took a deep breath and put his fears aside. 'It is traditional, it is the custom, to provide a wake for the departed on the even of their sad interment. It's, how can I put it, a last opportunity for paying one's respects.'

'And I suppose this wake takes the form of carousing with food and drink supplied to all comers by the Lord of the Manor?'

'*Carousing*, my Lord? Dear me, no. The village assembles in the Great Hall in a most solemn manner. Food and beer are provided, certainly.'

Giles, Lord Barthwick, laughed. 'I'll wager they're provided *and* consumed in great quantity. The village may assemble in a most solemn manner, but I cannot believe the solemnity lasts longer than the first quarts of ale. No, Bates, there'll be no carousing at my expense. If the villagers wish to hold a wake there's a perfectly good ale-house on the road where they can do all the carousing they wish for a coin or two. As for myself, I'll take a hot bath, sup at eight and be early to bed.'

'A *hot bath*, my Lord?'

'A *hot bath*, Bates,' Giles, Lord Barthwick, said, mimicking his steward. 'A tub, filled with hot water. Surely you know how to obtain such a thing?'

'I'll do my best, my Lord.'

'I'm certain you will, Bates, if you wish to retain your position here. Now, as to tomorrow. I'll rise at eight o'clock.'

'*Eight*, my Lord. Your uncle was about by six.'

'My uncle is dead, Bates. I'll rise at eight and I'd be obliged if you would prepare *another* hot bath for me. I swear it'll take an uncommon amount of bathing to get the dust of that road off my person.'

'Very good, my Lord.'

'And, Bates, I'll have the household account books immediately. Tomorrow, at ten, we'll start to go through them. Pray to God, Bates, they're in better order than the rest of the sheepfold you call a Manor House.'

Fortunately for Bates, with the help of Tobias Holroyd he had always kept the account books immaculately and was not afraid for Giles, Lord Barthwick, to peruse them as meticulously as he did. He snorted coarsely each time he came to an expenditure which related to the village in general and to the provision of common fare and drinks.

'I wager we shall save a hundred guineas a year,' he said, 'by cutting out all this rampaging at the Manor's expense.'

His eyes gleamed when he examined the tithe book. 'Pray explain all these null entries to me, Bates,' he asked, his voice cold as a moorland spring.

'It was his late Lordship's custom, my Lord, to defer the payment of tithes in bad times. Last year we had a serious outbreak of the blight and many were short at harvest time. His Lordship forgave them the tithe for a twelve-month.'

'I'll brook no such laxity,' Giles, Lord Barthwick, cried. 'We are not running a charity house, Maister Bates. You will set about the collection of those tithes by any possible means. I'll not have village louts growing fat at my expense.'

The next shock came when, under Bates' supervision, his Lordship's dinner was served and the cook provided an assortment of meats. Giles eyed the capon, the small saddle of mutton, the chine of beef, the shank of pork as they were placed on the table before him.

'Tell me, Bates,' he said, his voice dangerously quiet, 'what's to happen to the food I myself do not eat?'

'Why, my Lord, it is taken to the servants' hall to provide a garnishment for the servants' meal.'

'A *garnishment*?'

'Aye, my Lord. It is the custom in these parts that the

servants feed on stew, with a garnishment of leavings from the Master's table.'

'It is a custom that will end today!' Giles thundered. 'I'll not have my storerooms pillaged and plundered to put fat on servants' bellies.'

'Hardly fat, my Lord,' Bates was bold enough to say. 'We are twenty-eight in number – there'll be but a shaving for each one.'

'You question *me*, Bates?' his Lordship asked. 'You take leave of your senses, I'll be bound, if you think you can *question* me like some insolent churl.'

'It was not my wish nor intention to give offence, my Lord. I did but wish to acquaint you with details of our local customs.'

'Very well, Bates. Henceforth you will send to the purveyor and the servants in Hall will fill their bellies with salt herring and potatoes, or oatmeal stew made with available root vegetables, both of which are most nourishing. While I am in residence, Cook will attend upon me daily and I shall choose my fare. Sufficient will be cooked to provide a meal for me and my guests in generous though not extravagant quantity. Self-denial, Maister Bates, is a quality much to be admired, and gluttony the most heinous sin of all. I'll have none of it below stairs! I'll have none of your rural rollicking and carousing at my expense. Each servant in my employ will be given a generous measure of ale each day, one measure, Maister Bates, the allotment of which you yourself will supervise. Have I made myself clear, Maister Bates?'

'Abundantly so, my Lord,' Bates said stiffly.

'Good. Now you may leave and tell Holroyd I want words with him after I have eaten.'

Bates coughed. 'Holroyd is no longer with us, my Lord,' he said hesitantly.

'No longer with us? Explain yourself, Bates.'

Bates certainly could not repeat the conversation he'd had with Holroyd. 'I'm off to London,' he'd said, 'by the next Flyer. I'll not stay here to serve a tyrant. I was indentured to his uncle – I have no fealty to this jackanapes.'

'What of your ten guineas, Tobias,' Bates had asked. 'You're to receive ten guineas from the estate.'

'It'll snow at Midsummer afore we'll see mite nor morsel of that, I'll be bound,' Holroyd had said. 'I'm away to London to find a place and prove myself before yon waspish half-maid has the opportunity to blacken my name. I shall place myself at the disposal of Lord Bristow and see what befalls. Dandy Jim will be here a week or two on the inventory and the counting, mark my words.'

'Tobias Holroyd, my Lord, was indentured to your uncle. He was not certain you would wish to renew the obligation and has gone to seek a situation elsewhere.'

'The blackguard! Where's he gone, Bates? I'll blacken his name for this.'

Bates shuddered at the prescience Holroyd had shown, using those exact words. 'I do not know, my Lord,' he said, 'though I've a feeling he'll seek employment in York where he's already well-known.' He deliberately kept his back to the window – *Who lies by the light of the moon will die by the light of the following sun* was a local saying too awesome and revered to be ignored.

'We are not without influence even in that rural outpost,' Giles, Lord Barthwick, said. 'I'll soon root him out, I'll be bound.'

Lord Stonebridge came the following morning to express his condolences and to discuss what arrangements were to be made for the funeral of his dear old friend.

He was stunned when he heard from Giles that the interment had already taken place without any of the county present.

'Ye mean to tell me,' he said, on the brink of apoplexy, 'you've already entombed his Lordship, without benefit of clergy nor ceremony as befits his rank and station. Why, you young whelp, are ye insane, totally bereft of all sense of decency? Is this the arrogant way they teach you in

London?'

'Sir, you go too far,' Giles, Lord Barthwick, said stiffly.

'Dammit, *Sir*,' Stonebridge retorted, 'it's thee with thy churlish ways that go too far. Your uncle was a much respected man in these parts. His daughter, your cousin dammit, was betrothed to *my son*! Have you no shred of humanity in ye?'

'I had heard of your desire to weld the two estates together to your greater advantage,' Giles said.

Now Stonebridge couldn't speak. He slapped his hand against his coarse woollen riding breeches in frustrated rage, struggling for breath, his face suffused with the blood of his anger. When, finally, he managed to control his rage, his words were precise and haughty.

'Damned thou art for an upstart,' he said. 'I prithee accustom thyself to solitude, for there's not a house in Yorkshire will open its door to thee after this day's work. Th'art an offence to the grand name tha bears, a traitor to thy blood, a stink i' the nostrils of civilized men!'

'I'll call you for that, Lord Stonebridge,' Giles said, his face white with anger.

'Tha'll *call* me? Tha'll call *me*!' Stonebridge thundered. 'Now I know th'art nobbut fit for Bedlam! I don't respond when *dogs* yelp and whine. I instruct my kennelman to reach for a whip to thrash them. Just as I'll have my kennelman thrash thee, if ever I clap e'en on thee again.'

He turned on his heel to march out. Giles made to follow him but Lord Stonebridge stopped him with a gesture. 'Tha needn't show me out,' he said. 'I was walking these corridors in love and friendship for thy dear departed uncle when thou wert sucking a vixen's tit.'

The fences and rails were going up all around the newly allocated fields and already the land belonging to the Manor was being broken with a horse pulling a metal plough of a kind never seen in the village before that dug deeper than the villagers had ever seen. The estate manager had recruited three itinerants; one of them must have been

101

used to the horse method for his furrows were straighter than any man believed possible, and at least two hands span deep in the first passing. The loam he turned over was rich and friable as they could see. The other itinerants took turns to lift the stones the plough pulled to the surface and stack them in neat piles; they'd come in handy for wall-building later.

A week passed before John Aysgill thought it suitable to call on his Lordship, who'd stayed inside the Manor house after the visit of Lord Stonebridge. Bates, who'd listened to the whole exchange between their two Lordships with great glee, had recounted it word for word in every cottage in the village. He himself was sorely tried; a week before her death, Lady Barthwick had misplaced one of her rings and they had made every attempt to find it in her rooms without avail. It was on the inventory, of course, and when it couldn't be produced for Giles's inspection, he'd ranted and accused Bates of stealing it.

Even when it was found at the bottom of a sewing box he hadn't retracted his accusation, merely sneered that Bates had come to his senses and had returned the stolen property before the bailiffs were called in. 'I'd seek my fortune elsewhere,' Bates had said many times, 'but the years have passed me by and I know Dandy Jim would hunt me down and blacken my name. What chance would I have against a noble Lord?'

Now Bates met John Aysgill at the back door. 'I've prepared him for your coming as best I can,' he said. 'I've told him his uncle held you in special esteem, and even caused you to accompany her Ladyship sometimes on her journeys since you were a man he could trust to guard his loved ones. But be warned, he's such a wayward mind to him, one can never know what he'll say next. It's my belief that Lord Stonebridge's words, however well-deserved, have left him with a permanent ill-humour.'

Giles, Lord Barthwick, was sitting in the barely furnished room in which he'd chosen to greet the petitioning villagers. It contained a table and a chair, on which he sat, and no other furniture, certainly nowhere the petitioner could rest his bones.

'John Aysgill,' he said mildly. 'Bates speaks well of you. What is it you want?'

A book was open on the desk before his Lordship. By its side was an inkwell, and a stand for goose quills. His Lordship had been writing on the folio of the book when John Aysgill arrived. He'd looked up briefly but now had returned to his scribbling, his head bent over the page in the light that came from the embrasure in the wall by his side. The room was cold but there was no trace of a fire in the black grate behind him.

'It concerns the fencing of my land, my Lord,' John Aysgill said.

'Aye? What of it? You've barely a fortnight.'

'Yes, my Lord. It was my intention to discuss this matter with the late Lord Barthwick.'

'From whom, Bates informs me, you had great success in the past of extracting favours and privileges past your station.'

'I was able to be of service to his Lordship on several occasions.'

'And, I'm certain, procured a more than ample recompense for your labours.'

John Aysgill was puzzled – such play of words was not for him, such hidden meanings and vituperations. 'Aye, my Lord, I was paid for my labours.'

'And now you come yet again, cap in hand, seeking some advantage?'

'No advantage, my Lord. I come to petition your help over the matter of providing a fence for my land, in terms that permit me to repay you to the full over a number of years since I have had the misfortune to be granted land with three sides exposed and none to share the cost of enclosure.'

'And if I provide the cost of the fencing, how shall I hope to recover my investment?'

'Through my reputation, my Lord. I am well-known

103

hereabout as a worker. I have three sons in good fig, and two daughters not yet wanting marriage. I pledge myself to pay the cost of the fencing, God willing, within five years.'

'And if God is *not* willing, Maister Aysgill? Am I then to sit and play cat's cradle for my investment?'

'We have other means, my Lord. My daughters are nimble with shuttle and thread, and we can weave fine homespuns most well.'

'Have you the Flying Shuttle?'

'No, my Lord, but nimble fingers, strong arms, and stout hearts. We have a cow, a ewe, and both have been well-covered.'

'Spare me these rural details, maister, for the habits of animals are not to my inclination. No, Maister Aysgill, you are the fourth man who's come to me with this request for capital for fencing. And I'm obliged to furnish the same answer. If I were to be soft hearted and provide capital for all who address me, why my coffers would soon be as empty as yours. I do not see my way to reward improvidence by permitting those who have not put a coin or two by to plunder my chest. The object of the Act of Enclosure is to permit each man to be self-sufficient, to teach him that only by his own endeavours, by self-denial, and by providence, can he succeed. I would assuredly be failing in my duty if I were to encourage any man to start the new life with a burden of debt to me. You have fourteen days, Maister Aysgill, in which to sink your first posts, to hang your first rails. After that I will give you a week of grace. If your land is not fully enclosed twenty-one days from now, then I shall be obliged to follow the provisions of the Act of Parliament, call in the bailiffs, and command you to vacate your land and your dwelling.'

'You'd dispose of us, my Lord.'

'It's not I who ordered these matters, Maister. The Petition was invoked by a majority of your own making. Now you all must learn to accept its provisions. The Law in all its majesty is a ponderous mighty instrument. Those of you who so lightly set it in motion must not be aghast when occasionally you are crushed by its intractability. I bid you good-day, Maister Aysgill!'

John stumbled from the Manor with a pain in his chest that was not entirely caused by his Lordship's words. What was this daemon the village had called down upon itself? If only his Lordship, his late Lordship, had still been alive John knew he would have done his best to shield the villagers, to protect them from the harsh rigours of this monstrous Act of Parliament. Could his late Lordship but have known the evil that was being unleashed in their midst, would he have persisted in forcing it through?

'How did it go, John?' Fred Ottershaw said. He'd been waiting in the stand of yews by the entrance to the Manor drive.

'He refused any help,' John said.

'Refused?'

'Aye, he wouldn't even contemplate it, and gave me a sermon on providence and self-denial.'

Fred fell in beside him and the two walked disconsolately together among the village houses. John heard the clack of the loom as he walked up to his own door after bidding Fred Ottershaw goodbye, and the whirr of the spinning. Gertrude stopped when she saw him, and Dodie let the end of the yarn twist in her fingers. The lads came through from the back; Peter was still carrying the withies with which he was making a cladding for one of the new bottles; Simon had an iron in his hand and, John knew, he'd been fashioning a gate hook in the blacksmith's fire, with Matthew to blow the bellows they'd made from a pig bladder to make the flames glow hotter.

'He refused,' John said to his assembled family. There was no point in beating around the bush.

Gertrude gave a sob and quickly stifled it with a piece of cloth from her apron pocket.

Simon looked dumbfounded. 'Refused – how can he refuse. The damned scheme started in the Manor.'

'I'll have no cursing i' the house,' John said instinctively, though his thoughts were elsewhere.

Only Peter had a practical suggestion. 'I've been working it out,' he said, 'and for half the cost we could put up a temporary structure in withies and reeds. It'd last nobbut a year.'

'Nay lad, get thy cap on right. We don't have money for even half the cost. And the Petition clearly says the fence has to be "of a permanent nature". Withies and reeds will not hold back a lusting bull, nor even a ram.'

Only Dodie was practical. She saw her father's needs, brought his chair forward, stirred the fire on which the food pot was bubbling, and went to the store to draw him a pot of ale. She sat him down, fussing over him, fetching his clay pipe and his pot of herbs to smoke in it. 'Now tha sit there,' she said, 'and rest thyself, Father. At thy age, tha shouldn't tire thyself.'

'Nay, lass, I'm not dead yet!'

'Tha looked half dead when tha came through that door, Father. Tha freetened the life out of me. Now sit there quiet and I'll give thee a bowl of soup when it's ready. Meanwhile, close thy eyes, smoke thy pipe, drink thy ale, and let the world quietly pass by.'

When she saw he had settled, she took down her warm cloak and placed it round her shoulders. 'I'm going out for a few minutes,' she whispered to Gertrude. 'Watch over our father – I'm that worried for him.'

The lads had gone out to the back to resume their work in silence, each thinking about the future without being able to settle on anything positive. Dodie looked round, then stepped out of the door and walked across the green to Fanny Colborn's house. Fanny was at the back, bending over a large iron pan in which she was heating water for the washing. Polly from the Manor was helping her fold the clothes that had dried on the line. Polly had been discharged from service at the Manor the day after Giles, Lord Barthwick, arrived and no reason given. She'd been given an hour to pack her bags, along with Maisie, who came from Betlaby and was a girl similar to Polly in many respects, open hearted, full of figure, with bright shining eyes.

'What do you reckon about Dandy Jim?' Dodie asked Polly. 'Is he a man a *girl* would likely to take an advantage from? Is he open to blandishment?'

Polly pushed a wisp of her blond hair back from her forehead. She'd fallen lucky to be taken in by Fanny Colborn, who'd needed help not only with the washing but also with the number of back-door admirers who came seeking entertainment and relaxation. Polly had already gained more in her purse than in a whole quarter of employment at the Manor. When Dodie arrived they had been talking together about the possibility of renting the house that stood beside the ale-house on the main road, midway between Betlaby and Barthwick. Fanny had already seen the premises which would comprise three rooms. 'We'd get no end of trade there,' Fanny had said. 'We could give up the washing, and spend our time entertaining the travellers and ale-house customers.'

'Blandishment?' Polly said. 'Do you mean what I think you mean? Has he got an eye for a pretty figure?'

'Aye, that's what I mean. You know . . .'

'I do know,' Polly said. 'He does have an eye for a pretty figure. He is open to blandishment, I'll be bound. But, like me, you have one failing . . .'

'And what's that?'

'It's the reason he discharged Maisie and me, quick as could be! The reason he couldn't bear to have us under his roof. We were born wrong for that one, I'll be bound, just as you were. He's one of them unnatural creatures as prefers lads to lasses, I'll stake my life on it!'

Dodie was astonished. 'Nay, Polly,' she said, 'th'art making it up since he threw you out!'

'Making it up, am I?' Polly said with a toss of her bright curly hair. 'If you think *that*, Dodie Aysgill, you've much to learn about lads and men. In the matter I'm speaking of, Lords is no better than any other as walks on two legs proud as a peacock, only more rapacious, more demanding, and more inclined to take their pleasures in

107

whatever curious dark corner they may find them. Believe me, I was bended over the beds of a few of them while I was in service up there and I know what I'm talking about. I could tell thee tales of the nobility and their wicked ways as would send thee straightways into the nearest nunnery.'

The gloom that had descended on the Aysgill household could not be lifted. Peter collected all the cloth the girls had woven and took it to market, haggling for every penny until he obtained the best price. Sam Weighton made them an offer for the cow but they refused to sell for such a pittance. Sam's eyes glittered. 'I'm prepared to wait,' he said. 'You'll be glad to take what I'm prepared to pay, ere long!' It seems he hadn't forgiven John Aysgill for besting him at knurr and spell, and was determined to wreak his revenge on the entire family.

Two weeks went by, with no hope showing. Despite what Polly had told her, Dodie had tricked herself out in her finest clothes and had gone up to the Manor. Giles, Lord Barthwick, had seen her but his distaste at addressing her became immediately apparent, and he dismissed her with the same words he'd used to her father. When John discovered what she'd done, he took his hand to her for the first time in many years, and she went to her bed bruised and crying at what she thought was his ingratitude. A lethargy seemed to have fallen on him during these last days; he would sit by the fireplace for hours, sucking his empty pipe, presumably reflecting on his life, only coming back when the food was served, and then pecking at it with no appetite. Simon went about his tasks as if oblivious to the situation they faced. Matthew and Peter tried all the ways they knew to raise the fencing money, but none of the village had a coin to spare, nor any suggestions to offer. Too many people were requiring their own coin too quickly, and were in a mood to buy, to realize on what capital they had. Now that they had more land that could yield more, they purchased more seeds to supplement what they had in their own stores. They bought more animals to run on the extra land, knowing that was the way to prosperity. When his Lordship had finished ploughing his own ground he let it be known that his plough and his labourers were available for hire, but only on payment of cash. Sam Weighton dug into his store of coins and was the first to have his new allotment furrowed. From the ploughing, he obtained a yield of stone, with which he announced his intention of building a hut on his own ground, to use as a storehouse.

The season moved into March and John lifted himself from his chair and walked out into the cold air. The biting winds of February were ended but his breath still brought mist from his mouth. He walked out of the village and stood on the corner of his new land; the spring growth had already started and he could see it was good land, in good heart, sloping gently upwards but easy to work across the slight slope. He bent and plucked a stalk of rape – even untouched there'd have been supply for all his animals, aye, and for the new born.

His cow and his ewe had been tethered to stop them straying; both were munching contentedly as he rubbed their backs with his workworn gnarled hand.

He sat on a stone that marked the corner of his boundary, and looked back at the huddle of houses of the village beneath the high walls of the Manor, the green isolated in the middle and Simple Tom driving a flock of unruly geese across it. Smoke from some of the chimneys hovered spiralling in the air without a wind. Farther he could see the track going down towards the river, and the stand of timber his late Lordship had planted as a covert for his pheasants and grouse. He could see, in the distance, the road and the smoke from the chimney of the ale-house where they'd be roasting the travellers' fare. The scenes of his life walked slowly by his memory, the hundreds of triumphs and disappointments, the good times and the bad, the rich times and the lean. He remembered when he'd been showing Walt Smith how to bend a bow, almost from this very spot, and had aimed for the bole of the tree he could see, a hundred paces distant. In those days it had been a weak and puny oak; now it was large and full of majesty. At the moment of letting the arrow fly, a wind had come from behind and had lifted the arrow and carried it. When they'd paced its flight to where it had stuck in the thatch of Job Hirst's father's cottage, it had flown well over six hundred. 'I'll never be able to pull a bow like yon,' Walt had said dispirited, and John, most unkindly, had not told him the wind had helped.

One of the new lambs came across to where he sat, mother's milk dribbling from the corner of her mouth. Three ewes born this season – what untold luck!

He held out his finger and the lamb sucked vigorously, its own spittle deceiving it into thinking it was drawing milk. 'Nay, lass,' John said, 'you're working yourself to death, and drawing no profit from it!'

Fred Ottershaw had seen him sitting there and walked across the field. 'I can't fence this side, John,' he said, the misery showing on his face. 'I've tried all roads. Is there *nowt* you can do for us? Yon devil in the Manor has already sent for the bailiffs – I understand three of them comes tomorrow. Jonathan Phillips has already sold out to the Manor – Dandy Jim has given him seven days to get out of his cottage. You can hardly blame him with no bairns. He says he's going to Whitby, and get himself employment on a boat. James Waterton is talking of selling now that his cow and his bullocks have all died of the bloat from the wet spring grass, and his ewe has turned barren. Sam Weighton says he'll take the land since it abuts his own, on a ten-year note of hand. They reckon that shed he's talking about building wi' the stones is going to be a house for hisself to live in, so's he can come away from the village. That way, he'll be independent of the patronage of the Manor in all particulars. They say Dandy Jim is furious with Sam Weighton, but there's nowt he can do about it. It's in the Act that a man can sell to any man – only if he refuses to sell can the bailiffs come in and eject him, when the land goes to the Manor. If the folks go on

110

giving their land to Sam, afore we know it, he'll own half the land of the village. Then some will be sorry they pushed the Act through, I'll be bound!'

Mark Ottershaw came running across the field towards them, his uncapped hair flying in the wind behind him as he ran. 'Father,' he said, 'I've done it . . .'

'What's tha done, lad?' Fred asked anxiously. 'What's tha done . . .?'

'I've talked to Sam Weighton. He'll lend us the money to fence this side.'

Fred's face cleared. 'He'll *lend* it to us?'

'Aye. We can have it!'

John held up his hand to stem the words bubbling from the lad. 'Wait a minute, lad,' he said. 'I've knowed Sam Weighton a bit longer than tha has. What's the terms of the borrowing?'

'The terms . . .?'

'Aye, the *terms*, lad. Nowt is for nowt in this world, especially when Sam Weighton has a hand in it.'

'Oh, the terms. Well, we have to pay back after a year, double the amount.'

'And if you can't pay?'

'Well, we have to give him a Deed of Gift, for his security.'

John Aysgill shrugged his shoulders. 'That's not a loan,' he said. 'That's usury. How are you going to earn enough in this first year to pay Sam Weighton *twice* the cost of the fencing. You're not, I'll be bound! And then what happens when you default on the payment? He takes the land you've so kindly broken in for him.'

Mark Ottershaw's face was saddened as he worked out the details of the arrangement Sam Weighton had offered. John Aysgill was right – it *was* usury.

'Nay, Father,' he said miserably, 'I did the best I could.'

'I know tha did, lad,' Fred said. He stared across the fields with blind eyes, his feelings drowned in a pit of sorrow. 'Seems like some of us was meant by the good God as made us never to see advantage,' he said. 'Us have

111

worked all us lives, and garnered nowt but hunger, pain, and misery, aye, and a belly laugh or two along the way to delude us into thinking that all was well with our world.'

'Doan't take on so, Father,' Mark said, putting his arm round his father's work-thinned shoulders, looking at his wind-dried skin, his bony-knuckled hands.

'I mind when your mother were alive, before the twins killed her and themselves by coming too soon. "All I want, Fred," she'd say, "is a bit of comfort and the truth about our next crumb." She were a noble woman and bore me six of you. Now you're the only one as survives!' Tears ran down his bony cheeks and he raised his fist in the air. 'There's no God,' he said. 'Only a Devil as leads us on wi' false hopes. There's no God if he can drink deep off the sweat of a man's honest brow, if he can feed off a man's muscles and consume the flesh from his body.'

'Nay, Fred, tha mustn't deny God that way,' John said. There was little conviction in his voice since his thoughts had been running down the same path a time or two recently.

'And whyfor not?' Fred demanded, his angry voice rising in pitch. 'We labour day and neet, following the seasons, and for what? For nowt. When we seek to gain advantage for ourselves, it's ta'en away from us by bits of London paper. We didn't want *fences* when we made our mark for the Petition; we wanted our bits of land joined together to ease our work and gain us the advantage. I had four bits of land no bigger than would take half a day to plough. Putting them together was meant to make life easier for Mark and me, to give us an *advantage* however small. And what happens? Him as has never worked in his life gets the land, else him up the hill, that bloated bullock of a Sam Weighton, uses his bits o' coin to *buy* the advantage. We sit at the loom all winter wi' our eyes crying of tiredness in the dark, and the cloth we sell earns more for the man who buys it than the man who laboured to make it. Well, I've seen my way. I'm leaving the damned land and I'm going into the town. I've heard they pay a working man good regular wages in Leeds and Bradford. I can read and write a bit though not as good as thee, John. I'll make something of myself, if only that my lad here shall not have the same life I've had myself. Damn the land, damn the seasons, damn the back-breaking work in the cold and wet. I'll sell my land to Dandy Jim and spend my life cursing the day God made me a countryman to be used and abused by all.'

He marched wildly away without a backwards glance. 'Go after your father,' John said. 'He has sore need of thee, I'll be bound.'

He sat down as he watched Mark hurry after his father, feeling short of breath, with no energy in his legs. He shook his head to clear it and immediately felt dizzy. His mind was confused and he couldn't work out what he was doing sitting on a stone at the corner of Billy Fogg's farthest strip. Aye, and what was all that noise of hammering that sounded in his ears?

He sat still, confused. He looked down at his hands and was shocked to see the veins sticking up, and his skin puckered and gathered tight over bony fingers. Nay, and what were the boots he was wearing. He'd never owned boots like these in all his forty, or was it, forty-five years; he couldn't remember; what was he thinking about? He'd better get back to the cottage, aye, but why? – there'd be nobody there since his Father and Mother had died, was it ten years back?

It was Gertrude who, worried by his non-return, came up to find him. 'Father,' she said anxiously, 'are you all right?'

'He looked at me,' she said to Dodie when she got him home and into bed, 'as if he'd never seen me before, as if he didn't recognize me and I was a stranger to him.'

'His hands are that cold,' Dodie said, rubbing them as her father lay back on the straw sack that formed his pillow, his eyes open but his senses elsewhere.

The boys gathered round the truckle bed, looking at their father, who stared back at them with

113

uncomprehending eyes. 'Give him a bowl of something to warm his vitals,' Matthew said. 'He stayed too long on that cold hillside without moving. I reckon the wind has chilled him. It don't do a man any good to sit still in that cold. According to what Mark said, Father were there for hours, never moving from Billy Fogg's stone. Happen the sense has been frozen out of him. We mun get up a big fire, and pour something hot in him, get him to sweat and break out the chill from his bones.'

'Rub him wi' goose grease, that's the best way to warm him,' Simon said. 'Then wrap him in hay the way they do new-born babes wi' no blood in 'em.'

The girls left the room while the boys stripped their father and each worked on parts of him, vigorously rubbing the goose-grease into his flesh. They were shocked to see how thin their father had become, the bones protruding across his ribs and his back, his hip bones jutting out. 'Nay, he's nobbut skin and bones,' Simon said. 'Us'll have to get some food inside him soon as we can.'

They wrapped the best of last season's hay round their father's body and wound a calico sheet around him. Peter stoked up the fire. 'Nay,' Simon said, 'don't be so mean. Chuck a bit more on. We want to get him good and roasting.'

They dragged his truckle nearer the fire, spread the straw in his mattress to make him more comfortable.

'Here,' Matthew said, dragging his own mattress across, 'put him on this as well. It can't be any comfort for his old bones to be scraping on the withies.'

When the girls came back, they gently held their father's mouth open, and spooned broth between his few remaining teeth, holding his tongue down to make certain it slipped down his throat a drop at a time. Dodie had spooned some of the bone jelly into the broth, and thickened it with a couple of spoonsful of oats from the scant store left to them after the hard winter. When they had fed him, they laid him back, and piled his hide coat on top of him, then Dodie's woollen cloak. They all sat

114

around, not speaking. Occasionally, Gertrude would lean forward and touch her father's face where it protruded from the wisps of hay escaping from his wrappings. Once she poked her hand down into the calico and the hay on each side of his body, and when she withdrew it from his right side, her face wore a worried frown.

'That right side's not warming,' she said. 'The left side's broken with sweat but the right side's cold as the grave.'

'Nay, don't talk like that,' Matthew said. 'Tha puts a shiver right down my spine.'

'Give it time,' Peter said. 'It takes time for the warmth to spread.'

They pressed in closer, watching intently. Now they could see the colour begin to suffuse through the right side of their father's face. 'See!' Peter said triumphantly. 'See his colour coming back?'

'Aye, but nobbut on't right side,' Simon said. 'Left side's pale as ever . . .'

Gertrude pushed her hand back in among the wrappings. 'Right side's still cold,' she said. 'Left side's warm as't fire back and I can feel his heart thumping fit to burst.' She turned tearfully to Dodie, who, though a year younger than she was, seemed to give her strength. 'Father's going to be all right isn't he?' she whispered. 'He's going to be all right?'

Dodie hugged her and Gertrude gratefully enfolded herself in her sister's ample warmth. 'Aye, Gertrude, he's going to be all right,' Dodie whispered back. 'Just give him time. Tha moan't worry, tha moan't be impatient.'

The vigil lasted all night with the fire going lower since they didn't have much kindling left and were reluctant to leave the house in the night to look for more. Each one of them dozed on and off, all shaking themselves guiltily as they woke. When the first light of dawn came over the green, Dodie shook herself. Gertrude was lying at her feet, fast asleep on the earthen floor, her head resting against the flock of wool Dodie had been spinning. Peter was asleep leaning against Simon, also asleep. Matthew was wide awake, the dull red light from the embers of the fire reflecting in his eyes, which were fixed fanatically on his father as if he were trying to will him back. John Aysgill was breathing with a laboured gurgle in his chest and now it seemed to Dodie as if the shape of his face was changing, almost as if the left side was slipping, was melting, losing the firmness of the outline of his features. His mouth had dropped open at the left corner, and a drool of spittle had coagulated in the corner of his close-cropped grizzled beard.

'I'm going to fetch Fanny Colborn,' Dodie said. 'She'll know what's amiss.'

'Pray to God she will,' Matthew said. Now it was light he felt a need of comfort and reached down the worn Bible from which his father had so many times read to them. He sat there watching his father twitching in his false sleep, the breath rattling from his bony frame, and could not open the Bible to read.

For the first time, Matthew had doubts. Could this be the work of the God of love, the God of forgiveness, the God who watched over all? His father had been, was, a God-fearing man who'd lifted his hand against no man in anger, in lust, in self-seeking. John Aysgill had been a good, godly, man. Why, then, had God forsaken them?

The Bible lay heavy and unopened in his hand and he put it back on the shelf as he waited for Dodie to return with Fanny Colborn. If God couldn't help, then perhaps an earthly, world-wise, sinner could. They had no other hope.

When Fanny Colborn saw John Aysgill she turned to the lads. 'Quick,' she said, 'get down to the river and fetch me as many leeches as you can. Make haste, now, if we're to save your father.'

When the lads hastened away she stripped the calico sheet from her patient, removed the hay, wiped him dry of the goose-grease. 'You've done a good thing to get the flow of blood started again,' she said, 'but now we must

116

drain off the pressure. There's obviously a block somewhere and the pressure has built up. We must get the pressure down, else the block will never clear.'

'How do you know all such things?' Gertrude asked in amazement.

'Aye, Gertrude, you'd be surprised at what men talk about when they've sated their lusts. There's many a surgeon and physician I've embraced, helping them relax after they've cut a body apart.'

'Oh, Fanny, how *could* you?' Gertrude asked, horrified but yet fascinated.

'It comes easy when you have a tithe to find in the morn,' Fanny said, smiling mischievously. 'Now bring in more kindling, for we moan't freeze to death while we're physicking your father, moan we?'

The lads returned with ten leeches in a bag and the marks of the leeches' teeth around their ankles where they'd stood in the stream offering themselves as human bait. Fanny laid her gentle hands on John Aysgill's body, trying to trace the flow of warmth from one side to the other. Matthew watched her long delicate fingers in fascination as she moved them slowly over his father's emaciated frame. 'Aye, we'll have one here,' she said. Cautiously, he took one of the leeches from the bag, holding it behind its head. The long slim slimy thing, like an undergrown eel, twisted and curled in his hand as he pressed its head against his father's skin. The leech sank its teeth into John's flesh, anchoring itself there and beginning immediately to pulse as it located the blood vessel within. Fanny stroked John's body. 'Another here,' she said. By the time she'd worked all the body, she'd found eight places and now a leech pulsed and throbbed at each one. Already the leeches were growing in size as they drained John Aysgill's blood from him, front and back. All this time his eyes had been closed and he was lost to the world.

'Now stoke the fire,' Fanny said, 'and hang yon kettle over it.'

She opened the bag she'd brought with her, and from it

117

drew metal cups the size of the breasts of a small woman.

'Turn him onto his face,' she said, 'but you, Peter, hold his head so's he can breathe easy.'

She held the cup in the steam from the iron kettle until it was hot and filled with vapour. When she was satisfied that all the air had been driven from it, she clapped the cup on John's flesh below his shoulder blade. As the steam condensed, a vacuum was formed inside the cup which, she hoped, would draw the blood to the surface of the skin. Instinctively she knew it was important to get John's blood moving; she'd seen at once that parts of his body were being denied, and knew enough to realize that without blood, the flesh would die.

She prepared another cup, and slapped it on John's body on the other side of his back. A third and a fourth went on the front, on the flat parts of his flesh below and to the side of his chest.

She looked at the three lads. Simon, though the oldest, was fat and she doubted his strength. Matthew looked strong enough for her purpose. She placed her fingers delicately on each side of John's heart cavity, confirming her diagnosis. 'Right,' she said, 'I want you to press on his rib cage as hard as you can, then let go. Press and let go, press and let go, with all the force you can.'

Matthew did as she told him. 'That'll move the spit in his chest,' she said. 'It should break it up, make it flow.'

Sure enough, John coughed once weakly. 'It's working,' she said, 'it's working.'

Matthew thought his hand would fall from his wrist during the next fifteen minutes as alternately he pressed and released, pressed and released. After fifteen minutes, his father suddenly started to cough and his features suffused with extra blood as he struggled. 'That's it,' Fanny shouted, excited. 'Get him sitting up, quick.'

They pulled John into a sitting position; Fanny broke the cups from his back and each gave a strong sucking sound as it came away, leaving bright red blood weals behind it. 'Get his head forward,' she said, 'and you,

118

Matthew, start on his back the same way.'

Matthew was pressing his father's back in and out, in and out. Fanny looked worried.

'It's not working,' she said. 'Stand him up. You, Simon and you, Peter, get your arms under his and lift him!'

They did as they were told and their father hung between them like Christ on the Cross.

'Dodie,' Fanny said, 'pull your father's legs back so's he's leaning forward!'

Dodie did as she instructed.

'Now, Gertrude, bend your father's head forward, but not too far. You Matthew, keep on pumping!'

Now John was trying desperately to cough and couldn't and Fanny realized that if she didn't do something, he'd choke. In desperation she forced his mouth open and pushed her finger as far as it would go down his throat. She pounded his shoulder blades with her other hand, banging him vigorously to get him to cough and clear his lungs. When his chest began to heave she pulled out her finger. 'Legs farther back, Dodie,' she shouted and Dodie pulled hard so that her father was suspended between the three of them, practically face down.

John gave one almighty cough and a retch and a great flood came from his throat. Fanny kept pounding until he shuddered, retched and bile flowed.

'By God's grace,' Fanny shouted, exhilarated by her success, 'I believe we've done it, we've done it. Lay him back on the truckle, but gentle.' She snatched a brand from the fire and applied it to each leech's tail. It was the only way to make them release their interlocked teeth without tearing out a chunk of flesh. Each one writhed and let go, and she grabbed it behind its head and stuffed them, bloated with blood, into the bag.

She looked at John's face; already the difference could be seen and the muscle at the left side of his mouth had begun to tighten, drawing his face back into its normal shape. The white-green colour of death was being radiated with a soft flesh colour. His blood was flowing again, his lungs were empty of spittle and phlegm.

'I think he'll live,' she said, wiping her sweat-laden brow on the hem of the night-shift in which Dodie had found her and brought her on her errand of mercy.

As if to confirm what she had just said, John Aysgill opened his eyes, though, as yet, there was no sense in them.

Simon, as the first-born, went up to the Manor and was seen by Giles, Lord Barthwick.

'On the matter of the fencing, my Lord,' Simon said, 'since my father's illness we have been able to make no steps forward. I humbly petition you to give us more time, or to permit us to cut the wood we need, against our family promise to pay the cost when we have crops.'

Giles sighed impatiently. 'It seems to me,' he said, 'that your father's *illness* comes at a most convenient time, with only the word of Mistress Colborn as to the nature of it. Well, Maister Aysgill, it may be convenient to you to use your father's malady as an excuse for a further petition, but it is deuced inconvenient to me and I'll not countenance it. What was said to your father, and to that chit of a sister of yours who sought to importune me in this matter, must remain. I will buy the land from you, but you must vacate the cottage within the week, else I'll have the bailiffs eject you by force. Do not trouble to petition me again, Maister Aysgill, nor any other of your family, for you'll find my door closed to you henceforth, as to all you indigent folk who have failed to learn to provide for yourselves.'

Simon didn't move though it was apparent he'd been dismissed. 'Can you not find places for us in your employment, my Lord?' he said desperately. 'We can work for wages, like the men you are employing to plough your land and build your walls, Irishmen who can have no first claim to service with you.'

'It is no matter of yours, you impudent churl, whom I employ. *I* will say who has first *and* last claim to service with me.'

120

Giles, Lord Barthwick, had risen in his seat and his voice was shrill. 'Steward,' he called. 'Bates, get in here, man.'

Bates was in the next room attempting to do work that once had belonged to Tobias Holroyd. He dropped the quill when he heard his master's voice and rushed through.

'Throw this churl from the Manor,' Giles screeched, 'and give instructions that neither he, nor any other of the Aysgill family, is to be permitted to molest us with their petitions. Aye, and place the Aysgill name at the top of the list of matters for the attention of the bailiffs.'

As Simon walked down the slope that led from the Manor, he saw Peter hurrying towards him.

'Come quickly,' Peter said. 'Our Father wants to speak to thee.'

His disappointment forgotten, Simon hurried home with Peter, to find his father had recovered consciousness but had lost the colour from his cheeks again.

'Has someone gone for Fanny Colborn?' Simon asked anxiously, but his father's quiet voice drew him near the bed.

'There's nothing Mistress Colborn nor any other could do for me, Simon,' he said. 'I'm going, lad, and there's an end to it. I've had more than my full term, and now the good Lord is calling me; I moan listen to him.'

'Nay, Father,' Simon said, tears streaming down his face. The others all stood round the bed; he'd looked briefly at Dodie's face and had read there the confirmation of what his father was saying.

'His heart beats faint,' Dodie said, 'like a little bird's. There's no feeling in his limbs.'

Simon laid his hand alongside his father's cheek. 'Tha's been a good father to us,' he sobbed. 'We'll be heartbroken if tha leaves us.'

'Leave you all I must,' John said slowly. 'It makes my heart sore to know there's nowt for you, save what we own. You'll have to do the best you can wi' that. His Lordship will come round, mark my words. He'll come to know our country ways. You must learn to serve him as, man and boy, the Aysgills have always served the Lord of the Manor. Nay, come closer, Simon, for I can hardly see thee. Is Gertie there? And Dodie? Matthew and Peter?'

'We're all here, Father,' Matthew said, but John Aysgill didn't seem to hear.

'Tha mun tell them, when tha sees them, Simon, as I blessed them all at the end, just as I bless thee, my first born. Tell them I bless them and hope they'll be right godly in all they do . . .'

His voice had trailed away to an inaudible whisper, and his eyes had lost their focus. He slipped away into death as effortlessly as if he'd welcomed the parting. His body didn't move, didn't slump in the bed, and only Simon, close by him, actually saw the moment when life left his body and his spirit began its ascent.

Simon reached in and closed his father's eyes, and then they all knew. Peter, the only one with coin in his purse, took two of them and placed one on each eyelid. Matthew knelt beside the bed in the shaft of bright February sunlight that came through the aperture by the fireplace. 'Dear Lord,' he said strongly, 'we commend our father's soul to thee. Take him into Thy Blessing. Guard him and give him rest for ever more for he has been Thy humble servant in this life as we know he will be in the life hereafter.'

'Amen,' his sisters and brothers said, all kneeling beside the truckle bed on which their father lay, his snow-white hair touched by the same shaft of sunlight that illuminated the heads of his children. Gertrude and Dodie were both crying quietly, and Simon had placed his arm around Peter's shoulder in his grief. John Aysgill's skin had drawn tightly on his skull and already his head had the waxen look of an effigy.

'I thought he was better,' Simon said. 'I thought Fanny Colborn had brung him round.'

Dodie had spoken with Fanny when she'd accompanied her home and had been told his recovery was only temporary.

'The truth of the matter, Dodie,' Fanny had said, 'is that your father is wore out and there's nowt that man nor maid can do for him. The loss of his land has hit him harder than most, and the death of Lord Barthwick who was his friend. This Giles will be friend to no man, mark my words, nor maid either. We must all guard ourselves against him and his perverted ways.'

'Fanny did her best,' Dodie said. 'Nobody could have done more.'

'Aye, I'm not complaining. It just took me suddenly . . .'

'We can only be glad he didn't go screaming in pain.'

'Aye, that's the blessing.'

Gertrude was already busy preparing the shroud in which they'd bury John Aysgill.

'We'd better be away for the digging, Matthew,' Peter said.

'There's no hurry for that.'

'Aye, but father wouldn't like to linger.'

'I suppose not.'

They took the mattock and the spade from the shed at the back and went through the village. All who saw them knew what they were doing, and one or two folks touched them in sympathy. 'You'll be wanting the cart?' Missis Cryer said.

'Aye . . .'

'I'll get it ready.'

'Aye.'

They laboured all the afternoon, digging deep into the rocky ground of the village cemetery by the chapel wall. Despite the problem with the roots, they'd picked a place under the tree, near where their mother had been buried all those years before. It was hard labour but they were glad of it and spoke little to each other, both occupied with their thoughts. One or two of the villagers stopped and watched them, but none offered to help – it was the privilege of the lads to bury their own father.

When they returned home the cart had been delivered, decorated with laurel leaves, its rails intertwined with greenery, its bed strewn with clean hay and moss, with spring crocuses and asphodels, daffodils and narcissus.

Gertrude and Dodie had sewn their father into the shroud of good calico, binding the edges neatly with a ribbon Dodie had been saving for herself.

'Us'll get going then, shall us?' Simon said, his voice heavy with grief.

'Aye,' Matthew said. 'But I do so wish we'd had a coffin for him.'

The three lads picked up the shroud and carried it outside, laying their father feet first in the cart. Dodie had sewn a posy into the stuff of the shroud; the colour of the primroses and violets splashed life on the oatmeal-coloured fabric. Simon and Matthew hauled the cart, with Peter holding on behind. The two girls walked by the side, their heads cast down, tears raining from Gertrude's face unheeded.

One by one the villagers came from their cottages and walked along behind the cart, the childrens' voices hushed, all heads bowed. They'd all known John and, more than any other man of the village, respected him. They'd sent to the fields and the men had stopped work, hurrying back into the village in their muck and sweat. By common consent, the lads avoided the track that ran up to the Manor but made their way through the cottages once they'd crossed the green. They halted the cart by the new-dug grave and the village women flung in the flowers they had been carrying. Simon lowered himself into the hole, and they passed the shroud with his father in it feet first down to him. He caught the top end of the shroud, and lowered that to the bottom so that his father lay flat, his head towards the chapel, his feet towards the village and the cottage that once had been his.

'Aye, he'll need to look over his shoulder afore he'll see yon Manor,' Matthew said.

It was a fitting comment. All knew their father had been killed by the events of the last weeks, that the will to live had been driven from him by the Petition of Enclosure, the death of Lord Barthwick, the difficulty with the fencing, the harsh uncomprehending attitude of the upstart Giles, Lord Barthwick. All their hatred focused on the Manor and its new occupant.

When they returned home, three bailiffs were already in the cottage.

PART TWO

Book Two

Book Two

Simon Aysgill was tall and loose-limbed like his father. He had his father's wide open eyes, his same lazy smile, his same soft manner of speech.

As John Aysgill's first-born he had inherited all his father's possessions, but he had permitted Peter, the brainy one, to negotiate the sale of their unfenced land, to Giles, Lord Barthwick, and their livestock for which, much to their surprise, Charles Cryer had given a good price. No-one had known that Charles had a few coins put by; he'd never been a man to squander money, and they'd all assumed he had little of it.

'I were saving for a sunny day,' he said when he paid them from his leather purse. 'I always knew that one day the coin would come in handy. Now I'm going to do as Sam Weighton is doing; I'm going to build myself a house and a barn on my land, so that I can cock a snook at yon devil in the Manor. I'll pay no more cottage tithe to him, you can be certain.'

Simon had been genuinely pleased, though he could read the sour expression of envy on Peter's face. 'I'm reet glad you've won your independence, Maister Cryer,' he said, 'and I wish you good fortune and heavy crops according to thy merit. There's nowt left in Barthwick for us Aysgills, and we're away to the town. We may not find fame and fortune, but at least, like you, we'll be freed of the yoke of his Lordship.' With that, they'd divided the inheritance five ways.

Simon shivered with the cold as he pulled on his work shirt and breeches, tying a neckerchief round his throat. It'd be light soon enough, and he had three miles to walk to his work at the textile mill. It was good to spend this first half hour of the morn alone in his house. He looked round the rooms he had found for himself, counting his good fortune. One sitting-room and one bedroom, with a fireplace. Why, he even had running water of a sort since the spring up the hill fed down the open trough at the back of his yard. No doubt it was the spring that made the walls of his bedroom slimy to the touch but the same was true of all the houses in this street in Hunslet, Leeds. Come the summer, his neighbours told him, the walls would dry out and the smell would disappear.

He couldn't complain; he'd only been in Leeds two weeks and already he'd found himself somewhere to live and a job of work to go to each day. He'd had extreme good fortune, he told himself, refusing to let his mean city surroundings depress him. He straightened the straw mattress on his bed and piled his few clothes on top of it, the better to keep out the damp, before he opened the door and stepped into the cobbled street. Already the folk were up and about and he could see smoke rising from some of the chimneys. His neighbour, he knew, always had a bowl of oatmeal before he left for work but then he'd married a grand lass who seemed to look after him in all particulars.

He walked along the street, joining the trickle of working folks going his way, men, women and children. As he drew near to the factory the sun rose over the city and he could see the spires of the churches catch the first rays of light. My, what a bewildering place he'd found it when he'd first arrived, with Matthew and Peter. Such a vast crowd of people, of waggons loaded to the top with woollen stuffs, with beer barrels. Half the stuff he saw was strange to him, coming fresh from the country. He'd wandered about the city all the day, his eyes widening with every passing hour. He'd never seen so much magnificence as in the coaches of the rich folk, in the rooms they occupied, far grander than anything you'd find in the Manor at Barthwick. He'd stumbled upon a procession of dignitaries, walking along the soiled pavements in their gold, silver and ermine-trimmed robes when they descended from their ceremonial waggons, as he thought of them, carrying a variety of objects the like of which he'd never seen before. Sticks with what might have been lanthorns atop them, but these were encrusted with gold and sparkling jewels, some looking like orbs, some like crowns.

'Why,' he'd told himself, 'there's enough wealth in any one of the sticks to fence *all* the land of Barthwick, aye, and give every man a pair of ewes and a cow and a bull!'

A man wearing a tall billy-hat, with silver buttons on his long frock coat, had grabbed Simon's shoulder and had poked his stomach with a short billy-club.

'And where does tha think tha's going?' he'd said. pushing Simon back into the crowd.

More than anything else, it had been the crowds that had amazed Simon – he'd never believed the world could contain so many folks, all crammed into the one place. Then he'd found the river and had stood amazed on the bridge, seeing the boats passing beneath with all manner of goods. Many carried coal, and split wooden planks, but there were open grain barges and even some private boats carrying fine gentlemen and ladies. The buildings were all magnificent and many floors high in places, with elaborate entrances, canopies held up by thick pillars. Almost all the windows had glass in them – not the thick green twirly glass of the Manor, but glass so flat you could see through it. Many times he'd lost himself in the maze of alleyways north of the river along a thoroughfare that led from the street at the Bridge. He'd passed over the bridge and headed away from the bustle of the inner city, his head in a whirl. And then he had become exhausted, and had gone into an ale-house with a horse-yard, where he'd drunk a pint of strong beer and had eaten a stew that tasted mostly of oatmeal and rabbit. It had been bubbling in a big pot in the corner of the yard under a chimney hood, and they'd given him a chunk of coarse bread with it to mop up the gravy. He'd been flabbergasted at the price they'd asked

131

him to pay for it but, he reasoned, in the city the price of everything is bound to be higher since it all has to be brought in from the countryside. He didn't realize, mercifully, that they'd seen his garb, recognized him for a countryman fresh from home, and had doubled the price accordingly.

It was in the ale-house, after his food, that he'd had the greatest fortune.

A large man had been sitting morosely, eating a plate of the food. He carried his weight heavily, moving ponderously across to the pot to fill the plate again, returning to sit on the bench next to Simon, who was unashamedly gazing about him in wonderment. A coach had arrived in the outer yard, and six passengers had climbed from it. The horses had been uncoupled and led to stalls at the side of the yard; Simon's eyes had widened with interest – he'd never seen horses of this quality before, except occasionally on the Flyer going along the Great North Road. The Lords of the Manor had always kept good horses, but not big and strong like these, which were much fuller in the chest and had greater flanks than the ones he knew. The people descending from the coach had gone inside the ale-house, all seeming wearied by their journey.

The ostler came out with two more horses, and his helper guided them between the shafts of the coach while the ostler put on their bits and bridles, avoiding their impatiently kicking hooves, grabbing their nostrils when they tossed their heads so vigorously he couldn't get the leathers over their ears, even fetching one a clout across its nose when it persisted in misbehaving.

Simon had been drawn by the scene and sat back on the bench watching every detail of it, drinking in the familiar horse smell, the odour of leathers, the clean whiffs of ammonia dung that had followed the horses from the stable.

'Just in, are ye?' the fat man sitting next to him asked him.

132

'Aye, that I am.'

'I could tell it from thy clothes, and the look on thy face. Tha's a healthy skin and that always reveals a lad from the countryside. Me, I'm going back.'

'Back? Where to . . .?'

'Back to the village where I was born. My lad's going to take me in.'

'Don't you like it here, then?' Simon asked incredulously. How could anyone want to return to the country after what he'd found here in the city, the throb and excitement of it all, the busy bustling scenes. Why, as compared to *this*, even Barthwick was the back of nowhere.

'Like it? I've hated every minute of the time I've spent here. I came here to try my hand at merchanting, turned my small holding over to my son and came here to try my hand. It's a hard mean life, I can tell you. I've spent my last weeks longing to get back, and I'm going back, soon as that coach leaves. It'll drop me nobbut six miles from my lad's place and I'll sleep quiet and dry tonight.'

Simon looked at the world-weary eyes of his companion. 'If you've been here so long,' he said, 'could I solicit your advice. I'll need a lodging while I'm here, something fitting to a man who seeks employment. Where would you suggest I look?'

'Aye,' the man said, 'you've fallen right on your feet. There's my place, as I've walked out on not two hours ago. It'll not be let, yet, because I never said I was going. I didn't know if I'd have the courage to book my place when the time came. Well, now I've paid them, and ta'en a seat, and that means for certain I'm away. Tha can have my place.'

'Is it . . . grand?' Simon asked shyly. 'I'm not well furnished with coin.'

'Grand it is not,' the man said. 'At twopence a week it could hardly be grand! But it's a roof over your head and, apart from a few roaches, and a rat or two, it's clean of lice.'

133

The next good fortune had come after Simon had taken occupation of Number Twelve, Turkey Street, Hunslet, a single-storey house in an alleyway of similar houses, built for a speculation by a City Merchant on land he'd inherited. The house was clean, and the departing tenant, Will Moorsom, had left a pile of clothing on the bed that Simon knew he could alter to fit. They were pantaloons, and shirts, more suited to city wear than his country breeches and waistcoat. He'd swept the place out with a besom Moorsom had also left, when he saw his neighbour eyeing him from his own doorway.

'New, are you?' the neighbour asked. 'My name's Sid Fletcher. What's yours?'

Simon was taken aback by the citified directness of speech, but pleased to have someone to talk to. 'Simon Aysgill o' Barthwick,' he said, giving his name country style.

'Aysgill o' Barthwick – now that's grand for a start. What's a lad wi' a grand name like that doing in a mucky hole like this?'

Simon coloured. 'I meant no offence,' he said. 'It's country style, you see, to say where you're from!'

'And, from the look of you, you haven't been long from there?'

Again the directness of blunt speech. Simon saw he'd have to get used to their ways. 'No,' he said, 'I just came from there. But I'm no country bumpkin, mark my words. I can read and I can write. I've not much in my pocket, but I can work alongside any man.'

'That's if tha can find a job.'

'Aye,' Simon said. 'I mean to start looking first thing in the morn.'

'Tha has no need to go looking, if tha's happy to work in the textile mill. Tha can take my job since I'm leaving it come Saturday. I've gotten a better job minding a machine in't printing.'

'Are you serious? Do you mean it? You've a job I can go to?'

'Aye, I mean it. The overlooker was asking if I knew a good honest worker. And tha looks strong enough.'

The two of them had walked the three miles to the textile mill the following morning; Simon of course had never seen anything like the factory that greeted his eyes. It appeared to have been built across a stream – 'That's for the water wheel,' Sid Fletcher explained, and to be three storeys high, about a hundred feet long and forty feet deep. It was made of dark brown bricks at the top and large stone pieces at ground-floor level, with a vast number of gaping holes on each level, each stone lined and painted white with lime.

As he drew near the mill he heard the noise that was to become such a part of his life in the city, the noise that would fill his head all day and every day, even continuing in his head at night when he returned home, dog-tired, to sleep. In those early days, however, the noise was stimulating, even exciting. It spoke to him of energy and activity, of the opportunity to better himself by working hard and earning money. It meant prospects in his new life, no matter how much he might be inconvenienced by it.

'Aye, Mr Tomlinson, this is a lad you might like to take on to replace me after Saturday.'

Mrs Fletcher had quickly sewn some of the working garments for Simon and had lopped his hair so that he no longer looked such a country bumpkin.

'Have you worked in a mill previously?' Mr Tomlinson asked, eyeing him doubtfully. Certainly the new recruit seemed strong and agile, but a bit gormless in the way he was looking at the rows of lasses at the carding benches.

'No, he hasn't,' Sid said, 'but he's a good worker, take my word for it.'

'I s'all have to, wain't I, since he doesn't seem to have a tongue in his head!'

Sid gave Simon's sleeve a tug. 'Come on, Simon,' he said. 'Tha'll have all the time in the world to look at the lasses if tha get's the job. But first you'll have to speak up for yourself.'

135

Simon was entranced by the sight of all the activity.

'Tha'd be carting,' Tommy Tomlinson said. 'Same as Sid. It's all go, and not for a lad as isn't nimble on his feet. I'd give thee 'prentice wages.'

All the way along Sid had talked to him about the job, about Tomlinson, about the meanness of the mill owner. 'Tha'll never see the owner,' he said, 'but somehow he seems to know everything that goes on and tha'll have to watch out for him. Aye, and if Tomlinson offers thee 'prentice wages, don't accept it. Say tha works for a full man's wage. They always try to set people on wi' 'prentice wages, with the promise they'll review it after a six-month, but they never do. So, stick out for a man's wage. That way, Tomlinson will know you're not to be trampled underfoot. Aye, and say you'll work hourly, and not piece work.'

'What's piece work?' Simon asked, quite bewildered by all the new information he was receiving so quickly.

'Piece work is when he gives you a job to do. When he says, you'll do this, and that, and this, and that, and doesn't mention hours. Tell him as you'll work from bell to bell, and what's not done, doesn't get done until the next bell.'

'Nay, they'll never give me the job if I tell 'em what I won't do.'

'Take my word for it,' Sid had insisted. 'Just do as I tell you, speak as I tell you to speak, and tha'll not go far wrong.'

'I'm accustomed to getting a man's wage, Mr Tomlinson,' Simon said, gulping at his own temerity.

'A man's wage, eh? I hope tha's able to give a man's work.'

Simon plucked up his courage. 'I am that, Mr Tomlinson,' he said firmly but respectfully. 'From bell to bell, I'll give you a man's work.'

'From bell to bell, eh? Tha's not as daft as tha looks, eh?'

'A man's work, Mr Tomlinson, I'll pledge myself to it,

136

from bell to bell!'

'Right. Tha can start right away,' Mr Tomlinson said. 'I like thy spirit. I'll set thee on, but mark tha'art on trial, until Sid goes.'

Those early days were everything Simon had hoped. His job was carting; he carted the wool when it arrived, carted it to the combers who separated it into long and short strands – the long to be used for worsteds, the short for coarser woollens. When the wool had been combed, he carted it to the spinners, an entire room of men and women who spun the combings into fibres on the big Saxony wheels. It was the first time Simon had seen such a wheel, which not only spun the yarn but also wound it onto cops. Simon then loaded his cart with the cops and raced up onto the next floor via a steep ramp that took all his energy. Here he gave the cops to the weavers who operated the Flying Shuttle machines he'd heard much about but never seen. In the Flying Shuttle system, the shuttle containing the weft yarn was flung from one side of the loom to the other by pulling a handle hanging before the operator's head. The shuttle was caught in a box and then another jerk would spring it back after the warp threads had been moved. The plain weave cloth was being woven at a rate unbelievable to Simon, who'd been accustomed only to the hand-loom they'd had at home. Multiply the faster weft shuttle movement by the number of girls and men working the machines, he told himself, and he'd have some idea of the furlongs the Mill turned out in a year. He couldn't do the sum and his mind reeled even to try.

All around the mill iron shafts whirled, their cog wheels engaging other shafts, leading to machines. All the threads were being spun in thesé machines, from cop to shuttle, from cop to bobbin. The shafts were turned by the power of the giant water wheel below which rumbled and grumbled with a continuous whoosh of water from the tributary of the River Aire. On the very top floor were the teasing machines, which took the cloth and brought up the nap by rubbing the wiry heads of plants known as *teasels*

137

over the fabric. From there the cloth was taken to the shearers who stretched it out and clipped the nap with giant shears sharp enough to take off a man's hand.

The whole building with its wooden beams and floors reverberated with the constant sound of the machines, the grinding of the gears, the splash of the water, the slap and clack of the flying shuttles as the operators pulled the picking pegs, the demanding voices of the workers as they shouted for more of whatever supply they needed, the run and rumble of the carters' trolleys.

Simon, that first week, loved it! It was exciting, it was active. For the first week he ran everywhere with his cart, seeing everybody, smiling at everything, eager, anxious to please everyone, to keep everyone supplied with their needs. He had no time to stop and exchange words with Sid as they passed each other, or with any other of the carters. When the bell rang each morning for the start of work, he was there, pushing his cart into the low level, racing it up the ramps to the top. When the bell rang again for the meal break, he flopped down where he was and took out an oatmeal cake he'd bought on his way to work, fresh from a baker's oven. When he'd eaten he'd go down to the river, to the weir above the mill where the water was passably clean, and scoop handfuls of it to slake his thirst.

The mill started each morning at seven o'clock and work continued until nine o'clock at night. It was a long day, but Simon got used to it, since he'd been accustomed to long hours in Barthwick, when work continued as long as there was light to see by. He didn't know how the lasses and the children could stand it – they were pale and listless folk by his country standard and seemed to lack energy, dragging themselves around the place, often perspiring. Each day at least two women would suddenly keel over, no doubt under pressure of work, and often a hand, an arm, their hair, would go into the machinery. There'd be screams, and shouts, and a section of the machinery would be stopped, but only for so long as it took to clear the person from the machine's grasp. Then a carter would be called –

138

sometimes Simon himself, to cart the body down to the back of the mill to a room where the doctor would come. What happened to the person after that would depend on the extent of the injuries, but the following day, another lass would be standing there, to take her place.

In all sections of the mill the children worked, retying broken threads, clearing machines, setting up the warp of the looms, their deft nimble fingers moving fast along the threads, their small backs straining to lift trays of cops into position. After his first week, Simon was on nodding acquaintance with one of them, a ginger-haired kid whose clothing was all in rags, who had a perpetually dirty face and running nose, but a lovely smile.

'Aye, and what's thy name then?' Simon asked, as the kid flopped beside him eyeing his oatcake with evident hunger.

'Ezra . . .'

'Ezra what?'

'Just Ezra. I don't rightly know any other name.'

Simon took pity on him, broke off half his oatcake and gave it to the lad, who set to and devoured it.

'Where do ye live, then?'

Ezra looked surprised. 'Live?' he asked. 'Why, I live here, of course.'

The bell rang at that moment and both sprang up to start work again.

Lizzie Fletcher, Sid's wife, had started cooking for Simon, and each evening when he returned from work he'd spruce himself up a bit in the running spring water and then go next door where Sid would have returned from his new job in the printing works. Sid was making seven shillings a week as against Simon's five and they were talking of finding a better place somewhere nearer where he worked. 'Aye, I'm on my way up,' Sid predicted confidently. 'If I keep my nose clean, I shall get a job as an overseer, and that'll give me all of eight bob.'

'I'm saving the coppers,' Lizzie said proudly. 'We mean to get away from here, and live respectably.'

Simon was giving her a shilling a week from his wages and she was feeding him. It was a lot better than buying a meal in an ale-house, or making something for himself – he'd never been a dab hand at cooking.

'I was talking with Ezra today,' he said to Sid. 'Remember him? Little red-haired lad?'

'Aye, tha means Ginger,' Sid said, sucking on the pork knuckle in the stew. 'Watch it when you take your snap – he'll come round with them moon shaped eyes of his and rob the nourishment from you.'

'Aye, he had half my oatmeal cake this morn.'

'Daft devil,' Lizzie said, chiding him. 'A man needs all the eating he can get if he's going to survive working. Tha mun be kind to thy stomach and give nowt away.'

'Especially to the 'prentices,' Sid said. 'Yon's a thieving lot of devils, mark my words. The only reason they don't rob you is that you've nothing worth stealing.'

'He said something that puzzles me,' Simon said. 'He told me he lived there at the mill.'

'They do,' Sid said. 'They live up in't attic. Didn't tha know it?'

'Have they no homes?'

'Aye, they have a home in the mill. Who do you think does all the cleaning and clearing after we go at night, and greases the machinery in the morn afore we hear the bell ring? The mill owner buys them from the orphanage. He's supposed to teach them, feed them, learn them about mill work. He does little of any of that, of course. So far as he's concerned, they're cheap labour.'

Simon thought about the apprentices after he returned next door to his own home and fell, exhausted, onto his straw-filled mattress. He couldn't get to sleep despite being tired. The air of the room smelled dank and stale and when he put out his hands he could feel the slime on the walls thicker than ever. He could hear the rats scurrying in the corners but they didn't bother him much since he knew there was no food in the place to attract them. Doubtless the ones he was hearing were passing through the walls of

140

the houses from one to the other in search of food. The bed bugs were more active that night and he felt them biting at his flesh, though he was used to that and his body didn't break into rashes, like some he'd seen among the 'prentices and the pale-faced lasses who worked in the mill. When the sun came, he'd change the straw in the mattress, take the palliasse out and hang it in the sunshine all day. Aye, and come a sunny Sunday, he'd walk out towards Middleton, lie in the fields all day just breathing the fresh air.

For the first time he missed Barthwick, missed his clean bed in a dry room beneath the window through which, often, he could see the moon. It seemed like paradise to him at that moment.

He felt a tug on the cloth that covered him and knew an intrepid rat was starting to climb. 'Get thee off,' he said loudly, slapping at the cloth. 'Get thee off, tha dirty city-bred devil.'

The mist had crept slowly in, covering the water with its soft light grey blanket from which only the roofs of the highest buildings peeped, and the masts of several tall ships anchored down there in the harbour.

Gertrude sat at the window of her attic room, enchanted by the scene spread out before her, the empty streets, the empty fish-markets, the silent still North Sea extending to the distant coast-line of the Continent of Europe. Even after a month, it was still incredibly romantic to her. She hugged herself in her cotton nightshift, reluctant to break the spell to put on the thick warm woollen robe her Mistress had bought for her.

She didn't need to start her work until half past five, but she liked to get up early, to sit here and count her blessings, thinking of the days behind, the day ahead. She shuddered again when she thought of where she might have been, remembering the dirt and slime of that hovel in which her brother Simon had been content, even happy, to live. Gertrude's heart had sunk when she'd seen it, smelled the decay of the open drain at the back of the house, seen the rat droppings in corners, the cockroaches and lice that always accompany dirt. She could feel again how she'd recoiled when her hand had touched the slime-greened walls with their crumbling plaster, the half fallen ceiling in one of the rooms. God was merciful, she reminded herself, to spare her all that.

She'd come from Simon's house, refusing his offer of sharing his lodging until she found something for herself, and left the mean streets of Hunslet as quickly as she could, seeing the slatterns in the doorways of the gin-shops and ale-house yards, the drunken men, the crushed women and children seeking employment. She'd clutched her reticule to her as she'd hurried through the vile streets of this low-class quarter, fearful some fleet-footed child bag-snatcher would snip it from her wrist and run with all her possessions. She'd sewn all the coins of her division of their father's estate into the hems of her petticoats save two she carried in a purse hanging beneath her dress from a cord round her neck. Her dress was clean but shabby, her bonnet a simple straw she'd woven and blocked herself and covered with a scrap of cambric dyed dark with logwood chippings. Superficially, she resembled a number of matrons walking the streets of the quarter in their respectability, though her complexion had the ruddy tint of the country as compared to their white-skinned, sallow, features. Her frightened, downcast eyes peeked out from beneath her bonnet, looking in this direction and that, fearing some dreadful onslaught.

She gasped when she saw a man in his twenties step out from a doorway ahead of her with a grin on his face as if to accost her, his arms beginning to spread wide. She turned down an alleyway and quickened her pace, fearful to run.

Halfway down the alleyway she turned and saw the man entering the end of it. She hastened, turned at the far end, moved quickly through the throngs of what seemed to be a street market, past the door of an ale-house, along the

142

street and the side of a river with crowded wharves and jetties. After going half a mile she turned and looked back again and her pursuer, if that's what he had been, seemed to have disappeared. Now she could slacken her pace and choose her steps more carefully since her shoes and the hem of her gown had become soiled by the mud and the ordure through which she'd hastened in her anxiety.

She lifted her eyes and to her horror saw ahead of her at a distance of about a hundred paces, the same young man whom she instantly recognized.

On her right was the yard of a coaching inn. She entered rapidly with no thought in mind except to surround herself with what she hoped were goodly honest people. The ostler leered at her as he flicked the bridle of the lead horse attached to the large coach that waited in the yard.

The agent was standing there, a big bluff man wearing a long bottle-green coat, with a brown stove-pipe hat, pale beige breeches and two-coloured boots. He looked so like a country gentleman that she approached him for protection.

'Are you for the Flyer, mistress?' he asked, his kindly eyes searching her face.

'Aye,' she said, not thinking logically but needing desperately to escape from the Hades in which she found herself, 'aye. Which are your least expensive seats?'

He eyed her shabby neat clothing, the string reticule in which she was carrying what he judged to be her entire possessions.

'Tha can sit inside, mistress, for sixpence,' he said. She gasped at the price but knew she'd be obliged to pay it if she were to hope to escape.

'I'm obliged, Sir,' she said. 'If you'll but give me a moment . . .'

She went into the corner of the yard and, as inconspicuously as possible, lifted the hem of her petticoat, opened the stitches, and took out the coin.

Thus had begun the odyssey that carried her from Leeds to York, from York to Malton, from Malton to Whitby.

The sight of the sea had stopped her headlong flight at Whitby – she'd been entranced immediately by the smell of the salt and of fish, the sight of the vessels at their moorings and anchorages, the ruddy-featured fisher-folk so different from the pasty-faced slum-rats of Leeds. When she'd descended from the coach in the yard by the south side of the river which debouched into the sea at that point, she was bewildered and tired, but had a great sense of coming home. She'd made enquiries of the wife of the innkeeper, who'd eyed her simple but clean clothing and placed her accurately as a God-fearing girl unlike the many who arrived in the seafaring port hoping to ply their ancient profession among the gullible foreign sailors.

'Mistress Edgecombe was asking if I knew of any respectable girl who wished a post in her service. I think she had in mind someone younger, but I could send you along to speak to her, if you've a mind. You'd find her a severe and demanding mistress, but fair and correct in all her dealings.'

Mistress Edgecombe was a large imposing lady in her late forties, Gertrude judged, with a matriarchal bosom clad in ivory coloured silk without decoration of lace at wrists or throat. Her hair had been pulled severely back from her face and she wore it, without wig, in a style Gertrude had never seen before with the length plaited into coils and wound round, held in position, so far as Gertrude could judge, by a number of pins and covered with a fine, almost invisible, veil. It was a severe and practical method of styling the hair, Gertrude thought, resolving to do the same herself if it would not be considered above her station in life.

'To what do you owe your present misfortune?' Mistress Edgecombe asked severely when Gertrude had introduced herself to the housekeeper and had been shown, after much whispering and coming and going, into the sitting-room on the first floor where Mistress Edgecombe was drinking a cordial from a fluted glass.

'My present *misfortune*, ma'am?' Gertrude asked.

'To be abroad unprotected, to travel alone to a strange place on the Flyer, to have lost one's female dignity, can surely be described as no other than a misfortune?' Mistress Edgecombe asked, though in a kindly voice and without hauteur or criticism.

Gertrude had told her everything, from the Petition of Enclosure, the lack of funds for financing the fence, the death of her father, the separation of the family, her brother's mean lodging, the pursuit by the young man in the streets of the slums of Leeds.

It was a piteous recital that left neither with dry eyes.

'My poor dear,' Mistress Edgecombe said finally, when the terrible tale had unfolded itself, 'how much you must have suffered. But the Lord *is* good, and has guided your steps to a safe anchorage. If you would care to do so, we shall give you a haven here, a harbour secure from the storms.'

It was only when Gertrude had met Mr Edgecombe, or Captain Edgecombe as he was still called despite having retired from the sea, that Gertrude began to understand the source of many of her Mistress's colourful allusions to storms, harbours, anchors and tides. The job she was given paid the unbelievable sum of five whole shillings a year; she had a room to herself in the attic which overlooked the harbour out to sea, and she ate table leavings with the other six servants below stairs. The Edgecombes kept a fine table at which fish, something of a novelty to Gertrude, prevailed, and did much entertaining. Gertrude had never eaten so well in her life, nor slept so warm and dry, since the bed in her small room was covered by a down-filled embroidered covering, skilfully worked in coloured wools. On the second day, the housekeeper had taken her to the draper who kept his tiny shop in a small square not far from the house, and there she was asked to select materials for clothing, and a uniform which the draper had already made. It was the first time in her life that Gertrude had been in such an exciting shop, or seen the ready-made liveries for the servants of the grand houses of Whitby. She was soon to learn that many sea captains, after a life spent afloat, liked to have prettily dressed servants about them, and maintained a style of living which had much to commend it.

Whitby, she soon learned, was a port trading with many other ports. Much wool was exported from there to the Continent of Europe; much timber came in to be used in the building of grand houses farther inland. There were several active ship-building concerns along the river, and much ship repairing. Though some of the docks were in a state of ill-repair, much work and profit was derived from the alum trade and coal shipments, and from the whale fishing fleet that went to the Arctic Ocean.

The job she had been given began at half-past five; she climbed from her window seat reluctantly and washed herself in the cold water in the ewer before dressing and combing her hair, winding it and securing it beneath the white mob cap she wore when not serving at table. Her thick woollen stockings prickled her legs but she was grateful for their warmth. She gave her shoes a quick rub before slipping them on her feet, and then put on the overall that covered her from neck to toes, tying it round the waist so that it fell full over her petticoats. She went down into the basement and came back upstairs with the ash bucket into which she emptied the remains of the coal fire in the living-room, after sifting out the larger, re-usable, pieces. Her mistress had an eagle eye for profligacy and waste. She relaid the fire with sticks and fresh coals; the master would light it when he came down at six thirty.

One by one she cleaned the ashes out of the other grates, polishing them with the blacking powder, rubbing the bronze of their ornamentation so that it shone. It was very modern to have these iron firebacks – she had been told that their's was the only house in Whitby in which commonplace chimneys and grates were thus decorated.

She kept a careful eye on the huge clock in the sitting-room, listening to it signal each quarter hour with satis-faction, or panic, depending on whether she was ahead or behind with her work. Promptly at six fifteen the Housekeeper, Mrs Watts appeared and began to check that each task had been carried out conscientiously. Gertrude waited – she knew there would be one point of dissatisfaction, since Mrs Watts couldn't let a morning inspection pass by without in some way asserting her authority. The words came when Mrs Watts arrived in the kitchen, where Gertrude was cleaning the vegetables for Cook, who sat by the stove drinking a bowl of soup into which, to Gertrude's amazement, she tipped a measure of rum from a keg in the store, reputed to have been brought back from one of Captain Edgecombe's voyages to the West Indies.

'It has been my misfortune to see slovenly, even slatternly, work,' Mrs Watts said in her morning icy voice, 'but never to witness anything that compares with the way you have cleaned the sitting-room hearth, Mistress Gertrude. Lest our dear Master should have a fit of apoplexy when he comes to warm himself by the fire in the full expectation that those who take his coin will give him service for it, and discovers how shoddily you have honoured that expectation, I suggest you go back upstairs and repair your omission at once.'

Gertrude couldn't resist the mischievous impulse that escaped from her. 'Fie, Mrs Watts,' she said, 'I could understand you more readily if you'd speak more plainly.'

Mrs Watts gasped. 'Are you being *impertinent*, Gertrude,' she asked, clasping her hand dramatically to her thin bosom. She turned. 'I'll not stand here to be insulted by a chit of a maid,' she said as she stormed from the kitchen.

Cook was watching Gertrude shrewdly. 'You're not always what you seem,' she said. 'But I warn you, you'll have to learn to keep a curb on your tongue if you hope to remain in service. Some may think you a timid maid without a word to say for herself, but I've seen a wink in your eyes a time or two you'd do better to save for some attentive lad.'

The kitchen door opened again. 'Come *along*,

Gertrude,' Mrs Watts said angrily. 'Impertinence is one thing, but *disobedience* is something I neither can nor will tolerate . . .'

Gertrude didn't mind; she was shrewd enough to realize that only by commanding those beneath her could Mrs Watts justify herself to her employers. She was a good-hearted woman who'd been embittered by being abandoned by her husband in childbirth, many years previously. The child had been born dead. 'Her heart was double-broke, you see,' Cook had said when she related the story to Gertrude over a hot rum toddy one evening. 'No way a healthy babby can come from a mother whose heart is broke.'

Following his successful career on the sea, Captain Edgecombe, on his early retirement, had taken over a ship-building yard, investing the money he'd earned carrying rich cargoes for part-shares. The yard was prospering, never lacked for orders for all manner of vessels for the coal trade, for the wool-exporters, for those who ventured all over the world in search of rich trade. Every time Edgecombe built a ship he took shares in it himself and already had become a wealthy man. Gertrude had heard all this from Cook, who, though she always behaved in a superior manner to the other servants in view of her unique position, seemed to have taken a fancy to the shy timid lass from Barthwick, who was unlike the other pert young ladies. It could perhaps have been that Cook felt a greater affinity for the older girl, since Gertrude was twenty-four and some servant lasses were as young as fifteen and sixteen. Cook was forty, and she and Gertrude soon became great cronies, though Gertrude had little time, nor indeed had Cook herself, to sit and gossip.

The Edgecombe household was a happy one; Gertrude counted herself lucky to have found such a haven. She hastened back to the sitting-room and gave the hearth a quick wipe with her duster, polishing the knobs of the fender yet again, though she could already see her face in them. She was on her way down the back stairs when she heard the Captain coughing as he came from his quarters on the third floor; he wouldn't have approved of finding her still in the sitting-room when he came, morning grumpy, from his bed.

Gertrude sped down to the kitchen and picked up the knife to peel the mountain of potatoes that awaited her attention. She hugged her pleasure to herself as she worked deftly and quickly. Today, she had been granted her first day off since she'd started work a month ago. Today, she'd promised herself, she'd explore the whole of Whitby, every nook, every cranny, and even get the ferryman to take her to the other side of the river. Today, she was on holiday.

Cook had been watching her; she came across and took the second tub of potatoes away. 'I'll find that again later,' she said. 'I believe Mrs High-and-Mighty Watts said you could go out when the tatties were done?'

'Oh, thank you, Cook,' Gertrude said, greedy for every moment of her free day.

She went upstairs, took off her overall and put on her outside coat over her dress of plain green fustian. When she was ready, she walked along the attic corridor to Selina's room, since the servants were only permitted to leave the house in twos lest misfortune befall them in the teeming streets. Selina, already dressed for out-of-doors, pouted when she saw Gertrude. 'You've taken forever!'

They presented themselves in the servants' dining-room, where they were inspected by Mrs Watts, who pronounced them decent enough to leave the house. Then they stepped out into the morning air after hearing her lecture and her admonishment that they return at five o'clock, not a moment later, 'by which hour all decent bodies are inside their houses and only ragamuffins and trollops stalk the streets'.

'Where shall we go first?' Selina asked. She was a tall girl with blond locks now hidden beneath her plain velvet cap. Gertrude found her lackadaisical, inclined to be moody and bored, and certainly her manner this morning showed

149

little enthusiasm for their venture.

'Let's go and look at the ships in the river,' Gertrude said.

'If that's what pleases thee . . .'

They walked along the side of the river, seeing the many vessels they couldn't identify, hearing the well-meant whistles and cat-calls of the foreign sailors who'd be leaving on the tide. They saw three-masters hovering off Whitby, waiting for the river mouth to fill before they could come in, while the men already moored were impatient for the tide to rise so they could cast off and be away. They saw jolly boats plying along the river carrying men to larger vessels anchored off the bar, their oarsmen plying the sweeps with that consummate skill that seems to remove all effort. They saw the fishing boats, their shallower draught enabling them to leave at three-quarter tide, their decks covered by nets and withy creels. Most of them had small sails of a rectangular shape though cut thinner at the top and unlike the sails on the big square riggers. The dockside was an exciting mixture of nets, creels, baskets and ropes, hordes of men knotting and repairing their equipment, laying ropes into wooden sheaves, securing rope-ends onto sheave boxes. Though Gertrude knew nothing of the names, she found her head spinning with the different shapes of all the artifacts that lay on the side of a busy port where boats and ships of all sizes and shapes ply their trade.

Above it all was the clean sharp tang of the ocean, the cleansing smell of the wrack in the air, the fresh odour of the fish.

She stood near a box of cod, delighted by the colour of their scales, by the flash and glitter of them. When a man put a monster before her face in joke she shrieked and jumped back.

'Nay, mistress,' the man said, ''tis nobbut a lobster.' He took her round the shed, showed her the lobsters, black and wriggling mysteriously, the crabs still snapping their claws despite the knot the fishermen had tied round them.

'You don't mean to tell me folks eat things like that?' she asked.

'Aye, and pay a fine price for them, my dear,' he said. 'These'll all finish on some gentleman's table, being cracked and sucked and devoured by them, washed down with a pint of best ale, or some of that pale Gascony, or happen a sherry wine.'

He was a fascinating man and Gertrude would have loved to talk more with him, but Selina pulled her coat. 'Come on, Gertrude,' she whined, 'I don't like it here. I don't want to spend my day off in this stink.'

They left the fish dock and climbed the hill side by side, to where the houses were set out in small rows and squares. This was the part of the town where the successful shop-keepers and others lived. Here was a saddler, next door a shop that sold clothing for fishermen. There was an ale-house at the corner of one of the squares. Gertrude peeped in through the yard gate and saw the outside courtyard, with a balcony round it. The morning had fled and already noon was past.

'Let's go in here,' Selina said, now quite vitalized. Gertrude glanced at her, wondering what could have caused the change of mood.

They went into the ale-house and saw a number of gentlemen dressed for business, sitting at the plain wooden tables, drinking ale from pewter pots. The pot-boy rushed in with another tray of pots he set on one of the tables. The men had looked at the two girls as they came in and mostly had ignored them, continuing their brisk talk one with the other.

'What is it?' Gertrude whispered.

'They do business here,' Selina whispered. 'These gentlemen are all taking shares in cargoes, buying and selling interests. It's an Exchange – you know, like a Corn Exchange, or a Woollen Exchange, only these men are selling risks, not goods.' Selina was chattering in a most animated voice, her sparkling eyes looking boldly round the room, in which were half a dozen other women all

151

finely dressed, sitting in pairs or threes.

Gertrude glanced up and suddenly caught the eye of one of two men, sprawling relaxed on a bench across the room with a pot of ale before him. When he saw she had noticed him, he winked and tossed his head suggestively.

'Did you see that?' Gertrude asked, outraged. 'I think yon man is making overtures to me!'

Before she had time to think Selina, instead of replying as Gertrude had expected, rose and crossed the room, to disappear through a door at the side of the bench whereon the men were sitting. The man who'd winked at Gertrude, or so she thought, immediately rose from the bench and followed Selina through the door.

Gertrude didn't know what to do. Certainly she felt it was most improper to be sitting there alone in this room filled with men, but what could she do? She could hardly follow Selina through the door now that the man had gone there, lest he think that she were following *him*. As she kept her head down but her eyes alert beneath her bonnet, one by one, three of the other ladies got up and went through the door and three individual men followed them. Oh dear, it was impossible to understand what *could* be happening.

She was astounded to hear a voice at her elbow and see a man sit in Selina's place. 'Sir,' she asked, outraged, 'what will you with me?'

'How can I catch your e'en if you keep your head bowed. You bain't in Chapel now, you know.'

She blushed in her confusion, not knowing what to say. The man was big, and looked strong and, in truth, was just a bit handsome, but he'd no right to approach her this way as if she were a trollop that any man could address his coarse remarks to without disadvantage.

'Sir, I have no wish to talk to thee,' she said. 'I'd be obliged if you'd leave me be. I'm but waiting for the return of my friend before going back to my respectable employment at the home of a gentleman who, I feel certain, would protect me from all offence could he but be here . . .' Her voice tailed away before his disarming, amused, regard.

''Tis a pity to keep such e'en downcast,' he said, 'for a more rare and lively tint of cobalt it has never been my privilege to see.'

'Sir, you *must* not, you *shall* not speak of these matters for 'tis most unseemly.' She pretended to look anxiously for Selina. 'Oh, if only my friend and companion would return, I could bring this improper adventure to a rapid close.' She had to admit she was thrilled beyond measure. No man had ever told her she had fine blue eyes. What had he said, rare and lively! He must have had an education to be able to speak his mind so fluently, so strongly and fine. But, it would not do, in truth it would *not* do!

'I am most vexed,' she said, 'that my companion should have left me this way. I beg of you, sir, if you have honour, to sit quietly here as if we were acquainted, to protect me from further molestation. I shall not speak to you, for that would not be seemly, but from time to time until my friend returns to rescue me from this dreadful situation, I shall *smile in your direction*. Not, you understand, *at you*, for that would be most improper and immodest. You are to read nothing in my smile but gratitude for your continuing gentlemanly and protective behaviour. Is that understood, sir, or must I seek elsewhere the protection my friend's untimely absence has obliged me to solicit?'

'By your style of speech, Mistress,' he said, 'I can assume you are an educated lady. I shall do as you request and sit here accepting your smiles for what they are meant to be, a token of our proximity rather than a mark of your affection. I shall, however, take the opportunity to pray . . .'

'To pray, sir?'

'Yes, to pray.'

He seemed inclined to say no more but his remark had intrigued her. Men do not usually address the Lord in prayer with a pot by their hand, with their heads erect, their eyes wide-open and sparkling – though his were a delicate shade of amber, not blue – and sitting formally, though relaxed, at table. Still, a man's prayers were a matter for himself and his Lord alone, surely?

'To pray, sir?'

'Aye, to pray.'

Most intriguing, Gertrude thought. Why should a man nearing thirty, wearing a blue livery jacket over a fine shirt laced with silver, almost white pantaloons and black shoes with silver buckles, a man with light coloured and crinkling hair tied behind his collar in a neat knot, a man whose healthy complexion bespoke a clean life, though his hand, toying lightly with the handle of his ale-pot showed evidence of manual labour such as her own hands showed, why should such a *handsome* man take this opportunity for prayer?

'To pray, you said, sir?'

'Aye, to pray.'

Oh, it was so *vexing* that he volunteered no further information. 'Are your sins of such a magnitude, sir, do they weigh so heavily upon your shoulders, that you needs must pray all day to seek forgiveness?'

He shrugged those sturdy shoulders. 'I pray, not for forgiveness, but for the granting of a boon.'

'A boon, sir? I would have thought such a matter bespoke more humility in the address than you appear to give. I would have thought that . . .'

'. . . that I should only ask a boon on my knees i' the Chapel o' Sunday. I pray to a God much more lenient than that, one who is . . .' He half rose. 'But, alas, I see my prayers have not been answered, for your companion returns. Tell me quick, what is the name of your employer?'

'Captain Edgecombe, sir, but what business is that of yours?'

'I'm obliged, Mistress,' he said hurriedly and, without waiting for Selina to cross the room, he turned and walked out of the ale-house with determined, even jaunty, strides.

'You were quick,' Selina said. 'And I though you an old maid stick-i'-the-mud!'

154

Gertrude looked at Selina's flushed face, noted the way her petticoat gaped from the unbuttoned front of her dress. 'You mean to say you came out wi' a button undone, and Mistress Watts never saw it,' she gasped. 'You must fasten it at once, Selina.'

Selina looked at her in a strange manner as she fastened the button. 'I lack understanding of thee Gertrude,' she said. 'Either th'art such a nincompoop, else . . .'

'Else what . . .?' Gertrude asked.

'Nay, never mind,' Selina said quickly. 'Let's leave this place, shall we. It fair gives one the creeps.'

Cook was scandalized. 'Tha went into Waley's Ale House,' she gasped. 'Nay, Gertrude, I thought better on thee. Thy first day out . . .'

Gertrude was downcast and wished she had not spoken. She hadn't mentioned the young man who'd spoken so freely with her, thank God, or Cook would have fallen of apoplexy, to judge from her reaction.

'It was only to rest our feet,' she said.

They'd returned early, since, after the ale-house, Selina seemed in ill humour and somewhat fatigued, pleading a headache as her reason for coming home. Cook was busy in the kitchen preparing the supper for ten, a small table by the Captain's standards. Willy the pot lad had stoked the fire with coal, of which there seemed to be an abundance in Whitby, and the vast ovens were heating well for the roasts, with the many pots bubbling on it. She was in the middle of rolling a pastry on a board but she dropped the wooden pin and collapsed into a chair.

'Willy,' she said sternly, 'get thee out of here and doan't come back until I tell thee.'

He snatched a piece of the raw pastry as he ran out of the kitchen but Cook only grunted at him. 'I've failed in my duty,' she said. 'I thought, somehow, as tha knew more than tha does, since tha has such a pretty way o' talking, and has obviously been learned to read, which I never was. Tha knows nowt of Waley's, tell me the truth.'

155

'Only what Selina told me. That it's an ale-house rather like an Exchange. A Corn Exchange or a Woollens Exchange, except that the men buy and sell risks in boats, shares of cargoes, and such like.'

'Aye, it's that right enough,' Cook said, nodding vigorously. 'And tha knows nowt else about it?' She was obviously mortally embarrassed.

When the door started to open she shouted, 'Get out of my kitchen until I open the door to thee, whoever th'art!'

The door was slammed closed, whoever was there assuming Cook was having one of her moods.

'Tha knows nowt else?' she said softly to Gertrude, reaching across the table and taking her hand.

'I didn't find it very agreeable in there,' Gertrude said.

'I'm not surprised,' Cook said. 'It's a House of Ill Fame, of Assignation. It's frequented by businessmen, aye, buying and selling cargoes and risks and boat shares, but it's also frequented by trollops selling *themselves*!'

'Trollops . . .?'

'Aye, trollops like Selina. Has tha never wondered where she disappears to, sometimes; what she's doing when the bell rings and it takes her thirty minutes in the answering of it; why she has the room at the end of the corridor in the attics, at the head of the stairs?'

Gertrude was puzzled. None of this meant anything to her. Cook could see her innocence and went to the door of the servants' hall, knowing she'd find Selina sitting in there. 'Selina,' she bawled. 'Come here.'

Selina came in. 'How much did yon lad give you i' Waley's today?'

Selina looked spitefully at Gertrude. 'Why, is she complaining she didn't get owt off her fellah?'

The back of Cook's hand smashing across her mouth silenced her and brought tears to her eyes. 'How much,' Cook demanded.

'Sixpence. I asked a shilling.'

'Tha's not worth a penny. You see, Gertrude, what happens when trollops like this prowl the street, seeking

156

advantage and a filthy coin. Aye, my lass, and did he gi' ya a good . . .?'

Cook used a word so vile, so foul, that Gertrude clapped her hands over her ears and cried, 'No, no!'

Selina smirked. 'How would you know anything about that, you dry old stick?' she asked insultingly. 'The only thing you've had between your knees these many a long year is a pudding basin!'

This time the Cook's backhand brought blood to the corner of her mouth.

'It's true,' she sobbed, 'it's true. Tha's a frustrated old maid as longs for a man and can't catch one. That one there does better than thee. She caught a fellow soon as I'd gone, and if I hadn't returned when I did and spoiled it for her, she'd have been bent over the bed wi' her skirts up, mark my words. And come away wi' a coin in her hand.'

Cook was flabbergasted. 'No, Gertrude,' she said. 'It ain't true, tell me it ain't true . . . Not thee!'

'Go on, Gertrude, tell Cook it ain't true,' Selina sneered, wiping the blood from the corner of her mouth. 'Tell her it ain't true what I say, that when I come back with my coin in my purse and my dress unbuttoned, you had a fellow sitting at the table beside you, speaking with you bold as brass. And you were addressing him, and smiling at him.'

'Nay!' Cook shouted. 'Tha weren't. It ain't true.'

Gertrude's eyes were cast down. Oh, how could she have done so many bad things on her first day out? Would anyone ever trust her again? She'd gone into a house of ill-fame with trollops, she'd permitted a man to admire her, to sit at her table and address her, had even conversed with him and had solicited his help. Tears of bitter sorrow ran down her face. She felt sullied by her own badness, defiled. 'Aye,' she sobbed, 'I mun confess the truth. 'Tis true, 'tis true.'

She turned and fled from the room with Selina's mocking laugh echoing in her ears. She raced up the back stairs and flung herself, sobbing, on her bed feeling utterly,

utterly, depraved and soiled.

Mrs Watts found her still there, five minutes after the inspection of servants for the dinner table. 'What, pray, are you doing here?' she demanded, her voice icy and haughty as ever. 'Is this how you repay your mistress's kindness and generosity for giving you a day of leisure, by continued idleness and sloth? I give you five minutes to appear before me in the servants' hall, Mistress Gertrude, or I'll speak to Mistress Edgecombe, who has been an *angel of charity* to you, and seek permission to send you packing.'

Gertrude's eyes were red, and she couldn't avoid sniffing when she held out her hands, back and front, for inspection. Mrs Watts tugged at the corner of her long apron with its two straps that crossed her breast, and set her cap to rights, adjusting the pinned-up lappets that topped the pleated frill. Her face softened as she looked into Gertrude's eyes.

'If you have problems, Gertrude, I'm at your disposal, you know. We pride ourselves on being a *happy* family here. Nor Captain Edgecombe nor his lady would like to see unhappy faces about them.'

Gertrude smiled bravely, but couldn't trust herself to speak. In her heart she'd realized she had nothing with which to reproach herself, save the sin of vanity for having thought the young man was expressing an interest in her. From what Selina and Cook had said, she could see him now for what he was, a vile person who frequented evil places, and as such, she could put him from her mind. Selina was what she was; Gertrude could remember Fanny Colborn, and Polly at the Manor. She reminded herself of what Dodie had said to her, whispering together one evening behind the curtain, that many such women would seek advantage in that way. Dodie had told her many stories of women who went with men in that way to earn a dowry, else how could a poor-born woman hope to better her situation?

The attraction of male for female was natural. The beasts in the field did it, all animals did it, and basically, mankind were animals, or so the travelling preacher had often thundered from the pulpit of the Manor Chapel.

The only difference, she told herself, was that human beings should do it with love. Aye, well, that would be a perfect world. How many girls in Barthwick had ever married for love? Mostly they'd married for the advantage, to give their unborn child a name, to escape from home and harrying parents, to find a bit of space in which to live. Perhaps Selina and her kind were of a similar mind. Looking for a dowry, an advantage. She saw the younger girl looking at her across the room. Tonight was a special night, and the Mayor was seated at table, wearing his elegant robes. His wife wore a gown of white brocade and jewels sparkled from her. The girls had been bidden to stand against the wall with their hands crossed, while Enoch, James and Lemuel, the footmen, approached the guests wearing their pale lemon liveries, with blue facings to their jackets and white hose. Captain Edgecombe's Steward had served at sea with him and was therefore privileged not to wear livery. His long black frock-coat, with black breeches, his tied-wig well powdered, gave him a clerical look which the rolling gate of his sea legs promptly denied.

Gertrude caught Selina's eye, and the younger girl cocked her head slightly to one side, like a puppy looking at its master not knowing whether a curse or a caress will be its portion. 'Oh, Selina,' Gertrude thought, 'that you should choose to earn your dowry in that way . . . That you are so impatient and cannot wait until you meet correctly a man with whom you can join your life,' as Gertrude herself hoped to do. But the die was cast, the girl had chosen her path.

Anyway, Gertrude asked herself, who was she to stand in judgement of another girl and her way of life. She remembered the words of Cook the day she'd been cheeky to Mrs Watts. She herself had not always been so perfect that she could criticize Selina. Once again the irresistible impulse burst from her, and she smiled and winked saucily at Selina across the room. Selina, recognizing forgiveness, smiled back, friends in complicity.

The footman had turned and was frowning at Gertrude. 'What's tha winking at, lass,' he whispered fiercely.

'Not at thee, I'll be bound,' she said, boldness escaping from her.

Robert, the Steward, coughed his disapproval behind his gloved hand . . .

Now that Gertrude had, in a sense, forgiven Selina she was able, also, to forgive herself, to drop the immense burden of guilt she had been bearing. She sped down to the kitchen with the plates, to return with the first of the trays of capons. The Edgecombes used the modern method of serving meals, learned by the Captain on his voyages abroad, where the courses were brought separately to table, rather than being all combined on the board. The Captain had also brought Baccarat glassware from France and even the new porcelain with which they were experimenting. The large dark oak table shone with Gertrude's own efforts since she loved it best of all her jobs. The guests were elegant people, wearing many different pastel coloured gowns in silks and brocades, with lace trimmings and jewels that must have cost many fortunes. The men all looked handsome with their clean white linen stocks, their velvet jackets in dark colours contrasting with the pretty pastels of their ladies. The conversation flowed and sparkled, and many times Gertrude had to drag her mind away from attempts to understand what was being said in order to fetch or carry something.

'I am so lucky,' she told herself, 'so wonderfully lucky.' She remembered all that she had escaped from in the slums of Leeds, and though her heart went out to the members of her family still living there, she couldn't let that spoil the thought she hugged to herself. 'I am so fortunate,' she said to herself, 'so very fortunate.'

'What's wrong wi' thee tonight,' Enoch whispered fiercely. 'If tha can't hear when I click my fingers, I'll seek somebody else to serve my station.'

'It's the gloves you're wearing,' Gertrude said cheekily, in her eyes a sparkle to match any jewel around that elegant, opulent, table.

Among the women fighting to get into the small terrace house, none was more active nor fought with greater vehemence than Dodie Ottershaw. 'You stay out here,' she'd said to Mark, her husband, 'and don't start your dreaming. Be *ready* when I shout to you.'

'Nay, Dodie,' he'd protested, 'are you certain we want the sticks of an old woman who could have died of owt so far as we know?'

'I *want* them!' she'd said passionately. 'Do your share, and we'll have them.'

Mark had shrugged his shoulders in resignation. In the two months he'd been married to Dodie he'd learned she could show a strong will when she'd a mind, and would brook no disappointment once she'd set herself to a task. In part he blamed himself. When first they'd arrived in Leeds, Dodie had been grieving the death of her father and the sundering of her family ties. She'd moped about the small place they'd found, with no energy, no effort to do anything. He'd wandered the district looking for a job with no success and each time he'd returned to their mean house he'd found the evidence of tears on her cheeks. Her talk had been all of Barthwick and their life together. Finally Mark, mild though his nature might be, had lost his temper with her. 'The days of Barthwick are gone,' he said. 'Do you think I don't grieve for my own father as killed himself rather than come away. We mun put all that behind us, lass, if we're to make a new life for ourselves.'

He'd put his arm around her to soften his words and she'd clung to him, crying bitterly. 'Tha mun drag thyself out of it, lass. Tha mun be brave and forget thy father and the life we all had in Barthwick, else us'll sink wi' the rest of them!'

He knew it had taken a great effort of will on her part though he couldn't even begin to understand what a complex person she was and, he now realized, always had been. Sometimes she seemed soft and tender; at others she appeared to be hard and scheming.

Losing his temper had had the effect he'd desired, but he hadn't been prepared for the wild swing of character that had followed it. Dodie had looked up at him, seeing him ill-humoured for the first time and recognizing she'd been the cause of it.

'Tha's right,' she said, 'tha's right. It *is* dead, and over with. I've no cause to go on grieving, just as I've no cause to make you live in a place like this!' She'd set to and cleaned the little house top to bottom, going through the two rooms in a whirlwind of energy that seemed to set the walls vibrating.

It was a return to the old Dodie he'd known. He'd never forget finding his own father, the day after John Aysgill died, lying in the river with his throat cut, the knife still clutched in his hands. He knew why his father had done it; Barthwick was life to Fred Ottershaw and he was too weak a character to start elsewhere. Dodie had taken charge; she'd thrown away the knife and put about the story that Fred had been killed by footpads and robbed. She'd seen to the arrangements for Fred's funeral and had moved into the house to take care of things, while her brothers and her sister had started their long trek to Leeds, too independent to fight the bailiffs who'd occupied John Aysgill's home.

Yes, in those days, Dodie had shown great strength and determination. He had to admit, as he thought ruefully, that despite the way she'd taken *him* over, so far he'd had no regrets. He hadn't been prepared for such a quick marriage as Dodie had arranged when they knew they'd have to leave Barthwick.

'Why don't we travel together to Leeds and see what comes of it?' he'd said.

But she had pretended to be scandalized. 'Why, Mark Ottershaw, don't you love me enough, then, to make an honest woman of me? Do you want to start our lives in *sin*?'

She'd made it sound such a heinous crime that he'd had no alternative. 'Aye,' he'd stammered. 'Well, if tha wants to be wedded wi' me!'

'I want nothing more!' she'd said. He'd been surprised by the intensity of her voice, but quite dumbfounded when she'd marched him off to Betlaby that same day and waylaid the cleric on his way to evensong.

'We'd like to be married,' she'd said simply.

The cleric had immediately eyed her waistline. 'Right away?' he'd asked.

'You needn't look at me like that,' she'd said pertly. 'We want to be married right away but not for the reason you think.'

Although Dodie had always given her family cause to think she was confident of herself, that she was the strong one who could face anything, in truth she was the one least able to contemplate a life on her own in the insecure future she knew must follow when they left Barthwick. She was the one who'd bound the strands of the family together, but mostly to safeguard her own security. When the lads had quarrelled with each other, she had always been the one to mediate between them, to bring domestic peace and family harmony back again. Now that she saw a bleak future in Leeds, she wanted a man by her side, someone she could rely on to be her companion. She'd chosen Mark Ottershaw the night of the Harvest Fayre, when the first clouds of uncertainty had begun to gather over them all.

'Are you there?' he heard her voice calling and looked up at the first-floor windows of the little house.

'Aye, lass, I'm here,' he said.

He saw Dodie turn back and plunge into the room and then, through the aperture, a cloud of white linen began to descend. He caught it, gathered it in his arms.

'Take care of it,' she said.

163

Next he saw the wooden end of a bed, which came out, went back in, came out again, as a woman's voice screeched – 'it ain't thine, it were promised.'

'Promises are nowt,' Dodie's voice bellowed. 'It's hands, not promises.'

The bed end came out with a run and fell down. It was all Mark could do to stand up after it hit him on the shoulder, but he staggered with the carved wood piece and laid it on the pile of sheets. Next came the bedhead in two parts, and then the bed-rails, then the wooden straps.

When Dodie appeared out of the front door she was awry, flushed with triumph, carrying a large ewer and basin *and* a wooden stand with turned legs.

'You have it all safe?' she asked, eyeing the bed parts. 'Daft lad, you ought to have put the sheets on top of the bed, keep them from being soiled.'

'We shouldn't be doing this on the Sabbath,' he said.

'You can bless your fortune I sat up half the night outside the hospital and heard the news first,' she said, 'else there'd have been nowt left by chapel time.'

They'd heard the news of Mrs Cowgill's incarceration in the hospital with sorrow. Since they'd come to live in this street in Meanwood, Leeds, they'd often visited her. Now she was a poor lady, abandoned by her family, but once she must have been quite well-to-do, since she had a bed with a wooden foot and head and strappings just like a nobleman's bed. And she had linen sheets in which she slept, the first Dodie had ever touched. 'Aye, Mark, just think how grand it would be,' she'd said a time or two, 'to sleep between *sheets* of *linen*!'

'I've got nobody left,' Mrs Cowgill had often said to Dodie, who frequently sat with the old lady and even drank *tea* with her, listening spellbound to her stories of life with her husband who had worked in the office of the iron foundry. It had been by using the names Mrs Cowgill had given them, and pushing Mark forward, that Dodie had got him the job in the foundry when they weren't supposed to be taking on any new people. It was Mrs Cowgill who induced Dodie to say *thee*, *tha* and *thy*. 'Now Dodie,' she'd say, 'you don't want people to know where you come from the moment you open your mouth.'

'But the Squire, Lord Barthwick himself, wasn't above saying a thee, or a tha!' Dodie protested at first.

'Yes, well you can do anything if you're a Squire,' Mrs Cowgill had said.

For the two months Dodie had known her, the old lady had been going steadily down in health. The previous week she'd asked Dodie to fetch the doctor, and Dodie had learned she'd already paid him for his last services, knowing she was dying. After the doctor had examined her, he'd ordered her into the hospital, and Dodie had visited her there. By now Mrs Cowgill's condition had so deteriorated that she was not able to recognize her visitor, nor answer any of Dodie's questions.

'What's to be done with your furniture, Mrs Cowgill,' Dodie had asked. 'All your fine linens, your crockeries?'

Mrs Cowgill couldn't understand, couldn't respond, and Dodie had made up her own mind about what was to happen to them! She'd waited outside until she'd been told that Mrs Cowgill had died and was to be disposed of by the hospital according to her last wishes. That meant the surgeons would get her remains for their experiments, Dodie knew, but she had no sentimental interest in Mrs Cowgill, now that she was dead. She'd raced back to Mrs Cowgill's house, pausing only to collect Mark, who'd been lying abed after his week at the foundry, and had hoped to clear much from the house before others knew. But the minute they'd seen her going in, the neighbours had realized what had happened and had descended on the premises like a pack of wolves. Dodie had managed to extract one set of linens; her second foray had produced some crockery; her third the bed and bed linens, the ewer and jug and stand. She was amply satisfied as they made their way home beside the carter to whom she'd promised a coin when they arrived.

She squeezed Mark's elbow affectionately. 'Aye, Mark,

it won't take long,' she said, 'afore us'll be able to live wi' a bit of dignity.'

They weren't the first young couple to start their married life with nothing except what they could find. Mark had made them a bed of a couple of packing crates stuffed with flock from a mill and covered with paper broadsheets from the back of a printing shop.

Now they'd have a proper bed, and sleep between sheets.

The place they'd found had two rooms, one up and one down, with a yard at the back in which was a privy shared by all the people in the row, down which they poured water from the spring. The privy came out in an open drain, but at least it had a door to it and a body could take care of her necessities in private. Number 6 Grape Street, Hunslet had become home to Dodie Ottershaw. At first she'd been apprehensive about living in such close proximity with other people since the walls were only a brick thick and anything said louder than a whisper could be heard by the folks next door. But the house did have a slate roof and was dry, unlike the slum in which her brother Simon chose to live. Dodie had shuddered in horror when she'd seen Simon's home and quite understood why Gertrude had bolted. She'd have bolted herself if she hadn't had Mark to turn to. Her little place now meant everything to her and when she wasn't working in the Mill, she scoured the streets, going nearer and nearer the town, looking for things she could use, in back alleys, behind emporiums. Any scraps of cloth were put to service and she'd been able to find many in the Mill. Once or twice in the Mill she'd failed to repair a thread or to pull a warp and the piece had been spoiled before the overlooker saw it. That way she'd provided enough material when joined together by deft stitches to make a palliasse for their bed *and* a cover. Mark had turned out to be very good with his hands and she'd found many things for him to repair. Now they even had two chairs, and a table.

When they arrived home she paid the carter from their scant supply of coins and took the goods inside. The house, though small and mean, was thoroughly clean and even smelled fresh with the lavender she'd found behind an apothecary's shop. The room downstairs was four paces by three, with a staircase leading off in the corner to the upstairs room beneath the roof. There was a chimney breast at one side of the downstairs room, with a back wall shared with the house next door.

Usually, of a Sunday, Dodie and Mark took their creels with them and walked the three miles to the coal grading yard behind the blast furnace. Here, the coal was hand separated by the blast furnace workers into a quality that would make the new coke they were using in the furnace, with the unusable slag tossed down a steep bank they called the slag heap. If a person scrabbled about among the shale and stones of the slag heap, occasionally they could come across a piece of coal the size of a walnut or a maid's fist. Bit by bit Dodie and Mark, and many other people from the houses with a fireplace in which coal could be burned, would clamber over the heap, digging deep into the surface to find a forgotten nugget. Together, working all Sunday afternoon, Dodie and Mark could usually get enough coal to give them a fire each morning on which to cook their food. In the evening, they were mostly too tired from working at the foundry and the mill to bother cooking, and they'd eat the stew that was in the pot barely warm from having sat all day on the remains of the coals.

'What do you think, Mark?' she asked, as she showed him the bed nicely made up with the linen sheet folded over at the top the way she'd seen Mrs Cowgill do it.

He looked at her then looked at the bed with his eyes glinting. 'That's a sight I'm proud to see,' he said. 'Nobbut one thing wrong wi' it.'

'What's that?' Dodie asked anxiously.

'Tha's not in it, waiting for thy husband to come take his pleasure of a Sunday!'

She blushed prettily. She still hadn't accustomed herself to Mark's sexual hunger, to him wanting her every day of his life. She'd have thought the hardness of the work they both did would have tired him, but every night when they came to bed, no matter how exhausted they might both be, he wanted his pleasure. She'd found it very difficult at first because often she was so tired she'd be content just to lie there and let him have the use of her body. But she'd learned that she couldn't do that – he always became so excited towards the end of it that he'd lie there and pump everything into her insides.

'Nay,' she'd said, the first time he'd done that. 'We moan't take chances on having a babby. I don't want a babby, else I shan't be able to go to work and then what'll us do?'

The wages they paid him in the foundry were miserly, since there were many people wanting work. She managed to earn a little in the weaving shed of the mill but often there'd be no work while they were waiting for the spinners to catch up. It took six or seven spinners to keep her going with the Flying Shuttle – too bad they couldn't invent, or so it seemed, a machine to do the spinning that would keep up, since she spent so much time idle for which she received no money at all.

She'd quite determined there'd be no babby until such time as they had a home and a bit put by. That first time her womanlies were late in coming she'd spent a coin or two on Geneva spirit, and had bounced herself up and down. She'd drunk so much hot gin she'd made herself ill for a day or two, but then her womanlies had come and she'd known there'd be no babby. Ever since then she'd stayed alert, no matter how sleepy she might be, listening to his breathing getting more and more excited, waiting in fairness until the last moment before heaving him off. He always groaned, of course, but now he'd come to accept it and didn't object when she took the bit of cloth into the bed to catch his outpourings. When he grumbled, as he sometimes did, she'd always console him, play with his parts a while, and tell him that one day, one day afore she got too old, he could have the making of a babby inside her.

'Tha can take thy pleasure tonight,' she said, 'when we've been to't tip for coal . . .'

Mark always preferred her when she relaxed, and he knew the signs; she'd revert to the style of speech they'd known in Barthwick, she'd be more tender, not quite so thrusting and ambitious. Sometimes he felt overawed by her drive and energy, like a man who's mounted a placid mare only to find that between his knees she becomes a galloper. He remembered a filly Lord Barthwick had brought on, who'd never been properly curbed. Many times they'd seen her streaming over the countryside, even with the full weight of Lord Barthwick on her back, him holding the reins with his iron hand and belabouring her head with his whip as still she bolted at full gallop. When that one went, there was no stopping her until she'd jumped every obstacle in sight and had exhausted herself. Many times Dodie made him feel like that.

'Nay, Dodie,' he said, 'I missed my sleep this morn to fetch Mrs Cowgill's bits and bobs. A body's entitled to his rest.'

'I reckon you're right,' she said, unfastening the top of her bodice, 'though it's thee will be grousing when tha goes to work on a cold belly.'

'Nay, lass, thy belly is never cold,' he said, deliberately misunderstanding.

'Tha'll know well enough what I mean,' she said, 'when tha gets cold pobbies in *thy* belly of a morn.'

There was a terrible scream which no-one at first could locate. When it came again, they all looked across at the cog and rung gin, and saw Jamie Milner lying on the ground by the giant cog wheel next to the windlass.

'It's Jamie. He caught his arm,' someone shouted, but they were all rushing forward to see the lad. He was lying on the ground amidst the horse-droppings, still screaming though he had almost lost his senses from the pain.

Matthew dashed in. 'Grab the horse, somebody,' he yelled, since the animal, scared by the noise and the rushing of people, was continuing to race round the gin, causing the cog to continue turning within inches of Jamie's head.

The horse's head was grabbed. It reared, but stopped, trembling. Matthew bent under the stationary cog and lay Jamie back on the ground. Jamie screamed again but this time he lost consciousness. Matthew looked at the blood-soaked sleeve of Jamie's work-shirt from which the mangled ends of bone and flesh protruded.

'I reckon as he were laikin' wi't horse,' Bob Norris said. 'I've told him times to leave't beast alone.'

The horse was harnessed to the overhead rail and spent its life walking round and round the circle, the baulk of timber to which it was attached driving the twelve-foot-wide wooden cog, whose pins engaged in the rung of the shaft of the windlass to draw the buckets out of the shallow mine. The second rope, wound round the windlass in the opposite direction, was let down as the first was drawn up. Jamie had no doubt been interfering with the placid horse which had probably shied its head sideways to avoid his tormenting and knocked him over. In falling, Jamie must have flung out his arm which had been trapped between the cog and the rung, held tight while the cog rotated. The whole of Jamie's arm from above his elbow to below his shoulder had been smashed by the hard oak of the machine and now flopped useless in his shirt.

The mine owner, Jabez Broadley, had heard the commotion and came out of his office beyond the winding machine. 'Now then,' he called as he came through the group, 'why are ye all stopped from work?'

The Broadley Colliery on the southern edge of the sprawling industrial district of Hunslet had both open-cast seams and bell-pits which went down thirty or more feet. The men from the open-cast had downed tools when they'd heard the screams; Jabez waved his arms and shouted at them as he walked through them. 'Whatever's amiss,' he siad, 'it's no occasion to neglect your work.'

Matthew didn't know what to do for the lad lying on the

ground. Certainly he ought to do something for the lad was losing blood copiously from his wound.

Jabez forced his way through the miners. 'Aye, it's young Jamie Milner, is it?' he grunted. 'Many's the time I've had to warn him for playing with the horses. You've all heard me a time or two I wouldn't wonder?'

He glanced down at the boy. 'Two of you,' he said quickly, 'get a hold of him and bring him across by't side of my shed. Then we can get the horse moving again. Thee, Silas, grab his back, and thee, Matthew, grab his legs.'

'He ought to be put on something, Maister,' Matthew muttered.

'Put on something. Why? He's not long for this world wi' an injury like that. Believe me, I've seen it oft enough. Come on, then, pick him up and bring him over.' He looked round at the rest of the men. 'And you can all get back to work,' he said. 'It only takes two to carry a slip of a lad like that.'

Grumbling, the men went back to the open-cast trough they'd been cutting, that gradually went to a depth of six feet or more. Two caught in one of the bell pits the previous week when a slab of stone fell from a shoulder of the bell, seven a month ago when one of the bells collapsed entirely . . . And Jabez never altering his expression, never finding a word of sympathy when the relatives arrived to cart the bodies home.

'Has he any folks that you know of, Matthew?' Jabez asked.

'Only his mother,' Matthew said. 'His father was one of the Duke of York's men and they never knew what happened to him.' Matthew remembered the conversations he'd had with the lad as they'd walked to and from the mine. The lad and his mother lived in the next street to him; Jamie had been intrigued when he'd learned that Matthew had left the country only four months ago, and asked hundreds of questions about rural life. Mostly he was interested in horses.

'Aye,' he had said, 'it must be grand to cock thy leg over

171

a horse's back and set him going towards the distant horizon, wi' nowt between you and there save rolling fields and woods and streams. Aye, and not pulling a cart behind you, neither. Go on, Maister, tell us about it.'

The lad had mopped up all Matthew Aysgill's stories of life in the country even though invention had run dry and Matthew had had to draw on the few books he'd read.

'Tha can *read*,' Jamie had said incredulously when he'd seen Matthew's Bible one Sunday when he'd come round to Matthew's house. 'Can tha learn me to read?'

'I can that,' Matthew had promised. So each of the three previous Sundays Jamie had spent the afternoon at Matthew's being 'learned' to read – a labour of love that had given as much pleasure to the teacher as the pupil.

'I'll take him to the doctor,' Matthew said firmly.

'Tha'rt wasting thy time,' Jabez said. 'I've seen that many . . .'

'*I'll take him to the doctor*,' Matthew said firmly. 'You'll not deny me the right to do that, Maister.'

Jabez could see Matthew Aysgill was determined. 'Well,' he said, 'if tha's a mind to waste thy time trying to save somebody who's already past hope. . . Mind you, tha'll not be earning while tha's doing it.'

Matthew didn't reply but took the cart and wheeled it closer to the lad. 'Give me a helping hand, Silas,' he pleaded, seeing that Silas was already going back to work and leaving him to his own devices. 'Take his feet, but gentle, mind.'

Together they lifted the lad onto the flat bed of the cart. 'I can't spare thee a horse,' Jabez said. 'It's time yon had a change . . . And tha'd better bring the cart back quick . . .'

Matthew couldn't bring himself to speak as he set off between the shafts of the cart to take Jamie for medical help. His mind was working as he walked along hurriedly, tallying the coins left to him with what Jabez Broadley owed him. Had he enough to pay the doctor for his attention? Should he risk Jamie's life and pull him the extra two miles to the free hospital. With blood pouring

172

from him at its present rate he knew he didn't have the time; he'd have to go to the doctor and offer him a pledge. Fortunately the first two miles were all downhill and his major task was preventing the cart slipping rather than pushing it along. He watched Jamie all the time, but the lad never stirred. It looked as if the blood had stopped flowing quite so strongly; the thong Matthew had bound round his shoulder had perhaps helped the blood to clot in Jamie's shirt.

Matthew was in a storm of indecision. Should he stop and leave Jamie, running on himself to bring the doctor to Jamie's side? No, he couldn't do that. If he left, Jamie would be the prey of every animal, every body robber who passed by. He prayed as he raced through the streets that the doctor would be in his shop, would agree to see him, would accept a pledge for his services.

'Dear Lord,' Matthew prayed over and over again, 'help us in this our hour of need.'

In some strange way, since he'd come to the city Matthew had a feeling that God was closer to him than when he'd lived in the country. There had been precious little need for the intercession of God in the country with its slow paced and even rhythms. Here amidst the clash and clatter of too many people doing too many violent things in too small a place, the need for God seemed greater and He appeared closer. Certainly Matthew had found himself thinking more about God since he'd left Barthwick and come to the city. He hadn't wanted the family to break apart but the decision had been taken, and each had gone his or her own way. It had seemed somehow sinful to Matthew, against God's Will, that brothers and sisters should separate, should act independently. He'd had good fortune; he'd been awed by the size of the Parish Church and had entered it. Afraid to penetrate too far into its dark interior, he'd knelt on the floor at the back of the last open pew, seeing the magnificence of the stone work and the wooden decorations.

When, after a half an hour, he'd tried to stand up, he'd

found an ague in his knee which had caused him to stumble. A man passing behind him, wearing the black frock-coat, black breeches and white cravat of a clerical gentleman, had assisted him to his feet and had shown him into a pew. Something about Matthew must have caught his attention for he also sat down in the pew, clasping his Bible and Prayer Book, seeing the Bible Matthew held in his hands.

'Where do you belong?' he'd asked in a soft educated voice.

'Not from nowhere,' Matthew had stammered in his confusion. 'I mean, not from anywhere, your Reverence.'

Slowly the priest had drawn the story from Matthew of his father's death, their flight from Barthwick, their separation. 'Yes, 'tis sad when a family goes separate ways,' the priest had said. 'What are your intentions?'

'I seek work, and a place to live,' Matthew had said, 'since I have but few coins in my purse.'

'I may be able to help you,' the priest had said. 'I've been given a living in a village not far from the city. The family who have the living are rich merchants and can, I am sure, offer you some work if you are honest and not afraid of toil?'

Thus had Matthew met the agent for the Broadleys, and been given a job by one of their nephews, Jabez Broadley. The Broadley family had built speculative houses near the mines but none was vacant at that time; the Reverend John Shipton had called on another of his parishioners, who'd offered Matthew – a good God-fearing workman, the priest had called him – the rental of one of his houses.

Work in the mines was hard but as a countryman, Matthew was more used to toil than many of the others who came. He could dig with a smooth easy movement, could wield a hammer to crack the coal seams, could carry a hundredweight back to the carts which the younger lasses and lads pushed along to the graders. Most of the coal went for coke-burning for use in the furnaces and had to be picked free of shale and stones – Matthew developed a

174

skill at avoiding the larger stones in his picking, since he was paid by result and not by time. For digging and carting twenty hundredweight of coal he was paid a penny. In a good week he could sometimes earn as much as three shillings.

His only regret was that working in the open-cast mine all week left him too little energy on the Sunday to attend the church of which his benefactor had the living. He'd done it once, walking the ten miles to the Broadley village only to find himself nodding with fatigue during his benefactor's sermon. 'Aye, Lord,' he'd said in his prayer that night, 'the Spirit indeed is willing, but the flesh is almighty weak.' Now he went to Church twice each Sunday at the local parish church a mere mile from his home and spent much of the rest of the day sitting on his pallet, intending to read the Bible but more often than not falling asleep over its pages until Jamie had come with his hunger for knowledge, to waken Matthew with his interminable questions.

Matthew had had the further good fortune that the house he had found possessed a few sticks of furniture and was clean. His tastes were simple, almost ascetic, and he ate sparsely. In the few months he'd lived in the street he'd been surprised how many people came to his house to see him, to hear him talk, and read from his few books. Few of them could even write their names though some of them were sending their children to the local school that had been endowed by a Leeds-born magnate who'd gone on to make his fortune in the City of London as a wool merchant. The school was divided into two parts; one was a Grammar School in which several subjects were taught; the other part taught reading, writing and arithmetic only and was attended by several members of artisans' families who wished to learn how to calculate quantities for the work their fathers did.

He groaned when he remembered how he'd tried to persuade Jamie's mother to permit Jamie to go to the free school, but she was crippled with bone ague and they

175

needed the miserable pennies he earned from Broadley to live.

'If only tha'd gone to school,' he muttered into the cart, 'tha'd not be here now!'

He pushed the cart into the yard of the doctor's house, a grand three-storey building with glass in the windows, a porticoed door with steps leading to the front entrance, a yard with two coach houses and five stalls for the horses. The doctor's ostler saw Matthew enter with his burden. 'Tha mun bring him over here,' he said. 'The doctor would not care to have you litter the yard.'

Over here was a long low shed containing a table with a flat marbled top, tilted at an angle presumably so that the blood would run off it into a large stone trough at its foot; the ostler and Matthew lifted Jamie and laid him on the slab; Jamie didn't stir and the ostler whistled beneath his breath when he saw his condition.

'I reckon as you'd have done better to take him to the mortuary,' he said. 'I don't see signs of life left in him.'

When the doctor came out ten minutes later, still belching from the food he'd been eating, he crossed the yard in his black frock-coat, rolling back the braided cuffs and unbuttoning his white linen sleeves. He took one look at the patient.

'There's nothing I can do for *him*,' he said and started to turn away.

'*Try*, Doctor, won't you please *try*?' Matthew asked, his voice agonized.

The doctor looked at him. 'Is he your lad?' he asked.

'No, but a dear friend and companion. He's a good boy, doctor, who cares for his mother with great devotion.'

The doctor turned and looked at the lad. He reached over and placed his hand on Jamie's throat beneath his chin. 'Aye, well, there's life yet in him, but he's gone far into death. I don't know as he could be brought back.'

He looked at Matthew. 'I suppose you've no money for my fee?' he asked.

'I can pledge myself to work. I'll labour for your

worship. I'm accustomed to horses and could help your ostler in aught he may require. I'm not afeard of hard tasks.'

'And how would you live while these tasks are being performed?'

'The good Lord will provide,' Matthew said simply. 'I have but few needs . . .'

'Aye, you look undernourished, but strong.'

The doctor was impressed by the fanatic who faced him. He could sense Matthew would give him full measure of work. 'Th'art no Catholic?' he asked.

'God forbid I should come to Him in such a false way, your worship,' Matthew said fervently. 'I'm but a simple man who seeks to serve the Lord as best I may in my own parish, neither Catholic, Jacobite nor Quaker in their dire extremities.'

The doctor slapped his leg. 'Well said for a simple man,' he laughed. 'Come, let us delay no further. You're not afraid o' the sight of blood, I trust, for thee and me shall shortly be taking a bath in it if the lad's heart continues to beat.'

The doctor amputated Jamie's arm just below the shoulder, leaving as much as he could of the unbroken part as a stump which he cauterized with a hot iron that brought the vomit and bile to Matthew's throat. He struggled valiantly to hold both down since the doctor had need of his help. Jamie had recovered consciousness briefly, had moaned and struggled then screamed and fainted away again. When the stump had been cauterized and greased, the doctor wrapped it with clean cloths.

'You'll need to change the cloths as oft as you can,' he said, 'and to keep them clean to take away the risk of infection, you understand. If the gangrene gets in, the lad's gone, I'll be bound. He'll be fevered for a day or two but make no mind; if you have access to clean water, wash him down as regularly as you can. Aye, and the good Lord go wi' you. The lad will need His Grace in the days to come.'

Jamie seemed to be breathing more regularly, more

sturdily, and the doctor was satisfied with what they'd done. His jacket front gleamed with blood and the cuffs of his shirt were covered in its startling red.

'When shall I start my work?' Matthew asked, but the doctor shook his head.

'You've no call to work for me,' he said. 'You'll have work enough bringing the lad back to life. You're a good man, Matthew, a blessing and an inspiration to us all. Now, leave the lad be for a minute or two, go see my cook and ask her for the leavings. Aye, and get yourself a glass of spirit from the barrel. I reckon as you need it from the colour of your face.'

The doctor stalked away leaving Matthew speechless. God moves in His mysterious ways, he thought, and men of Love and Charity are to be found everywhere. He dropped to one knee despite the blood and bone sawings that lay beneath the bench, and bowed his head to the Almighty God in prayer.

Three days and three nights Matthew sat by Jamie's pallet and tended the lad who recovered consciousness a few hours after his operation but moaned with pain. The shock had so affected Jamie's mother that she took to her bed in a flood of tears. Matthew had, for the first time in his life, to use harsh words to get her to rise and cook a bowl of nourishing soup for the lad; he sent her hobbling out with a coin in her hand to buy stock bones and a bit of beef. When she returned her breath smelled of gin and the bones were a pitifully small pile in her basket; Matthew forced her to get water and set the bones to stew with the few scraps of beef, a couple of stringy onions and a carrot, a slice of turnip and a few potatoes.

In the afternoon of the second day Matthew noticed the offensive smell emanating from the bandages and tore the strips of cloth away. The green slime below told him the worst – the wound had become infected and had turned gangrenous.

'Aye, that's it, he's not long for this world now,' Jamie's

178

mother whined, but Matthew silenced her. 'Get thee to the apothecary,' he said, 'and fetch a handful of alum powder. Aye, and to the baker for bread.'

'What s'all I use for coin,' she asked tearfully. Matthew had none to give her.

'Tha mun beg,' he said. 'Tha mun promise to work for them. Tha mun borrow. Even, tha mun steal.'

'Nay and be transported to Ameriky.'

Matthew seized hold of her. 'Your son's life is in danger,' he said. 'Go out and get bread, get alum, and bring it back sharply unless you want to bend over the edge of a pauper's grave.'

She went out and returned a half hour later, again with the smell of gin on her. Well, at least, he thought, she'd been able to beg in the gin house. She brought enough alum to fill the palm of a babby's hand, and a crust of hard mildewed bread. 'It'll have to do,' he said, scraping the green off with his knife. He'd boiled a small pot of water over the fire and used drops of it to soften the bread and mix it into a stiff paste with the alum.

'What's that for . . .?' she asked querulously. 'That'll do him a mischief.'

'It cures horses,' Matthew said grimly. 'We shall have to pray to God it does the same for human beings.' He took the dressings that had been boiled in water to cleanse them and dried before the fire; he smeared the alum bread paste in them and slapped it on the stump of Jamie's arm, binding it firmly but not too tightly into position. Jamie was lying back on the bed seeming unconscious of what was being done for him though he twitched when the warm poultice was applied to the raw end of his wound. Matthew's cheeks were hollow with fatigue and worry; the only food in the house had been given to Jamie in sips, though he'd seen Jamie's slatternly mother stick her finger in the pot to take out the marrow bones which she'd sucked noisily and hungrily.

As soon as the lad settled back into his coma-like sleep, Matthew straightened the coverings of the pallet. 'I've a

179

mind to go outside for an hour,' he said. 'Keep an eye on the lad. It'll be a while afore the poultice starts to pull the poison out, but I'll be back afore then.'

He walked rapidly to the Parish Church through the warmth of the July day, easing his way through the busy crowds. As always he wondered where so many folks came from to be abroad in the middle of the afternoon – in the country you knew where every man would be at each different time of day. Certainly in mid-afternoon they'd all be in the fields labouring. Did these people, bustling along so busily, have no work to go to?

He slipped into the back of the Church, which was empty. The beams of sunlight came down through the patterns of coloured glass that had been inserted into the embrasures above the altar and the nave quite recently, designed, so he'd been told, by some foreign gentlemen the burghers had brought here. He sat in the pew at the back of the Church, too tired, too dispirited to kneel. He clasped his head in his hands. 'Dear Lord,' he prayed, 'I beseech thee to draw the poison from out of Jamie's arm, to heal him as only Thou can do. Forgive us all our sins, and for the brevity of my prayers, for I must quickly return.'

He walked rapidly back feeling eased by the visit to Church, sensing once again the close proximity of the Lord in this place though the tired pallid faces of those about him gave little suggestion of awareness. As he walked he thought about Jabez Broadley, the mine working, and the all too frequent injuries and deaths among the workers. Though he couldn't put his finger on the reason, he felt a sense of injustice. Of course, men must work to earn money to stay alive and hope to better themselves, and work was dangerous. The woodman's task was dangerous – how many had he known who'd lost a finger, even a hand. But then such naturally ordained events as childbirth were dangerous – how many women had died in the normal process of reproduction.

But there was something not normal about the coal

180

workings, and Jabez Broadley's attitude to the men who worked for him. Jabez had no respect for human life, Matthew decided, and that was ungodly and sinful. A man must love his neighbour and respect him, even if he were bereft of worldly wealth. Witness the way the doctor had respected Jamie's life and had worked to save it.

With these musings and half-formed opinions fresh in his mind, Matthew went inside the cottage where Jamie was lying. There was colour in his cheeks and the bandage was a sodden mess of blood and pus. Matthew took it off and saw the wound had drained of impurity; the clean flesh looked as wholesome as fresh raw beef.

'Tha's going to be all right, Jamie,' Matthew whispered, 'by the Lord's Grace, tha's going to be all right!' He smiled. 'Though tha wain't be playing the lute, I'll be bound!' he said as he took out his Bible and settled down to read.

Gertrude had taken the glasses below stairs for washing and was stacking the cut-crystal decanters neatly on the sideboard, ready for refilling by the Steward after an evening of cards to which her master, Captain Edgecombe, had invited three of his ship-building friends. They had all been smoking cigars and pipes and she'd opened the windows to clear the air. Strictly speaking the task could have been left until the morning when she rose early but she didn't enjoy coming into the room with its stale stink of wine and tobacco when she rose fresh from bed and had waited until her master's guests had departed before sneaking down to clear the room. She knew that if any other servant should see her, they'd chide her for over-conscientiousness.

Mrs Edgecombe had taken the family coach to London to spend the week-end with their son before despatching him to college; it was a matter of pride to Gertrude to be even more meticulous about her work during her mistress's infrequent absences from the house.

She had placed the decanters in a line, ready for the

Steward, when suddenly she was startled by a noise from the door of this first-floor drawing-room. She turned hurriedly and saw the Captain standing there, looking at her.

'I beg pardon, sir,' she said as she bobbed a curtsy. 'I thought you had retired for the night and wished to place the room in order before going to my bed. I pray you forgive me.' She knew Mrs Watts would be furious at the knowledge that a member of the staff had been caught by their employer – household tasks were to be completed out of sight and sound of the master and mistress who might be discommoded by the glimpse of mob-cap and the flurry of dust. 'Servants at work,' she'd so often said, 'should neither be seen nor heard.'

The Captain did not enter; he was swaying gently backwards and forwards, and from side to side, his thumb thrust into the pocket of his waistcoat, his fingers drumming on his ample stomach. 'Ah, 'tis thee, Gertrude? I heard the clink of glass as I was on my way to my bed, and wondered what rascal was at my sideboard!'

Gertrude was shocked. She blushed furiously, suddenly realizing how it must look to the Captain to find her at the sideboard with a decanter in her hand. Did he truly believe she'd been *stealing* his fine French cognac, his Spanish sherry, his West Indian rum . . .?

'Sir!' she exclaimed in a scandalized voice. 'I am but *clearing* the room, *nothing* more. I am not a *thief*, to steal down in the night and *rob* my benefactor!'

She spoke with such vehemence that he was obliged to chuckle. He walked across the room and placed his hand on her shoulder. She stiffened beneath his touch but forced herself not to flinch. 'They told me tha wert a spirited lass,' he said, still smiling. 'I'm not accusing thee of stealing owt.' His hand stayed on her shoulder and, as he looked into her eyes, more close to her than ever he'd placed himself before, she suddenly realized he'd taken a drop too much of the wines in the decanters and was using his hand on her shoulder to balance himself.

182

'Shall I fetch the Steward, Captain Edgecombe,' she asked quietly, 'to see you to your bed?'

His eyes opened wider and gleamed, as if he were seeing her for the first time. 'Nay, Gertrude,' he said, moistening his lips, 'tha can take me to bed, right enough. Yes, tha can take me to bed this neet!'

'Oh, sir,' she protested. 'That would hardly be proper.'

'Not *proper*, Gertrude, to do as thy master bids? To render him this small service?'

He managed to stand without the benefit of his hand on her shoulder, and turned himself clumsily about like a barque under full sail lumbering through the wind to the other quarter. 'Come along, Gertrude,' he said, 'I'll lead the way and tha mun follow in line.'

Her heart sank as he set out, step by step, to negotiate the passage between the drawing-room and his bed-chamber on the floor above.

'Shall I not fetch the Steward, Captain,' she urged as she followed him.

'The Steward, lass? What need have I for a steward's services. I'll swear tha can do all he could, aye, and more.' He chuckled in his drunkenness; the sound came horrible to her ears. He banged open the door of his bed-chamber, in which she had never previously set foot. His enormous bed seemed to stare accusingly at her; she caught a glimpse of her own reflection in a silvered glass on the wall and gasped in fright at it, thinking at first that another was in the room. He turned, directed his posterior carefully towards the edge of the bed and fell backwards so that he was lying sprawled upon the counterpane. He struggled upright so that he was sitting on the edge of the bed, and beckoned for her to come across the room. She did as he bid, trembling in fear and shame, sorely afraid that at any moment the door might open to reveal the accusing eyes of Mrs Edgecombe or, what would be even worse, Mrs Watts.

'The boots, lass,' he said gently. 'The boots come off first.'

She bent down, glad of some excuse to hide her blushing face, and pulled the soft leather boots from his feet and calves. Even in the extremity of her anxiety, she told herself she'd never felt such fine leather in her hands. When she lifted her head she was horrified to see the Captain was already unfastening the drawstring at the waist of his breeches.

'Let me bring the Steward to assist you, Captain,' she pleaded, her voice issuing thinly from her fear-dried throat.

'Nay, Gertrude,' he said. 'Tha mun take off thy clothes if we're to have the pleasure of each other. And sharp about it, for I've a lust in my loins that bids fair to burst me.'

'I'm a maid, Captain,' she wailed. 'I've never known a man.' The tears ran unbidden down her face as she stood there, looking across at him as he started to lower his breeches while he was struggling to his feet. He stopped at her words and looked across at her. She knew that now she'd be discharged in disgrace, that she'd lose her position and be thrown into the street, but she couldn't accede to his desires, she truly couldn't. Oh, if only she could be like Selina or, so tattle-tale told it, a couple of the other new girls. If only she could be obedient, and give the master his *right*.

'I'm a *good* girl, Captain,' she said, trying to muster what was left of her dignity. 'I'll serve you loyally in any way God permits. But, in all conscience, I cannot do as you bid, I just cannot!'

There, it was out. She had refused the master. She trembled, awed by her own temerity, her audacity. Very well, the die was cast. She'd pack her bag first thing in the morning. She bent down and took the boots, turning to place them in the rack where she'd noticed several other pairs. She heard the crash behind her and trembled, fearing his angry hands on her. If only he would take her by force at least she would be able to settle her conscience. She heard his deep and doubtless passionately enflamed

184

breathing. Oh, men, she thought. Why must they be such lustful creatures? Why must a man so gentle, so kind and understanding as Captain Edgecombe debase himself when his passions were stimulated by drinking? She turned swiftly to meet his onslaught, and saw him lying face down on the floor-covering.

He was fast asleep.

September 1741 turned into October and the streets glistened with rain that stood in puddles between the cobblestones. Folks without homes huddled in doorways until beaten away by broomsticks; a crowd of lads gathered outside the back of the baker's seeking the warmth of his oven, huddled together in hopelessness. The waggons rolled along the streets with horses slipping in the mud and urchins ever ready to assist in freeing a stuck wheel in the hopes of a coin that never came. Men wearing sackcloth triangles on their heads to keep out the rain pushed carts of fish, meat, muffins, loaves, ever ready to catch a sly hand trying to snatch beneath the covering. Each carter carried a whip in one hand, and lashes were frequent. Day had but recently come and the air was night-cold and damp. A mist of factory smoke rolled along the streets at the level of the house-tops, occasionally wafting its sulphurous vapour down to scour the lungs of the passers-by. The horses of the Flyer urinated in the yard, champing in the harness, ready for their run to Doncaster after a night cooped up in the stables. The ostler wore three capes of felted wool, one upon the other, and still felt the damp chill.

The coachman, as a man of consequence, was in the dining-room eating a leg of chicken hot from the stove, a tankard of wine beside him. The pot-boy appeared brandishing a red-hot poker. He sprinkled expensive imported pepper into the pot and stirred it vigorously with the poker. It foamed and the smell seeped across the yard, rich and pungent. The coachman raised it to his lips; his gorge gulped and gulped again before he set the drained

185

pot back on the table with a crash that indicated the coach was ready to leave. The agent scurried about, hastening the last of the eight passengers on board, before helping the coachman into his enormous caped coat and offering him his elegant green and black top-hat. The coach departed in a rush and flurry that spattered mud against the knot of bystanders watching from the gate of the inn; one of them exclaimed harshly before he hastened away up the street without regard for the weather despite being clad in a meagre jacket over breeches and leggings, though he did have the benefit of calf-high boots tied with thongs at the top. He plunged into the early morning traffic heading into the city's centre, walking briskly through the throng despite the mud that lay everywhere on the cobbled streets. He turned west after the Bridge Gate, and made his way towards the Corn Exchange, turned off into a mean alley just after the Exchange and entered a tall building, climbing the stairs rapidly to the second floor.

When he entered the door, the clerks all standing at their tall desks looked up at him. Mr Percy rapped his desk with his ruler and they all looked down again and resumed work on the ledgers. Mr Percy came from behind his low desk where he had been sitting comfortably on his chair and eyed Peter Aysgill askance.

'I'm to see Mister Shepley at once,' Peter said with the self important air of someone who bears tidings.

'I cannot permit you to see Mister Shepley looking like that,' Mr Percy said in his waspish, unmanly voice. 'Man, you look and smell like a dung-heap, not that it has ever been my misfortune to smell such a thing.'

Mister Shepley's voice boomed behind him. 'Permit Maister Aysgill to enter at once,' he said. 'Don't impede him on a matter of dress, Mr Percy.'

Peter Aysgill bounded forward like a whippet released from its handler.

'Shut the door behind thee,' Mister Shepley commanded, 'and tha'd better stand away for, in truth, tha does smell o' the yard!'

Shepley was a self-made man and now his enterprises were many and greatly varied in their interests. He'd started out as a buyer of wool from the cottage industry around Leeds, then had realized there was money to be made exporting it. This had led to him speculating in shares in the vessels that carried the goods to distant places. Now he was a wealthy man, with his finger on the throbbing pulse of everything. 'Come, man, speak out. What did tha uncover?'

Peter hesitated. All along the route from the inn yard he'd been thinking of a way in which he could put his newly acquired knowledge to greater advantage, and now he knew he had the answer, if only he had the courage to carry out his daring scheme.

'Come along, man, what did you see? What can you report? Or wert as blind as now tha'rt dumbfounded?'

'I saw Mister Frederick board the coach,' Peter Aysgill said.

'Good. Good. And . . .?'

'Another boarded the coach, closely muffled against the rain.'

'But tha wert able to catch a glimpse of his features, eh? Tha saw who it were, eh? Come on, tha's e'en like a fox! That's why I reward thee so greatly.'

'Aye, Maister, I saw his features. I had the great misfortune to stumble against him as he crossed the yard.'

'Well done, man, well done. Tha'll get a sovereign for this morn's work. Who was it?' Shepley's thick lips were moist and trembling with anticipation. His bright eyes glittered at the thought of the profit to come, if only he'd wagered right.

'It was Peabody all right!'

'No mistake, man?'

'No mistake. It was Steven Peabody.'

Shepley's mutton chop hand came crashing down on the table. 'I knew it,' he roared with pleasure and self-satisfaction. 'I knew yon pair were conspiring. But I'll have the advantage of 'em yet, mark my words.' He reached into the pocket of his fine coat and drew out a coin which he put on the table before him. 'You've served me right well, Peter Aysgill,' he said approvingly. 'You've kept your eyes and your ears open and served me right well in the six months since I took you in as a country bumpkin, to run my errands.'

Now was the moment for daring. Peter had never been as afeared of any man as he was of Shepley at this moment. Shepley had been his benefactor but only because Peter had proved himself of great use. No-one took note of the country bumpkin, as Shepley called him, standing at the edge of a group of merchants discussing future prospects for alliance and profit on the steps of the Corn Exchange, making business deals. By informing Shepley of what he heard, Peter Aysgill had put him in the way of several profitable business ventures recently. Shepley had been generous and Peter had already amassed a purse of coins he was guarding zealously against the future. He had been living in a room at the back of the offices, eating his meals in taverns and ale-houses, ever alert for the whiffs of gossip that, added together, made for commercial intelligence.

Peabody and Frederick were going to London together. They were rivals in business and doubtless had now formed an unholy alliance. That could be for only one reason. They intended to try to make a joint bid for Carpenter's Mill now that old Ezekiel Carpenter had died. His son lived the high life in London; he had no interest in the mill and would be happy to sell it for a reasonable price, which Peabody and Frederick *together* could offer him.

Shepley was scrawling figures on a board with chalk, seeming to have forgotten Peter Aysgill's presence. 'Send Walt Goodman in here,' he shouted.

Goodman appeared almost immediately, a lean stringy man nearing thirty years of age, wearing a light coloured jacket that didn't quite reach his knees, a pale green waistcoat, a red scarf tied into the throat of his oatmeal coloured shirt, breeches and calf-length boots in scuffed leather. He had a wide-brimmed hat in his hand, stove-pipe shaped but of a soft and floppy material. His face was burned brown and his eyes had the sharp look of an independent man.

'Tha'll hie thee to London,' Shepley growled, 'and sharp about it. Tha mun beat this morn's Flyer.' Goodman said nothing but bent his head in acquiescence. He was used to being sent to distant places, always in a hurry, always with a letter of instructions. It was said that no man could push a horse farther nor faster than he. 'Mister Percy,' Shepley shouted. 'Now you can complete the offer to Carpenter at ten thousand pounds, and enclose the draft on the Leadenhall Street Bank.'

When Goodman had been despatched, he sat back in his chair and chuckled. Without doubt Goodman would secure the mill at that price since Carpenter was fond of the London gaming. When Frederick and Peabody arrived they'd discover they'd been forestalled and would need to return and do business with Shepley. They needs must have the mill if they were to hope to expand. They'd pay his price, eventually, for the Carpenter property. He'd take them up, and up, finally let them close at twenty thousand, giving himself a neat quick painless profit of ten thousand pounds, with nowt on the other side of the ledger but Goodman's ride to London, and a coin for Peter Aysgill. He heard a cough, looked up and round, and saw Aysgill was still standing there. . . 'Dammit, Aysgill, I thought tha'd left . . . Truly, tha has the ability to vanish into the background when tha's a mind.'

'I reckon, Mister Shepley, as you'll make upwards of twelve thousand pounds on that Mill,' Aysgill said.

'I'll close it with a profit of ten, but what's that to thee?'

'Nothing, Mister Shepley. I wanted only to show I could have a value to you, and that my information could put you in the way of profit. As I recall, it was my word that revealed the Frederick/Peabody alliance . . .'

'That it was, Maister, and here's another coin for thee in token,' Shepley said, his eyes narrowing. He'd been too long in business, had fought too hard to make himself, not to recognize the pinch when it came.

Peter Aysgill let both coins lie on the table. 'I have another piece of intelligence,' he said nervously. Now came the moment of endeavour – would he have the courage to carry it through against such a strong man as Shepley?

'By God, tha'rt a treasure,' Shepley said, reaching into his pocket again. 'If this goes on, tha'll soon be a wealthy man.' He threw another coin near the other two. 'How many men of thy acquaintance can boast an earning such as that, in one morn?'

'I was hoping to come to an arrangement, Mister Shepley,' Peter said.

'An *arrangement*?' Shepley roared. 'Has tha no faith in my good intentions towards thee, then? Didn't I take thee in as a runner, feed thee, house thee, even buy thee clothes to put on thy back? And now we're talking of arrangements? Come on now, lad. What's this new intelligence tha'rt concealing from me as has treated thee always like one of his own kin? Don't tell me tha's another who's turning from me with ingratitude.'

'My intelligence has always been reliable, Mister Shepley,' Peter said, clinging desperately to his courage in the face of Shepley's bombast, his wheedling, his emotional appeals. 'I'd like to come to an arrangement.'

Shepley had risen in his seat. Now he collapsed back into it like a defeated man. 'I never thought the sun would rise on such a day,' he said, 'that I should be held to ransom by an ingrate I'd considered a friend. I'll hear the terms of your arrangement, though wi' sorrow in my heart.'

'I would like to be paid a percentage of the estimated profit resulting from any intelligence I might bring.' There, Peter had said it.

Shepley rose in his chair, his eyes bulging. 'Thief,' he shouted. 'Ingrate! You'll leave this office at once. You'll pack your bags and get out, hear me! If ever I see hide or hair of thee, I'll set the dogs on thee.'

Peter was more prepared to face this violence than the former pleading. He'd heard this violence used too often against others to take it seriously.

'Mr Shepley,' he said, 'you have no dogs. You won't turn me away. You're too intelligent a man not to realize that if I have information to sell I'll not lack for buyers prepared to consider an arrangement. Nor do I need to remind you that fifty per cent of something is much better than a hundred per cent of nothing.'

'Art trying to teach me arithmetic, then?' Shepley said, realizing he'd been bested, but admiring Peter Aysgill for having had the courage to stand against him.

'No, Mister Shepley. I'm trying to better myself, as I believe is every man's privilege and duty.'

'And how does tha hope to do that?'

'By supplying information to you and then taking half the profit resulting from my information.'

'Half, lad? Isn't that being greedy?'

'It's being fair, Mister Shepley.'

Shepley sat back in his chair looking at Peter Aysgill, marvelling at what he saw. Six months ago he'd found Aysgill on the pavement when he'd arrived at the office. Aysgill had known his name, known his business interests, and had even known his movements of the previous evening. All Aysgill had wanted, in those days, was a job. Well, he'd given him one as a runner, nothing more, carrying messages and documents. Aysgill had rapidly demonstrated he was a genius at making himself inconspicuous, at being in the right place at the right time, hearing and seeing things that Shepley, when he learned of them, could turn to his own advantage.

He had to admit that he'd made a lot of money from Aysgill's information during the past six months, but the thought of any fifty per cent share was anathema to him, bitter as wormwood.

'We use my capital,' Shepley said. 'I ought to have a consideration for that. Say, sixty/forty . . .?'

Peter almost sighed with relief. Now he had Shepley on

191

the hook. 'Mister Crosby is said to be looking for a runner,' he said.

'Nay, tha'll never desert me to work for Crosby . . .?'

'I seek only to better myself, Mister Shepley,' Peter said piously. 'If I can do so with advantage to another . . .'

'Mister Percy,' Shepley roared, 'come in here!'

Percy, the office manager, came rushing in. '*Mister* Aysgill and me are entering into an arrangement,' Shepley said. 'For any information *Mister* Aysgill may give me resulting in me taking a profit, *Mister* Aysgill is to receive fifty per cent of such profit, after the consideration of expenditures and so forth . . . you know the style and the wording. In consideration of this arrangement, *Mister* Aysgill is to agree to be bonded to me for five years . . .'

Peter was coughing. 'I had in mind other conditions, Mister Shepley,' he said.

Percy glared at him. 'You speak when you're spoken to,' he hissed.

'Nay, if I don't speak now you'll nobbut have it all to scribe again,' Peter said, smiling now that he had won his confidence. 'I'm not much of a one for the correct form of words, but I'm certain Mr Percy will repair my deficiencies. I had it in mind that our arrangement would provide for fifty per cent of the estimated profit to be paid to me in advance. I certainly had not thought to give you the burden of a bondsman . . . Perhaps I had better withdraw and seek employment where best I might find it . . .'

'Tha has me on the rack,' Shepley said sorrowfully. 'I'd be obliged if tha would draw me no further . . . Do as *Mister* Aysgill says, Mister Percy, right away.'

During the months that followed the *arrangement* worked to their mutual advantage. Shepley never ceased to grumble every time he despatched Peter Aysgill to the bank with a draft, which Peter promptly put to his own account. Despite the large sums of money standing to his credit, Peter continued in the same life style, still wandering about in his shabby clothing, eating in taverns and ale-houses, sleeping in the one room at the back of the office like a dog in a kennel, hanging about the Corn Exchange, the new-founded Coffee House, the Woollen Exchange, so inconspicuously that few ever knew he was there. One Sunday he saw Matthew in the street but quickly crossed to the other side before his brother noticed him. He saw Simon, who was drunk on ale at the time and easy to avoid. Only Dodie ever saw her younger brother but he pretended not to hear her cries and lost himself in the crowds thronging a side street before she could catch up with him. Peter had found himself; the Barthwick days were but a bad memory to him. He had no desire to be reminded of *that* humiliation! Now he was independent of everything to do with the Barthwick life, the drudgery of farming in all weathers for doubtful crops, the self-negation of touching the forelock to the Lord of the Manor.

One day, he told himself, he would be in a position to humble even the mightiest.

His ambition lay along the parallel paths of wealth and power; he wanted both as desperately as a thirsty man seeks a drink, a starving man a crust of bread. And he didn't need his indigent family hanging around his neck along the way. Now, when he eavesdropped on the merchants, he listened not only to commercial news but also to political and social gossip. He knew very well that his path would be considerably eased by the knowledge he was gaining, and expanded the scope of his activities to include the places where the gentlemen and ladies of Leeds sought their pleasures. Now he made his first investment, as he thought of it, in fine clothing. He bought a braided brown coat and white waistcoat from a man who'd had it from his master. With white hose and buckled shoes, scarlet breeches and fine white lawn tied elegantly at his throat, he was inconspicuous among the young bucks who sported themselves in the town, especially when worn with his short wig and tricorn hat braided with gold and silver.

Now as he went his nocturnal way, he began to feel the first stirrings of a secret strength. He already possessed a sufficient small fortune to enable him fully to share the life of these dandies, yet he saved his money, hoarding it as his future fuel, spending but little as he walked through their meeting rooms but observing, listening, noting everything with his keen eyes and ears. The more he learned of their life-style, the more he despised, but yet envied, them. He could barely thole to watch a dandy throw away a fortune at cards or at the tables in the Assembly Rooms – yet the mathematical side of the play interested him very much and soon he had another fascinating study with which to amuse himself. Soon he was able to calculate the odds and knew with certainty whether to advance at the game or consolidate, whether to strike a blot or leave one, whether to put an opponent on the back or contrive to have himself placed there as a delaying move. Though he had much confidence in his abilities, he never actually played but stood anonymously in the crowd watching and learning, careful neither to laugh nor groan when the dandy throwing the dice proved himself to be inept.

And always listening, always noting, always observing the conduct of gentlemen, listening to their speech, imitating their pronunciation in the sanctity of his room at Shepley's office. He had his first chance to practise his new manner one night coming out of the Assembly Rooms when the doorman called a chair for him, for it would never do to be seen leaving on foot. As he was waiting for the chair to be readied, his brother Simon, again the worse for drink, came lurching along the pavement towards him. 'Ain't tha my brother, Peter,' he said, attempting to clasp Peter's arm.

'What will you with me, my good man,' Peter said, drawing to the full on the hauteur he had so long practised, copying the bloods inside.

Simon looked perplexed, and the two footmen standing duty at the Rooms hustled him across the pavement.

'Insulting a gentleman like that,' one of them growled.

'Tha can count thy good fortune he hasn't had thee whipped.'

Simon turned his head despairingly, but Peter ignored him and stepped into the chair. 'My office,' he said. 'Make for Boar Lane . . .'

One footman turned to the other. 'Yon's a hard working gentleman,' he observed. 'Always goes back to his office when he leaves here. Some o' them inside, carousing day and neet, could learn from him . . .'

'What's his name?' the other footman asked.

'I don't rightly know. Never heard him give no name.'

'Never saw him give a coin, either,' the second one sniffed.

Shepley's affairs were going badly, Peter knew. Almost as if to slight Peter, or from resentment of their *arrangement*, Shepley was speculating more and more in ventures that had nothing to do with Peter's information. Often he went in deeply without a correct source of information and lost heavily. Peter realized that it was only the fifty per cent share that Shepley received from Peter's intelligence that kept his head above water.

One night Peter was sitting in an alcove of the Assembly Rooms, watching the passing parade of fashionable people in their evening finery, when he picked up the sound of voices from the next alcove. These alcove corners were Peter's favoured listening posts since many of the men who lounged in them were suffering the effects of excessive drinking and fatigue, seeking the opportunity to doze. He'd seen Marquand and Sir Ian Clether come past and had shut his eyes as if dozing. They'd taken seats close together in the next alcove without realizing their voices could be overheard.

'All's in readiness?' Sir Ian asked.

Peter knew Sir Ian was vastly in debt, that his family seat near Wakefield was pledged, that unless he could quickly acquire funds he would be disgraced and ruined.

'Aye, all's in readiness,' Marquand said. 'We can start as soon as you've a mind.'

Peter's dossier on Marquand was indeed a full one and included much knavery and commercial trickery. His ears pricked when he heard the next sentence.

'I'll try Shepley as you suggest,' Sir Ian said. 'He appears free with his investment money these days.'

'Aye, I think he'll be worth a sizeable sum. Say thirty thousand or thereabouts!'

Peter could have told them Shepley was no longer worth anything like thirty thousand pounds if all his pledges were reckoned.

Other names were mentioned and either suggested or discarded. Peter knew each one and concurred with the choice – all were men who liked a speculation. It seemed as if the two conspirators might have a good investment and Peter wondered how, if possible, he might get into it. Such investments rarely paid less than a hundred per cent on the investment capital, and the chance to double his money in one dramatic coup greatly appealed to him. His blood ran cold, however, when they continued:

'You're certain you have the skippers in your pocket?' Sir Ian asked nervously. 'You can guarantee they'll send back a report the ships have foundered?'

'As certain as if I were sailing them myself,' Marquand promised.

'And no man will suffer?'

'Only the fools who invest their money,' Marquand chuckled. 'I reckon this endeavour will bring a fortune to both of us and I shall be able to tear up your notes. You'll have Clether Hall free of encumbrance at last!'

Peter listened aghast as the scheme slowly unfolded itself through the men's words. He had to admit it had the merit of brilliance. A number of wealthy men were to be invited to take shares in a valuable cargo to be sent overseas in a fleet of newly-built vessels. They could also take shares, should they so wish, in the vessels themselves, believing the cargoes were being exported to the Continent of Europe.

But the goods would not be put on board! The vessels would sail in ballast, each with a crew on board. When they were but a few miles off shore, the crews would be put into boats and would return to port with a story of a terrible storm at sea in which all the vessels had foundered. Meanwhile, the goods would have been sent by a different route, for sale to the benefit of Marquand and Sir Ian. The vessels, too, would be sailed down the coast of France in convoy, and in Cadiz sold to Spanish customers anxious to buy ready-built vessels. Thus Marquand and Sir Ian would have the benefit not only of the value of the cargo, but of the vessels themselves.

Peter's head buzzed. He could see no reason the scheme should not succeed. Of course, Shepley would go down with it since he'd have to borrow heavily if he agreed to take shares from Sir Ian, a man of impeccable reputation. It developed that men from the City of London were also to be invited to take part in the speculation so that the effects of it could be spread wider, the better to avoid suspicion. How could he profit by this knowledge, Peter asked himself. He knew he could not approach the pair of scoundrels – it would be a simple matter for Marquand to engage a couple of footpads to murder him. He could, of course, inform Shepley, who'd go to a Magistrate, or send Walt Goodman post-haste to Bow Street to lay information before Colonel Sir Thomas de Veil. But, if Peter disclosed his knowledge, the reward he would gain for information would be a pittance. Surely he could put this knowledge to some better use to his own financial gain.

He lay awake at night on his pallet without arriving at any successful conclusion. He had been sitting in the outer office, where these days he was a privileged visitor, when Sir Ian Clether had been announced and had been closeted with Shepley for the better part of an hour. The two men had left the office together and a clandestine examination of the ledger a couple of nights later had revealed that Shepley had taken the shares Sir Ian had offered him, pledging his property to the extent of thirty thousand pounds to do so.

Still Peter Aysgill couldn't think of a way to advantage himself. If he informed Shepley, he would straightway withdraw since Peter saw a clause had been inserted permitting him to do so and holding the funds in a closed account until the sailing of the vessels had been confirmed with bills of lading for the goods.

He lay awake many nights, with the day of the supposed departure coming ever closer before, finally, the solution to the problem came to him. One afternoon he went to see Shepley in his office.

'Aye, Maister Aysgill, what's happened to the flood of information you used to bring in – your mind appears to be elsewhere these days, to the advantage of neither of us.'

Shepley was sorely troubled, that much was evident. Peter knew he had made a couple of bad investments recently and was pressed for cash. He'd even heard that the bank were pressing Shepley for the repayment of a trifling loan not secured by the shipment of woollens. 'I've been thinking of my money, Mister Shepley,' Peter said with pretended humility, 'and need to seek your advice as to how I might put it to advantageous use. I had a thought that perhaps I could deposit it with you, and you could use it in one of your investments. Thus, by using my money, we could become partners in a sense.'

Shepley composed his features, trying to hide the relief he felt. 'Aye, lad,' he said, 'you've come to the right man. Your money, and my business abilities . . .'

Peter had brought a draught on the bank, which he laid on the table before Shepley. He coughed in embarrassment. 'Of course, Mr Shepley, you'll understand that I would want the money to be secured. All men are mortal in these hard times, and I have but little money to lose.'

'I'll not die on thee,' Shepley said with a laugh, his hands itching to clasp the draft. 'Two thousand pounds, eh? You've amassed a tidy sum in our little transactions.'

'Aye, Mr Shepley, and I owe it all to you.'

198

'Nay, lad, tha's given me good service – I'd be the last to deny it. Tha'd better see Percy and get him to draw up a paper. Fetch it in here for me to sign then tha can have it notarized.'

When Shepley read the paper he was so anxious to lay hands on the cash, so befuddled by worry and his recent heavy drinking that he failed to read it correctly.

Peter knew that much depended on this agreement. 'You'll notice, Mr Shepley, that I've put the money on one-week call?'

'Aye, lad, though that's a short term.'

'Well, if you'd rather not have the money, Mr Shepley?'

Shepley was desperate. 'Nay, lad, one week's enough . . .' It would be, too, when the vessels sailed with their bills of lading, when he received his advance on the price for the sale of the goods.

'And you'll see that, to secure myself, solely in the event of your untimely death which I pray to God will never happen . . .'

'Amen to that, lad . . .'

'I've put in a clause which gives me control of the business, so that I may realize my assets again . . .'

'The whole business?'

'It would be hard to partition it, Mr Shepley. Anyway, it's only a formality.'

'Aye, I suppose it is.' Shepley dashed off his signature, calling on Percy to witness it; Peter Aysgill's signature was witnessed by one of the clerks; and the notary, who'd been waiting in the outer office, came in, notarized the document and witnessed both signatures. Now 'the agreement had the force of law, and the notary took it with him to make a legal copy of it and to deposit it in the archive.

Peter Aysgill was on tenterhooks for the next weeks. The two thousand pounds represented two-thirds of his small fortune and he knew he could not afford to lose it. Time and again he watched as Shepley made what he considered foolish investments with the money and, by the day the vessels sailed, he knew there would be none left in the bank.

Now was the time to start the second part of his plan and where better than in the Assembly Rooms where it had all begun. He prowled the Rooms waiting until Sir Walter Mounsey, the Head of the Bank Committee, was relaxing in one of the alcoves; then he seated himself in the next alcove, deliberately within earshot. Lord Grant was sitting in the alcove Peter Aysgill had chosen, his head nodding in sleep.

'I quite agree with you, my Lord,' Peter said, directing his voice away from his Lordship towards the adjoining alcove. 'Shepley came to me for a loan but I refused him. The man's insolvent enough as it is . . .'

'Wassatyersay . . .?' His Lordship opened one eye but immediately closed it again since it was inconceivable the fellow next to him on the bench, whom he didn't know, could be addressing him.

'Any man who'd loan money to Shepley nowadays would be a fool, in my opinion, and courting disaster. I know for a certain fact that the Notary Greaves has an agreement pledging Shepley's entire business . . .'

He rose quickly and left the Assembly Rooms before Sir Walter Mounsey could get a glimpse of his face.

News of the sinking of the vessels came from Hull, where the lifeboats landed the crews. The conspirators had chosen the time well since the previous night there had indeed been a fierce storm off the coast of England, and two colliers had foundered on Beachy Point. No one suspected a plot, and the whole dreadful affair was written off as yet another Act of God.

Shepley was ruined.

The bank had verified from the notary, with whom the bank did much business, that an agreement *was* in existence pledging Shepley's business for a trifling two thousand pounds – they refused to loan him any further money and called in the outstanding sums.

Peter went apologetically to Mr Shepley. 'I'm obliged to

call in my two thousand,' he said, 'or to invoke the terms of our agreement.'

Shepley looked at him. 'I know it in my bones, Maister Aysgill, that somehow tha has accomplished my downfall. I curse thee, Maister Aysgill, and pray to God tha'll never prosper.'

Shepley went to his home in Harehills. He sat in his study, apparently, for an hour before his manservant heard the blast of a weapon. He dashed in but already he was too late and the gaping hole in his master's chest, and the spreading of blood, signified the end of his life.

The next day Peter Aysgill moved into Shepley's office, and sent for Shepley's tailor to call upon him, bringing swatches of cloth.

Book Three

'How strange life can be!', Matthew Aysgill mused. Who would have thought that the Milner tree could have had two such dissimilar branches as Jamie's mother and her sister, Mildred. He watched her now as she sat beside her nephew, holding the book open between them, reading its contents with him. She must have felt his regard; she looked up and smiled across the room at him, a rich warm smile that offered a delicious intimacy. Though his bones ached from working at Broadley's, he managed a smile in return before she bent back over the book, commanding Jamie's attention. In the months since his accident, the lad had made steady improvement; Matthew had sewn a leather cap and strap which covered the stump of his arm; more importantly, however, the lad's mind had improved along with his arm and the nightmares and resulting truculence had disappeared. It had been very difficult to talk to Jamie in the first months while the wound was healing since he seemed to withdraw into himself. Matthew had tried to interest the lad in reading but had not been able to devote the time to him, since he'd had to work long hours to recover the money he'd lost by his absence from work. Broadley had taken his revenge for what he regarded as Matthew's insolence by offering employment only in the new mine which they were opening by the pillar-and-stall method. This meant back-breaking work chipping out the seam to leave a pillar which supported the roof, taking the coal only from the stall. It was by no means as easy, or as productive, as digging the open-cast seam – a man had to work twice as hard in dusty and dangerous underground conditions, to earn the same coins.

When Mildred came to the end of the chapter of Defoe's book, she closed it, and told Jamie it was time for him to go to bed. The lad was looking well; Mildred was a better provider than his own mother, who had gone into a total decline since the lad's accident, depending more and more on Matthew's generosity. Now the lad spent much of his time in Matthew's house and Mildred often accompanied him, book in hand, to eat by Matthew's fire of an evening when Matthew returned from work. More and more, Matthew had come to enjoy returning home to find Mildred there with Jamie, his place newly cleaned, his pot of stew or soup bubbling over the embers. Often these days, when they ate so late since Matthew returned late from work, Jamie would climb onto Matthew's bed around which Mildred had modestly hung curtains, to conceal it from the many folks who came on Sundays to hear Matthew talk, or read to them from the Bible. Many times the small house would be thronged with people. During the summer months Matthew had sat on the step and the folks had gathered around him in the street, often as many as thirty. Now the winter was upon them and people came inside; the miracle was that most would bring a small offering of meat, a couple of marrow bones, a turnip, a scrap of cloth filched from a mill as spoiled, a piece of hide with which to mend Matthew's boots. Truly, the Lord will provide, Mildred thought, as she helped Jamie onto the pallet and drew the curtains.

She and Matthew sat by the embers of the fire and, as usual, were at a loss for words knowing Jamie could overhear them. Matthew used his time unabashedly to gaze at Mildred, to admire her handsomeness, while she, though aware of his eyes upon her, modestly gazed into the fire.

'You are a good woman, Mildred,' Matthew finally said.

'By God's Grace I try to better myself each day,' she said. 'But the way is hard and long.'

'I have a dream which comes to me often,' Matthew

said. 'I have a dream that one day all men will be equal in the world, as I believe them to be in the sight of God.'

She looked up when he said that and the look in her eyes was challenging. 'They hang men for that sort of talk, Matthew Aysgill,' she said. 'Try to tell your Jabez Broadley that all men are equal in the world.'

'One day he will know it,' Matthew said with the confidence of a believer. 'But may I tell you the rest of my dream?'

'Pray do,' she said.

'I dream that when men become equal in the world, it will be possible to travel among them without let or hindrance, carrying the message of Brotherhood in the word of God.'

'You see yourself doing that, Matthew Aysgill?'

'Aye, I do. And let me tell you what is more. I see you, Mildred, travelling by my side, as my wife and my helpmate!'

She coloured and looked up at him again, though shyly this time with none of her former challenge. 'Do I understand you correctly, Matthew Aysgill?'

'Yes, you do. I am asking you to agree to become my wife. To pledge with me in Holy Matrimony.' He reached out his hand. 'I know I am behaving badly in addressing you this way, but I mean no mischief to you. These are modern times; everything we have ever known is changing; people are leaving the homes in which their families have lived for generations. There is need of guidance on all sides and I can think of no more noble task than devoting myself to that. I cannot do it alone. I need someone to guide *me*, to help *me*, aye, and someone I can love to *love* me. Dare I ask if *you* could ever love me, Mildred, as I love you?'

She gave him her answer with a hug and a kiss, leaping from the stool on which she sat to embrace him. 'I was afeared you would not speak,' she said, 'and how, then, could I have told you of the love that's in my heart *already* for thee?'

*

Matthew's head was filled with noble schemes which, each evening, he would sit and discuss with his bride. They had taken Jamie in to live with them, though Matthew insisted he visit his mother every day with a bowl of nourishment and that he pursue his education under Mildred's guidance. It was Matthew's hope that if Jamie could be brought along in Latin and French, perhaps he could be apprenticed to some lawyer's clerk, following an occupation in which the lack of a limb would be no detriment.

Matthew had thought much about the working of the coal mines. He was not an inventor, or a practical man, but it seemed to him that some systems could be changed. Under Mildred's prompting, he worked out a scheme in which each man would pay a small sum from his wages, trifling amounts which, when put together would add up to the fee for medical treatment at the mine-head. Many men forced to work underground, as Matthew himself now was, suffered from the amount of dust and coal black they breathed into their lungs each day. A doctor, coming regularly to visit the mine, paid for by 'the Fund', as Matthew called it, could examine each man who suffered this dreaded 'black lung', to help to cure him in time. It had been known for years that black lung caused early death, but the mine workers accepted it as a normal, inevitable hazard of work.

The doctor could also be fetched quickly to save men involved in mine accidents.

At first he began to air these opinions on Sundays when people were attracted to his house to hear him speak. Many accepted what he said, and suggested that similar systems might be used in other workings, in the mills, the foundries, both of which had their share of industrial accidents.

The crowd had gone one Sunday, and he was sitting in his chair, relaxing, while Mildred prepared their meal from the things people had brought. 'There's a cow-heel tonight,' she said, 'and a handful of oats! That'll make a nourishing broth that will last all week long.'

He held out his hand to her and she took it, using her other hand to push a wisp of hair back from her moist brow. 'Are you all right?' he said, indicating her big belly.

She nodded. 'I'll be glad when we turn the year into 1743,' she said. 'I'm looking forward to a spring baby.'

'You'll be well . . .?' he asked anxiously.

'Aye, I'll be fine,' she said. He let go of her hand and she bent as best she could over the pot in the fireplace, stirring its contents deeply, her eyes gazing reflectively into the coal blaze. She had no fear of childbirth, she told herself, but her mind was troubled by Matthew. She believed passionately that he was a good man, that he could do more with his goodness, his thoughts about improving the quality of life for most people. He couldn't see, however, that his ideas were unpractical and too far ahead of the time.

'What Colley said about the mills was interesting,' Matthew said, breaking in on her thoughts. 'That they should pay into a fund for a midwife or a nurse to be at the mill, to help the children and the women who take sick. How many women drag themselves to work each day when they are farther advanced than you are.'

Something in what he said struck a nerve in her. She turned round and her eyes looked strongly at him. 'You and Colley have much in common, *Maister* Aysgill,' she said, her voice as heated as the fire-pot. 'You both talk of the plight of women and children in the mills and the mines, but you do nothing about it. You talk of your Fund, yet make only half-hearted attempts to collect the coin from each man. Men are not ready to do these things themselves. They need a leader, someone who will tell them what's to be done. I'd like to see people talking less, and acting more.'

Matthew was shocked – though he'd known that some of Mildred's ideas were progressive, she'd never expressed them to him with such vehemence. Nor had she ever taken him to task in such an outspoken, unwomanly, manner.

209

'Tha'll do well, Mistress, to watch thy tongue,' he said. 'If folks cannot converse without the heat of anger or unseemly vehemence . . .'

'But don't you see, Matthew,' she said, 'that we have a need of *anger* and *vehemence* if anything is to be *done*. You're such a *good* man, my husband, but you are so *unworldly*. You think that all men can be as good as you if only you'll point the way.'

'Men need to be shown the path of enlightenment . . .'

'No, Matthew, no!' she said passionately as she crouched before his knees. 'Men need to be *led*, to be *driven*. Sloth and indifference are the greatest enemies to progress we shall encounter, if your vision of a life of noble service is to be achieved. People will listen to you as they did today for you have a spellbinding way with you and are so clearly a *good* man. They will bring small gifts to salve their consciences, and thank God for that for I know not how we'd feed Jamie, his mother and my child yet unborn with what Jabez Broadley pays you for your endeavours. But when the people go from here, back to their own lives, what do you think they'll take with them other than the benefit of an hour spent listening to a *good man*. You could recite a prayer in Latin, and I swear they'd attend your every word. But all without comprehension.'

He was of a mind to be offended by her forthright speech, but when he looked down at her sincere face, he couldn't find it in his heart to chide or reprove her.

'What would you have me do, Mistress?' he asked softly.

'I'd have you look at the money that Jabez Broadley is paying, and then examine the profit he makes from his coal. Your wages could be doubled and Jabez Broadley would still be an exceeding wealthy man.'

'What can I, one man, do about that,' Matthew said. 'When I protested that the work in the new pit would be ill-paid, Jabez but laughed at me and said that if I didn't want the opportunity of working, there were many others who'd be happy to wield a pick in my stead.'

'Aye, beloved, but if you *all* said the same thing . . .

'*All*?'

'Aye, if you were *all* in *accord*.'

'Nay, Mildred, that's the devil's gospel that we should combine in *revolt* against the Master.'

'I didn't mean revolt, Matthew. Merely that the men should combine their opinions, that some should be selected to speak for the majority, and that Jabez Broadley should be shown your intentions.'

'And what, pray, would they be?'

'It would be for a majority of the men, under your leadership, to decide. You could influence them of course. But it occurs to me that the pillar-and-stall lends itself to a form of persuasion. If someone were to weaken the pillars, the whole seam could be stopped. Jabez Broadley would lose his coal and that would bring him to his senses.'

'Nay, Mildred,' Matthew said in a shocked voice. 'Break down the pillars! I couldn't countenance owt like that. Tha'rt a regular firebrand, and no mistake.'

She sighed. Little had Matthew known when he'd married her what violent schemes lay in her heart. Little could he know how her woman's heart had turned at the sight of the injury to Jamie's shoulder, at the people daily being injured, their bodies torn and bleeding, to make a profit for the master. When she saw other women dragging themselves into factories in the last stages of their child-bearing, to earn the coin for a day's labours to feed an already large family, something within her told her that life should not be like this, that the whole message of the God she believed in much more fervently, even, than Matthew, had not created human kind for this terrible, dark, existence. As a woman she was helpless, but she longed to change with a man, to fight this oppression, this tyranny, this inhuman sacrifice of humanity. She had married Matthew because she thought she saw the same passion in him, but their life together so far had revealed a good but ineffectual man. Matthew was good; he was a saint in the way he didn't spare himself in the service of other people,

211

but he wasn't strong enough, wasn't bold or brave enough to fight for causes, to lead the revolt she felt was so necessary.

'Aye, Matthew,' she said, 'happen I am a firebrand. But more than words will be needed to light a flame under people prepared to accept the yoke of any Master who pays them a pittance. You said these are modern times, aye, and everything is changing. When you see the Flying Jenny making cloth faster than a body would have ever believed possible, when you see the giant water-wheels, the large ships I'm told they build though I've never seen them, when you hear about iron ore and coke being burned together to make melted iron, you could believe that that was all there was to it. But the same changes, Matthew, are taking place within people's spirits. It's not just machinery, Matthew, it's people and what's in their minds, what sort of lives they want to lead, what sort of food they want, clothes to wear on their backs. We've always accepted the seasons come, the seasons go; but here, Matthew, there are no seasons. Here we're locked in a perpetual winter of the spirit, with no spring to look for except what we shall create. There'll be no flowers for us, Matthew, unless we can gather the seeds and plant them ourselves in the hearts of men. Aye, and women!'

She looked up at him. 'Tha's gone away from me, my husband,' she said bitterly. 'It's not seemly I should speak so, it's not fitting that a mere woman should say these things, I know. But there's a life being born within me, Matthew, and I don't want to see my babby in a mine, a factory, a mill! I don't want to watch his little legs bend wi' rickets, his ribs showing from a shortage o' pobbies, his eyes large with hunger and pain . . .'

'There'll be money and enough to take care of the child,' Matthew said gruffly.

Mildred pulled from him. 'I'm not talking about *money*!' she said. 'I'm talking about the nature of his *life*! What does it serve if he has coin in his pocket, and chains and shackles around his heart and his mind?'

212

She rose with difficulty and went to stand by the fire, making a strong effort to control herself. 'I'm reet sorry,' she said finally. 'I forgot myself speaking to you, my husband, like that . . .'

'Th'art forgiven,' he said. It was all he could think of at that moment.

The Jacobite rebellion was at its height and the young Scottish Pretender came marching south; he reached Derby in December of 1745 and there he stopped. Charles Stuart, Bonnie Prince Charlie as he had been named, had realized that an unpopular Hanoverian King such as George II could nevertheless rally popular support to a Protestant cause, so engraved on the minds of people was their hatred and fear of the Catholics.

Though all of Europe was aflame with war, the British people were much more concerned with maintaining their burgeoning trade and there had never been so much opportunity for making wealth.

Mills had been opened to serve the needs of this commerce, and to clothe the armies engaged in conflict; it had never been easier to find employment in the mills, mines, foundries and factories of the prosperous city of Leeds.

Despite this sudden access of wealth and opportunity, Simon Aysgill's position remained the same. He still lived in the same house with its slimy and peeling walls though the open water sewer had now been covered by stones. He'd been from one job to another seeking at first to better himself, but latterly because he couldn't conquer his need of ale and often arrived at his job late and unfit to labour. The only change of note that had come to his life was that he was no longer alone. Somewhere along the way, and Simon had not been able to remember when it had happened, he'd picked up a girl who now shared his house and board. Amelia was seventeen years of age and had run away from a Foundling Home in Manchester. Something of a slattern, Amelia had been living the life of a bawd

213

when she'd encountered Simon. Some innate part of his Aysgill character must have been awakened by the girl's plight; she remembered well that, at the beginning, he'd treated her with a courtesy and kindness she'd never known from any other man. Of late the loss of jobs, the constant drinking, the poverty of his living, seemed to have soured him and his kindnesses and courtesies had become few and far between.

They were sitting at home one evening and she was attempting to repair his torn jacket by the last of the day's light, when she heard the knock on the door. She opened it.

Matthew and Mildred came in the room and' both wrinkled their noses at the foul odour. It was apparent the bedding hadn't been freshened for many a month, and a plate of scraps stood congealing on the table. Simon was sitting before a large pot of ale his woman had doubtless fetched for him.

'Aye, Matthew,' he said, 'come to preach a bit more?'

The two brothers didn't see each other often for Simon had no time for Matthew's mealy-mouthed spouting about the beauty of God. 'If God is so wonderful,' Simon had once asked him truculently, 'how is it he lets men live in the condition we do, thee and me both. Tha's down't mine, digging away, filling your lungs wi' poison. I'm either in't mill, or't foundry, running about till I drop. And neither of us has owt to show for it come Michaelmas.'

'No, I haven't come to preach,' Matthew said. 'I've come to put a simple fact to you, man to man, that has perhaps escaped your attention. This girl of yours is in her seventh month, unless my eyes deceive me. What are you going to do about it? Or will you make bastards to carry the Aysgill name forward? You're the oldest, your child takes the name down the line. Will you forsake our father's memory with a bastard?'

Simon looked at Amelia, amazed. 'Is it right what he says?' he asked her. 'That tha's i' thy seventh month?'

''Tis true,' she said in a whisper, her eyes cast down.

'Then why has tha said nowt?'

'I'll tell you why she said nowt to you, Simon,' Mildred said, putting her arm protectively round the young girl's waist. 'She was afeard you'd turn her out to fend for herself!'

Mildred didn't tell Simon that the girl had come to see her and Matthew one Sunday, had taken her quietly into a corner and had told her the sad story. 'He'll beat me, Mistress Aysgill, I know for sure. The first time he's in his cups he'll blame me and beat me. And then he'll put me to the door with a blow and a curse.'

'You'll marry the lass?' Matthew asked his brother. 'You'll not shame the Aysgills' name with a bastard?'

'How do I know the bastard is mine?' Simon roared. 'She were nowt but a bawd when I first knew her. Tha knows what they say, once a bawd, always a bawd.'

'That's a terrible and disgusting thing to say,' Mildred said with great heat. 'I don't know how any man could be so contemptible.'

'Is this the way tha lets a woman talk, Matthew? Is it the custom in thy house to let thy woman forget herself? For it ain't in this house. I'll pray thee to speak when tha's spoken to i' this house, Mistress,' Simon said to Mildred. 'Rattle thy pots as best tha might, and ride thy besom, but leave men's talk to men!'

'Mildred is right,' Matthew said. 'You shouldn't impugn the girl that way.'

'Impugn, eh. Fancy words. She's my woman, and I'll treat her the way I think is best.'

'You'll marry her?' Matthew insisted.

'Aye, that's as may be. I might wait till I see the babby's face and the colour of its hair afore I decide.'

Matthew tried ineffectually to force Simon to a commitment but his lack of seniority told against him; Simon was the first-born and as such was determined not to be pushed by his brother. Mildred said no more since she didn't want to prejudice Amelia's situation and knew that Simon would only take his vengeance on the poor girl after they had left.

215

When they returned the following evening, they could see the bruises on Amelia's face and she held her arm awkwardly.

They had brought Dodie and Mark Ottershaw with them. Dodie had not seen her brother Simon for over a year since she had little time to spare for social events. She was wearing a fine dress of dark green wool and a well-made and trimmed bonnet. Mark looked almost dapper in the clothes Dodie had found and altered to fit him, a coat that came to mid-thigh in beige wool with a matching waistcoat and the new style of trousers tucked into well-greased calf-length boots. His long hair had been pulled back below a black velour hat.

Dodie looked disapprovingly round the house.

'I do the best I can, ma'am,' Amelia sniffled, but Simon stopped her with a back-handed blow across her mouth which she was too slow to duck. It was apparent that Simon had been drinking again, though his ale-pot was empty.

Above all things, Dodie had become a practical woman. She'd smiled when Mildred had told her of Matthew's unsuccessful attempt to persuade Simon to do the correct thing. 'That one had his head in the clouds,' she'd said. 'He'll never persuade men to their earthly responsibilities. Mark and I will come, and I'll talk to Simon. He always used to listen to me.'

She sat beside him and he stared at her.

'What's tha come for?' he said. 'Tha needn't think tha's going to talk me round.'

'I know that,' she said. 'Nobody's trying to make you do anything you don't want to. Anything you think isn't right. What kind of a life would that be for poor Amelia, to be married to a man who'd done it only under sufferance. Aye, it'd be specially difficult for Amelia, seeing as she loves you so strongly, to know you'd taken her only under sufferance.'

'That's only women's blether,' he said, but she could see he hadn't considered the possibility that Amelia might actually *love* him.

'Of course it is, and I know it. But we women set more store by love than a man does you know, Simon. We think it's a wonderful thing to be loved, and to love. It doesn't happen much these days. Folks are thrown together these days, else they're put together by parents for a financial or commercial convenience. But to have a woman *love* you, and cherish you, and lay your first born baby in your arms, aye, that's something to warm a man's spirit. None of us has anything, Simon, except what we earn and save by our work. They can take our work away from us, throw us out of our homes, cause us to starve and die. But they can't spoil our blood, Simon, they can't spoil our name, and the way we can pass that blood on to another, and another. Provided we have someone to *love* us, the way Amelia *loves* you.'

'Aye, well, that's summat different, ain't it? I didn't know as the daft maid were smitten wi' me.'

'Well, she is,' Dodie persisted.

'Aye, well, in that case, I suppose we'd better get ourselves wed!'

'I thought you'd see it that way,' Dodie said, 'I thought, somehow, you would!'

Matthew and Mildred's two sons, Frank and Richard, were three and two years old when Simon and Amelia's son Arthur was born in the turbulent year of 1746. Europe was still at war and jobs were plentiful, though marriage had done but little to stabilize Simon's character. Dodie, the perpetual searcher for oddments, had found a small damaged loom behind a factory; Mark and Matthew had worked together to repair it and put it back into working condition, and it had been installed in the back yard of Simon's house beneath a cover that protected it from the rain. Mildred had taught Amelia how to spin and to weave, and Dodie had dipped into her small carefully hoarded store of coins to provide the first wool for Amelia to work into cloth.

217

'I'll loan thee the coin,' she said, 'and tha'll give me the cloth. I'll sell it for thee and take back my loan.'

'Nay, you can trust me, Dodie,' Amelia had said. 'I carry such a burden of gratitude for thee that I'll not let thee down.' She'd clutched the baby Arthur to her side when she spoke; despite the frugality of their life the baby had been born healthy and vigorous and now was contented and happy.

'It has nowt to do with trusting thee,' Dodie said. 'If you have coin in your hand, your husband will take it from you, and we'll never see profit from your labours. This way, if your husband asks, you'll be able to tell him truthfully that you have no money. What you must do is leave the money with me, and come here to draw it to buy food for yourself and the babby. That way, he'll not get the rickets and stands a chance of surviving.'

Amelia was happy with her spinning and her loom. It gave her something to do during the long days when Simon was away from home either working, which he did but rarely, or combing the ale-houses on the pretence he was looking for work. The piece of woollen cloth grew slowly between her hands but she was content to be doing something, to be creating something. Every evening when Simon came home she stopped since he didn't like to hear what he called 'the damned clacking of thy machine'. Many times during the afternoon while Simon was away, she'd wrap Arthur in her shawl and put him on her back to walk the three miles to the colliery tip Dodie had shown her. She'd climb the slope of the heap, digging in for the black nuggets with which she could keep the fire going for Simon. When she'd filled the basket, she'd take Arthur on one arm, the basket on the other, and start her walk home. If she'd had a good day on the slag heap, she'd take her coal to the butchers' shambles and there she could usually exchange some of it for a bit of meat and a few bones. One day, when she struck a full seam where a coal bearing cart must have spilled some of its contents, she filled the basket and hurried to the yard where she exchanged the whole basketful for a leg of pork she could salt down in the barrel in pieces. With careful management she knew she could make it last for many weeks. Then, with the leg tied round her waist, and the baby Arthur on her shoulder, she went back to the slag heap and filled her basket again. Unfortunately, the seam had been discovered by the other women scratching for fuel, and she had to fill her second basket piece by piece. She didn't mind; the leg of pork was such a joy to her that she found herself humming as she laboured her way home with her burdens.

When she arrived home, late in the evening, she found a gathering in the street where they lived. She hastened forward to see what could be amiss. Lizzie Fletcher was standing before her house; though for many months she hadn't spoken to the Aysgills because of an insult from Simon in his cups, she addressed Amelia now in her hard shrill voice. 'All these houses are coming down,' she said. 'They're throwing us all out.'

'Why is that?' Amelia asked. 'They can't pull down good houses, surely?'

'The owner wants to build a factory here. They say it's going to be four storeys high. Apparently, he needs the water from the spring.'

'A factory . . .?'

'Aye. He's given us all until quarter day to find somewhere else.'

The notice had been pinned to their door – Amelia couldn't read it so she took it into the house to await Simon's return. She didn't think he had found a job this week even though work was plentiful. His reputation had gone before him and most factory owners and the men who set people on knew that he was unreliable.

He came back at eight o'clock and, she could see, had not been drinking. She guessed he hadn't even had the money to go into the ale-house, though he could usually earn a drink or two by helping clean out the stables. She'd used some of her coal to light a fire no bigger than a man's hand, and on it the blackened pot was bubbling. The rest of the pork was already in the barrel, being salted, and she'd hidden it away in the yard out of sight. Her piece of cloth was nearing completion and she knew that within a few days she'd be able to lift it from the loom and Dodie could sell it at the Woollen Exchange, though they'd say nowt to Simon. She'd do it during the day when he was out, to make certain he didn't come with her and snatch the coins out of her hand.

He read the notice slowly, not at first understanding its import. When it came to him, he smashed his hand on the table, frightening the child whose voice she rapidly stilled.

'We shall have to go, Simon,' she said fearfully. 'But where shall we find anything as cheap as this?'

The rental of houses was increasing all the time – now you had to pay at least threepence a week to get anywhere good since more and more people were flocking into the town from the countryside, where the new farming methods were throwing so many men out of work. Using the new plough behind horses, one man could do the work of three or four planting the seed in drills, cultivating the land.

Simon looked at her tear-stained face and for once was moved to compassion. He had had nothing to drink now for two days since he had nothing with which to pay even for a pot of ale. No-one would give him work since all believed him unreliable and told him so. Even the ale-houses, which had been kindly and generous to him, refused to give him the hard work no self-respecting ostler would willingly countenance doing. He held out his hand and she flinched from him, expecting a curse and a blow. He held her neck and dragged her head to his breast, hugging her so tight and with such unaccustomed fervour she thought that she and the babby would be choked.

'Tha mustn't worry, lass,' he said. 'Us has fallen on hard times, right enough, but I'll do summat for thee, mark my words. I'll do summat to find us a place where we can live decent. I'll start a-working. You'll see, it'll all be different.'

All afternoon he'd been thinking about their situation and now the news of the house had hardened his resolve. 'Come sit down,' he said, 'and let me tell you what I've a mind to do.'

She was so overwhelmed by the change in him that she did as she was bid, squatting on the box she'd hammered together and covered with a rag to make a seat for herself. He took Arthur and held him on his lap. She was afeared he'd drop the babby and kept her hands nervously clasped on her lap to catch him.

'I was thinking today,' he said, 'that one man who always has work to do, always has a coin in his pocket, is a carter. Whenever did you see an unemployed carter?'

'Never,' she said. It was true; the carters were an elite since so many of the new goods needed to be carried from one place to the other. The cry of 'carter' was a common one in the streets of the city.

'You remember Dick the waggoner . . .'

'Aye,' she said, 'I remember him.' Dick the Waggoner was a well-known local character who kept his horse and cart in a stable at the end of the next street. Often Dick had mounted folk on the back of his cart of a Sunday, and had taken them for a ride into the countryside. He was popular with all the ragamuffins of the district since he'd always lift a child onto the seat beside him for a thrilling ride behind the horse. His horse, as well known as Dick himself, had recently perished of old age and been taken to the knackers, while Dick had bought a new, young, strong horse to carry on his business. Unfortunately, the new horse had not been broken to Dick's ways and one day, about two weeks ago, when Dick had been bent down beside the cart greasing the wheel-boxes, it had let fly with a back leg and had stoved in the top of his head. Dick had been lucky to die instantly – if he'd recovered from such a blow he'd have been an idiot for sure.

'Aye, I remember him, but what about him?'

'I were talking wi' his widow this morning.' He didn't tell Amelia of his shame when not even Dick's widow

221

would give him the job of cleaning out the stable.

'You'll take my coin and vanish into't nearest ale-house,' she'd said. 'If I thought the coin would go to the benefit of thy wife and that bairn of hers . . .'

Humiliated, he'd wanted to march out of there but she'd detained him. 'Why don't you try to make a man of yourself,' she said, 'like my Dick did in his lifetime. I'll sell you his business for four pounds, horse, waggon, stable an' all. And if you can raise another ten pounds, you can have my house. I'm going back to Wakefield to be with my kith and kin; now that my beloved has been taken from me there's nowt here for me.'

'If we could buy the business,' he said. 'There's a list of addresses on which Dick had first call for work. He could have been carting morn, noon, and neet, if he'd a mind.'

'Nay, Simon, I'd not want to see yon horse kick out your brains,' Amelia said fearfully.

'I was brought up wi' horses, lass,' he said boisterously. 'There's not a horse standing on four legs I couldn't handle.'

'Aye, well if you think it's all right. But you might as well put it out of your mind. We'd never raise fourteen pounds.' To Amelia's mind the sum of money was impossible to contemplate – it represented vast wealth to her, so used to surviving for days on what she could procure for a penny.

'That's what I've been thinking about,' he said triumphantly. 'I put it out of mind straightway but then I got to thinking. Our Peter is a wealthy man. Why, he lives in a house with *six* rooms. He had that Shepley's business. Surely, fourteen pounds will be as nowt to him. I can get a loan of it, pay it back each quarter day, aye, and give him a good interest on it.'

'Peter! I never thought of him. Do you think he'd do it?'

'Of course he will,' Simon said. 'He's my young brother, ain't he. My flesh and blood! Why, it was probably the few pun he received from the break-up ot father's mite that gave him his start them years ago.'

222

'He's never been to see us,' Amelia said. 'He's never even seen our Arthur.'

'Aye, well, he's no doubt been busy wi' Shepley's business, and keeping in with the swells. I mind the time I saw him outside the Assembly Rooms one evening. You couldn't see a difference between him and the nobles who were parading in and out, so elegant did he look. Aye, I shall go to see my young brother Peter, first thing in't morn. And by the setting o' the sun, mark my words, we shall have our own business. 'It'll be Simon the Waggoner, and no mistake . . .'

When Simon climbed from his pallet the following morning, Amelia had already cleaned and brushed his clothes for him, sewn the tears in his breeches, greased his boots to a fine lustre, even washed a neckcloth for him and pressed it with a stone she'd heated in the ashes of the fire, so that it tied flat to his throat. She'd filled the leather bucket with water from the spring, and even procured a piece of soap for him to use. Despite his protests she washed his hair with the soap and water and combed it to get out the many tangles. She sheared the ends to a neat line across his neck with the snips she used in her weaving.

'Now, let's take a look at thee,' she said as she eyed him with pride. At thirty-one years of age he was a handsome, well set-up man, with broad shoulders and a fine figure. His waistline and belly had thickened out, doubtless with the beer and the lack of hard work, but he looked solid and, thanks to her endeavours, respectable and clean.

'Tha'll do,' she said, not wishing to discomfit him by too close a scrutiny. 'Now away tha goes, Maister Carter-to-be! My heart goes wi' thee!'

Peter had kept on Mr Percy and most of the clerks though his familiarity with many of the ways of the staff who'd worked for Shepley caused him to get rid of a few of them. Percy, he knew, had always been assiduous in protecting Mr Shepley's interest – Peter wisely gave him an extra shilling on his wages and bought his loyalty by giving him a title and a screen round part of his desk.

Percy came from his office, as he liked to call his quarters, when Simon entered the counting room. He was surprised to see such a coarse fellow but knew he must have passed the scrutiny of the doorman below to advance this far into the premises.

'I'd like to see Maister Aysgill,' Simon said, taking his hat in his hand and nervously smoothing the back of his fresh-cut hair.

'I'm afraid that will not be possible,' Percy said disdainfully. 'Mr Aysgill never sees *anyone*, except by appointment. I doubt he would grant an appointment to such as you.'

'You snivelling tyke,' Simon said, angered by the slur, by the man's womanish ways and his precious manners. 'Tell my brother that Simon is out here to see him.'

Percy looked astonished, but turned on his heel and went into Peter Aysgill's private room. 'Mr Aysgill,' he said hurriedly. 'Forgive the interruption, but there's a *person* out there claiming to be your brother Simon.'

Peter had been reading his ledgers and hated to be interrupted. 'I'll speak to you in ten minutes, Mister Percy,' he said, without looking up from the ledger pages.

'What shall I say to your brother, Mister Aysgill?' Percy said, more agitated than ever.

'Tell him to go away, of course. You know well enough I never see anyone except by appointment.' There, so far as Peter Aysgill was concerned, the matter was closed.

Percy backed out, shut the door, and turned to Simon Aysgill, who stood half a head taller at least than he did, whose shoulders were twice as broad, whose whole stance bespoke an aggressive, even pugilistic nature. 'I'm afraid your brother is very occupied at the moment,' he said. 'May I suggest you write to him, stating the nature of your business, and we'll see what can be arranged?'

As he had guessed, Simon was a violent man. His hand

224

shot out and he clasped the front of Percy's coat before pushing him aside. 'An appointment, to see my own kith and kin,' he roared. He went forward quickly, grasped the knob of the inner door, and threw it open. 'An arrangement, to see my own brother,' he said, his voice unnaturally loud. The clerks had all dropped their pens and were congregating around the door, which he shut in their faces. He advanced across the room with his hand outstretched – Peter ignored it as he looked up into his brother's face, noting the puffiness of drink, the shabbiness of his clothing, the smell of cheap soap on him.

'Aye, Simon,' he said coldly. 'What do you want?'

Simon let his hand fall back by his side. 'Want, Peter, me that hasn't clapped e'en on thee this twelve month. I want to see my own young brother, the son of my father, that's what I want. Haven't you a friendly word for me?'

'Aye, good to see you, Simon, good to see you! Now, you'll have to excuse me. You catch me at a most unfortunate moment. I'll send one of my clerks around with a note when I have more liberty.'

He bent his head again over the page and Simon stood there aghast. 'Nay, Peter,' he said. 'It's me. Thy brother . . . I've come to see thee, to tell thee about thy nephew tha hasn't even seen.'

Peter realized he had to speak his mind in a most direct way. 'Simon,' he said, 'it was by accident that we were both born of the same parents all those years ago. We have nothing in common with each other except our blood and, frankly, blood is something that leaks from me when I cut myself. Nothing more. I've made a life for myself, and you've done the same for yourself. I have friends I have *chosen*, Simon. You, I regret to say, are not among them. Nor is my sanctimonious brother Matthew, nor my domineering sister Dodie, though of all my blood relations I admire her the most. Am I making myself clear, Simon?'

'Tha'rt making thy meaning known to me, Peter, though I can't say as it's clear. I never thought I'd see the day an Aysgill would deny his own blood.' Simon could

225

have said more, could have lost his temper with the anger that seethed within him, but for once he had a purpose so meaningful that he was able to control himself.

'If tha won't won't consider me as a brother,' he said, cold as Peter himself had been, 'perhaps you'd consider me in a business sense. I have the opportunity to go into business for myself as a carter. The business will cost fourteen pounds with a house, a stable, a horse and a cart. Will you loan me the money on business terms, to be repaid each quarter day in part, along with interest. A business arrangement, Peter, and nowt to do with our dead father?'

'No,' Peter said.

Simon looked at him, bewildered. 'What does tha mean, no?'

'I mean, no!' Peter said. 'I will not lend you fourteen pounds to invest in a carter's business. I will not lend you *any* money, Simon, to invest in *any* business.'

'Why not?'

'Because I do not think you are a man to be supported with money,' Peter said. 'I never have, and never will. And, while you are talking of our dead father, let me tell you, I would not lend the money to our father, either, for I consider him . . .'

The rest of his sentence was lost as Simon's fist crashed into his face and slammed him back against his chair, which toppled over and left him sprawling on the floor. That probably saved his life, for Simon, berserk, was in a mood to kill him and would have done so had not Percy, who'd been at his usual listening post at the door, brought in all the trembling clerks who managed by sheer force of numbers to overwhelm the brawling giant, force him across the office and down the stairs before tossing him into the mud of the alley outside the premises.

Despite himself, Percy felt compassion for the burly man, shamed and humiliated, lying with his clothing soiled in the gutter. He reached into his pocket, took out a coin, and flung it towards Simon Aysgill's head.

'You needn't come back,' he said, 'for I'll leave

226

instructions you are not to be admitted.'

Amelia waited all day for the return of Simon, believing at first that everything had gone well and he'd gone to see Dick the Waggoner's widow, had even started work with his new-bought cart. As the day lengthened, however, she began to have her doubts. Surely, she told herself, if he obtained the waggon his first trip would be here, to give her and the babby a triumphal ride . . .? Then she consoled herself by saying that perhaps Peter Aysgill had been out on business and that Simon had had to wait in his office till his brother returned.

When the evening came, she began to suspect something was wrong. She walked round the streets with her shawl on her shoulders and Arthur wrapped snug beneath it, but the horse was still in its stall and Dick's widow was sitting reading by the light of a mutton-fat candle.

Amelia went round the district, peering into each of the ale-houses she knew Simon frequented, but didn't see him. When Arthur began to whimper with the cold she returned home, fed him a mite of the pork-leg broth, and laid him to sleep in the cot she had made for him of withies.

She went out to the back to finish her piece of wool but the light was insufficient and she didn't care to leave a flaw in it, though by now she could have operated the loom without any light at all.

It was almost break of day, to judge from the heavens, when Simon returned with his clothes, on which she had lavished so much care, completely soiled and ruined. He'd obviously been drinking and, as so often happened in his cups, had been in a fight. One sleeve was almost torn from his jerkin and his neckcloth had gone. His trousers were coated at the knee with foul smelling ordure, doubtless where he'd fallen into dog's mess. She dare say nothing since she could smell the gin on him; she placed a bowl of broth on the table with a big knuckle bone in it and a hunk of bread she'd had baked in the oven at the street end. He slumped on his chair, looked owlishly at the food set before him and, with a broad sweep of his arm, dashed it all to the floor. 'Pestilential muck!' he said. 'Slop fit for pigs.'

She didn't know if he had been celebrating because he had obtained the loan, or commiserating with himself because he had not, but she knew that to ask would only invite yet another blow from his cruel hands.

'Aye, well, missis,' he said finally. 'Yon brother of mine, my own flesh and blood as ever was, had me thrown out of his plaguy office. He said he wouldn't back nor me, nor our dear dead father, in any sort of business venture. Tha'd better take thyself, and the bairn, away. You're young yet, and a good catch for some bright lad as can look after you better than seems to be in *my* ability.'

'Nay, Simon, I'll stay by thee. Through thick and thin, I'll stay by thee. Now, take thyself to bed, and I'll join thee presently.'

He was already fast asleep and snoring well by the time she'd washed his breeches clean of the foul smelling muck, and climbed wearily onto the pallet beside him, blessing God that her man was too far gone to desire her that night.

Gertrude Aysgill walked slowly up what she felt certain had once been the street in which her brother lived but now was a mess of rubble of houses being knocked down. She walked to the end of the street and, seeing a woman come out of a house, addressed herself to her. 'Pardon me, Mistress,' she said, 'but I'm looking for a man who used to live here. Simon Aysgill? Do you recall him by any chance . . .?'

The woman looked shrewdly at her, guessing by the style of her dress and her manner that she was no doxy come to plague a lover who'd wronged her. 'Might I ask, pray, what is your connection with Maister Aysgill?'

'I am his sister, come from Whitby to solicit his advice.'

'Then you'd better look for him in the Mill Cottages,' she said, 'for they were fortunate enough to gain a place there, largely, I'll be bound, through the entreaties of that wife of his.'

'Wife?' Gertrude said, 'I had no notion he was married.'

'Married, aye, and wi' a bairn too, as bonnie a lad as ever you'd see.'

The woman would have liked to linger and talk, Gertrude could see, but she was doubly impatient, now, to find her brother. She hurried along towards the Mill Cottages – if Simon were living there, it must mean he was in steady employ since she knew that such dwellings were usually reserved to faithful servants.

When she arrived at the cottages and enquired again, she was directed to Number 4, a two-storey house in the centre of a terrace, with a passageway that led to the back through the terrace itself. The house appeared clean from the outside and she walked through the passageway to knock on the back door. From within she heard the sound of a child's voice of about three years saying a version of 'There's someone at the door'. The door was flung open and at first she didn't recognize the hulk of the man who stood there.

It was obvious that he didn't recall his visitor, either. 'What does tha want?' he asked truculently. 'I'll not have maids knocking on *my* door, bold as can be.'

'Don't you recognize me, Simon,' she said. 'It's Gertrude, your sister. Gertie?'

'Gertie? Aye, lass, 'tis thee, right enow. Bai gow, tha mun come in, right away. I thought tha wert lost to us for ever.'

She came in and sat in the largish room, seeing the weaving loom, the spinning wheel, the crib in the corner, the table and chairs. The place, however, had the awful sour damp smell she knew so well of unclean drains and inadequate foundations – the furniture was mean and rude, the cooking arrangements crude and primitive.

'I'd offer thee summat, but we have nowt,' he said, 'save a glass of water. Tha's all right; it comes from a fresh well the company dug.'

'I need nothing,' she said, 'except to look at you. How long has it been?'

'Aye, well, it's the year 1749, so that makes it nine years, doesn't it?'

'Nine years . . . How the time has gone.'

She didn't tell him that she'd already called on Matthew and Mildred, on Dodie and Mark, and had even taken a carriage out to Peter's splendid home which stood in its own grounds behind a wall. Peter had received her somewhat brusquely, but he'd been polite enough to offer her a cordial and then had asked to be excused since he was about to dress to go to dinner at the Town House of Sir Ian Clether, or so he'd told her. She'd been overawed at the thought of her brother dining with a baronet, but pleased that he had made such a wonderful success of his life. She had no trace of envy or jealousy – life had been good to her and she would not have changed her situation. Except in one respect . . . And that was the reason she'd come to see her family. To solicit their advice.

'Mildred and Matthew are making a meal for me tomorrow, Sunday,' she said. 'I'd like to ask you if you'd care to come? Dodie and Mark will be there.'

'Tha's not invited Peter, then?'

'I did speak of it, but he is going to the country on Sunday and won't be back in time.'

'Aye, well, if yon young devil ain't going to be there . . . Though I tell you the truth as we can't fetch nowt wi' us!'

'There is no need,' Gertrude said. 'I have recently had a small good fortune and seek to share it with you.'

Her 'good fortune', as she put it, had come about in a most surprising way. Mrs Edgecombe, her employer, had selected Gertrude one day to accompany her to the shops, taking along a maid to carry the purchase, and a footman to protect them. Coming through Baxter Gate, they had suddenly been set on by a bunch of knavish footpads, and the footman had been clubbed to the ground by one of them. This had so enraged Gertrude that, without thinking what she was doing, she had seized the cudgel from one of the footpads' hands and belaboured him with it about his shoulders. Taken aback to be assaulted by a slip of a lass, the footpads had turned on their heels and fled. A carriage had been called and they'd returned home, where the doctor was called to examine the footman's injuries.

The house had buzzed with the story of Gertrude's bravery and, after dinner, Captain Edgecombe had called her to his study.

'Mrs Edgecombe has given me an account of your bravery today,' he said. 'I congratulate you on having honoured the position we have given you, and the trust we have placed in you. It is not my custom to reward brave service, for I feel that such is the necessity, the obligation, for which we must all strive. But Mrs Edgecombe takes a different line and has beseeched me to give you a token.' With that, to her great astonishment, he'd placed a golden sovereign in her hand. A whole sovereign . . !

She spent many hours sitting on the chair in her room, looking at the coin which she kept wrapped in a scrap of cambric, before she made her final decision.

The bravery needed to tackle the footpads was nothing as compared to that she needed to approach Mrs Watts, who, as the years passed, seemed to be developing into more of an autocrat than ever before. 'Mrs Watts,' she'd said, humbly and fumblingly, 'I have been in employ now for nine years and hope I have given adequate service to my master and mistress . . .'

'I grant you your failings have, for the large part, been minor ones.'

'I was wondering . . .'

'I cannot read your mind, my girl. If you persist in wasting my time . . .'

'Could I take a journey to Leeds, to visit my brothers and sister whom I have not spoken to for nine long years?'

'Years are all the same length, my girl. It is only foolish romanticizing that stretches some and abbreviates others. I shall put your request to Mrs Edgecombe if and when an opportunity to do so presents itself.'

Mrs Watts had made Gertrude wait four whole days before she'd summoned her. 'You are permitted a week's leave of absence from your duties,' she said, 'on the condition you travel by coach and stay with your brothers. You are to behave correctly at all times remembering the good house whose name, by association, you bear and are to do nothing to bring it into discredit. You will keep an account of your movements, since you can write, and I will scrutinize the account when you return, since I can swiftly discern lies from the truth. Is all that clear?'

'Most clear, Mrs Watts.'

'And you agree to the terms?'

'Without reservation, Mrs Watts. And I thank thee and Mrs Edgecombe for your great charity and kindness.'

The 'thee' had slipped out but, for once, it brought a smile to Mrs Watts' craggy, wintry, features. 'I hope you'll take much pleasure from being with your family again,' she said softly. 'I have not seen mine these last twenty years and sometimes miss them sorely. I will lend you my travel box. It will serve you well on the coach.'

Simon's already dulled eyes seemed to lose what little life she'd brought to them at the mention of Gertrude's good fortune. 'Aye, good fortune seems to have passed us by lately, sister,' he said. 'It'll be good to share yours wi' you – though I pray that Matthew will not physic us with his heavenly aspirations after the feast.'

'I think he, too, will share my joy at seeing you again.'

Mildred had told her about the tragedy of the lost carter's business. They'd gone to see Amelia and Arthur, and there had been such a scene when Simon found them there – gloating over his tragedy, he'd said, like the rest of the Aysgills – that Amelia had pleaded with them not to return. When, finally, they had gone back, Simon had moved to the cottages. None knew better than Mildred how Simon felt. He couldn't find employment anywhere, except for a few days from people who didn't know him; but Amelia, little brave Amelia, had left her baby with Lizzie Fletcher and marched into the mill as bold as could be. 'I can work,' she'd said, 'I can work a loom, or a spinning wheel. I can do any job you have!'

The overseer had been impressed by her enthusiasm and her obvious energy. 'Aye, missis,' he'd said, 'I don't doubt tha can work ten months of the year, but what happens when tha's having thy babbies?' It was an argument they all used to reduce the pittance they paid to their work-people.

'There'll be no more babbies,' she'd said bitterly. 'That was taken care of when I had the last one . . . The crone of a midwife would have been better employed in the butchers' shambles.'

So impressed had the overseer been with the sprightly slip of a lass, who seemed to know and speak her mind with such determination, that he'd also spoken to the mill owner's agent and obtained the renting of the Mill Cottage for her.

It had been another pain, another knife twisted in the self-respect of her husband Simon, especially when they refused to employ him except casually, and only in the meanest and dirtiest work, for which he was paid a mere pittance. Most of his time he spent at home, looking after Arthur who could now walk and talk. When he was in work, which was seldom, Amelia took Arthur with her and let him play at her feet while she tended the Flying Shuttle loom and harried the spinners to keep her supplied with cops of thread.

'Say you'll come tomorrow,' Gertrude pleaded to Simon. 'It will be a blessing for us all to sit round a board again, as we did in Barthwick, though I promise a richer fare than was our portion there.'

When Mildred had told her of Simon's plight, her instinct had been to give what was left of her sovereign, after her fare from Whitby and the food she'd consumed on the way, to him and his wife, possibly for the benefit of them and the bairn, but Mildred had advised against it.

'Simon is so unpredictable these days,' she'd said. 'Who's to know what he would do with such a vast sum at his disposal. The good Lord knows he could do anything – he could use it to travel to London and desert his hearth and home . . .'

Gertrude felt guilty at the amount of money she'd spent to provide the feast for them all, with good beef, a pork leg, a cut of lamb, meat coffins, even a pastry cake baked in the oven with fruit in its centre. She'd spent almost five shillings just providing the food! It had seemed a wicked waste until she'd reminded herself it happened only once in nine years! And the money was hers, rightly earned, a token of reward for what she'd done. At least, she'd resisted her first impulses to spend the money on clothing for herself! That would, indeed, have been wicked!

They sat round the table in Matthew's house, their eyes gleaming at the sight of such a spread. 'Many a noble will not eat so well this day,' Amelia said in appreciation. Gertrude had thought carefully about providing ale in view of Simon's predilection, but Amelia had obviously spruced him up and had talked to him; he sat there white-faced and subdued, his hollow cheeks sunken, his eyes deep in their sockets like some man recovering from a near mortal illness. He sipped the beer slowly and all were conscious of Amelia's eyes on him, though all tried to talk cheerfully to cover any embarrassment they might feel. Only when they'd eaten their bellies full did they push back from the table on which enough food was still left to see the three families through the next week. If the truth were told, all were out of the habit of eating such rich fare in such quantities; their stomachs had shrunk during the years of enforced privation.

'Now, Gertie,' Dodie said cheerfully when the food had all been taken from the table and portioned to take away. 'I have a feeling that all this is but a preliminary. I sense you have another surprise for us all that you haven't yet revealed?'

Gertrude blushed and turned her head to look at the fire. In the years that had passed, she'd continued to think of the family as a unit. She'd imagined them all living in Leeds, seeing each other, talking with each other as a family will, taking all their decisions in consultation with each other. She couldn't realize that the years had dealt unkindly with them, that the family ties had sundered and they no longer thought of themselves as belonging to a whole. What she had to say now seemed out of place, trivial, without consequence. Each of them had married, independent of the others. Matthew and Simon had started families of their own. What part of the tremendous story that was in her breast should she, could she, reveal to them?

'I've met a gentleman,' she said hesitantly. 'To be truthful, I met him many years ago . . .'

That wasn't the full truth, was it? She couldn't bring herself to reveal the whole awful story, and its beginnings in the whore-house in Whitby.

She'd been astounded that evening, after the dinner, when she'd gone down to the kitchen to drink an illicit first brewing of tea from Cook's pot, to find her tormentor of that afternoon sitting, large as life, at Cook's table.

'Nay, Gertrude,' Cook had said cheerily, 'you never told me as it was Luke Fossett tha were talking wi' this afternoon. Luke's mother and me started in service together all them years ago, afore I took a fancy to better my position by becoming a cook!'

'How dare you come here, sir,' Gertrude had asked. 'I have nothing more to say to a man who persecutes a young lady, forcing his evil intentions upon her.'

'Oh, fie, Gertrude,' Cook had said. 'This is the eighteenth century, not the Dark Ages!'

Gertrude had wanted to remind Cook of how outraged she had been a few hours earlier when she imagined Gertrude capable of the worst kind of conduct. She'd left the kitchen at once and had retired to her room. There was a smile on her face as she lay abed, unable to sleep. So, he had asked her employer's name because he had a fancy to see her again, had he? He was a honourable man, was he, to judge by what Cook had said?

Over the weeks she had joined in the conversations in the kitchen, for he began to come on each of his free evenings. He worked as a footman for Sir Edward Wilson, who, at ninety years of age, never stirred from his house after dark and was usually abed and asleep by six o'clock. Over the years a friendship had developed between them in which each could converse freely with the other. Gertrude realized that several times Cook had endeavoured to leave them alone together, by inventing a pretext of going to the store-room, but on each occasion Gertrude had risen and had quickly left the room. Though she suspected that Luke Fossett would have liked to speak with her in private, she'd never permitted it. She was too unsure of herself to welcome any intimacy, however friendly and well-intentioned it might be.

The years had rolled by; Gertrude was so well pleased with her situation that she longed for no change to endanger it – she wanted life to roll on exactly as it did at present, feeling secure in the bosom of the Edgecombe family. Other servants came, and went, usually to be married, to give their unborn babies a father and a name. Selina had caught an Army Officer for herself and had departed in a coach in great splendour; only Cook, Mrs Watts and Gertrude had stayed on, with the three loyal footmen, Enoch, James and Lemuel. In these circumstances, all Gertrude's natural shyness had reasserted itself; she told herself she had no interest in changing her situation to take on a husband, to start a family. Cook had dropped many hints to her about the passing years; it was only when Gertrude realized she had become thirty years of age and saw that Luke had never married and still appeared in the kitchen with loyal regularity, that she started to question her motives in refusing to accept his advances. Of course, she was afraid; she'd had to admit that to herself. She was afraid of wifeliness, of the responsibilities of pleasing and pleasuring a man, of bearing him children. She was also afraid of the responsibility of making a home for him. Though she enjoyed all the tasks she did in the Edgecombes' house, she doubted she would have the ability to carry out the same procedures in a home of her own.

Two things had combined to make up her mind. Luke

Fossett's employer, Sir Edward Wilson, had died, leaving no provision for Luke, who'd been turned from the door with only his wages by Sir Edward's younger, avaricious, pleasure loving widow who intended to move to the Colonies with a fancy man she'd taken to herself.

Luke had little difficulty finding another position and had come to the kitchen one evening full of news. Though he'd spoken with Cook, Gertrude had sensed his words were for her. She'd listened with utter dismay as he told them he had signed on as a deck-hand, and would be going to sea on a cargo vessel sailing to the Continent of Europe, perhaps down and round the Cape as far as India. The places were all but names to Gertrude, terrifying in their distance.

'Aye, you'll no longer be bothered o' an evening wi' me,' he said. 'Though I don't reckon as it'll make a mite o' difference to some folks.'

Cook had seen the bitterness in his eyes and had grieved for him many a time. This evening, when she found it necessary to go to the store-room, Gertrude stayed in the kitchen. It was the first time they'd been alone together in seven years.

'I can't go on the way I am,' Luke had said, standing perfectly still, making no move to approach her. 'I've loved thee, Gertrude Aysgill, since the first moment I clapped e'en on thee.'

'In a house of Ill-Fame.'

'Where I was waiting for my master who was transacting business. You never gave me chance to explain,' Luke said. 'Ah, well, it's too late now. They say as I can sign on in the morn, and be away on the even-tide. I'll take my hopeless love wi' me in the best traditions, and try to forget.'

Even then she could not speak, but rose quickly and left the room, a fluttering bird escaping back to its own nest.

The next morning, when he went to sign on at the ship-master's office on the dock-side, he found a pale figure waiting by the door, a shopping basket in her hand.

'I haven't a moment,' Gertrude had said. 'I'm supposed to be buying for Cook.'

She hadn't slept all night long and finally had come down with rings beneath her eyes.

Cook had looked shrewdly at her, had thrust the basket into her arms. 'Go out and get a breath of air,' she'd said. 'A good sea-breeze would do thee good.'

Luke held her arm and steered her to the side of the office into the shelter of the doorway. All round in the morning mist they could see men walking like grey ghosts, many with their wives beside them, seeing them away on the tide, their sad faces closed against the knowledge they might never see their men again.

'Tha's come to see me off,' he said, deliberately not assuming anything lest he frighten her away again.

'Nay, I came to tell thee . . . I love thee . . . as thou loves me it seems . . . When tha returns . . . if tha's still of a mind . . . tha can speak . . . to Captain Edgecombe . . . since he's the only father I know . . .'

He clutched her in his arms, feeling her stiffen, blaming himself for a clumsy hasty fool, then feeling her relax. 'I hope tha'll come back, Luke Fossett,' she said. 'I've a notion as I'll miss thee while tha's away . . .'

'I've met this gentleman,' Gertrude told her brothers and sister. She looked round the table at her family, at the wives and husbands they had married, at the children they had made in love together. Surely, it couldn't be wrong for her to marry Luke Fossett.

'He is a fine man, with a good Christian disposition.'

'How does he earn a living?' Dodie asked, ever practical.

'He goes to sea on a cargo vessel. He's well thought of by his Master and can always be certain of a vessel.'

'It's a dangerous occupation,' Mildred said. 'We hear such stories of storms at sea. You could be a widow before you are a bride.'

'Nay, Mildred,' Matthew growled. 'A man is taken according to God's Will. Many a man spends his life going to sea and retires to a ripe old age. Your gentleman is a good Christian, you said.'

238

'Aye.'

'A Protestant?'

'Of course; you don't think I'd let myself be addressed by a Papist. Captain Edgecombe, my employer, has vouched for him and would have taken him into his service had Luke so desired.'

'He bears a good name,' Matthew said, and they all laughed, relieving the tension.

'All we need,' Mark Ottershaw said, 'is another John and we shall have the books of the Bible . . .'

'So, what do *you* think, Simon,' Gertrude said, addressing herself directly to him as the oldest of the Aysgill family. 'What do you think, Simon? Should I marry him. Do I have your permission and your blessing?'

Simon was embarrassed to be thus addressed, since it had been a long time since anyone had respected him enough to ask his opinion on anything. His eye caught Amelia's eye; their son Arthur had climbed on her knee and was sucking his thumb while the adults talked. Matthew's sons Frank and Richard, now grown to six and five, were standing by their mother's leg. He turned his head to look at Dodie and Mark. They'd had no children, maybe never would or could. He thought of the three marriages. Dodie, who'd wanted a husband to shield her from the rough life of the city and had chosen Mark. Matthew and Mildred, who'd met in a common churching, both waving the banners of the Lord above their heads on all occasions, though Mildred was a sight more practical than Matthew. And then his gaze came back to his Amelia, and his Arthur. Aye, well, it had been a rotten start, and had gone badly for both of them. He'd not been a good husband to Amelia, nor a good father to Arthur, in the way of providing. But one thing stood out clear in his mind.

'Do you *love* him, Gertrude,' he asked softly.

'Yes, Simon, I do.'

'Then *wed* him, and a blessing be on both of you . . .'

*

239

Gertrude and Luke Fossett were wed in the church near the Edgecombe house, in the presence of the Captain himself, who stood witness for Gertrude. Since Luke was leaving in a few days for an extended voyage, it had been agreed that Gertrude would continue in her employment at least until he returned, meanwhile looking for a house for them. Captain Edgecombe further assisted them by the loan of a cottage he kept in Robin Hood's Bay in which they could spend their few days of honeymoon alone together, an unheard of luxury to Gertrude's mind.

Cook had taken her on one side before the ceremony and had explained certain womanly matters to her, astounded by Gertrude's naïveté, her complete lack of knowledge of the ways of the marriage bed. In the event, Luke proved to be as patient in that matter as in all others and Gertrude found herself able to respond to him without fear or embarrassment, happy that Luke seemed to have enjoyed himself and taken satisfaction from her. They quickly established a pleasing relationship that, as yet, was merely an extension of their long-standing friendship with the addition of intimacy in small matters. Many heads turned in the small fishing village when they walked down from the small cottage on Tommy Baxter Street hand-in-hand, to watch the fishermen come and go from the slip, or to walk out on the scaurs at low-tide, looking at the strange marine life that inhabited the pools between the rocks, splashing each other with sea-water like children, exclaiming with glee when they found a sea anemone or a starfish, sometimes even a small crab.

Mrs Edgecombe had said that Gertrude could take an extra two days in the cottage after her husband had sailed; she went to the Whitby docks to see him depart in what seemed to her to be an enormous cargo vessel rigged with so many sails she couldn't count them. She climbed the point to the Abbey and watched his boat sail towards the horizon until she could see it no longer. She cried all the way along the cliff-top path back to Robin Hood's Bay, but when she arrived her eyes were dry and she'd exhausted her emotions. She set to and cleaned the cottage from top to bottom before falling, exhausted but lonely, into bed.

When Gertrude arrived back in the Edgecombe house she was startled to see the doctor coming from Mrs Watts' cottage, which occupied one corner of the stable and carriage house yard. That cottage had always been the prerogative of the Housekeeper, with another one at the other corner for the Captain's Steward, and quarters above the coach house for the coachman. All the other servants, except Cook, lived in the attic rooms. Cook had her own room behind the kitchen and next to the storeroom which she guarded jealously.

'Forgive me, sir, is something amiss with Mrs Watts?' she asked the doctor anxiously.

He nodded and paused. 'Aye, Mistress Gertrude, she's not long for this world,' he said. 'You best go in and comfort her.'

Mrs Watts was lying pale in her bed. 'I wasn't feeling up to much,' she said, 'at your wedding but I didn't want to speak. I've talked with Mrs Edgecombe. You're to take over my keys while I lie abed. I charge you do well, for I'd take it amiss to find disorder when I return.'

Cook was weeping, and several of the new girls were sitting round the kitchen table taking advantage of the housekeeper's sickness to neglect their duties. Gertrude had taken the housekeeper's keys and key belt, which she'd fixed round her waist. 'I'll thank you all to get back to your duties,' she said severely.

When the bell rang that had been connected by wires to Mrs Edgecombe's sitting-room, Gertrude primped her hair a little, examined her hands, brushed down her apron with its cross straps, and went upstairs. Mrs Edgecombe was sitting stony-eyed; it was Gertrude's guess that even she had shed a tear on hearing the doctor's news, for Mrs Watts had been with her all her married life.

'Ah, you've taken possession of the keys. I'd be obliged if you'd assume the responsibility of housekeeper until . . . until we can think about it . . .'

'It is my privilege, ma'am, to serve you in whatever capacity you choose,' Gertrude said with obvious sincerity. 'Would it be impertinent of me to ask what ails Mistress Watts?'

'I fear it's the wasting disease,' Mrs Edgecombe said sadly, 'for which there can be no cure. Mrs Watts has suffered from it this past year, with much pain. It will be a comfort for the poor body when the good Lord takes her.'

When the household assembled that evening, as they did every evening when no guests were invited, the Bible stayed closed while the Captain composed his own prayer.

'Almighty God,' he said, 'we have but one thought in mind this evening and that is to commend the soul and the spirit of our dearly beloved Emmeline Watts to Thy forgiving Mercy. In Thy Mercy and Charity, deliver her of this noisome pestilence, this all-destroying sickness. For Emmeline Watts has been thy good and devout servant all the days of her life and worthy of Thy good Grace.'

He opened his Book of Common Prayer at its prepared place and began to read to them. ' "... they cried unto the Lord in their trouble: and he delivered them from their distress. He led them forth by the right way: that they might go to the city where they dwelt. O that men would therefore praise the Lord for his goodness: and declare the wonders that he doeth for the children of men!" '

He closed the book and looked at their bowed heads. 'You will all oblige me, and cleanse your own spirits, if this night you would devote part of your prayers to Mrs Watts, who has aye been a model of virtue and understanding to us all ...'

The doctor had dosed Mrs Watts heavily with laudanum but it worked only intermittently to stifle her interior pain. Her groans grew weaker by the hour and, just before the coming of the new day, she slipped quietly and peacefully into death. Cook, Gertrude and Mrs Edgecombe were by her side in the last hours. Mrs Edgecombe drew the linen sheet up and over her face after kissing her gently on her forehead. None spoke as the footmen took up station

242

outside the cottage to thwart body-snatchers, and the three women stumbled wearily to bed.

Gertrude had intended to leave the Captain's employ now that she was married to Luke Fossett but Mrs Edgecombe spoke strongly against the idea. 'You can live in the stable-yard cottage,' she said firmly, 'and continue with your employment here while your husband is away at sea. And if you're thinking of the other matter, well, when nature takes its course as inevitably it must since you both seem normal healthy souls, why, you can do your lying-in in greater comfort here with folks to look after you, and return to work when you are able.'

The idea represented unbelievable luxury to Gertrude for it meant she could stay in the Edgecombe house and still be a wife to Luke Fossett when he returned from over the sea. She accepted the post; all her food and clothing were to be provided, even when her man returned from sea. In addition she was to receive the incredible sum of five pounds per year. Not only would they be happy and comfortable – they'd also be rich!

The first three months went by rapidly, with Gertrude cleaning her new cottage from top to bottom to remove the unmistakeable odour of death that lingered in the rooms. Mrs Edgecombe permitted her to order new bedlinens; she polished all the woodwork until her arms ached but the surfaces shone like glass. Meanwhile she assumed the rank, if not yet the total dignity, of housekeeper, firm, severe, experienced enough in all the tasks the maids had to do to see immediately if any scrimped. Captain Edgecombe's Steward accepted her fully and there was none of the back-stairs tension that so often occurs in large houses. After her trial period of three months, Mrs Edgecombe sent for her and she stood demurely before her in the sitting-room, remembering all those years ago when first she'd stood there with trembling heart.

'You'd best start one of the maids to look to your

243

responsibilities,' she said, 'for I note you already have a handsome bloom to your cheeks.'

'Oh, ma'am. I am so sorry. . . '

'You needn't "oh ma'am" me, Gertrude,' Mrs Edgecombe said with mock severity. 'I've seen too many girls blush prettily as you blush now, and they without benefit of wedlock. How long has yon rascal been at sea?'

''Tis three months now, ma'am.'

'Aye, so it is, and the end of your probation. Well, if it's a satisfaction to you, the Captain and I are agreed you're to stay in your post as housekeeper. From henceforth I shall call you Missis Fossett, as befits your new station in life, and shall instruct the staff to do the same. Now, pray sit down, Missis Fossett, and do me the kindness to take tea with me. You may pour.'

When the ceremony, which Gertrude had often practised in the kitchen against this moment, was completed and Mrs Edgecombe was chewing at a piece of cake, she looked at Gertrude with a kindly eye.

'I imagine your mind was elsewhere,' she said, 'but I remember the day you were wed and two magpies flew over the house as you set out. That means you'll have mirth all your wedded life, you know.'

Gertrude hadn't known the local lore and was delighted.

'Aye, and you were married on a Wednesday, and that's the best day of all. Monday for health, Tuesday for wealth, and Wednesday the best day of all. You'll carry your child all through the cold winter to keep you warm, and be delivered of the mite in the spring, and that's a blessing, believe me. You'd best go to the draper tomorrow, to order cloth for your swaddling clothes, for you'll need them come spring-time.'

When Luke Fossett came home in the spring, he already had a fine son, Walter.

'I hope you approve the name,' Gertrude said fearfully. 'I couldn't leave the poor mite unchristened.'

Luke was too delighted with his new fatherhood to

concern himself with trifles; he'd jibbed a bit at first at the thought of living in Captain Edgecombe's cottage rather than seeking a place of their own, but then, he told himself sensibly, how many men could boast a wife prudent enough to provide them with free living, free food and five pounds a year. And give him a lusty babby to come home to, the spitting image of himself.

'Aye,' Gertrude said in response to his question, 'he does look like thee.'

He'd bent over the tub of water in the stable yard holding the child beside him, looking at their reflections side by side. 'You're the spitting image of thy dad, Walter,' he crowed in happiness.

One evening when Gertrude had carried their meal from the kitchen to their own cottage, so that they could eat together in solitude, he reached and took her hand as they seated themselves while she said prayers.

'Tha'rt a wonderful wife to me, Gertrude,' he said. 'And I want to try to do something for thee. Nay, don't interrupt me when I'm talking. I long to try to better myself in some way; I long to try to better our station in life. But I'll be damned if I know how.'

'You shouldn't curse at table, Luke,' she said, mildly reproving him. 'I know how, if you're interested to hear me speak?'

'I am that, lass.'

'I've been talking with Captain Edgecombe. He's of the opinion that since you have much time on your voyages when you're not on watch, you could use the opportunity to study for advancement. The Captain thinks you could become a mate, if you studied hard, and then, who knows, a captain with the command of your own vessel.'

'Nay, I'd never manage that,' Luke said. 'I can barely read and write, and do my sums.'

'The Captain says that is all you need to make a beginning. He has such a library of books up there and will help you learn them, I know. He's well-disposed towards you, Luke, very well-disposed. He seems to take a special

245

interest in anybody trying to better himself. We've a coin or two, now. You could buy some books for yourself, and a book box, to take on your next voyage. Just think, Luke Fossett, you could make yourself an educated man, the Captain of your own vessel sailing out of Whitby. I'd be that proud of you!'

He looked at her eager face, her firm devoted expression, her shining eyes urging him on.

'Dammit, I'll do it! You'll see, Mistress Fossett, I'll make thee proud of me yet!'

Peter Aysgill had been dressed most carefully – his clothing had been bought only after he'd spent long hours studying what gentlemen were wearing in this day of changing fashion, when what was suitable today could already be *démodé* by the morrow. His carriage had been called for seven o'clock and promptly, three minutes before the hour struck, his Steward came into the study to inform him. 'Your carriage awaits, Sire,' he said gravely.

'Thank you, Mister Willerby,' Peter replied. He knew that little love was lost between Willerby and himself. Willerby had served in the country houses of titled gentlemen; only the larger sum of money Aysgill paid him would keep him in a commoner's service. Willerby was a man with ideas greatly above his station, Peter knew, but he had much information of a practical nature to impart; Peter would extract every scrap of it before he discarded him.

'How do I look, Mister Willerby?' Peter asked. The green velvet ensemble had cost him all of twenty-five pounds with its braided coat, its lace-trimmed collar and cuffs, the breeches dropping fashionably low over white silk hose. He held his black ebony cane by its silver top as he twirled around.

'Very fitting, sir, for an Assembly at the home of Sir Ian Clether,' Willerby, a master of obfuscation, said.

Peter Aysgill realized that once again he'd been set down, bested by a damned lick-spittling steward. He'd have discharged the man instantly, but still had much need of him in the difficult times that lay ahead.

The Assembly at the Town House in Leeds of Sir Ian Clether was a most grand and brilliant affair, provincial no doubt by London standards – as several of the guests were later heard to observe – but still impressive. There must have been at least two hundred beeswax candles burning in the crystal chandeliers newly imported from the Continent. The food table was twenty paces long and piled high with all manner of comestibles, meats, fish, vegetables, all manner of fruits and pies, coffins of chicken and meats, partridges and pheasants, ducks with several sorts of forcemeat. Six footmen stood in blue and silver livery behind the table, helping guests to platters of the food which were carried in the hand, a skewer being provided with which to pick and eat the slivers and slices. The dining was in the latest 'buffet' style and considered most advanced. But then, Sir Ian was always advanced in his pursuits and pleasures, informed guests said knowingly.

Since the untimely death of his wife, Sir Ian kept his daughter Tessa beside him on these occasions. A large boned, rather plain girl, she made up in costume what she lacked in beauty, and jewels sparkled from her wig, her neck and her bodice like sprinklings of dew.

Peter advanced across the room after being greeted by Sir Ian and Tessa. He avoided the buffet since his confidence didn't yet extend in that direction and strolled, seemingly aimlessly, through the rooms of the grand house.

He stopped when suddenly he heard his name called: 'I say, Aysgill, is that you?'

He turned and found himself confronted by a figure he instantly recognized as Frederick, the man he'd seen climbing onto the coach all those years ago, the man to whom, he supposed, he owed his present prosperity. For wasn't it the observation of the Peabody/Frederick encounter that had emboldened him to strike for an arrangement with Shepley?

247

'Why, Mister Frederick. There's many a year I haven't set eyes on you.'

'There is that, Aysgill,' Frederick said with enthusiasm. 'Come, let's find a drink together away from all this gallivanting.'

The house had been built with an elaborate ballroom on the first floor; the sound of the orchestra playing, and the shuffle of feet, echoed through the adjacent rooms, drowning out the tones of fashionable voices in the social conversations that consisted in the main of gossip and scandal.

'I've been watching your progress since Shepley, God rest his soul, bested us in that deal. I don't know how you managed to do him down and take over his enterprise but I take my hat off to ye, for that was a strategy greatly to be applauded. Folks are talking about you, you know, saying you're becoming a commercial force to be reckoned with.'

'I have had the good fortune to be at the right places at the right times,' Peter said modestly.

'Aye, that's as may be, but you've done a few shrewd transactions and that will never *harm* a man's reputation in this city. 'Tis reckoned you're on your way to becoming a wealthy man, and there are those who'll set a cap at ye.'

Peter smiled. Finally, the burghers of Leeds were coming round to him, instead of his having to solicit them. It was a time for making money and none recognized it more clearly than he. It was a time when a hundred pounds ventured could return itself a hundred fold, given good management, a sharp eye and impeccable information. Now Peter employed three men where Shepley had employed only one, Peter, to carry out his spying work; none knew faster than he when a new venture was being floated; none knew more about the commercial, social, and sexual status of the participants than he did.

'I've a mind to put a proposition to you,' Frederick continued. His voice was unctuous, his manner seemed to indicate an ease of friendship, of mutual trust and opportunity. His glance, when he looked round the room in which they'd found a private corner in which to sip their cognac and talk, excluded all others in a private intimacy. 'Since we are both engaged in similar enterprises, I have a mind we'd carry far more weight if we were to join our forces . . .'

Peter chuckled to himself; he had guessed that Frederick intended to talk terms with him. It was Frederick's only way out of a situation in which he'd found himself by over-extension. So many of these men, he reflected, were greedy and spread their capital too thinly with no safe position to retreat to when an investment soured. He knew Frederick had invested much money in a prototype of a new spinning machine that could multiply the work of one person and supply the thread for a whole bank of Flying Jennies, instead of the present hand spinning method that employed six people to keep one Jenny working. The machine had not been a success; the engineer was an unpractical man, a dreamer who couldn't translate his drawings into reality. Frederick had backed him heavily and would see no return for his investment.

'You mean, partners?' he asked innocently.

'Aye, that's it, partners in a new enterprise. We could call it Aysgill and Frederick, though, since it's rightly my idea, it might look better to have my name come first . . .'

'Frederick and Aysgill. Aye, it has a ring to it, I suppose. But I thought you already had a partner in Mr Peabody . . .'

'Aye, well, Peabody didn't work out too well. He wasn't my sort at all.'

Peter knew that Peabody had been Frederick's only hope of salvation, since he was a cautious investor who studied matters much more carefully than Frederick did. Frederick often went at things like a bull at a gate. The two partners had finally fallen out over the morality of Frederick's committing Peabody funds to one of his more foolish enterprises. Peabody, Peter knew from his intelligence sources, had pulled out of the partnership and taken himself off to London.

'I think you and me, we'd get on much better,' Frederick said.

'My money and your brains, is that it?'

Frederick coloured. 'Nay, Maister Aysgill, I'd be bringing into the partnership a full inventory of investments. Aye, and a few lucrative patents that'll yield fortunes when they mature.'

Peter had been playing with Frederick, but now he'd seen his principal reason for coming to the Assembly approaching across the room. He started to slide from his seat. 'These are grave matters, Mr Frederick,' he said. 'I shall need to give them my fullest consideration. And now, sir, if you'll excuse me . . .'

'Well, I'll be damned!' Frederick said. 'What a boorish . . .'

Peter leaned towards him. 'Even the most rapid calculation, *Mister* Frederick, shows that you are at least forty thousand pounds in debt to the banks and the Jews, so I'd be careful whom you call boorish. Now, I bid you good-day!'

Sir Ian Clether, walking through the rooms, was very satisfied with the way the party was proceeding, with everyone seeming to enjoy himself. The dancing was well-attended and a popular innovation, the food table had been greatly admired before it was decimated. There must be at least two hundred people here, he thought, and could tell himself that no-one he had invited had stayed away. It'd be the talk of the Leeds social season and no doubt. If his present enterprises succeeded as well as they might, he really would have to think of buying one of the two Yorkshire seats in Parliament and opening a London house.

'Ah, yes, Aylesford, isn't it? Peter Aylesford?'

'Peter Aysgill, Sir Ian . . .'

'Ah, yes, Aysgill. How foolish of me not to remember. Aren't you the fellow who's taken over Shepley's place?'

'Yes, Sir Ian.'

'Tragic matter, that . . .' Sir Ian said, shaking his head

250

sorrowfully while his eyes flicked everywhere looking at his guests. 'Now, Mister Aysgill, if you'll excuse me. Good to see you here.' Sir Ian would have walked away had Aysgill not detained him.

'Sir Ian,' he said, 'I'd be obliged if you could grant me a couple of minutes of private conversation!'

Sir Ian, checked, looked surprised at the overt request.

'By all means, Aysgill. Some time soon, eh? Have a word with my Steward one of these days . . .'

'I meant, now, Sir Ian,' Peter said quietly.

'Oh, quite impossible, alas. I have duties to my guests.'

'I wanted to show you a letter from Mister Marquand giving instructions to the Captain of a vessel, the *Aphrodite*. That's what she's called now, though she was the *Leeds Daffodil* when she foundered at sea on her maiden voyage . . .'

Sir Ian knew immediately what he was talking about. 'Come with me,' he said tersely, and led the way across the rooms, raising his hand to greet a few people, but stopping to talk to none.

When they arrived in his study, surrounded by calf-bound volumes in shelves against the wall, Sir Ian threw himself into an easy chair and beckoned for Aysgill to begin. Peter sat down.

'Come on, man, out with it. What is it ye' want of me?' Sir Ian said.

Peter looked with distaste at the man slumped opposite him. His face had the dissolute look of a man who cares more for drink and food than for his appearance, a hedonist who relentlessly pursues the pleasures of the flesh. Peter's spies told him of seeing Sir Ian wager a thousand pounds on a cock-fight, squatting in the dust surrounding the ring urging the two birds to kill each other.

They'd told him of other things, too, which Peter held in reserve, like a trump card at whist.

'Do ye want money, is that it?'

Now that he had paid his large debts, Sir Ian was making

money from enterprises which people brought to him. He'd begun to realize that his previous error had been to involve himself in matters he didn't fully understand. Now he merely waited until people came to him with a proposition. He'd always had a shrewd eye for a villain, an honourable man, a man who could be bought and seduced, one who couldn't. Now he put it to use in the loaning of his capital, all of which was returning to him vastly multiplied.

'Anyway, what do ye know of the *Leeds Daffodil*?' he asked. He knew he'd summed up Aysgill a-right. This was a strong man, a man of some sort of principle, certainly, but a man prepared to see a thing through to the end, no matter how hard the way. He could tell at a glance that Aysgill stemmed from peasant stock, but then, so had so many people one met these days. It was usually a sign of strength and shrewdness.

'I have made it my business to know *all* about it,' Peter said. 'I have compiled a dossier on it which, following the return of my agents from Spain, is now complete. Alas, Sir Ian, some men are venal and, once bought, can be bought again for a higher sum. The Captain of the *Daffodil* is such a man. Though he now resides in Jerez in Spain, and has married a local lady despite the wife he already has in England, his memory of events is as keen as ever. I have an affidavit from him with his signature attested by a Spanish notary who, mercifully, cannot read English . . .'

'And this instruction from Marquand?'

'Mr Marquand cheated you, Sir Ian. When he told you the cloth had been sold cheaply for lack of provenance, he lied. It was sold in Paris for a respectable sum, and Marquand pocketed the difference on a forged Bill of Sale – 'tis an old trick.'

'And so is blackmail, Mr Aysgill. What are your terms? I presume the dossier of which you spoke is for sale? Together with the original materials, I trust?'

Peter was shaking his head and the smile on his face was huge. 'No, Sir Ian, it is not for sale, not even to you.'

'Then, dammit, what *do* you require of me?'

252

'I will give you the dossier, and all the original material, with my pledge never to speak of this matter again, on one condition.'

'And that is?'

'I've a mind to be married,' Peter said. 'I've amassed a tidy fortune. I have a neat house with good servants, carriages, horses, everything I require. Except a bride, someone to keep me company, to warm my bed at nights. Alas, Sir Ian, I do not have your taste for my own sex.'

Sir Ian sat bolt upright. 'That's a damned scandalous lie, Aysgill, and I'll have you thrashed for it!'

'It's not a lie, Sir Ian, since I hold the evidence of unimpeachable sources. And you will not have me thrashed. You'll offer me, of your own free will, the hand of your daughter, Tessa, in marriage. We will form an alliance, not only of our families, but also of our businesses. It can be named, Clether and Aysgill, if you have a mind, or perhaps you would prefer not to be visibly associated with such an enterprise, in which case we'll call it Aysgills.'

Sir Ian had slumped back in his chair, knowing himself to be defeated by this damned upstart tyke. Though society condoned all manner of libidinous sex practices, it frowned on people who had those practices exposed to the public scorn. His title, he knew, would prevent any possibility of a prosecution at the Assize but he would be tried and found wanting in the salons of his peers and his entrée taken from him. He would become a social outcast and that, to Sir Ian, would be worse than transportation to America. The other charge, he guessed he could get away with by attributing all to Marquand. He could play the role of the gullible gentleman who'd been deceived by a venal man of affairs. The two combined, however, would undo him.

'I could have thee done to death, Aysgill,' he said.

'You could, Sir Ian, 'tis true, but I fancy my judgement of character is not so amiss. There are things that even you, Sir Ian, would not do, and murder is one of them.

You will realize, of course, that the dossier of which I speak has been lodged in the safest place, to be opened and read in the event of my sudden demise.'

Sir Ian put both hands on the desk. 'Very well, Aysgill,' he said. 'I can see I have no choice in the matter. Now tell me, what sort of a man are you? Tell me a little about yourself and your interests, your beliefs and convictions, for I'm to get to know something about you afore I offer you to my daughter as her future husband. You'll want an early wedding, I presume?'

Peter laughed. 'Far from it, Sir Ian. First I would like to join our business interests to our mutual benefit and satisfaction.'

The wedding of Peter Aysgill to Tessa, daughter of Sir Ian Clether, was the highlight of the Leeds 1755 social season. Their business affairs had greatly prospered in the years of the betrothal, and Aysgill and Clether was one of the most active, if not the richest, merchant houses of the city. Sir Ian had no cause for complaint on the score of business; Peter had used the prestige of the Clether name to great advantage and now they were virtually acting as a private bank, loaning money to other merchants, taking shares in enterprises, supporting new developments in the industrial field. Peter had always felt that mechanization of some of the common processes would come sooner than expected. He realized Frederick had been on the right track when he'd backed the spinning invention, but had foolishly allowed himself to be dragged in too deep, with too little capital. Peter estimated, also, that the new growth would need sources of new energy, and had backed the Newcomen steam engine with a factory making them in Hunslet, the Aysgill and Clether Steam Engine Works.

Little had changed in his home life; before his marriage he'd moved to a larger house in the same residential district and now had a four-storey home with a gabled front entrance, a stable yard and carriage house. He had refused any attempt at ostentation though all his windows contained clear glass in leaded lights. He knew that, somehow, Tessa had discovered the background to their betrothal and despised him for it and for his humble origins. He didn't care about that. He had not married her for love or convenience but for the opportunity to associate himself with her much respected family name.

At first she had asked, in her autocratic voice, to be given her own quarters including her own bedroom; he'd compromised by allowing her to install a bed of sorts in her dressing-room, to be used when she was unwell, as she delicately put it, but for the majority of the time he insisted they share a common bedroom.

He quickly realized that he had little appetite for sexual matters, but made a point of exercising his husbandly prerogative at regular intervals. For her part Tessa responded without emotion; he knew she had not been a virgin when he married her, but could hardly blame her for that considering the godlessness of her father and the home in which she'd been brought up. Her mother had been dead for many years and her father had shown no inclination to remarry.

On one thing Peter had insisted, and for many months had engaged two footmen to follow Sir Ian everywhere he went. When he tried to sneak incognito into a brothel in Meanwood noted for the variety of the sexual diversions it offered, including small boys, he'd found his way barred by the two. After a few such incidents, he realized that such places were out of bounds to him. One day he tackled Peter in the office, charging him with unwarranted interference in his private life, but Peter was quite adamant. 'What you do in the privacy of your home, Sir Ian, has nothing to do with me, but I'll not have my father-in-law dragging our family through the gutters of low bawdy houses.' Now, when Sir Ian was so inclined, he travelled to London, leaving the business more and more in his son-in-law's capable hands.

He had no reason to fear; Peter Aysgill had retained all of his peasant cunning and had combined it with a shrewd business ability. This plus his unscrupulous method of gathering scraps of information and putting them together in the way of business intelligence, made him a force to be reckoned with. He never used his information directly, but hoarded it and only brought it out to assist him in making decisions. 'I don't know how Aysgill does it,' businessmen in Leeds would say admiringly and, it should be said, with envy, 'but nothing goes on without his knowledge.'

By now he had suborned a host of people – the footmen in the Assembly Rooms were not above earning a coin by giving him information, the pot boys in the ale-houses, even the coachmen on the Flyer, who could hear privileged conversations taking place in the coach interior behind them much better than any of the passengers ever knew.

In only one way was he constantly bested and slighted. Despite having married Tessa and having the entry to all the high-class salons and meeting places, he could still be wounded by a reminder of his past. 'Oh, Aysgill the peasant', was always enough to injure him, to hurt his self-esteem. Even Tessa used it sometimes in moods of high dudgeon, and suffered the consequence of blows to the face that kept her out of circulation for days, until the bruises had healed.

One day he was sitting in his office in the building they had taken in Boar Lane when one of his footmen breached Percy's screen and was admitted to see him.

'Sir,' he said, obviously having ridden hard for his livery was spattered with mud, 'we have been obliged to bring the doctor to madam.'

Aysgill left the office hurriedly, mounted the horse his footman had brought for him, and headed northward through the busy streets, cursing the people who got in his way, beating them aside with his stick like a man demented.

He dashed into the house when he leaped from the horse in the stableyard, and upstairs to his wife's dressing-room, guessing they would have lain her there for the doctor's inspection. He dispelled the knot of girls on the upper landing with a curse and burst into the room. His wife was lying back in bed with Mrs Lakeham, their housekeeper, and Jenny, her personal maid, standing beside her. The doctor was bending over a tub containing foul smelling liquid; when he saw Aysgill he tried, ineffectually, to cover it.

'What is it, doctor?' Peter demanded harshly of him.

'I think everything will be all right now,' the doctor said, dissimulating to the best of his ability.

'That's not what I asked. What is, or was it?'

The doctor didn't know what to say but glanced at the servants. Aysgill dismissed them with a wave of his hand and waited until the door had closed behind them. 'Well, Doctor, now will you speak, dammit?'

'It would appear, Mr Aysgill,' the doctor said, mustering his professional dignity, 'that, quite by accident I am sure, your wife had swallowed a quantity of some noxious infusion, which had poisoned her. Fortunately the housekeeper was able to recognize the misfortune and summoned me promptly. I was able to administer an emetic in time and now your wife's stomach has been voided. I do not think there will be any further results of this unfortunate error, though your wife will be quite exhausted and in a condition of weakness for some time to come. She will need much care and attention, and nourishing broths would be of the greatest assistance. You may also give her a little wine from time to time . . . Now I bid you good-day.'

He had put his phials back into the leather bag he carried for the purpose; he snapped the bag shut and left the room. Aysgill didn't bid him good-bye; he stood beside the bed looking down at his wife, watching the beads of sweat trace a path across her aristocratic upper lip. Her face was flushed and damp with her endeavours; he saw the puffiness beneath her eyes and her straggly hair, wet with sweat, fell in disorder about her. He felt no feelings of compassion for her, only regret that he hadn't appreciated how foolish she could be, and how headstrong.

'The doctor's gone now and we're alone.' he said. 'You can open your eyes.'

She did so and looked up at him; he had never seen such hatred, not even on Shepley's face that last day of his life.

'Why?' he asked her. 'Why did you try to take your own life?'

There was a strong vein of madness in her, of a wild passion he had not seen before, and a loathing for him. 'It wasn't my own life I was trying to take,' she shrieked, 'It was the life of your damned unborn peasant brat growing within me! And would have, too, if the sawbones, damned be his hide, hadn't arrived too soon . . .'

Book Four

Simon Aysgill came from Mill Cottages before the sun was up and walked slowly along the cobbled streets past ghostly figures huddled against the cold, seeking the shelter of the buildings against the cutting morning wind. He walked slowly past the mill that had become so much a part of their lives in the recent years; icicles hung from the overhanging roof and the first rays of the sun flashed coloured lights from them and gave a touch of beauty to the drab façade of the building. Hoar frost clung to the bushes on the waste ground beside the road on the way down to the river; Simon turned left towards what was locally called the Moor, leaving the already thronged streets behind him. The moor was not the wide expanse such as he'd known a few miles from Barthwick in his youth, where the lads used to go to snare rabbits, play knurr and spell, while the lasses walked past in company showing occasional smiles from beneath their bright country bonnets; Hunslet Moor housed cock-fights and was the haunt of footpads and evil doers, and no woman, or man of quality, would ever risk being there later in the day.

As he climbed onto the moor, he passed a tinker making his morning meal on a fire beside his cart, his horse already harnessed and eating from a hay bag, his children sprawled on the ground around him sucking on knuckle bones he'd taken from the brewis, his wife sitting on the edge of the cart with her arms folded over her ample child-bearing stomach. When the day had begun, they'd go down into the streets seeking pots to repair, selling their plaited straw ware, the kids thieving if the opportunity presented itself.

Many tinkers trained their children to be nimble fingered at cutting a pursestring, or lifting a watch.

'Good morning to ye,' the tinker said with the cheeriness habitual to members of his craft.

Simon didn't reply – not from rudeness but because he was occupied with his own thoughts, weighed down by his own despair.

The years had dealt unkindly with him and already, in this year of 1756, he looked twenty years older than his forty years. His cheeks had sunk in on his skull and his hair, untidied, had the consistency of dank straw. He'd lost most of his bottom teeth and those that remained were browned and blackened stumps since often he couldn't afford the salt to rub them with, and was idle with a tooth stick.

A thin sheet of ice covered the dew pond high on the moors. It was surrounded by natural banks and trees, and the water in the centre was at least eight feet deep. No-one ever knew how minnows and sticklebacks found their way into such a pond but they were there in profusion and Simon's ten-year-old son Arthur used to try to catch them, when he wasn't working in the mill to earn a coin to supplement the family's earnings.

Simon turned and looked back and saw Hunslet spread before him, coming rapidly to life. Smoke was pouring from the chimney on the roof of the Mill, casting its pall over the surrounding streets, throwing its soot onto the house roofs. Even up here, he could hear the clatter and the cacophony of the carts already being dragged over the cobbles, the noise of the water-wheel of the mill, the crowing of cockerels, the fretful fitful mooing and bellowing of the animals condemned to spend their lives in stalls until, standing ankle deep in their own mire, they failed to give milk and were taken to the butcher's shambles to be slaughtered. He couldn't forget the life of the country, the days he'd spent behind their simple plough tilling the soil. He saw the face of his father again, already a benign old man when they were young lads, and recalled the kindly rhythm of country life that compared so starkly with the hectic clatter and pace of life in a stinking city where a man couldn't breathe, couldn't fill his lungs for fear of coughing to death or inhaling some foul pestilence. Two people had died of a plague in the Cottages only a three-month ago.

The future stretched before him, bleak and hopeless. He knew that now he'd never have the opportunity to better himself. He had become a dried-out husk, or so he told himself, lacking the energy or the opportunity to make anything better of himself as his brother Peter, his sister Gertrude and, to a lesser extent, Matthew and Dodie had done.

Now he took the jar he'd carried up the hill and drank deep from the gin it contained. Now that ale-houses were being taxed, he could no longer afford ale, even if he had any money. He'd filled the jar with gin for a penny he'd taken from Amelia's purse without her knowing. When she found out, she'd scold him again in what he thought was becoming her shrewish voice. When he'd drunk the last of the gin and could feel its strength flowing through his head and the confidence it gave him, he set the jar down then slowly walked down the slope and into the pond, cracking the thin coating of ice; it crunched under his feet and against his legs as he moved forward, against his waist and chest, finally against his face and the top of his head as he went under.

The tinker had been leaving Leeds, not entering it. When his family had eaten breakfast, which he always liked to take before they set out on the track to their next destination, he settled them aboard the cart and then, with a cheery whistle, followed the path up and into the Moor, walking beside the horse's head, a man at peace with the world of his own choosing. When he reached the summit of the short incline he turned and looked back over the city. Leeds had been good to him and he'd earned a useful sum of money, as well as the sacks of oats he'd bartered.

He fingered the gold watch in his pocket; that would sell for a tidy sum in Wakefield, he told himself – his oldest girl at thirteen was a dab hand at wheedling the bucks eager to plunge a hand into her amply filled bodice, captivated by her rogueish eyes. Mother Douglas would give a fair price, he knew, to take her into the Covent Garden brothel when next they went to London.

He saw the gleam of the pond through the trees and stopped the cart. 'Take the skin, Nellie,' he commanded, 'and fill it wi' watter for the journey. There's nowt like dew for slaking a man's thirst!'

Nellie leaped from the cart clutching the bladder in which they carried water hanging from the back of the cart to keep its contents cool.

'And wash thysen *after* tha's filled the skin – tha might make us a coin or two in the next ale-house – happen tha can pay us a meal on thy back.'

He settled himself on the ground, his ever-busy hands plaiting a snaffle for the horse with strips of pig-skin. When he heard his daughter's shout, he turned and ran over the mound to the side of the pond. 'What ails thee, lass?' he said, looking to where she was pointing but seeing nothing but what seemed to be a log floating on the water midst the cracked ice top.

'It's a man, Father,' she shouted.

He went down and stood beside her. Now he could see the arm floating beside the body, which lay face down. 'Fetch a bit of rope, Alfie,' he shouted.

Alfie and the others had already started down the bank when they'd heard Nellie's shouts; one of them ran back and brought a coil of twisted hemp. The tinker weighted the end with a flat stone and cast it over the body; its weight was sufficient to float the body slowly nearer to the bank until they could drag it ashore.

'Quick, see if there's owt in't pockets,' the tinker said.

The pockets were empty; the tinker looked down at the remains of Simon Aysgill, recognizing the man who'd passed him a short while ago. 'Are we going to take him down to't hospital?' Nellie asked. 'They'd give us a sovereign for the body, down there.'

'Nay,' the tinker said. 'He's but recently dead. They'd say we'd pushed him in and lay an information with the magistrate, to avoid having to pay our money. We'll leave him – somebody's bound to come by, ere long. Meanwhile, let's put as much distance between ourselves and this place as we can.'

Several of the merchants of establishments in Hunslet had combined to build and finance a Charity School, with yearly endowments drawn from rentings of premises that had been made over to the School Board, on which three local dignitaries, including the vicar of the church, sat. The school, however, was managed by Titus Waverley, an educated son of a gentleman from Wakefield who'd been obliged by a small scandal to leave his father's home. The school had a yearly provision of uniform for five boys which included a blue hat, blue coat and trousers with waistcoat, one pair of shoes, two shirts, two neckcloths, two pocket handkerchiefs and two pairs of stockings.

The school building comprised a teaching room some twenty feet in length and twelve in width, a study for the Master, a dormitory for the boys, and an outside wash-house. Next door was the Master's own house, which also contained his office and the school dining-room.

The teaching room had long desks at which the boys were permitted to sit on a bench. The desk had separated tops with a drawer beneath each section in which the boys kept their books and writing utensils. There was a metal inkwell let into the desktop, filled with ink made from boiled walnut skins, brown/black in tint. Each boy was responsible for maintaining his own quill and each had a knife in a sheath for that purpose.

Dodie Aysgill saw the building start, and watched it grow each day as she passed on her way to work. The new school occupied many of her thoughts as she worked her loom all day; her three children had been born in 1750, '51 and '53, and she was determined that the two older ones, the boys Stanley and Claude, would have an education. The school seemed to be her only hope of providing one for them. She was already teaching them what little she could on the Sunday, and at six years of age Stanley could already read slowly and write a passable hand. Claude, at five, was more slow in learning and often fell asleep over his books to be woken by his mother's angry scolding.

'You'll bless me hereafter,' she said sternly. 'You can be nothing unless you have an education in this life. You'll never have a fine house with a carriage, like your Uncle Peter.' Uncle Peter was always held up to them as an example of virtue and diligence; they'd never actually seen him and, on their occasional walks past his fine house, had never even ventured inside the gate.

'If you can read and write so well, Mother, why don't you have a fine house and a carriage?'

Dodie would look round their house, which she contrived still to keep clean, and sigh, for no-one could call it *fine*. 'Aye,' she'd say, 'your Father is a wonderful man, but he does lack ambition.'

Mark had matured into a contented man, going each day to his work in the foundry, returning late at night when his work was done to sit by his hearth, listening to the children prattle, watching as Dodie prepared their evening meal. Old Missis Scobie who lived next door was content to earn her food and rent by looking after the children while Dodie went to work to earn her mite in the mill. Mark felt he lacked for nothing; he had work to go to, a loving wife, and food in his belly; a man who demanded more was a malcontent. He knew Dodie was not happy with this life and scratted and scrimped to put a few coins by. She was still a most handsome woman with a finely developed figure; child-bearing had enhanced her natural beauty rather than making a drudge of her – if anything she looked much younger than her thirty-eight years and could still turn a head or two.

When Dodie looked at her children, especially the

youngest, Caroline, she never regretted her decision to have them. The sight of Simon's son, Arthur, and of Matthew and Mildred's family of two boys, had proved too much for her motherly instinct. She'd wanted to save money, to try to find a way to better themselves without the burden of young ones, but now she didn't regret them. Though they did try her patience when they fell asleep over their books . . .!

If only she could get them into that school. Well, at least, the two boys – Caroline was pretty enough that she wouldn't need an education to make her way in life. Dodie had never wanted anything as passionately as to get her two sons into the Charity School; she absorbed every word she could hear about it and became more excited when she learned they were to admit a few children of the poorer classes, to teach them reading, writing and arithmetic. With that much knowledge, the boys would be able to go anywhere, could start in an office in the city the way her brother Peter had, could aspire to reach his great heights. It was a dream that sustained her during her long hours of drudgery at the mill. She'd watched the school finally finished, had stood with all the others when the fine-robed men came to make speeches, when the first five pupils were shown to the public in their neat blue clothing. One day, she dressed herself with great care in her good clothing, including the cloak she'd made all those years ago from the piece of wool she'd persuaded her father to let her have. Her tightly bodiced dress showed her still firm figure to good advantage, her bonnet was clean and well pressed.

'Where are *you* going, my dear?' old Missis Scobie had asked with a cackling leer. 'Off to see some fancy man, I'll be bound.'

'Fancy man,' Dodie snorted. 'At my age, wi' three bairns?'

She hoisted her skirt as she walked along the pavements towards the school, not wanting to arrive travel-stained by mud. People jostled her as she passed along the crowded street, and many cast bold glances in her direction. She had to step frequently into doorways to avoid being splashed by the passing horses drawing carts and even carriages. Though she went quickly she avoided hurrying too much since she didn't wish to arrive flustered and dishevelled.

Titus Waverley was in the teaching room with his charges when he saw the woman halt at the gate that led to the front door of his house. Intrigued, he stood at the leaded panes and observed her as she walked up to the front door and boldly pulled the bell. She was a fine figure of a woman, he had to admit, as he wondered what she was doing calling unescorted on him.

'Keep at your books,' he said out loud. 'I shall chastise any who makes noise before my return!' He left the teaching room and crossed the connecting corridor, opening the front door of his house to confront his visitor. 'You come at a bad time,' he said, 'when my servants are both out at market, acquiring victuals for the boys.'

'I am sorry to disturb you during your instruction,' she said. He was impressed by her firm manner, by her directness, which was not presumptuously bold but quite respectful. 'Come along in, ma'am, I beseech you,' he said. 'For 'tis a cold morning to converse on doorsteps.'

She came past him and he smelled the delicate lavender on her; he showed her into his office and offered her a seat before his desk. His manners, she thought, were quite exquisite. How she longed to see her sons taught such fineness and elegance.

'On which subject did you wish to speak?' he asked when she was seated comfortably, though somewhat perched on the edge of the chair.

'On the education of my two sons,' she said, 'who are aged six years and five. They are well-mannered boys, sir, and despite the humbleness of our station, have been educated to fear God and respect authority. I myself have given them the rudiments of language, and they can spell out the alphabet and even read and write. Of arithmetic, alas, I have little, save what needs for domestic reckoning.'

He looked at this strange lady sitting opposite him. He

268

himself was forty-five and estimated she could not be much younger than he, though she held herself like a younger lady and certainly had a mature beauty. 'I find it hard to countenance,' he said, 'that you have two *sons* of schoolable age? You appear so young.'

She accepted his flattery, bowing her head and attempting to blush, though it had been many a long moon since a man's overtures had brought the bloom to her cheeks. At least she knew she had achieved the effect she wished, had caught his eye in a personal way.

'You must not embarrass me, sir,' she said, 'for I'm a respectable married lady. It is my belief that there are opportunities for boys to be educated here?'

He shook himself as if trying to come quickly from reverie. 'There are indeed opportunities,' he said. 'I am permitted to take in as many fee-paying scholars as I can teach, to give myself an income.'

'Fee-paying?'

'Aye. School-pence. You understand that the Endowment of the school gives me no income, only my board and lodging. I am obliged to earn for myself by asking modest fees of as many as possible. I could take your boys, aye, and most willingly, but I'll be obliged to ask ninepence a week for each of them!'

Dodie's heart sank. She had known that education would be expensive but had not envisaged it would be *so* expensive. She made a quick mental calculation; the coins in her pot would last, at most, three months. After that, there would be no possibility of sparing *two* ninepences each week from the pittances she and Mark earned.

'I fear I am spending your time rashly,' Dodie said sadly, 'for there is no possibility we could afford such a sum of money.'

''Tis but a modest amount, Ma'am,' he said. She could not know how desperately he was fighting within himself. Though nothing of it, he hoped, was apparent in his mien, he had found her so attracting, so stimulating to his earthly manly feelings. Once again he felt the fires of lust, which he

269

had hoped banked after his disgrace and dismissal from his parental home for offences against his father's maids, rise fiercely within him. 'Oh, God,' he prayed silently, 'help this Thy tormented servant in his hour of need!'

The lady seated opposite him leaned forward and his eyes burned at the cleft between her well-endowed breasts. He began to find it difficult to breathe, to keep his composure. He bent his head forward and clasped his hands to his temple. 'Oh God,' he prayed.

'Sir,' she said, her voice low and most appealing. 'I have a lust to see my boys educated that gainsays all thoughts of prudence. It is a desperate hunger within me that overcomes all other considerations!'

He opened his eyes, saw those twin orbs so close to him, looked up into her face.

'Madam,' he said hoarsely, 'you tempt me most sorely to accede to your request. I am but a human man, who can give but must take in equal measure. I have a desire for thee that, now that I have clapped eyes on thee, will give me no peace till I take thee into my arms.'

'And to thy bed, sir?' she asked quietly.

'Aye, I must confess myself . . .'

Dodie had ever been a practical woman; that no advantage could ever be gained without an equivalent sacrifice had been her conviction since she had left Barthwick. She knew men for what they were, the victims of appetites and lusts they could rarely control. This much and more she had learned as a young girl from Fanny Colborn and Polly at the Manor. Even as moral and kindly a man as Lord Barthwick himself had not been above cocking a leg over Polly when the desire was upon him. As Lord of the Manor it was his right and he could not be gainsayed. In the urgent matter of the schooling, Titus Waverley could be considered the Lord of his Manor, and could not be gainsayed. Dodie's only concern was that she should obtain the best price for the only commodity she possessed with which she could bargain – herself.

'Since you are being so forthright, sir,' she said, 'I must

270

be equally so. I have a lust to see my sons educated. You have a lust that perhaps I can assuage . . .'

'Madam,' he said, tormented, 'I implore you to save me from my dishonour.'

If only she would be outraged . . . If only she would leave . . . If only she would remove herself from his eyes . . .

'Where is the dishonour, sir? I would count myself a poor thing indeed if I no longer possessed the ability to appeal to the natural desires of a gentleman of breeding and discernment. Come, sir, we are mature people, neither in the first impetuous hasty gallop of youth; should we not both advantage ourselves by striking a bargain?'

He groaned again, knowing he was lost. In truth her manner of speech and her voice were as seductive as the rich ripeness of her form. 'Aye, ma'am,' he said with despair. 'Should we not both advantage ourselves? I'll give your lads the benefit of my knowledge . . .'

'And I pledge you, sir, the best of my ability, for I have scant knowledge of the ways of the world of gentlemen, save that one can always count upon their discretion and reliability in matters of arrangement.'

'I'll not renege on you, ma'am,' he said brusquely. 'A bargain is a bargain only when each side honours the pledge. You'll not find me wanting.'

'Nor you me, sir. There's my hand on it.'

'Yon lips would serve me better,' he said with evident hunger.

'And so they shall, sir, so they shall, when my lads are conning their books.'

'Why am I a Methodist?' the man said, his powerful voice carrying over the crowd to the faint-hearted folks standing at the back. 'Why do they call me a *Methodist*?'

He looked out from the knoll on which he was standing over the Hunslet Moor, gratified that so many people had come to listen to him preach. Jonas Sotherby had assembled a good local group of loyal workers, he thought, if they could pull out a hundred people on a

271

Sunday, the only free day most of them had for resting after the week's labours. More and more he saw that people wanted to hear his alternative message; more and more people were becoming disenchanted with the conventional church, which seemed only to care for its own. How often he had encountered the antagonism of the local clergy, who saw in his popularity a challenge to themselves in their easy going ways of privilege.

'I am a Methodist,' he said, 'because when my brother Charles and I were students at Oxford's great University, we realized even then that a love of the Lord could not support a man who didn't put some of his own effort and energy into thinking about his fellow man. My brother and I used to meet in what doubting students called 'The Holy Club.' They meant it disparagingly, but we took it as a compliment, a testament to our faith. And we worked out a timetable for the meetings of the Holy Club. We arranged our lives *methodically*, so that we could better serve the Lord efficiently. We had *method*, and that is why they call us *Methodists*. Now, of course, people are starting to use my name, and call us Wesleyans. *I do not mind what people call us, so long as they listen to us*!'

Matthew and Mildred stood side by side in the front rank of people thronging the moor to listen to John Wesley. Here, Matthew thought, is the answer. This was the second time he'd heard John Wesley preach and he was enflamed by the man's simple message. This was no fox-hunting preacher more concerned with keeping in with the Lord of the Manor than in ministering to the poorer parishioners. This was no bishop who rarely, if ever, saw his See. This was a man who carried his message to the people where the people congregated, not in cold barren churches.

Several times Matthew had engaged the Reverend John Shipton, his early benefactor, in conversation, asking him why *he* did nothing to halt the abuses of the Broadley family, the enslavement of the workmen, their use of women and children in degrading jobs. Each time John Shipton had used words to avoid the issue, had preached

272

to Matthew that he must be humble, that he mustn't speak out against the established order of things. More and more, Matthew had become dissatisfied with John Shipton, and his own local parson's approach to religion. When he'd heard John Wesley, who'd largely abandoned the churches and carried his message to where men worked, to where men lived and congregated, he'd realized that this was not a man who would compromise for a coin, as Shipton had done.

'They ought to call you the Antichrists,' a voice from the back bellowed. 'You're nothing but devils trying to pull down the established Church, to destroy it with your loose talk. No wonder you travel the country. Nowhere will have you twice in a row.'

The murmur from the back of the crowd grew louder.

'Ignore them,' John Wesley said. 'Wherever we go to preach we find a few lost souls who haven't yet found their way into the Brotherhood of Man in Jesus Christ.'

Matthew and Mildred turned round to see the source of the fracas at the back, and were astounded to see a group of men from the local parish church.

'I want to tell you about that Brotherhood,' John Wesley said, his strong voice carrying over the crowd. He was not to be shouted down by one group of malcontents, his stance said. Nor would he descend to their level of abuse.

'The Brotherhood of men is no club reserved exclusively for the rich, for the privileged, for the high-born . . .'

A billet of wood, skilfully aimed from the back of the crowd, came sailing across the heads of those in front and struck him on the chest. He was visibly shaken by it but he made an effort to recover and continue.

'It has been my rule,' he said firmly, 'confirmed by long experience, always to look a mob in the face. A few loud voices and billets of wood, coming always from the hiding place at the back of a number of faithful listeners, will not frighten me, nor cause me to be silent, for I know Jesus Christ, and he compels me to speak!'

It was apparent to Mildred that the rowdies at the back

of the crowd would not permit him to carry on, as other billets of wood began to rain over their heads onto the knoll. Slowly, she started to sing. Matthew heard her, and he sang too. He held his two sons' hands in his, and they sang the well-known hymn whose hopeful words had been written by the brother of this divine who stood before them. The folks immediately about them heard them, and they too sang. Gradually the sound rose from the front and rolled back through the crowd. John Wesley himself, recognizing what was happening, began to sing in his melodious voice, and the words of his brother, poet Charles, echoed over the moor. 'Gentle Jesus, meek and mild . . .'

A better aim than most smashed a billet like an arrow across their heads, hitting John Wesley in his face. They all saw the blood spurt, and then he was down. Now the turbulence from the back developed into a brawl in which the Church interlopers were at an advantage since they'd prepared themselves for the encounter with clubs. They laid about them, hitting heads, intent only on fighting a path through to the platform, where, doubtless, they would have killed the preacher they had dubbed the Anti-Christ in their ignorance and fear. There were about thirty of them, and not all were from the Church. Matthew knew bullies and hucksters were sometimes paid a coin to break up the Methodist meetings, usually urged on by the local clergy, who saw a danger to their easy way of life in the rallying cries of the Methodists, now pulling more and more people to their support. He turned to face the rowdies and linked arms with Mildred, pushing his sons behind him towards the knoll. Others saw what they were doing and they linked arms to form a solid barrier between the rowdies and the fallen preacher, who was being tended by two of his disciples. The mercenaries didn't have the heart to lay into women and children of that solid wall of folks; they knew they had set out to do what they were paid for by breaking up the meeting in disorder. The church folk, infinitely more fanatical, laid about them with their clubs. Some of the mercenaries had thrown their clubs down and the Methodist supporters grabbed them and began to assail the church folk. Soon the fight had spread outwards into a number of small pockets and here the superior numbers of those who had been listening to John Wesley began to tell.

One churchman, however, recognizing Matthew, screamed at him and came charging forward with his blackthorn club; before Matthew could disengage his arms from those beside him the club had hit him on the cheek breaking the skin and causing the blood to flow. Mildred went for the churchman like a wild cat, her fingers raking his face, the work-broken edges of her fingernails drawing weals in his skin that sprang with blood. Others went in, kicking the churchman's legs, hitting his shoulders, pummelling him unmercifully until he managed to turn round and run away defeated.

Mildred picked Matthew from the ground where he'd fallen under the impact of the blow. Her eyes were flashing and sparkling. 'Aye, that were grand,' she said. 'That bit of violence will win more converts for John Wesley than all the words in the world . . .'

Arthur Aysgill, Simon's son, was only eleven years of age when he was given his first opportunity to do an adult's work, though Thomas Tomlinson, the overseer who had hired his father all those years ago and now had moved to be head overseer at the mill, would pay him only a boy's wages.

'There 'tis, lad,' he'd said. 'I'll start thee on a machine. If tha shapes up I'll give thee a man's wage. But first tha'll have to show me tha can do a man's job.'

Amelia protested when Arthur told her at home that night what had been agreed. 'Nay,' she protested weakly, 'they ought to have set thee on a bit better than that. Thy father would never have agreed . . .'

More and more as she thought about Simon, she endowed him with qualities he had never possessed. She forgot that he had basically been a weak person, with little

275

ability to fend for himself, revealing the aspect of the Aysgill character that had flawed John Aysgill of Barthwick. She knew that Simon's brother Peter had been right when he'd refused to give Simon a loan, and had asserted he wouldn't have loaned money to his father, John. She knew that if Simon had taken over the carter's business he would not have made a success of it. Every time he'd been paid for a load he would have gone into the nearest ale-house and, with money in his pocket, would have treated everyone in sight to a pot of ale.

'Tha moan be stronger,' she said to Arthur. 'Tha mun stick up for thysen. Tha moan't be overgenerous. Look after thysen first. Be prudent, and set a sum by – not that there'll be owt left over from the bairn's mite they're paying thee. Above all, keep thy hand in thy pocket.'

Arthur's job at the mill was to run the fulling machine, which took the woven woollen cloth and pounded it under water with fuller's earth to make the threads stick together and to shrink them. The machine, which could accept a full six-feet width of the cloth on a roller, was run by the power of the water-wheel, which also supplied the necessary deluge of water. The hammers, each a foot round, were lifted and dropped by a system of rods worked from the shaft of the wheel to rise and fall as the cloth slowly moved along under the tension of Arthur's winding. At the same time as he had to maintain the heavy turning of the roller handle, he had to ensure that sufficient of the fuller's earth mixed with the water in the fulling trough to fix the threads together. There were twelve hammers, each going up and down every few seconds, thumping the cloth solidly against the heavy oaken base-board six inches thick. When a piece of cloth came off the roller, Arthur had to work swiftly to take away the roller, which weighed at least fifty pounds, and to substitute another which weighed upwards of a hundred and fifty. He rapidly became adept at engaging one end of the roller in the semi-circular slot designed to accept it, and lifting the other with one heave to drop it into its own slot, remembering always to move his hands quickly away lest they be trapped between roller and slot. Then he had to go along the two edges of cloth with his bodkin, sewing them coarsely together so that the cloth already in the fulling machine would drag the new cloth after it. If any of his coarse stitching was not properly done and the two sections of cloth parted under the drag of the drawing wheel, he'd have to leap into the mud of the trough and connect the two again, while the water and fuller's earth splashed around him. He knew that the overseer was watching him constantly, measuring his work according to the length of cloth he was able to full during a working day.

The pounding of the hammers never ceased except when he had to slacken the collar on the driving shaft to stop the hammers so that he could climb into the frame when a piece of cloth ruched and would have been spoiled. Each time the hammers were stopped the lack of noise permeated the other noises of the mill and the overseer would come to find out what had happened. 'Tha'll have to keep the hammers working, Arthur,' he'd say severely, 'if tha expects me to consider paying thee a man's wages.'

Arthur thought he had the answer to the problem. 'Aye, Mr Tomlinson,' he said, 'if I could nobbut have another lad here, or a strong lass, to help lift the rollers and to piece them together more slowly. Then we'd never need to stop the hammers at all . . .'

'*Another* lad, Arthur? Art telling me tha can't cope with the work, is that it? Art telling me the job's too much for thee? If that's the case, I can soon set somebody else on as can manage it by hisself, I'll be bound!' Thomas Tomlinson was a God-fearing man who regarded it as his God-given duty to stamp out the evils of self-indulgence in any of the people who worked at the mill. We're put on this earth to work, was his conviction, and that meant, to work as hard as we could for as long as we could. A regular attender at Church on the Sabbath, he regarded the great mass of folk who never went there as heathens, with sloth, laziness, greed and self-indulgence as their greatest sins.

277

He put it down, of course, to the breakdown of family life, to the excessive migration caused by greed. People weren't content, he told himself, to accept their station in life but must always seek to improve themselves. People had a hunger that amounted to greed in that matter. He himself had a family of nine children, and had taught each to be God-fearing, to say prayers at night and morn, to respect their parents. Each was being given instruction in reading and writing, but only the boys were being taught anything else. None of them would ever come into the mill, of course, but that was only a matter of discipline – he wouldn't like the owner to think he was favouring anyone by setting on his own.

'Tha mun learn, Arthur,' he said, 'to move a bit more sharply. To stop wasting time and energy in playing foolish games when tha breaks for thy snap. Many an Owner would make thee take thy snap at the machine. Bless the Lord tha works for a lenient master as lets thee take a quarter of an hour in the middle of the day so use the time more wisely. I know it's no good asking thee to bow thy head in prayer and gratitude for the good life tha's been given wi' paid employment and the benefice of a cottage to live in, but tha ought to sit quiet and gather thy strength for the rest of the day, rather than laiking about wi' the others i' the yard. The way to advancement don't come through laiking about, Arthur. It comes through sticking to thy job, to working hard for thy master. Aye, and following thy Uncle Matthew into the Church would do thee no harm!'

'As you say, Mr Tomlinson,' Arthur said meekly, though his thoughts were rebellious. Sanctimonious old prig! He didn't know what the words meant but he'd heard older men saying them behind Mr Tomlinson's back and they had a good taste in his mouth at moments like this.

When daylight began to fade and the bell sounded for work to end, he slipped the collar from the shaft of the water-wheel rod, stopping the hammers for the night. He'd devised a system he'd not mentioned to Mr Tomlinson, to

278

save him having to start his day in the cold wet trough. When the light reached a certain gloom, he attached long strings to the cloth on the next roller, and allowed the strings to be pulled through the trough. That way, in the morning, he could pull on the strings and the new length of cloth came through without his having to climb into the trough to feed it. He'd always hated starting work standing in the squidge, freezing his feet and his legs which never seemed to warm properly for the rest of the day. No wonder the lads laiked about in the snap break to warm themselves after the cold dankness of the mill, especially the part where he worked which was constantly splashed with water from the stream and the water wheel. Always, when he arrived home at night after running some of the way to give himself a start on his mother, he'd set the tinder to the dry fronds in the hearth, striking it desperately and blowing on it until it caught. It was his pride to have the fire started by the time his mother came into the cottage, and sometimes the pot hanging over it with the brewis starting to heat.

Some nights, of course, there was nothing with which to make the brewis, and they'd make a supper of a handful of boiled oats. On those nights, he'd slip out after he and his mother had eaten their frugal meal.

'Where are *you* going?' she'd always ask, but he'd laugh cheekily at her. 'I'm going to Church, like Mr Tomlinson says,' he'd reply, knowing she wouldn't believe him. It was a game they played together.

Amelia these days had little energy to argue with him. He was growing into a big lad and earning money – surely he had the right to take himself out for an hour or two if he'd a mind. On those nights, she wouldn't douse the fire – if they'd had any coal to burn – but would leave a couple of tiny cobs to warm the room against his return.

On this night, Arthur came out of the cottage, turned left and went round the back of the terrace, along the side of the wall of the mill to the centre where the water-wheel arch divided the building. All was dark in the vast structure and he walked carefully along the brick edge taking great care not to slip. When he was beneath the shaft housing, he gave a low whistle, which was answered immediately. Straining his eyes in the gloom of the pitch-black arch, he saw a flash of white hose. He held up his hand. 'Steady now,' he called softly, and then saw a foot. He grasped the foot and swung it over so that it rested in a hole in the brickwork of the arch, then another foot appeared. He guided that one, too, and steadied both legs. Wally was puffing and grunting horribly.

'Be quiet,' Arthur said softly, 'else they'll hear you below . . .'

Below was the wall of the house of the overseer who was also in charge of locking in the apprentices. The mill owner had taken twenty of them; they lived in the top floor of the mill and were not permitted to leave. Wally and Arthur had talked together when they'd grown tired of laiking in the snap break, and together, after much discussion and investigation, had devised this route down through the mill's water wheel, by which Wally could escape at night sometimes.

'I'm hungry,' Wally said when Arthur had helped to set his feet firmly on safe ground. 'They only gave us slops for supper.'

Wally was eleven, a thin lad with large hands, large eyes and a whippet look about him. The owner never took on large apprentices – he maintained they ate too much and their bulk didn't necessarily imply they could do more work. Thin lads were quicker and ate less and were therefore a better buy. Different orphanages demanded different rates for the sale of their charges. The mill owner bought his in Morley and paid only half a sovereign for them. He housed them in the mill and fed them and they worked for him until they reached fourteen. After that they were free to leave and try their luck elsewhere. During the time of apprenticeship, they were not permitted to leave the mill, since that, the owner believed, would expose them to moral dangers. Each had a plate and a spoon and their meals were carried up into their dormitory by the overseer's man. The overseer usually came with him, and took the opportunity to read a chapter from the Bible to them, or to get them to bend a knee in prayer. Most of them had but one prayer. 'Let him finish and leave quickly, before the supper grows cold . . .'

'Aye, what we had was mostly oats. So we'll get off to the ale-house, shall us?'

'I favour the coaching inn myself,' Wally said. 'Us allus gets good pickings there.'

'Aye, but we mun be sensible. It don't do to go to the same place too often, lest they become familiar with our faces.'

After much discussion on the way, they settled for the coaching inn. Wally liked it best there. He liked the light and the warmth, he liked the constant coming and going, the smell of the horses in the yard.

The November night was cold and there was already a suggestion of snow in the air. They bunched together, keeping near to the walls of the houses as much for warmth as for safety. You could never tell who was abroad at that time of night when most respectable people were abed, and their youth was no protection from the marauding bands of homeless lads who'd kill them in a back alley for the sake of their boots and jerkins. They passed one alley mouth and heard a scream from the blackness within, quickly stifled. They ran quickly away, dodging the few travellers still abroad, the carts still trundling along behind tired horses.

One coach was going along quite briskly. 'Come on, Wally,' Arthur said, and they ran after it.

The coach seemed empty, for there were no footmen. They could see the top hat of the coachman, who flicked his whip along the twin horses' flanks keeping them going. He had two lanterns of candles behind shaved horn 'windows'. They gave out a feeble light but enough to warn others of his passage. Arthur and Wally ran deftly behind it, then leaped up and stood on the outriders' bench, though crouched down out of sight of the coachman. Now they would see how awake he was, how sober. This one, unfortunately, must have been still fresh enough to feel the slight movement when they jumped on. After a couple of flourishes of his whip along the horses' flanks he flicked it backwards in the well-known 'whip behind'. The tip of the lash snaked over the top of the coach and cracked against the back of the woodwork, not a thumb's width from Arthur's face. He knew the coachman, alert, would cover the whole back of the coach with his lash. 'Come on, Wally,' he said as he dropped off.

Wally wasn't as quick as Arthur and the hesitation cost him dear. The lash came over again and exploded against his cheek. He called out as he dropped off the outriders' bench, and clapped his hand to his face where Arthur knew from experience a fierce red weal would be showing.

'You've got to learn to drop quicker,' he said. 'Directly you hear the whip whistle, you mun drop off, else you'll lose an eye one of these days, like John o' Pudsey.'

John o' Pudsey was one of their heroes, like the legendary Dick Turpin. There were many differing accounts of how he'd lost his eye but Arthur favoured the story that he'd lost it in 'whip-behind' off the back of a coach when he was a boy. Somehow, it made their adventures more real, more exciting, if they could connect them in this way with a known figure.

The coaching inn was full since the Flyer had just arrived, bringing stories of adventure; they'd been held up crossing the Yorkshire Moors but the coachman had refused to halt, even when a ball was discharged over his head. He'd bellowed for them all to hang on and had galloped the coach wildly with the three highwaymen in fast pursuit though unable to pass on the narrow track. Another ball had gone through the wood at the back of the coach, narrowly missing the head of one of the passengers and the shoulder of one of the outriders clinging to the back. The pursuit had finally ended when a woman riding on the top of the coach clutching a goose beside her had of necessity let the goose go; it had fallen with such an explosion of feathers and cackling, landing square in the pursuing horse's face and causing the horse to rear and throw the highwayman riding it. The other two had galloped into the back of the rearing horse and they too had been dismounted and the chase had ended in ignominy. The woman whose goose had saved them all was delighted, since the passengers, thinking she had bravely thrown the goose at the highwayman, had subscribed its cost to her at a much higher price than she would have obtained in any market. Now she was sitting at the long bench in the inn, being feted and fed on the best the table could provide.

As soon as Arthur appraised the situation, he clutched at Wally's hand. 'Come on,' he said urgently as he wriggled his way through the press of bodies until they were beside the woman, who was becoming befuddled with all the ale and food, the praise and adulation. 'That were a right brave thing you did, ma'am,' Arthur said. 'I thought you were very brave.'

'Aye, lad,' she said, 'it were nowt . . .'

He was standing beside her overfilled plate and his hand reached out to touch a succulent leg of chicken.

'Help thyself, lad,' she said, 'for I s'all never finish it.' Arthur took the leg and bit hungrily into it. Wally, more timid, reached in.

'Go on, lad,' she said, 'help thysen.' He needed no prompting and took a pig's kidney in his fingers.

'Put it on the trencher,' Arthur hissed, indicating the large slice of bread.

'Aye, then, why are a couple of waifs like you travelling alone?' the woman asked, making room for them on the bench beside her.

''Tis our dearly beloved mother,' Arthur said, his face solemn, his manner one of suppressed tragedy. 'My brother and I just hope as the good Lord will allow us to arrive in time . . .'

'Lord have mercy!' she said. 'Come on, eat. There's

nowt like eating when you've had bad news.' The boys needed no more telling, but tucked in to the various plates. Others, thinking they were the woman's relatives, treated them with the same honour and respect they'd accorded her, and both soon found themselves quaffing ale from pots, eating a mountain of food that had been placed before them. From time to time when no-one was watching them closely, both Arthur and Wally slipped pieces of meat into the pockets of their jerkins. The ale, the warmth of the inn, the surfeit of food, soon began to take its toll and both were nodding in sleep before the table was cleared.

The woman shook their shoulders. 'You'll have to find yourselves a place in the straw of the stables,' she said. 'They'll not let you sleep here! This place is reserved to the gentlemen for sleeping.'

One stout man wearing the frock-coat and breeches of a dandy, was already nodding in the chair beside the fire.

'Aye, we mun find a place,' Arthur said. They went outside after giving their benefactress a buss on the cheek, and soon were scampering back through the night towards the mill. It had started to snow, and the streets were already dusted with the white flakes that temporarily hid the ugliness of the mud. Few people were about at that hour, though they could see the will-o'-the-wisp lights of lanthorns being carried by servants seeing their masters home. Arthur couldn't remember when he'd had a better night. Certainly, he'd never seen as much food at one time apart from the dim memory of the time his Auntie Gertrude who lived in Whitby had come that once to give them all a feast. Now, Arthur had been told, she had three sons of her own, Walter, Reuben, and Daniel. 'Aye, Wally,' he said as they walked along. 'I've got cousins in Whitby as live in a grand house by the ocean . . .'

'Tha never!'

'I have! And I have an uncle lives right here in Leeds, has his own carriage and a house wi' six rooms!'

'Tha never!'

'Aye, 'tis true.' Arthur walked along in the glow of Wally's envy, his feet scuffing the thin layer of powdered snow. When he heard the noise he turned and looked at Wally, who was sniffling as he struggled along beside him.

'What ails *thee*?' Arthur asked. 'Why art tha making that noise?'

'Tha's got everything,' Wally said. 'Tha's got an uncle wi' a carriage, an aunt as looks out over the ocean, and tha lives in a cottage wi' thy mam! And me, I've got nowt. I'm nobbut a foundling orphan, sold to work in't mill. I've got nowt and nobody!'

'Nay, Wally,' Arthur said as he linked his arm in Wally's. 'In truth tha can't say that when tha's got me for thy friend.'

There was a rushlight showing in the room when Arthur turned to the Cottages and he set out running, slipping over the snowy cobbles, wondering what could be amiss. When he arrived he opened the door and went quietly in. His mother was lying on her pallet in the living-room and Ann Stanbury from the next cottage was standing over her.

'Nay, Mam, what is it?' he asked as he hurried across to the bed.

'Tha ought to be skelped,' Ann Stanbury said. 'Stopping out till this hour . . .'

'What is it, Mam?' Arthur asked again. His mam's face was a grey/yellow colour and her lips were so tight on her mouth he fancied he could see the outline of her teeth on them. Her deep-set eyes, sunken in their sockets, looked out at him.

''Tis nowt, lad,' she whispered. 'I'm nobbut a bit tired, that's all.'

'Her heart's wore out,' Ann Stanbury said, 'wi' all the work of looking after thee and that no-good dad o' thine.'

Without thinking, Arthur did what he and Wally tried to do to each other as they walked along. He turned his foot sharply on his heel and the side of his boot smashed against her ankle. She howled and leaped away. 'And that's nowt

285

to what I'll do, Missis,' he said grimly, 'if tha calls my dad again.'

'You young tyke,' she said as she swung her hand at him. He dodged back and she missed him. 'Nay, tha moant hit my lad, Ann,' Amelia said weakly. 'He can't abide hearing owt said against his dad.'

'Aye, well, now that the young rapscallion has deigned to come home, there's no need for me to lose my sleep,' Ann said as she bundled her coat about her and swept out of the cottage.

'I had to fetch her,' Amelia said. 'I thought my time had come . . .'

'Nay, Mam,' he said, 'thy time will be a long time coming. Look what I've fotched for thee.' He dug into his jerkin and brought out the hunks of meat he'd taken from the table.

'You haven't been stealing from some gentleman's table, have you lad?' his mother asked anxiously. ''Tis transportation for life for that.'

'It were all gi'en to me,' he said, 'and much more. And pots of ale.'

'I could smell *that* on thee,' she said, 'as soon as tha' came through't door! Tha' moant get like thy dad.'

He sat beside the bed and, while she picked delicately at the beautiful cold meat, the like of which they hadn't been able to afford for many a year, he regaled her with the story of their adventure at the coaching inn. He enlarged the account to make it funny for her and more interesting, since he could see she'd been worried when she'd taken ill and he hadn't been there to comfort or help her. He noticed how much she was eating in her small nibbles, leaving each bone stripped clean of flesh.

'Why, Mam,' he said when he'd finished the story. 'Tha were starved. I reckon that's what were wrong wi' thee!'

She looked guiltily at the pile of bones. 'I've *never* eaten all *that*,' she said, 'I were that interested in what you were telling me. May the good Lord forgive me my gluttony!'

'I don't reckon the good Lord has much time to spare on

folks like us, Mam,' Arthur said gravely. 'I reckon us'll have to look after ourselves henceforth.'

She held out her arms and hugged him to her chest. 'Tha'rt too young, Arthur, to blaspheme the Lord,' she said. 'Tha mun have faith.'

'Aye, a quick wit and nimble fingers is better than all the faith, Mam,' he said. 'I heard that in't mill and never knew what it meant until this evening, when we cozened them out of that meat by making pretence!'

'Don't tell me tha's an Unbeliever, Arthur.'

'Not yet, Mam, but it's getting harder and harder wi' every passing day. Happen there's one God for the rich and another for the poor folks like us. I wouldn't mind swapping them over, now and again. Any road, I'm glad of one thing . . .'

'What's that, lad?'

'Unless tha's squashed it beyond recognition, I've a rabbit pie in't other pocket as'll do us nicely for tomorrow.'

When work finished the next day and Arthur had raced home to light the fire for Amelia, he sat thinking in the doorway, watching for her to arrive. He saw her turn the terrace and start to walk towards their cottage, remembering all the evenings he'd waited here like this for a sight of her. He was shocked as he saw her, as he looked with greater perception at the way she moved, like an old crone. He remembered her coming fast along the street from the mill with a smile on her face, her tripping footsteps hastening her home to her husband, son, fireside and hearth. Now it seemed as much as she could do to drag herself along, each step visibly needing great determination and draining her of energy. Aye, he thought, the meat did her good. It helped her climb from bed this morn, helped her get through the day's work at the mill. But she needed more of it than they had hope of providing. He felt guilty that he had been unable to resist a slice of the cold rabbit pie – he should have left it all for her. His mind was taxed to know what to do. Chances like

287

the previous evening probably came only once in a lifetime. If everyone hadn't been so absorbed in hearing the account of the highwaymen they'd soon have noticed the two interlopers and thrown them out. If the woman hadn't been in such a state of euphoria she would have asked who and what they were, would have seen through their pretence and sent them packing with a box on the ears.

He thought of his aunt in Whitby and her fine house overlooking the ocean, which, they'd told him, smelled clean and fresh with air you could breathe. If only his mam could go to that house and enjoy a few days of an easier life, eating good food, not having to stand by the loom as long as the day was light, not having to survive on the pobbies they had.

When she arrived at the cottage her face lightened for a moment at the sight of him. 'Don't forget the rabbit pie,' he said cheerfully. 'I'm off out . . .'

'Doan't be late, lad,' she said. 'Tha needs thy rest if tha's working all day long. And tha should have a bit of pie afore tha goes out.'

'I've had my share,' he said cheerfully. 'Tha mun eat the rest.'

It had snowed most of the day and he'd been frozen at the fulling machine. He pushed his hands deep in the pockets of his jerkin, feeling the grease from the meat, picking out specks to eat as he walked quickly along. He passed the back of the ale-house and looked in through the yard gate. The potman saw him almost immediately. Before he could get to the first table on which somebody had left a part-eaten chop on a trencher of bread, the potman came at him, waving a wooden board as if to smash it on his head.

'Out of here, you ragamuffin!' he shouted, and Arthur fled.

His route took him past many ale-houses but he quickly recognized that fortune wasn't his portion that night – in each one he was chased away before he had the opportunity to grab anything to satisfy his aching belly.

It took over an hour to reach his uncle's house. He stood by the large wooden gate, which was open, and looked up the drive to the house itself, as he had often stood with his mother in the past, never daring to enter. A carriage was waiting by the door, a small one pulled by one horse only. Arthur plunged his hands deep into his pockets, and tried to summon courage to go up the drive. Afraid of the imposing front door entrance with its stone pillars and canopy, he walked round the wall to the back; but the large gate that gave admittance to the coachyard and stable block was tightly closed. He returned to the front, then, with fear-spittle threatening to choke him as he gulped, started up the drive towards the house. No sooner had he started through the darkness of the bushes, lightened by the dusting of fine snow they carried, than the front door opened. A servant stood there with a lanthorn when a gentleman came out, most finely dressed, to enter the coach, which the gentleman himself was driving. As soon as the coach started, the servant went back inside with the lanthorn, and the front door slammed behind him. The gentleman turned his coach and started down the drive. Arthur, caught, tried to push his way into the bushes, which shivered against his pressure and caused the snow on them to fly. The gentleman stopped the coach, and Arthur heard a cultured voice speaking.

'Who is in there?' the voice demanded imperiously. 'Come out of there, you scoundrel! I have my gun pointing at you and will shoot without hesitation unless you show yourself!'

Arthur came slowly from the bushes and dusted the snow from his face. The gentleman was part leaning out of the coach and holding a long pistol pointing at Arthur.

'Nay, sir, doant thee shoot,' Arthur said, terrified. 'I mean thee no harm!'

'Who are you, you scoundrel, and what do you intend, lurking thus in the bushes. Are you hoping to rob the house?'

'Nay, sir, I am no robber.'

'Then what? I grant you are a mite small for robbery, or are your confederates lurking hereabout?'

The pistol waved back and forth, settling on each arc on the cold trembling figure of Arthur. 'Art thou a 'scaped 'prentice, for I see thou wears working clothes?'

'I'm an honest boy,' Arthur said, 'come to visit my uncle and meaning no harm nor mischief.'

'His *uncle*?'

'Aye, sir. I'm an Aysgill. Maister Peter Aysgill is my uncle.'

The gentleman's eyebrows rose. 'Peter Aysgill is thy uncle? In truth, I can see a family resemblance in thy grimy face. Well, young *Maister* Aysgill, th'art out of luck, since thy uncle is away to Hull on matters of business, and will not be back these two nights. Come, climb alongside me and we'll find an ale-house to warm thy frozen bones, for there is much I would know of thee, and thy uncle.'

Arthur scrambled up with alacrity, riding on the step beside the coach hood, his hand holding the wooden whip-rack. The gentleman slapped the horse's rump gently with the stock of his whip, put the pistol back into its leather boot, and they trundled slowly down the path between bushes that separated the house from the road. Arthur hung there bemused; the turn in the events of the evening had been too much for him. He couldn't believe his good fortune when he found himself, for the second night in succession, sitting at an ale-house table with a plate of food before him, a pot of ale in his hand and a very smart gentleman talking to him as an equal, asking all manner of questions about the Aysgill family with enormous interest. Arthur told him of his father's death, of his uncle Peter's refusal to lend him money for a carter's business, of his mother's ill health, of their privations. He didn't remember when he'd talked so much. When he found himself dropping with sleep, the gentleman assisted him from the ale-house and even drove his carriage to the Mill Cottages before departing for the night, leaving Arthur on the stoop of the cottage with a bundle of food for his mother and a pair of coins in his hand.

'What was his name,' his mother asked him anxiously when he told her the story of the previous night in a rushing flood of words. It all seemed unbelievable to her, and extremely suspicious. Why should a gentleman buy food for her son, give him a pair of coins, bring him home on the step of his carriage, ask so many questions about the Aysgill family. 'He didn't do nowt to you?' she asked.

'Nay, Mam. He were very good to me. I reckon he could see as I was cold and hungry and in need.'

'The gentry don't *do* that, Arthur,' she said. 'It's not their place to talk with the likes of us any more than it's fitting for us to go above our station and try to talk wi' them. The gentry is the gentry, Arthur. They're not like us. It's something they are born to.'

'My uncle Peter wasn't born to it,' Arthur said stubbornly, but could say no more since the first bell was ringing, and Thomas Tomlinson would be standing beside the fulling machine watching for him to start.

If only Tessa had remembered her husband's impeccable sources of information, she would not have thought to deceive him with Lord D'Arcy's son, Percival. She and Percival had known each other all their lives since their fathers had been friends and frequent colleagues in business ventures. The D'Arcy money came from extensive land-holdings in the West Riding of Yorkshire; it was old wealth carrying rank and privilege, as the Clether fortune had been before it passed into the hands of the degenerate and profligate Sir Ian. Percival and Tessa spoke the same language, laughed at the same follies, had tumbled into the same bed together at house parties. Percival had travelled extensively on the Continent of Europe after he left Oxford and had returned a well informed young rake. Lord D'Arcy had despatched him promptly to the American Colonies, whence he'd made his way to Bermuda and the West Indies. The Colonial life didn't suit him well; though he found the people of Yorkshire utterly provincial, boorish and backward, at least the D'Arcy estates were within a coach ride of London where all pleasures were open to him from their Town House in Piccadilly.

He'd first flushed out a discontented Tessa more as someone to help while away the long tedious provincial evenings; her husband was frequently away and there were many opportunities of spending time together. To his great surprise, he found the gauche girl of his early twenties had matured into a woman eager for any sexual experimentation, with a hunger for the more exotic pastimes he'd rarely found in any woman save a well-tutored Covent Garden or Paris doxy. It was as if the birth of her child Gavin in 1757 had awoken strange latent desires; he'd never been better amused or diverted nor, he had to admit, more fatigued at bed play.

Matters had been made easy for them by Willerby, the arch snob whom Peter Aysgill had retained without in any way earning his loyalty or approval. Willerby was delighted to introduce Percival D'Arcy into the household – his presence brought a touch of quality Willerby sorely needed. Both Mrs Lakeham and Jenny had been instantly discharged by Aysgill after the attempt at abortion with the brew of foxgloves that had almost cost Tessa Aysgill her life; at Willerby's and Mrs Aysgill's suggestion, they had been replaced by Mrs Davies and Selena, a formidable couple from the estate of Lord Chepstow. All three were wise in the ways of the gentry, and did nothing to interfere in the relationship between Percival and Tessa. Willerby welcomed it; to cuckold his upstart ill-bred master was meat and drink to him.

Peter returned from Hull in a glow of personal satisfaction at an investment he considered making to improve the docks. There'd been talk of forming a dock company with the Hull City Corporation and Trinity House having an interest. Peter knew that to be associated with such a venture would bring social as well as financial rewards; he felt he was making an adequate amount of money, which could only increase in proportion as the years went by. Now he sought ventures that attached prestige to themselves and those who supported them; he'd been told that he would be given a seat on the board of the dock company – all the other gentlemen on the board were either peers or baronets and he knew the association of his name with theirs would greatly advantage him. It wouldn't happen immediately since they needed to seek Royal Assent, but at least he'd started matters rolling and had lodged a Letter of Intent with them.

As always when he returned from a voyage he called at his office, where Percy, now promoted to the full title of Assistant with a salary of one hundred pounds a year, waited for him. Quickly he scanned the sheets of information Percy had prepared, commercial and industrial intelligence on which the organization of his affairs depended. He'd given Percy his instructions and was preparing to leave to go to his home when Percy coughed nervously. 'One other item of news, Mister Aysgill,' he said. 'I didn't think I should commit it to paper.'

Aysgill laughed good-humouredly. 'Nay, Percy,' he said, 'there can be nothing more discreet than the papers you prepare for me. If any of them should be seen by the folks who appear on them, they'd set a pack of hounds on us, to be sure. When I'm dead and gone, we shall have to direct that they are published as a scandal sheet, to let folks know what we know of the ways of the so-called gentry in moral, as well as commercial, matters. What's this tidbit you have to offer? Some scandal, I'll be bound.'

Percy had no desire to tell his master the news. Over the years he'd conceived an affection for Aysgill who, despite all his failings, had always behaved well to Percy, advancing him steadily to his present trusted and well-paid position.

'It concerns Lord D'Arcy's son, Percival,' the clerk said.

'Aye, and who has yon rake been cocking his leg over this time?' Peter asked, without much interest. He'd long ago closed his dossier on the D'Arcy family, realizing they

293

were too exalted in their position to advantage him greatly. Now that he was seeking respectability in equal measure with fortune, he had no desire to expose himself to any of the powerful magnates as a blackmailer.

'I regret to inform you,' Percy said miserably, 'but Percival D'Arcy has been calling, and leaving late at night, at your own house, Mister Aysgill.'

Peter sat down quickly, since his senses suddenly were spinning. Percival D'Arcy and Tessa . . .?

Percy felt an enormous compassion when Peter Aysgill lifted his face. ''Tis true, Master,' Percy said softly. 'Little though I care for the role of harbinger of bad tidings, I'm bound to confess 'tis true. Curvy advanced himself to the house itself and clambered up the beech tree.'

'I'll have all the details, Mister Percy,' Peter Aysgill cried, 'but spare me them now. Have Curvy dictate them to you and make his cross on the paper. If he lies, I'll have his skin. If he omits one single detail, I'll tear out his tongue.'

'It shall be a complete account,' Percy promised.

The house had been greatly expanded in recent years and now contained a score of rooms. Tessa had finally won her way and been given her own quarters of a bedroom, a dressing-room, a room for her personal maid Selena, a sitting-room, a nursery for Gavin, a room for his nurse Mrs Pocock. All these quarters were at the back of the house and faced a giant beech tree set in the edge of a lawn and gardens. Peter had given way over the matter of the quarters on Tessa's promise she'd do nothing further to injure her unborn child. She had not had the opportunity; after the dismissal of Mrs Lakeham and Jenny, Peter brought the daughter of his coachman, James Ponder, to tend his wife. Emily Ponder was a large-boned lass of twenty-five whose shoulders and hands resembled those of a boxer. She was instructed never to let Mrs Aysgill out of her sight, day and night. She was to sleep in a cot in Mrs Aysgill's dressing-room with the door open, to accompany Mrs Aysgill on her short walks in the garden. Tessa realized that she was the girl's prisoner and resigned herself to revenging herself on her husband by spending as much of his money as possible on the additions to their home. When her son Gavin was born, a sickly little fellow despite his peasant stock heritage, she abandoned him completely to the wet nurse and didn't see him for a month.

When Peter had finally ordered Emily Ponder to bring the child, Tessa looked at her son and her husband with equal disinterest. 'Yes indeed, *Maister*,' she said with contempt, 'your brat resembles you. You must be proud. Now, if you'll kindly remove your gaoler and brat from my sight I'd be obliged; in truth her bovine manner is as little to my taste as is the fruit of your lusts!'

Despite the frigidity of her manner, Peter had made a point of continuing to visit her at regular intervals, satisfying his needs in her cold indifferent body, filling her belly hopefully with his seed. They no longer took meals together except when he filled the house with the most glittering company he could get to accept his invitations; most of them were men in one way or another indebted to him in the commercial sense, or hopeful of his favours. Several times he succeeded in attracting a gentleman of title and social consequence; on those occasions, Tessa would don her finery, wear the jewellery he purchased for her so freely, and appear as a scintillating hostess.

Peter could remember the time Percival D'Arcy had come to one of his evenings. He'd often wondered why D'Arcy had approached him in the Assembly Rooms with friendly overtures; now he could understand that he had been concerned only to encounter Tessa again. His mind was working as the coachman drove him home from the office. Mostly he was wondering how many people knew of the relationship between D'Arcy and his wife, and how many were secretly laughing at his cuckolding.

Of one thing he was quite certain – none of this could have taken place without the connivance of Willerby, his Steward, and the devilish pair Mrs Davies and Selena. His anger boiled so against them that he resolved that nothing would satisfy him until he'd seen them transported on whatever charge and pretext he could devise. As for Tessa, he'd bring back Emily Ponder, and this time she would stay.

Percival D'Arcy could wait! Revenge, to be enjoyed, must be taken slowly and should advantage the taker in whatever way it might. He'd have the best of Percival D'Arcy in one way or the other in his own good time.

His wife, Tessa, was in her bed when he arrived at his house. 'Alone, my dear?' he asked as he approached the bedside.

'Do you mind to dress yourself properly before you come in here,' she snapped, looking at the mud marks his travel boots were making on her fine woven carpet. 'Go and wash,' she said. 'You stink of the road.'

He stood beside the bed, looking up at its decorated silk canopy, its elegant curtains, its plumped goosedown pillows encased in the finest lawn, with lace along the edges from Nottingham, the finest money could buy. He looked at the face of his wife, her eyes flaming at him madly, her long aristocratic lip wrinkled in contempt.

He grasped the edge of the covering blanket and flung it aside, revealing her body in its nightgown.

'And you, my dear, of what do *you* stink?'

He could see she was puzzled. He reached into the bed and clasped her nightgown at her bosom. With a quick pull, he rent it apart. He pulled and rent it again, carrying on until he reached the hem. She lay still, not frightened yet, amused at the thought that his blood had been aroused at the sight of her. The nightgown, in disarray, fell from her body, held only at the neck and shoulders. He pulled again, the gathering ribbon snapped, and she lay there naked.

Slowly and methodically, watched by her amused eyes, he removed his garments. He came and stood beside the bed.

The smile didn't leave her face; it showed contempt,

boredom, superiority.

'Now, my dear,' he said. 'I am acquainted with the desires of what you might call the Upper Classes. I know their constant pursuit of pleasure leads them into many byways.'

'My my, Maister Aysgill, don't tell me you are acquiring sophistication.'

'If it is sophistication to make no distinction between ladies and small boys in the gratification of carnality, I must confess myself most *un*sophisticated. However, I think help may be nearer at hand than I believed possible. You, my dearly beloved wife, are now going to do to me everything you have done to your poltroon, Percival D'Arcy, in my absence.'

Now the smile was wiped from her face, and fear had replaced it. 'It is a base lie,' she said. 'Whoever told it to you . . .'

It was his turn to smile. 'Don't be a traitor to your birth and your class, Tessa,' he said. 'You've been uncovered in a despicable breach of faith. Now admit it. And have the good breeding at least to face the consequences.'

'And, if I refuse?' she said with a toss of her head.

'Then I shall bring in a whip and beat you like a bitch on heat!'

Peter found Percival D'Arcy in a corner of the Assembly Rooms, sitting in bored tiredness on one of the benches. 'The tables have been damned unkind to me, Aysgill,' he confessed, as Peter took a seat on the bench alongside him. 'I fear we have a sharper amongst us. They let in all sorts of riff-raff these days.'

Damn Aysgill, he was thinking. Why doesn't he get himself away on business? A night between the energetic limbs of Tessa would cure all his malaise. He put a finger beneath his short wig and scratched vigorously, thoroughly out of humour with the world and himself.

'I was hoping to entice you to a game,' Peter Aysgill

297

said. 'Perhaps you could recoup your losses in that way, for I'm no hand at play.'

'Aye, Aysgill, we might while away an idle hour if you've a mind.'

They entered a private room; the hard surface of the polished table glittered in the reflection of the overhead light. Three men were standing around it, resting their elbows on the eight-inch deep wall, padded with straw and leather, that served to prevent the dice falling to the ground. The game they were playing was simple; each took the two dice in turn and threw them, wagering on the outcome. The man who threw the highest combination of numbers collected all the money. Percival D'Arcy looked round at the men; he knew none of them by sight but, as he'd been saying to Aysgill a short while ago, they were letting all sorts in the Assembly Rooms these days.

'D'Arcy,' he said gruffly. 'Pleased to make your acquaintance.'

They told off their names in turn, Holmby, Cartwright and Samuels.

Aysgill introduced himself to them, and they all settled round the table.

'Ten pounds,' D'Arcy asked, and they all nodded.

Holmby won the first round with a six and a four.

D'Arcy took the second, with a five and a three.

D'Arcy took the third, again with a five and a three.

They had played for half an hour, and the winnings were about even, when Aysgill nodded inconspicuously to Samuels, the man who took his turn before D'Arcy.

'Shall we make the game more interesting,' Holmby said. 'Shall we permit side bets among those who have yet to throw?'

'Anything you care to do,' D'Arcy said. He took the dice from Samuel and rolled them languidly. His eyes gleamed, however, when he saw the double six. 'I say, how's that?' he asked, his languor gone.

Cartwright, who followed him, scooped up the dice, took out his handkerchief to wipe his nose, and rolled them. A five and a four. 'Rotten luck, my dear fellow,' D'Arcy said.

Now the side bets began, some rather rash, D'Arcy thought.

When the last throw had gone – Aysgill with a double two – D'Arcy collected his winnings, which amounted to a hundred pounds. In the next three throws, he won three times on the double six, improving his winnings to a thousand pounds when the side bets were included.

'Anyone fancy increasing the stakes?' he asked nonchalantly. 'Five hundred a throw?'

They all agreed since it was the only way they could begin to recoup their losses, or so it seemed.

'You have the most amazing luck, D'Arcy,' Samuels said as he handed him the dice.

An air of tension had developed with the increased stake. Had they not been secure in a private room, the table would have been surrounded. Aysgill glanced around and saw the door to the public gaming rooms was firmly closed. The five of them were alone. He nodded again to Samuels.

D'Arcy rolled the dice. There was an expectant hush as the dice clattered across the table and bounced against the far edge, to spring back and land. Double six. It was the fourth successive time. D'Arcy, following the pattern of the game, reached onto the table to pick up the dice and give them to the next player, Cartwright, but as his hand reached out suddenly he found himself held by the wrist. He looked angrily up into the face of Holmby.

'With permission, D'Arcy,' Holmby said smoothly, 'I have a fancy to examine the dice before anyone touches them.' He picked up the two dice between his thumb and forefinger, where everyone could see them.

'Are you calling me?' D'Arcy said in shock and disbelief.

'No,' Holmby said. 'It is merely my intention to give the dice a roll for myself.'

D'Arcy settled back in righteous anger. 'Roll them,' he

said, 'and be damned to you!'

The dice remained in full view as Holmby flicked his wrist backwards and forwards before letting them roll. They tumbled across the board, bounced against the far end and landed. 'Double six,' Cartwright said solemnly.

The men pulled away from D'Arcy as if he had the plague. 'Try them, Aysgill,' D'Arcy called desperately, 'you try them.'

Aysgill did as he'd been bid and flicked the dice. Double six again.

'I swear I know nothing of it,' D'Arcy said desperately, but it was plain that no-one believed him.

'Are you acquainted with this man?' Cartwright demanded of Aysgill harshly, indicating D'Arcy.

'Why yes,' Aysgill said. 'I would not believe him capable of sharping.'

'In that case,' Holmby said, 'I am certain you would not object, sir, to turning out the side pockets of your jacket.'

D'Arcy's face was red with anger. 'I'll call the first man who terms *me* a sharper,' he said. He reached into his pocket with great disdain; but the look on his face clearly indicated what he had found there. Cartwright seized his wrist again and dragged his hand from his pocket. In it was another pair of dice, closely resembling the other pair. Cartwright flung them on the table and they came up five and four. He picked them up and flung them again and this time they showed a three and a one.

'That's enough for me,' Cartwright said. 'Enough anyway to fetch a magistrate and have him decide the rights and wrongs.'

D'Arcy looked desperately at Aysgill. 'My dear friend,' he said, 'surely you know I'm not, and never have been, a sharper?'

Holmby had been examining D'Arcy's features intently. 'I know thee,' he cried. 'Now my memory serves me aright. Was it not thee, my fine friend, who called a man in White's in London over a pair of cards he said had dropped from your sleeve . . . Burgess, weren't that his name? You stopped his mouth for him right enough, wi' a ball, on Highgate Fields. Everyone said as you were defending your honour. Wait until news of today's deed is bruited abroad. Or do you mean to stop our mouths with a ball, in like manner.'

'Give me your hand, Aysgill,' D'Arcy said. He took his hand. 'I swear by all that's holy that I know nothing of these dice. I swear on the honour of my family that I have never seen them before. Surely, old friend, *you* can believe me, can vouch for me to these gentlemen?' His tone was desperate. Yes, he had been called in White's over a pair of cards by the man Burgess, the younger son of Lord Burgess. Yes, he had duelled with him on Highgate Fields and had killed him, defending his honour as was the right and duty of a gentleman.

The news of Burgess's death had harmed his reputation somewhat since it was known that Burgess always drank to excess and was, in truth, incapable of holding himself, or a pistol, straight. He had genuinely sought only to wound him, but the pistol had kicked high and the ball had taken Burgess in the chest.

He knew he would be ruined even if he challenged all these men in defence of his honour, if news of this incident leaked out. 'Aysgill, dear friend,' he pleaded, 'tell them you know me for a man of honour. Tell them, dear friend.'

Aysgill smiled. Now he knew he had this aristocratic poltroon in the palm of his hand and could squeeze out a slow revenge for his cuckolding. 'Gentlemen,' he said. 'I must tell you I know Percival D'Arcy, who has been a frequent visitor, in love and honour to my house. I cannot say anything in the matter of the dice for we have all seen through our own eyes that the dice did, in truth, lie in his pocket, while the falsified dice were rolling the double six on his behalf. I suggest this must be the one occasion when none of us can believe the evidence of his eyes. I can make no better explanation than that.'

'You are the largest loser, Aysgill,' Samuels said.

''Tis but a trifling sum,' Aysgill said. 'Of no importance.'

'I still think you should have redress,' Samuels said.

D'Arcy reached for his pile of coin and hastily thrust it towards Aysgill. 'Take it, dear friend,' he said. 'Take it all.'

'I have a better solution,' Cartwright said. He went to the door and opened it. D'Arcy looked in despair at Aysgill who shrugged his shoulders as if helpless in the matter. When Cartwright clapped his hands, a servant hurried forward.

'Paper and pen,' Cartwright ordered harshly. The servant hurried away, for such a request was not unusual.

'Another poor devil signing away his fortune,' he said to the steward before he hurried back.

He placed the paper and pen on the table, which already carried an inkstand.

Cartwright examined the trim of the quill before seizing it and dipping it into the ink. 'I propose to write a statement relating to this day's events,' he said. 'I think we should all witness it and give it to our friend Aysgill, for him to use in the future according to his discretion, should such an event recur. For my part, *Mister* D'Arcy,' he said, 'I know what my eyes have seen and am not afraid to meet you at any time or place to our mutual convenience. I should say that I am not unaccustomed to handling a pistol as, if memory serves me right, the unfortunate Burgess was. You have greatly offended this gentleman, Aysgill, whom we have never before had the privilege of meeting, and he has behaved with the probity of angels. However, I intend to put into his hands the means by which, if such an affair should happen again, he will be able to obtain redress.'

'Damn you, sir,' D'Arcy said, provoked beyond measure. 'I'll call you, and be damned to you . . .'

'It is not my habit to stand for sharpers,' Cartwright said. 'I'll not accept your challenge.' He scribbled on the paper rapidly, then invited Samuels and Holmby to read it before signing it.

Aysgill was chuckling inside himself, though he held D'Arcy's arm and pretended affection for him. 'What are these men?' D'Arcy said quietly. 'I know nought of them.'

'I think Cartwright is well connected in the city of York,' Aysgill said, 'though I have no personal account of him.'

D'Arcy would never know that Cartwright, certainly well connected in the city of York having served for four years as an Alderman, was indebted to Aysgill and his Merchant Bank for ten thousand pounds, which sum was to be erased from the ledger now that Cartwright had successfully smuggled the weighted dice into D'Arcy's hand. Nor that Samuels, a merchant from the city of Hull, sought an advantage in the proposed Dock Company which Aysgill would give him for his part-share in the day's events. Of the three, only Holmby was what he seemed to be, an unimpeachable witness, a gentleman of irreproachable family visiting Leeds on behalf of his extensive cotton interests. He had been invited to the Assembly Rooms by Cartwright and in truth had never seen Aysgill before this day, though he had remembered the London incident, saving the others from having to bring it to the fore.

'Take this, sir,' Holmby said to Aysgill. 'I am a man reluctant to find fault in others and am most moved by your support of this gentleman in these trying circumstances.'

'May I pledge you to silence?' Aysgill insisted.

'You have my word and my hand on it.'

The four solemnly shook hands before the three departed. Aysgill sat beside the beaten D'Arcy on the bench.

'Am I dreaming, dear friend?' D'Arcy asked, quite bemused. 'Is this some horrible nightmare from which I shall soon awaken? Were the false dice in my hand, the correct ones in my pocket?'

'Nothing is ever what it seems,' Aysgill said smoothly. 'I

303

was pleased to be able to be of service to you in your hour of need.'

D'Arcy looked at him. 'I fear I have misjudged you, Aysgill,' he said. 'I hadn't seen your true quality. For a man to stand by a friend in such a circumstance, for him to disallow the evidence of his own eyes in the face of friendship and faith, bespeaks the true gentleman. Here's my hand on it, Peter, and my assurance of service.'

Aysgill shook hands again. Really, he thought, all these hand shakes and protestations of friendship were becoming quite boring. He had the folded paper in his pocket carrying three signatures. He needed no other token of future success in the exquisite revenge he planned to exact on this honour-burdened fellow!

'If we're to be friends, my dear fellow,' D'Arcy said querulously, 'you'll need to do something about the style of your dress.'

The two men met constantly, with Percival D'Arcy enjoying, at the first, his role of tutor to what he regarded as an uncouth peasant. Peter Aysgill blossomed under his tutelage, though his social graces, one could quickly discern, were but laid on the surface like a gilded cloth on a rough board.

'We must take ourselves away to London if we're to get you outfitted like a gentleman of taste and fashion.'

'I'll have none of these French fancies,' Peter said good humouredly, eyeing the lace and ruffles on Percival D'Arcy's long coat in dark brown silk. They had gone together to a *soirée* at the home of Lord Newsam, a spectacular affair attended only by the first rank of West Riding society. Peter had long ached to be invited to such occasions and knew that without the sponsorship of D'Arcy he would never have been admitted.

Tessa remained at home on these occasions. Since the night Aysgill had exposed her infidelity, she had been kept a virtual prisoner in their home under the ministration of Emily Ponder, who'd never forgiven her the use of the word *bovine*.

Tessa's outrage was completed when she discovered that that night had resulted in her pregnancy. She would dearly have liked to taunt her husband by claiming D'Arcy as the father, but Mrs Pocock, Gavin's nurse, knew differently, since she'd ministered to Tessa in her womanlies the days prior to Aysgill's return. Now the story was put about that Tessa was sickly and confined to their home on doctor's orders. Gradually, the myth was becoming the reality, as Tessa ceased caring for herself, refused to dress or take exercise, and seemed to be declining into a form of imbecility or madness. Aysgill didn't care – he had no further interest in her now that she was pregnant again, preferring to pursue his own design of social amelioration under the expert care of Percival D'Arcy. Thoughts of his revenge were fading – D'Arcy could be a most engaging fellow when he had a mind, and his gratitude to Aysgill over the dice incident was charming to behold though, of course, the cause of it was never mentioned. Nor was the paper Aysgill kept in a strongbox of iron in his office.

'Shall you dance, my dear fellow?' D'Arcy asked him as they stood on the edge of the crowd in the ballroom of Newsam Manor. Peter shook his head. Though he had engaged an Italian dancing master, he had not yet lost his embarrassment at dancing in public. He was also taking lessons with the foils, but fencing was little to his taste. D'Arcy had insisted that a gentleman must master what he called the *épée*, but Aysgill found the instrument as hard to handle as the word was to pronounce. French, another of the attainments D'Arcy was thrusting upon him, made no sense to him. He could say, *soirée, merci, ma foi*, but to construct any phrase in the language was, as yet, beyond him.

He turned instantly when he heard the voice behind him say, 'Ah, there you are, my dear D'Arcy.'

Giles, Lord Barthwick, was standing before them, holding out his languid hand.

Peter Aysgill couldn't believe his eyes – Lord Barthwick must have doubled in size since Peter had last seen him, the day of his departure from the village. Now his Lordship was fat, even bloated, and his piggy eyes stared out from monstrous folds of flesh. His small pudgy hands had little shape to them so blown up with fat were they.

'My dear Giles,' Percival said. 'How good to see you looking so well . . .'

Giles' reddened eyes were flicking over D'Arcy's companion, trying to decide if an introduction would be to his advantage; though the clothes were right, he decided, the manner was wrong. Really, so many gentlemen were engaging themselves with these upstart merchant princes these days, these magnates with only money to recommend them. This fellow was definitely of that category, of that there could be no doubt. He was about to turn away, to administer the slight but unmistakeable social snub, when D'Arcy spoke again.

'May I present my friend, Peter Aysgill,' he said.

Peter held out his hand, amused to touch the flaccid decadent flesh.

'Aysgill,' Giles said. 'Seems to me I've heard that name before . . .'

''Tis a name much to be reckoned with these days,' D'Arcy said gushingly. 'Aysgill and Sir Ian Clether are partners in a venture or two.'

Giles' eyes glittered. The whole County knew how the Clether fortunes had been increased of late, just when everyone thought Sir Ian was going to the wall. In truth, the Barthwick inheritance was not proving the cornucopia he had imagined it would be, though the title sat nicely on his shoulders with the ermine.

'Aye, perhaps we could essay a venture or two together,' he said patronizingly. 'I believe 'tis quite the custom these days to engage in the better sort of trade.'

Both looked at Aysgill expecting some polite response. The many hanging on, hoping to catch his Lordship's eye, nodded approval of his benevolence.

Finally, Aysgill smiled. 'Nothing would better suit,' he said, 'but alas, I have so many people seeking to venture

306

with me these days that I am obliged to be particular in whom I select.'

Barthwick gasped, and D'Arcy frowned. Really, it ill became his protégé to administer a snub before so many people, all of whom had heard it and were aghast. What was the world coming to! Barthwick was looking at him and he hastened to smooth the matter over.

'My dear friend Aysgill is much taxed these days by affairs of business,' he said hurriedly. 'I am certain it is his sole wish to save your Lordship the drudgery of such a tedious occupation.'

Barthwick grunted, not completely convinced, then turned on his heel and stalked away around the ballroom, pushing his way through the crowd without a word.

'That was foolish,' D'Arcy said to Peter Aysgill. 'You have made an enemy where you could have made a friend. What am I to do with you, my dear Peter?'

'Forget this nonsense of Barthwick for I have special cases against him which could not bear the repetition. Tell me instead more about our King, George Second, who, you were saying, is not long for this world. If I am to enter the world of politics, it behoves me well to know the Royal Family.'

D'Arcy laid his hand on Peter's arm. 'My dear friend,' he said earnestly. 'Your slight of Lord Barthwick shows how ill you are prepared for the politic life, where a single enemy can do more harm than can be repaired by a hundred friends. You must learn to hide your feelings more adequately if you are to seek political advancement. There are limits, even you must know, to what can be bought by money, even in these venal days. Prior to succeeding to the title, Lord Barthwick was a man much versed in political matters.'

'But no longer is so?'

'He seems to prefer the life on his estate here in Yorkshire . . .'

'. . . where he can neither advantage, nor disadvantage me in my political aspirations.'

307

D'Arcy laughed. 'You're an uncommonly direct fellow, Peter,' he said. '*I* find your forthrightness most refreshing, but I can assure you others will dub you rude and boorish unless you learn to hone your manners to a finer edge. Now, sithee, here comes our hostess, Lady Newsam. Let's see what a fine figure you can cut for *her*. You can essay all the French you wish, for she speaks not a word of it though she'll laugh gaily at each of your *bons mots* as if in complete comprehension and accord.'

Percival D'Arcy and Giles, Lord Barthwick, met by accident in the Club in Boar Lane the following day, a place strictly reserved for the gentry.

'I say, who was that frightful fellow you were squiring so avidly at Newsam's last evening?' Lord Barthwick asked petulantly. 'You must be in to him for a vast amount is all I can suppose.'

'I owe him a debt of honour, and no more,' Percival said. 'We share no financial transaction.'

'Unlike Sir Ian, eh? I must say that yon fellow has lined the Clether purse. He cuts quite a dash in London society these days, though I believe his health is not of the best. So, where does your fellow come from, eh? I've a notion I know his name from somewhere.'

'You should know it,' Percival said, smiling. 'His family was a victim of that foolish enclosure business a few years back. In your village . . .'

'Aysgill. John Aysgill? Had three sons, if memory serves me right.'

'And two daughters.'

'Both gone to the dogs, I'll be bound.'

'On the contrary. Both are respectable married women with families.'

'I suppose your fellow, Peter Aysgill, has seen to that, if he has so far advanced himself he can command the sponsorship of such as you.'

'I believe there is little contact between the members of the family these days. I had the opportunity of speaking with the nephew, Arthur, some short while ago and he informed me they go their separate ways.'

'I'd be most awfully obliged, my dear Percival, if you could tell me what you know about all and each of them. It behoves us all to know what has happened to our faithful retainers.'

'My, Lord Barthwick,' Percival said mockingly. 'I should never have suspected you of such a sentimentality!' While they ate together he told Lord Barthwick the substance of his discussion with the boy Arthur, for he saw no reason to keep the knowledge to himself.

Lord Barthwick grunted with satisfaction as the information was laid before him. The upstart Aysgill would have to be taught, he told himself, that no-one slights Lord Barthwick in public and gets away with it.

Sir Ian Clether died the week before his second grandson was born, and had already been buried when the news reached Leeds. His spleen, no longer able to take the excessive bouts of carousing and drinking, had finally burst, poisoning his entire system and killing him within minutes.

Tessa shed but few tears; she had never forgiven her father for marrying her into what she thought of as slavery, and was content to see him go. Since she had no brothers, the line died with him; when the lawyer came to read the deed of settlement they found the estate near Wakefield was so encumbered with debts newly contracted to support Sir Ian's London lifestyle that it was beyond salvage, even with Peter's money. Peter was content to let it go; the Clether home had been old-fashioned and unmanageable; when the time came he intended to find himself something much more elegant, much closer to the Leeds scene. He also had ambitions perhaps to buy in London.

The day after he received the news, he removed the Clether name from all his business premises and documents. Henceforth, it would be Aysgill and Sons.

Robert was born in the middle of the night amidst great comings and goings; unlike his brother, Gavin, he was a lusty boy and the resemblance to the stronger Aysgill line was much more pronounced than in his older brother, who, still weak and sickly at almost two years of age, looked more and more like his mother. Gavin, Peter realized, was a Clether, while Robert would always be an Aysgill in looks and temperament.

He came to see Tessa the day after the birth and seated himself on the edge of the bed. She looked at him with indifference as she rested her hands docilely on the covers.

'I shall trouble you no more for my husbandly right,' he announced to her.

She nodded, quite beyond caring.

'Emily Ponder will become housekeeper, and I'd be obliged if you will not interfere with her duties.'

'What of Mrs Davies and Selena?' she asked quietly. 'What of Willerby?'

'The magistrate has them,' he said. 'They will not be returning here.'

His revenge against them for permitting his wife to take a lover was complete. The previous evening he'd laid an information against them, charging them with the theft of his property. The Magistrate had sent his constable to the house, and the rooms of Willerby, Mrs Davies and Selena, had been searched. All had contained gold and jewellery which he had reported stolen. Each had sworn innocence; Selena had broken down crying, saying it was all a wicked plot, and had to be forcibly restrained by the constable and his two helpers. The three had been driven from the house in the constable's black coach, and were now in the Leeds Town gaol, where they would stay until the Assize Court heard the case and sentenced them to transportation to America. The Constable's evidence of finding the gold and jewellery concealed in the bedding of each of the accused would ensure such a verdict.

'You devil,' Tessa hissed at her husband. 'And what demonic revenge have you planned against my dear

Percival, who is ten times the man you will ever be?'

Aysgill smiled. 'Revenge, my dear, against Percival D'Arcy? I plan no such thing. Do you not know that he is become my best companion. We are inseparable as cousins on all occasions and he introduces me everywhere as his friend. He sponsors me politically since it is my intention to seek office as Alderman of the City, a position attracting much respect to itself. I believe he is greatly attracted by the daughter of Lord Newsam and will soon make his intentions known to her parents. She, of course, is a girl much younger than you, who takes greater pains with her appearance. Her dewy freshness recommends her to all and she is greatly admired for her poise and wit. Why, I do declare that at the moment, you look, and smell, old enough to be her mother! *Tu as veilli, ma chérie*!'

He didn't know if his French was correct and cared less; it was enough that he indicated to her the knowledge he was acquiring from her paramour to complete his education, and her humiliation.

The house had been cleaned from top to bottom and a bright fire burned in the grate from the coal that Matthew brought home from the mine. Each man was allowed a basket each day as part of his employment, though the coal had to be taken from sortings and was often flinty. The two boys, Frank aged sixteen and Richard aged fifteen, were sitting impatiently at the table, on which a modest feast had been spread, bought with contributions from all of them. Frank and Richard both worked in the mine alongside their father; the three of them working as a team could bring out enough money so that Mildred no longer needed to work full-time in the mill. She busied herself around the streets where they lived, helping when she could, nursing sick folks, taking care of babies whose parents were in trouble, teaching a class each evening to read and write.

Today, Jamie was coming back, from Oxford!

'What a day,' Mildred said to Matthew. 'Our very own, coming back from Oxford!'

Jamie's story had been a triumph; Mildred had taught him, and Jamie had lost all the bitterness and hatred he'd felt at the loss of his arm. The doctor had seen him in the street one day and had invited him into his house, to examine the stump of the operation he'd performed. He and Jamie had conversed and the Doctor had been most impressed by the lad, who had a great lust to better himself. He had finally taken him in as an assistant, though he realized the boy's surgical ability would be limited by the loss of his arm. It hadn't mattered; Jamie had become more interested in the pharmaceuticals, and was content to learn as much as he could about that branch of medicine. The doctor had insisted, however, that Jamie should take an education to himself, and had paid for him to go first to Grammar School for Latin and Greek, and then to Oxford.

Today, Jamie was coming home to them.

Matthew grasped Mildred's hand when the lad came through the door. He'd grown tall and handsome, looking in every way a modest gentleman of learning. He was wearing a black coat and black breeches, with stockings and shoes. His hat was black, but it carried a white band around it. The cotton at his throat was impeccably white, and he had a fashionable short bobbed wig.

'Oh, my Jamie,' Mildred said as she squeezed her husband's hand, unable to move for the happiness of the emotion that had overcome her. He took off his hat with a flourish and smiled at them.

Matthew held his hand forward. 'Aye, Jamie, th'art become a gentleman, it seems to me. Come on, lads, this is your coz Jamie, come back bursting with knowledge from Oxford, but he'll not be too proud to take you in his arms and give you a kiss, methinks.'

Jamie swept both lads into his arm and hugged them. Mildred couldn't resist and went into the tight group, kissing Jamie's cheek and crying on him.

'I'm that proud of thee,' she said, 'I'm fit to burst! If only your mother could have stayed alive to see this day.'

Jamie's mother had gone into a decline shortly after his mine injury; she'd never recovered from it.

Nothing could spoil the day; Jamie sat at the table and they ate the food sparingly, listening to his account of his years at Oxford, his life, the vast range of knowledge he'd acquired in those ancient halls of learning. Mostly his recitals were punctured with 'I say, you never . . .' from Matthew, or 'fancy that . . .' from Mildred as they listened spell-bound. The day ended but they couldn't bear him to stop. Mildred lit a mutton-fat candle which gave enough of a flickering light for them to see the gleam of his eyes and the movement of his lips. He'd enlarged his course to include philosophy as well as Greek and Latin, and something called The Humanities. More and more as Matthew listened to him, he became troubled, even dismayed. It seemed to him that Jamie was expressing dangerous ideas in much of what he was saying. So many of the Greek writers, poets and philosophers seemed to contradict much of what Matthew believed.

Democracy passes into despotism, Jamie quoted Plato as saying.

The Latins appeared to be little better. *The cobbler should not judge above his last*, Pliny had said, according to Jamie.

His education appeared to have made Jamie less understanding of the need for the lowly man to seek to improve his situation, to strive for amelioration any way he knew how. But, this night, Matthew was too happy at the return of his nephew to let his disquietude come to the fore and intrude itself upon their celebration.

'Ah, 'tis good to see thee again, Jamie,' he said when finally they were all obliged by fatigue to seek a bed in view of the following day's work.

All the way to the mine in the breaking daylight, the two boys talked of their cousin and the wonderful stories he had told them of his life. Neither felt envy; neither

313

expressed any dissatisfaction with their present situation, and that worried Matthew. It was his belief that discontent could only spur a man to greater endeavours without which a man's life was not worth living. He could fully understand why Simon had taken his own life; without a belief in God to nourish him, Simon had known no hope; it had been all too easy to slip into a trough of despond from which there was no salvation.

Matthew knew that matters must move slowly, as they had in his discussions with the men of the mine. This day he had a double cause for celebration; Jamie's return had inspired him and he'd been unable to sleep deeply during the night, but the work he hoped to do that day would, he knew, stimulate him beyond any fatigue. That day, if the men stood fast, they were going to confront Jabez Broadley!

The men had gathered before the mine gate when he arrived with his boys. He looked round at the twenty-five or so, seeing one or two absentees among the more faint hearted. He hadn't wanted to take the role of spokesman but Mildred had insisted he do so. She was afraid that any other man to whom they might entrust the role might be bought off, or bullied, by Broadley. The men knew Matthew would stand firm and in a sense had nailed their courage to his.

The gates opened when the mine hooter sounded and they streamed across the outer yard between the piles of coal awaiting the waggons that would cart them to the river for shipment by barge. There'd been much talk of expanding the river and even building new channels down which it could flow – canals they were being called; if and when the canals were built it would be a simple matter to load the coal direct onto barges and carry it anywhere it needed to go. Matthew had heard that the Duke of Bridgewater was connecting his mines at Worsley to a sea outlet at Manchester, so that the coal could go straight to the boats for export overseas. Here at Broadleys the outcrop of coal had been worked out, as had most of the

314

bell-pits, and now the men, and some women, worked underground cutting the rich seam of coal by the pillar and stall method. The air in the mine was habitually foul since the upcast shafts were improperly engined and couldn't draw out a sufficient quantity of foul air to permit the fresh air to come in.

That was their first target.

The men gathered at the entrance to the mine down which they would climb by long ladders attached to the side of the eight-foot diameter shaft, past the ropes of the cog and rung gin which, all those years ago, had taken Jamie's arm.

'We're not going down, lads,' Matthew said. 'Remember that. Tell it to yourselves. We are not going down until Jabez Broadley gives us satisfaction!'

Other men who had not been approached to join the group, scuttled hurriedly down the ladders, and women with them. All had been given a chance to back out of the group since Matthew wanted only stout-hearted, God-fearing men behind him. Jabez Broadley had ridden into the mine a few minutes before and his horse was being led to its stable, a vastly different animal from the big-boned cart-horses he employed to turn the gin. The gin had been attached to a pair of bellows; two horses were needed now to turn it to lift the coal scuttles up and down the shaft, and also to blow air down the shaft pipe, sucking the foul air up the upcast. For weeks now the bellows, made of concertinaed leather, had leaked and failed to deliver a full charge. Jabez Broadley had been asked to repair the bellows, but he'd not done so, saying leather was too expensive.

He walked across to the minehead and saw the group of men still standing there. 'Get down the shaft,' he said. 'The hooter's gone a time ago.'

The men made no move.

'Come on,' he said. 'You'll earn no coin standing about up here.'

'Nor will you, Maister,' Job Bentley said.

'What's that tha says, Job? Art tha bereft of thy senses to talk back to thy master?'

'Tha baint *my* master, sithee,' Job said, and spat on the ground. 'I work for thee for coin, nowt more, nowt less. And I'm my own maister, and allus s'all be.'

'We'll see about that,' Jabez Broadley said. 'Tha can get out of my mine this instant. I'll not have men working for me as talks back when I gie an order.'

Matthew cursed himself for not speaking earlier, for letting Job Bentley, a troublemaker, have the first say. 'If Bentley goes, Master, we all go,' he said belatedly, aware that the men were looking for a lead from him.

Broadley moved forward and planted himself in front of Matthew, his big hands clenched by his sides. 'You'll speak when you're spoken to, Aysgill,' he said. 'I'll thank thee to hold thy parson's tongue until I address thee direct. Now, all of you, get down the shaft and start to work.'

'We're not going down, Master,' Matthew said quietly. 'Not until we've had a talk with you.'

'A *talk*?' Jabez Broadley roared. 'This is no time for talking when there's coal waiting to be dug and fetched out. By now the first bucket ought to be on its way.'

'We want to talk,' Matthew persisted, 'about the conditions down in the mine. We want to know when the bellows are going to be mended.'

'Are you mad?' Jabez bellowed. 'What the devil does it have to do wi' you when the bellows are mended. *I* own this mine, and *I'll* decide when the bellows gets mended, and nobody else. And you, Aysgill, can head away out of that gate wi' yon Bentley beside you.'

It was Mildred who had decided on the timing of the strategy, pointing out that with so many new mines being opened, and so many old mines being worked at lower levels now that the Newcomen engine was being used to pump out water, labour to work the mines was becoming scarce. Jabez Broadley would have set on another twenty men if he could have found them, and already there was competition among the owners to buy orphans from the

316

foundling homes. If he lost twenty-five men from his work force, he would not be able to replace them for some time and his pocket would suffer. 'You must all threaten his pocket,' she'd said to Matthew, 'it's the only way you can affect him.'

'I'll be happy to go, Master,' Matthew said, 'and take these men with me. We're all in agreement that if one of us goes, we all go, and offer our services elsewhere.'

'Nobody would take you on if I spoke against it,' Jabez blustered, but he lacked conviction. Most mine-owners were like himself and interested only in what they could earn. Any mine-owner of any size would welcome a ready-made work force of twenty-five experienced and grown men. He looked round the group and cursed Aysgill, who'd chosen his men well. All were good workers, all capable of moving much coal. The loss of profit would cripple him!

'Tha said tha wanted to talk,' he said grudgingly. 'What about?'

'We want the bellows mended today,' Aysgill said quietly, 'so that we can breathe fresh air down there. Six women have fainted from that air in the last two weeks, and one of them will never recover from the poison that's been put in her lungs, so we're told.'

'I was going to mend the bellows today,' Jabez Broadley said. 'I already have the leather on order. As soon as it comes, I'll get the bellows mended.'

'Aye, and as soon as the bellows is mended, we'll go down the hole,' Job Bentley said.

'Th'art pushing me too far,' Jabez Broadley shouted. 'I'll have thee out of here! I'll not take any more of thy lip, that's for certain.'

Bentley looked at Matthew Aysgill. 'Right, Matthew, us'd better be on our way. If we're going to Robinson, we'll need to get a move on to put in a full shift today.'

'Nay,' Broadley said, 'I'll send for the leather right away. You, Bentley, can take the cart and fetch it right away. Are any of you skilled in working leather?'

317

Four hands shot up.

'Right. You four can stay up here while Bentley fetches the leather. You can set to right away by stripping off the upcast bellow – the downcast will keep some air going down while you make the repair. Then you can do the other.'

'What about payment for all this,' Job Bentley asked.

'Aye, I'll give you time money, based on what you'd have earned at the face.'

'That suits me,' Bentley said. 'What about thee, Matthew?'

'Aye, I reckon that'll suit,' Matthew said, realizing he had lost the initiative again. He ought to have suggested that he fetch the leather, though it would have been a doubtful strategy to leave the men alone to be harangued by Broadley.

'Right, Bentley, I'll just do thee an order paper,' Jabez said. 'And the rest of you can get down below where you're most needed.'

Matthew led the way down the ladder. The twenty men gathered round him when they reached the bottom of the shaft. 'We did it, Matthew, praise to thee and Job Bentley – we faced him down – made him agree.'

'There'll be a price to pay for this day's work,' Matthew said. He'd seen Jabez Broadley's eyes on him as he'd gone over the lip of the mine-shaft and knew he'd engendered a hatred in the mine-owner that would cost him dear.

Job Bentley was trundling along on the seat of the cart with the bales of leather behind him. 'Aye, this is a damned sight better than working,' he said, as he drove through the streets in the cool fresh September day. The mine would be hot and stinking by now, and every breath, laden with the dust from the coat face and the heavy gases the picking released from pockets in the coal itself, would sear a man's lungs. Job had been in the mines all his life, first as a boy in the bell-pits, and now down at the levels that were being opened by the use of pumping engines.

318

He'd seen his father and his brothers killed by a fall from a bell-pit arched roof; he'd seen people killed by being dropped when the windlass slipped, or the rope broke. He'd known no other way of life. Many times he'd been out of work when a seam ran dry, waiting for another seam to be opened. He'd never married – he'd been too much concerned to get himself down to the ale-house when he'd finished work, to try to quench the terrible thirst that the mine always gave him. With the drinking had come the fighting, and the conviction that the world was against him.

Aye, well, Matthew had started them all thinking but it remained to be seen if the new thoughts would do them any good; it had been Job's experience that you answered the master's beck and call if you wanted to keep your job and, while you didn't need to bend down before him like a lackey, you did what he said. If he said the mine was fit to work in, you went down and worked, no matter how many people dropped beside you from fatigue or poisoning in the bad air. You took your chances: if the mine caved in, you pulled out all that remained alive and untrapped, and you got on with digging the coal again. Matthew's ideas had sounded dangerous. The idea that you could talk back to the Master if enough of you were in agreement. The idea that you could band together with your coins to provide a doctor for injury and ill-health hadn't worked, had it? This new idea had worked with the bellows, and Job knew that Matthew had other ideas in mind, like propping up the coal overhead with timbers to keep the roof safe, like opening up more air holes to suck out the gases faster.

Well, this one had worked, and here he was riding a cart with a load of leather to mend the bellows to prove it.

He could see the mine about a mile ahead on the other side of the copse, and slackened his pace, since he was in no hurry to get back. He entered the copse, brought the horse to a willing stop, and left it with its reins over its head while he went off into the bushes to relieve himself. As he buttoned his breeches again and came through the glade, he saw four men standing by the cart, looking into the trees of the copse. He recognized one of the men as Tarn Fowles, Jabez Broadley's horse handler, who rode beside Jabez when he was abroad at night to protect him from footpads. Tarn was a giant of a man, wearing a leather doublet over thick leather breeches and leather boots. Legend had it that Tarn could lift a shire horse by putting his hands and arms under its belly. He had fists like lumps of pork meat, and one of them now clutched a blackthorn cudgel as thick as a man's arm at the end.

They all turned to face Job when he came from the protection of the trees.

'Aye, Tarn,' he said. 'Art tha chasing thieves then?'

'Aye, I reckon as we are,' Tarn said. 'Thieves as takes a Master's coin and then speaks badly to him. Thieves like thee, Job Bentley.'

The four men moved swiftly to surround him and his heart sank. He did the only thing he knew; he dived in quickly aiming for Tarn's privates, hoping to disable him quickly and perhaps rout the others, but Tarn swung swiftly aside and tapped the side of Job's head with the cudgel, tearing the skin and drawing blood. Suddenly they were on him, slamming him to the ground, picking him up by his arms and legs, throwing him up in the air and letting him land face down on the hard stony ground. Each time he tried to twist, one of them would kick his legs away. After the fourth toss he knew he was losing consciousness; his nose had broken and blood ran over his face.

'Us'll teach thee, Job Bentley, to speak back to thy Master,' Tarn said. 'Us'll teach thee to join with other men to fling defiance like dung into thy Master's face!'

The terrible pounding began as two of them held him up by his arms and the other two took turns to slam a heavy fist into his belly, forcing the air, spit, bile and vomit out of his mouth with each blow. They turned him round, and began to pound his kidneys, one on each side slamming in those monstrous hands. He felt his senses going but resolved to try to keep them for he knew that once he went

320

under, he was a dead man.

'That'll do,' Tarn said. 'I reckon as he's learned his lesson.' They threw Job on the leather on the back of the cart, picked up the reins and thrust them in his shaking hands. One of them slashed the horse over its rump, knowing it would head back to its stable at the mine. The horse clopped slowly away, and Job, unable to see for his injuries, unable to breathe for the pains in his lungs and his abdomen, heard the bellowing laughs of the four villains from the copse behind him.

Wilfred Oates, who'd been working on the leather of the bellows, was the first to see the cart and its dreadful burden. While the others hastened to help Job, Wilfred raced down the mine ladder; by the time he emerged with Matthew they'd spread Job Bentley on a pile of straw, and Jabez Broadley was standing beside him, looking down.

'Who did it to you?' Matthew said as he crouched by the body.

'Aye, Job,' Jabez said, 'tell 'em who did it to you.'

Job managed to open one eye and looked up at the ring of faces. His eye found that of Jabez Broadley, saw the cynical smile on his face. 'It were footpads,' Job said. 'I didn't recognize them. I think they were after the leather.'

'Footpads?' Matthew asked. 'You're sure? You didn't recognize them?'

'Nay, I didn't,' Job said from the edge of his failing strength, 'I didn't recognize them.'

Matthew and Jamie went to Job's house that night after work. Jabez Broadley had permitted a couple of the men to borrow the cart to take him home, provided they brought it straight back. Jamie examined Job, using the knowledge he'd acquired as the doctor's assistant.

'I can't find anything wrong with him,' he said, 'except his nose is flattened, and it seems as if the organs of his body have been badly beaten. Everything seems to be working all right, so we'll just have to wait. He'll need to lie down for a day or two and drink only broth; he shouldn't eat anything solid.'

Matthew sat beside the bed; Job was bruised all over and in obvious pain. Jamie had covered his abrasions with grease but there was little else he could do.

'Who did it to you?' Matthew asked quietly. 'Footpads don't beat a man as you've been beaten. If they can't rob a man, they run away to try elsewhere. You were beaten. Whoever did it was after you, not the leather.'

'It were footpads,' Job said with great effort. 'Now, leave me be.'

'It were Jabez Broadley's orders, I'll be bound, though he'd have used his own men to do it,' Matthew mused out loud. 'I'll bet it were Tarn Fowles . . . that's the sort of work he's suited to.'

'Nay,' Job said weakly with terror showing in his eyes. 'I never said that. I never bore witness against Tarn Fowles, and you can't put the words into my mouth.'

When Matthew left he was convinced that what he'd guessed was correct – it *had* been some of Tarn's doing, acting no doubt under orders from Jabez Broadley.

The following morning the men were gathered outside the gate again when Matthew and the boys arrived. 'Did you go to see Job?' they asked. 'How was he . . .?'

Matthew gathered the twenty-four men in a tight circle around him. The hooter would be sounding soon, he could tell by the sunrise, so he didn't have much time. Could he possibly convince them in such a short time?

'Job wasn't beaten by footpads,' he said. 'He was beaten by Tarn Fowles, under orders from Jabez Broadley.'

'Did Job say that . . .?' one of the men asked.

'Not in so many words. He's afeard that if he bears witness against Tarn, the next time they meet in a wood he'll be killed. But I know that's how it was worked.'

Wilfred Oates spoke up. 'I heard Jabez Broadley call Tarn Fowles into his office after Job left with the cart,' he said. 'When I was stripping the old leather off the bellows

Tarn left the mine with another man — that lad from Scarborough who used to be a prize-fighter, they say — the one who outrides Broadley's coach.'

'There 'tis!' Matthew said. 'Jabez wanted to teach Job a lesson . . .'

'It'll be thee next, Matthew,' Wilfred said. 'He has thee marked.'

Matthew knew that was true, but he was driven on with a compulsion he couldn't either define or ignore. 'I s'all have to take my chances on that,' he said, 'though I'll make certain I never go through yon copse without my lads beside me. We can't let Broadley get away with this. We've got to find some recompense for Job. Now, I hope as you're all still with me.'

He could see one or two were thinking about Job's beating and did not want to attract the same treatment to themselves.

'Nay, Sam, it's for Job,' he said. 'You can't back out now. Ezra, Silas, Willy . . .?'

'Aye,' Ezra said, 'it's for Job, I reckon.'

'What are you going to ask for?' Silas asked.

At that moment the hooter sounded and the gates were opened. 'I don't know,' Matthew said quickly, 'but I'll think of summat. We all stick together, mind!'

As if he'd been expecting trouble, Jabez Broadley had arrived at the mine early and was standing on the step of his office. Tarn and the prize-fighter they called Scarborough Bob were standing on the step beside him. The men gathered round the top of the mine-shaft, shuffling their feet, and making no attempt to climb down the ladder.

'Let's go over there and talk to him, Matthew,' Ezra said, but Matthew shook his head. 'Let the devil come over here and talk to us,' he said. 'We'll meet him on our ground, not his.'

Jabez slowly advanced across the yard, while Tarn Fowles and Scarborough Bob stayed where they were, told by the Master to stay, like two well-trained dogs.

'What is it this morn?' Jabez asked. 'I thought we'd had enough of laiking about yesterday.'

'We want to know what's to be done for Job Bentley,' Matthew said strongly.

'What's that got to do wi' me?' Jabez said. 'If tha wants to do owt for him, take him round a bowl of gruel and drop on thy knees by his bedside, for healing is a matter for the Lord, they tell me.'

'Is he to be paid, then?'

'Paid? Paid for what?'

'It was in thy service, Master, that he got his injuries. He should have face money.'

'*Face money*, while he's lying abed? Tha's got some funny ideas, Matthew. He'll get nowt from my purse till such time as he digs coal again.'

'He was injured in your service, Master. He has a right to . . .'

'A right, Matthew Aysgill?' Jabez roared. 'Who are you to tell me who has a right here? On my land. I decide who has rights here; and so far as I'm concerned, the only right tha has, is to take them two lads of yourn, and get off my property. If ever tha sets foot on it again, I s'all take a horsewhip to thee myself. Now, get off, and begone! And the rest of you, get down that mine-shaft. There's been enough of this laiking about to last my lifetime.'

Ezra looked at Matthew apologetically, and started for the ladders. Silas moved to follow him. Wilfred Oates held out his arms. 'Nay, we can't leave Matthew,' he said. 'We can't leave him now.'

The others gathered in a tighter knot and Matthew turned towards the gate. 'Come on,' he said disgustedly. 'Let's go to Robinsons. We shall not advantage ourselves here.'

Jabez let them all move a few paces, then he called out. 'I'm setting people on,' he called, 'to work the lower level. The gin has pumped out all the water and it's dry as a bone down there, I'm told. We're extending the air pipes, and putting the bellows on the gin!'

The men stopped, wondering what he was going to say next.

'I'm paying double wages to any man working the lower level,' he said. 'But the men as wants it has to sign on this morn. I'll get all the workers I want when the news goes round of what I'm paying.'

Matthew knew at once he was defeated. Jabez spoke the truth when he said he'd get all the men he wanted. It would mean twice the pay to take home and feed a family, for doing practically the same work. No man in his senses would refuse such an offer. He heard the men talking to each other.

Opening the new level, eh? Dry as a bone? More air from a gin? Twice the wages?

His heart was sick as he realized he'd lost his battle. He couldn't keep the men together in the face of increased wages.

Jabez set his eyes on Matthew. 'You, Matthew Aysgill, are you going to be the first to sign on for the new level? You and your two lads. Or is making a nuisance of yourself all you care about? Airing your notions about God and politics, and not caring what happens to the men if they follow you. You're a dreamer, Matthew Aysgill, leading astray men who could be earning twice what they're now getting for their wives and bairns. Are you going to be worldly, Matthew Aysgill, and sign on?'

The men were muttering again. Aye, he is a dreamer. All this talk about God. All this talk about men being the equal of other men. Where did it get Job Bentley? Where will it get us?

'Well, Matthew?' Wilfred Oates asked. 'You can't say but that the Master is being fair in offering you to sign.'

Jabez Broadley had the native cunning to know that his victory would be the more complete if it included Matthew and his sons. He couldn't arrange for them to be beaten, as he'd dealt with Job Bentley. But if he could show the rest of the men that he was being open-handed, then any decision Matthew took would be interpreted by the men as pig-headedness, as dreaming.

'You know, Matthew Aysgill, as it makes no difference to me,' he said. 'If you want to go to work for Robinson, you're free to do so. But I'd like to see the men as have opened up this mine alongside each other, take the advantage of the higher wage for the deeper level. It's their advantage by *right* and I'd not like to see you take it away from them to satisfy religious or political notions of your own imagining.'

'Nay, Matthew, th'art obliged to let us sign,' Wilfred Oates said. 'Like the Master says, it's our right to advantage ourselves and our bairns.'

What could Matthew do? He knew for certain it would, somehow, prove to be a false advantage but he couldn't say why at that moment. And the men wouldn't be interested in his unformed fears and theories.

'Very well, then, I'll sign,' he said. 'Though I'd have liked to see a bit of something given to Job Bentley.'

'I *will* gi'e him summat,' Jabez Broadley said, magnanimous in victory. 'The minute he's better and walks through that gate, I'll gi'e him a job alongside the rest of you. I'll let him sign, on the lower level!'

Matthew had never heard Mildred more scornful than she was that evening. 'Why, you daft lummox,' she said, 'don't you see what he's done? He's bested you. He got you to sign first for the lower level and that means that what happens down there is with your approval. Jabez will always be able to say now that Matthew Aysgill signed first and therefore it must be reet! But it isn't reet, Matthew. You're working at a lower level, and it takes longer to get down and up again. You don't get paid while you're climbing ladders, Matthew! You're opening up a new seam, which means you'll have to dig a lot more stuff out to get the seam in good shape. And you only get paid for coal, Matthew, not for flint and stone. The coal has to be lifted out, and that takes more time from the lower level. And, last of all, the Newcomen engine hasn't been tested down to that level. Why, from what I've heard it could barely lift the water from the top level.'

'He said it was dry down there,' Matthew said stubbornly.

'Of course it's dry. It's dry because nobody is opening it up yet. The minute the picks start to go into it you'll free more water and the pump will have to work harder. And what happens if the pump can't manage it? I'll tell you, Matthew. You and those boys of mine will drown, that's what will happen!'

'Nay, Mildred, tha's overstating thy case,' Matthew said, his masculine pride injured by her unremitting forcefulness. Who was she to tell him what happened in a mine, he asked her. She'd never, unlike some, been *down* a mine! And who was she to call him a fool and a lummox?

She came and knelt beside him. 'Nay, Matthew,' she said softly, trying to placate him, knowing that in her anger and enthusiasm she'd gone too far for his pride. 'I'm not telling thee anything tha doesn't know. I'm not setting myself as the expert. I'm asking you to work it out for yourself, that's all. To reason it out.'

He let his arm drop around her shoulder, not yet quite ready for conciliation.

'Th'art my man and my master,' she said. 'I'll stick by thee as tha knows, and by the two lads. But I ask thee to think a bit, while tha's down in the lower levels, and to keep an eye out for the lads' safety, that's all I ask.'

'Th'art a good woman, Mildred,' he said, 'but tha does get carried away wi' thy tongue sometimes.'

'Tha can lead a horse to water, aye, but tha can't make it drink.'

'Summat like that.'

'Then, I beg thy forgiveness,' she said.

The next day was a Feast Day, and the Fair came and parked on the edge of Hunslet Moor. In the last years, a number of people had banded together and travelled the country in their carts in company, offering a vast swirling entertainment that could pull coins out of the leanest purse. They all dressed early; Jamie arrived to go with them and Frank went to bring his cousin Arthur and his aunt Amelia. Dodie arrived later, with Stanley and Claude, who'd been given a day off from their schooling, and Caroline who was tricked out in a fine silk dress Dodie had made for her. At six she was already showing signs of a great beauty, and Mildred, who would dearly have liked to have a girl, felt tears prick her eyes when she saw the young maid and heard her piping voice. Mark Ottershaw, big and bluff, was carrying the little one on his shoulder. He set her down and Mildred quickly gathered her to her breast.

'Nay, Aunt Mildred, you mustn't crush my dress,' Caroline said, 'for I'm to guard it and look pretty the whole day long, so my Mam tells me.'

'Nay lass,' Mark Ottershaw, her father, said, 'tha's to have a happy day this day and don't worry about thy dress . . .'

The Aysgill family thronged the little house of Matthew, the leader of the Aysgill line now that Simon was no longer. He sat Amelia down, knowing she was not as strong as once she'd been. Since Simon's death the light seemed to have blown out in her lamp and she depended more and more, he knew, on Arthur to keep them going in Mill Cottages.

They set off together, gradually finding partners and stringing out along the road that led to the Moor, already crowded by excited families whose children ran ahead, came back again, ran ahead again in a lather of excitement to reach the feast ground. They were all some distance away when they saw the first attraction over the heads of the crowd; the slack wire man had tied one end of his wire to the very top of one tree, taken the other end to another tree, and was walking between the two higher than any house top. As they watched in petrified amazement, he stopped in the centre of the wire and then began to bounce up and down. They heard the roar from the feast ground and started forward again, eager to miss nothing.

Such a sight greeted the children's eyes as they'd never believed possible. All round the feast ground the itinerants had set up their shows, which were booths built on poles and hung with a light muslin, stained with many colours. The first booth they saw was a show between two characters, with a hollow voice issuing from the booth beneath the ledge on which they sat. Though obviously made of wood and straw, the figures were talking in human voices. The children couldn't believe the evidence of their ears, especially when one of the figures took a cudgel and appeared to berate one of the other figures with it. They all screamed with excitement and several of them shouted out.

''Tis Punch and Judy,' Mildred said. 'They've had it in Bartholomew Fair in London for many a year!'

They found a great difficulty pushing their way through the crowd as one family, and each parent kept his or her eyes peeled looking out for their own children. Mark Ottershaw carried Caroline on his shoulders to better her view, and the two lads clung to their mother's sleeves. In one corner of the ground they came upon a group of men, small and wizened like monkeys with brown skins, who formed themselves into the most amazing triangles, with one man standing on the shoulders of another, or balancing on his head, resting on his hands. At one time, so Stanley counted, there were thirty of them balanced like the branches of a tree on the arms and shoulders of one single man! People were throwing small coins onto the ground before the men as they performed; Arthur had never seen so much money in one place, he told Amelia, his mother.

'Happen I'd do better learning to balance like that than run the fulling machine,' he said, only half in jest.

Frank and Richard pulled Matthew to one side. They wanted to look at a booth in which, so the sign said, was a 'Fat Lady with a Beard Two Feet Long'.

'Nay,' Matthew said, 'we'll not encourage them in making a spectacle of God's less fortunate creatures!'

He himself was tempted, however, to see the twins who'd been born joined at the lower spine with one torso governed by two heads.

All the booths were jammed close together, some selling candies brought from as far as Crete, sweetmeats from Italy, others selling cheap toys of various kinds. Arthur, who had saved his coins against the day, bought a figure of a man carved in wood and painted. When he held the figure by its feet, the man collapsed in a heap in his hand, but when he pressed the ankles of the figure together, the man stood up again. Though several of the children examined it, none could say how it worked its miracle.

At one corner of the feast ground was a booth larger than the others to which Mildred hurried her family. One of her many public enterprises had been to assist the parson to collect money; they'd raised the wonderful sum of two pounds in a little over two months and the money had been devoted to the purchase of musical instruments. The parson himself had been trained to the voila d'amore and was now leading his group of musicians in a spirited rendition of music by an Italian composer, Vivaldi. She stood entranced since this was the first time she'd been able to hear them play together. Music was sweeping England at this time, she knew; she found it such a pleasure just to stand there and listen without comprehension to the beautiful sounds they were making. Matthew squeezed her hand, knowing what the experience meant to her as the flute, the haut-bois, the fiddle, the voila d'amore, the bassoon and the lute all played in consort. The design above the stand announced that music by Handel was also to be performed and that afterwards there would be a collection of monies 'for the benefice of the Church in All Its Godly Works'. Mildred found her two nephews, Dodie's sons Stanley and Claude, standing beside her spellbound by the musicians. She didn't know how Dodie had managed to find the only two free places in the school, as she termed them, but she suspected her sister-in-law's method. She knew Dodie to be ruthless in pursuit of her own and her family's ambitions and found little sympathy with her sister-in-law who often derided the work she did to help people, mostly without hope of a coin.

'Mam says we're to have music lessons later,' Stanley said with great enthusiasm.

'I'd like to learn that one first,' Claude said. At eight years of age, he liked the jolly puffing the instrumentalist was doing with such obvious pleasure.

'We have enough bairns between us,' Matthew said, 'to form an Aysgill Consort, if we've a mind.'

'And care to waste a shilling an hour on the training of each one of them,' Dodie said.

'Aye, Dodie, us can't all get it free in't school,' Amelia said.

Mark Ottershaw looked up quickly in defence of his wife. 'Now, Amelia,' he said, 'we're supposed to be at the feast today to forget our woes. Come wi' me and I'll get thee a coffin and a screw of them peas that smells so nice.'

They all crowded round the conjuror, watching him pull all manner of unlikely objects from a battered top hat he supported on a muslin covered table. They saw the jugglers with their coloured wooden tops, throwing them up in the air whirling so fast the eye couldn't distinguish the handle from the end, catching them when they came hurtling down, throwing them spinning to each other, tossing them under arm pits, between legs, always always catching them.

On one stretch of ground the tumblers performed, running and throwing themselves in tight balls, turning somersaults while standing on their feet, or hands, forwards and backwards, springing up and twisting around, falling or so it seemed then bouncing up again.

One man had a performing bear that would rear up on its hind legs and clap its hands when the man goaded it. Another had a little white dog with a black patch over one eye that would walk along a stick suspended between two Y-shaped forks. Another had two monkeys dressed in human clothes that swung from a set of rails and bars the man had erected; the man had dressed himself in the Italian style, and wore a long, much pomaded and twisted moustache whose ends stretched at least seven inches on each side of his face.

'Look at the poor monkeys,' Amelia said. 'See how their teeth chatter with the cold. Gi'e us a coin, there's a sweet boy,' she asked her son Arthur. 'I reckon as the poor mites are starved for food.'

Arthur searched his pockets. 'I'm sorry, Mam,' he said, 'but I've spent up.'

'Gi'e us a coin then, Stanley?' Amelia asked Dodie's lad, but he pushed his hand farther into the pocket of his jerkin. 'I'm saving mine,' he said truculently. He had enough of his mother in him not to want to waste precious coins on monkeys . . .

They wandered about all the day long, completing many circuits of the feast ground, finding something new to see on each circuit, some new animal act or feat of incredible human skill. The afternoon was beginning to fade when Amelia, looking more tired than any other, asked Arthur to take her home. He didn't argue, as he would have liked to do. He'd take her home, settle her down, and then come back again, for the evening promised more wonders on this marvellous, marvellous, day. He only wished he could have brought Wally from the mill with him, but he knew it would be impossible for Wally to escape during the daylight without Thomas Tomlinson catching him and giving him a drubbing.

There was a tremendous excitement shortly after Arthur and Amelia left when Frank, Matthew's sixteen-year-old son, got himself into the final shoot of the archery contest. Without saying anything to anyone, he'd resisted the blandishments of other booths in which he could have spent his few coins in order to try the archery. It cost two pence for three arrows, and his first shoot, at twenty paces, had put all three in the centre of the target. They'd advanced the targets now to thirty paces and three lads were drawing bows against each other. The Aysgill and

332

Ottershaw families rushed over to the archery ground to watch the final shoot. If Frank could win, he'd earn himself all the money back he'd paid for bow and arrows, plus a prize of a fine big clay pot.

The other two lads, both about his age, went first, each taking three arrows at the thirty paces. The first lad seemed upset by the crowd that had flocked around them and his first arrow went wild. The next two were clipping the inside rings. Disgruntled he threw the bow down. The second took up the bow, drew it to refresh his memory of its tension, and then put his three arrows in the centre of the target, though the adjudicators, three men from the district, noted that one clipped the line.

Frank took the bow and drew it experimentally a couple of times.

'Take thy time, lad,' Matthew said. 'Thy grandfather were a champion in his day . . .'

Frank did the opposite to what his father had recommended. He took up the arrows quickly, one after the other, drew rapidly, seemed hardly to aim, and put all three in the centre of the target in a space he could have covered with his fist. The man in charge of the booth didn't need the recommendations of the adjudicators. He hoisted Frank's arm. 'Th'art an instinctive archer,' he said. 'Tha'd go a long way in the country, lad . . . In the service of some fine Lord.'

Frank was flustered but accepted the man's praise, anxious to get his hands on the pot. When it was put into his arms, he noticed the large drying crack across its bottom, but he didn't care. It was *his*, and he'd *won* it! For him this wonderful, wonderful day would be an unforgettable memory.

Afternoon turned to evening, and evening turned to night, and now lanthorns were suspended above the booths as the travellers sought to con the visitors of their remaining coins. Dodie and Mark were still strolling arm in arm, with Mark holding Caroline on his shoulder. The child had been asleep an hour and the two boys were sitting

333

in a bale of straw, exhausted, waiting for their parents to make up their minds to go home.

'You remember Barthwick?' Mark asked as he squeezed his wife.

'How could I forget the place of my birth?' she asked.

'Nay, I didn't mean that. I were thinking of't Harvest Fayre.'

'I know what tha were thinking of, right enough.'

'Tha's kept me happy.'

She looked up at him, her face relaxing into a smile more tender than he had seen in a long time. 'That's what matters to you, Mark, isn't it?' she said. 'To be happy! If you could but know the number of times I've envied you that. It isn't in my nature to be happy, and I envy those who can be.'

'What *is* in thy nature, lass?' he asked, matching her tone of voice.

'To strive always to seek to advantage us all. It's simple as that,' she said. 'I can never be content, can never lie happy abed without asking myself what I could have done that I haven't, to improve our situation. I don't want my boys working in a foundry, Mark.' He heard the note of desperation in her voice.

'Nay, Dodie, there's nowt wrong wi' a foundry. 'Tis good honest work.'

'It's heavy work, Mark, and hot. How many times have you come home without the strength to drag yourself to table. How many times have you been running with . . .'

'Nay Dodie,' he pleaded. 'Not today. Us is having a Feast Day today.'

The boys had all been washed by Eleanor and dressed ready for bed, though Walter, at nine, didn't see why he should have to go to his room with the others, when Gertrude came to the cottage in the stableyard to say good-night to them.

'Now, you must all behave well,' she said, 'since the Captain and Mrs Edgecombe are having a party tonight and I shall be busy. If any noise comes from your bedroom, Eleanor has my instructions to come upstairs with a switch in her hands, and your father will see some red bottoms if his ship docks in the morn!'

'Do you think Dad will dock tomorrow?' six-year-old Daniel asked. His dad always brought wonderful presents from foreign parts and had lots of tales to tell of what he'd seen and done. Daniel had already decided he'd be a sailor like his dad when he grew up.

Reuben's face was wrinkled with thought. At eight, he was always full of questions. 'How is it, Mam, that the packet can get here quicker than Dad can? It's not such a big boat, nor carries as much sail, as Dad's boat.'

'Aye, and doesn't carry as much cargo,' Gertrude said, hoping that was the right answer or at least that it would satisfy him. 'You must write your question on the board and ask your dad.'

Luke had made a piece of board for them and had painted it with black so that it was dull. The lads would chalk their questions on it, ready for answers when Luke Fossett came back into port. Most of the questions, she had to admit, came from her second born, Reuben. Walter, the oldest, was a placid lad who rarely asked anything except why he should go to bed at the same time as his brothers since he was older and already onto his second book in arithmetic at school.

As Gertrude tucked her sons in she thought once again about the goodness of her benefactors, Captain and Mrs Edgecombe. Now that she was secure in her position of housekeeper and handled everything for them with an easy efficiency, they had permitted the new girl Eleanor to include the cottage in her duties, with no deduction of Gertrude's wages. Thus Gertrude was able to make a life for her boys and keep a home for Luke when he returned from sea, as he did almost every six months. When the boys had come of schooling age, Captain Edgecombe, who had been put on the Board of Governors of the local Charity School, had obtained positions for each one of them free of all charges. They were even given books from which to work though the books had to be returned. There was a Lending Library now in Whitby, and Gertrude sometimes went along to the wonderfully exciting room where the books were kept and borrowed one. She had tried to read the novels of Henry Fielding but had not known sufficient free time to make much headway in the massive volumes, which could only be loaned for a short period.

Luke always spent much time there when he was ashore since each voyage brought him nearer to his mate's ticket. Now he was studying the stars and the way in which a man may find his way by knowing them. It always seemed a miracle when they lay abed and he pointed through the window of clear glass, telling her the north by looking at a star. But then all such things, even the motion of a lodestone, was a miracle to her, and the thought that men could move across the vast ocean like flies on a counterpane and still know which way they went the greatest miracle of all.

Whitby was such a wonderful place to live, she thought. So clean and prosperous. She'd returned from Leeds still horrified at the squalor that had driven her away the first time with its stench of crowds. She'd told her brothers and sister of the great opportunities for work that Whitby afforded, but she had not been able to arouse any of them to move again. It was as if they were afraid they'd go from one bad situation to another and no longer had the courage to essay something new. Dodie had been the most interested, but even she had lost interest when Mark Ottershaw had said he wouldn't move from the foundry where he was so contented. Her blood quickened at the thought of Luke's return; Mrs Edgecombe always permitted her a day off when he arrived, and they usually went to the cottage in Robin Hood's Bay, leaving the children in the adequate care of Cook and Eleanor. Cook, in particular, doted on Gertrude's children and never missed an opportunity to spoil them with a sweetmeat or a piece of cake bought from the new baker. Gertrude had the daring idea that perhaps, when Luke obtained his Master's Ticket and was permitted to take cargo shares, they'd venture the money Gertrude had slowly put by over the years, in the hope of gaining sufficient to buy one of the cottages in the tiny village she so adored, since she and Luke had always been together there, always happy. Much would depend on the venture, for some were successful, some were not, and she trembled at the thought of perhaps losing her savings. When the time came she knew that Captain Edgecombe, if God spared him, would advise her.

The Edgecombes' son, Maurice, was now living in Whitby at the completion of his education. He'd taken a house for himself near the boat-building yard his father had bought for him, and the story went that he was proving quite successful in the enterprise. How wonderful, Gertrude thought, to be able to set one's son up in such a way, with a house and servants, his own carriage, his own business and money in the bank with which to finance it. No doubt Maurice would soon be looking for a wife. He'd better hurry. Captain Edgecombe seemed to grow older with each passing year, more stiff in the leg and arm, more irascible with wrongdoers. The boys had told her that the teacher in the school walked in great fear of him, since the Captain examined the boys from time to time and heaped scorn on the master for any failure of his pupils to know their arithmetic or their English verbs.

The dinner that evening was to be a most splendid affair and she was anxious to get the boys away to bed betimes. She hastened back into the house, to which a whole new wing in stone had recently been added, providing a most elegant, or so she thought, dining-room, with more rooms for more servants in the attics above. Now she commanded a staff of seven, and Enoch Farthingale, now promoted to Steward and permitted to wear plain clothes, ruled over five footmen, a coachman, two stable boys and a yard man ostler, who, alas, was not proving satisfactory since he drank heavily, and would have to be discharged. Gertrude and Enoch got on very well together since each greatly respected the other's position and ruled their domains with efficient authority. Even Cook now had a helper since she was growing old and not so nimble or agile. She no longer had the strength to get the great roasts of beef and lamb into and out of the hot ovens and several times had burned her arms quite badly on the hot drippings. Now she had a strapping lass from Danby to help her. Sally, from a farm, had an outdoors naturalness about her. Gertrude had become so sophisticated she hadn't even protested when she'd learned from Cook, who seemed to be first with all the backstairs scandals, that Sally could, and was, simultaneously keeping three of the footmen from straying by obliging each in turn.

Gertrude could remember the time before her marriage when she would have been greatly concerned to hear such a thing; now her only feelings were ones of relief that none of the men would be bringing in some dreadful disease, as prevalent in Whitby as in other ports-of-call. They said the doctors were constantly attending to people with all manner of oriental plagues and pests, brought back from voyages to the Far East and South America. There'd been an outbreak of cholera up the hill in the poor cottages, for which a recently returned sailor had been blamed and stoned to death in anger even though the doctor had said the man himself wasn't suffering from the disease. The Town Council had ordered the cottages burned to the ground and were, even now, building new ones up there for sale to speculators who'd rent them out.

She went into the dining-room to inspect that everything was ready and in order. The setting of the table depended on her and her staff; the service was the province of Mr Farthingale and the footmen. She checked the cleaning of the elaborate silver salt that was set two-thirds of the way up the long mahogany board, recently made from wood brought specially from the West Indies. How it did shine! She must remember to compliment the girls both on the salt and the table itself. She checked each of the crystal glasses

338

from the Continent. Each had been hand worked and shone with the lead that was in it. The candles had already been lighted to permit them to start to burn; they would be snuffed and only lighted again when the guests arrived. The candles themselves cost a king's ransom since they were beeswax and gave no smoke or smell, as mutton-fat candles did. The sideboards carried an array of plates and eating utensils all made of solid silver in one of the new factories at Sheffield. Enoch Farthingale, who'd travelled there with two footmen and the day coach to bring the large boxes under protection of four outriders, had told her of the many men sitting at their grinding wheels and benches, fashioning the silver into the most beautiful table-ware imaginable, buffing it on wheels, rubbing it with paste to bring up the final shine. The stillroom now contained a large vat of fine clay used solely to polish the silverware to maintain its original gloss, though the girls complained the clay drew their hands. Gertrude never told anyone, but before Luke came home from one of his voyages it was her habit to go secretly into the stillroom and massage her hands in the clay, to make them more smooth, more delicate to the touch. It was a vanity of which she spoke to no-one.

One of the mirrors on the wall had not been shone properly; she called one of the girls to do it immediately. One of the candles had been set in its sconce on an angle and would burn unevenly, possibly dripping onto a guest's wig; she called for a stool and had one of the girls climb up to straighten it. One of the footmen preparing his serving position took the opportunity to gaze openly at the girl's ankle as she reached up for the candle, and Gertrude drove him from the room, determined to report his boldness to Mr Farthingale, though she wouldn't go so far as to ask that he be docked a coin for his breach of discipline.

James and Lemuel, the two oldest footmen, were positioned in the front hall for the arrival of the guests. It was a cold night with a gusting wind and Gertrude's last personal thought was that perhaps Luke's boat might be delayed if the Captain deemed it too dangerous to try to cross the Whitby bar on the morn. After that she had no time for personal thoughts as she supervised the girls walking sedately among the guests with trays of sweetmeats and glasses of liqueur or cordial, to warm them against the cold October night. The footmen opened wide the door each time they heard the doorboy's quick knock, in time to permit the newly arriving guests to enter without check. Most wore heavy cloaks which they gave to the footmen who placed them in the cloaks room, an innovation of Mrs Edgecombe's on the corner at the end of the hall. A log fire burned in the vast grate in the hall; it sent its warm air up the staircase which had been incorporated into the new wing, lined with marble from Carrara in Italy, they said, and snowy white in colour, with merely a few flecks of pink or green or blue. The balustrade was of carved wood with gold-leaf-covered cherubs holding sprays of flowers as the supporting rails. They did say that Captain Edgecombe had spent a thousand pounds on the staircase alone but no-one denied its beauty.

The guests were greeted at the top of the staircase, in a small lobby where the Captain and Mrs Edgecombe stood to receive them. The Captain looked very dapper in his suit of black silk with yellow breeches, white stockings and yellow kid shoes; Mrs Edgecombe, grown even larger and more florid in her complexion with the years, stood in a dark green silk gown with a pinched waist and a figured bodice worked with gold and silver threads and pearls. She'd given up wearing any sort of hoop or bustle; nature had so generously endowed her that the skirt stood full from her hips without artifice. She wore no wig over her hair, which had been braided and dressed in an elegant circle around her forehead. On the top of her head she wore a flat headdress of white cambric edged with pretty lace, on which tiny flowers had been raised in the most delicate crotchet. Mrs Edgecombe didn't enjoy the modern fashion for spending so much time with the hairdressers;

she had her hair treated by her own maid, curled and braided, plaited and stitched into position by delicate threads; except when they entertained such a treatment would last her several days, even weeks, until the itch caused her to unwind it and have it washed and powdered.

The guests continued to arrive in all their splendour; the Mayor of Whitby arrived with his lady and several of the Aldermen; the glitter of their apparel completely outshone that of the Lord Lieutenant of the County, who wore a simple suit of the best violet satin in a tint difficult to achieve by dyeing. He was gracious and affable as befitted his superior station; he'd known Edgecombe for years and thought him the best kind of burgher, a rich man with a deep sense of charity and an interest in the welfare of the city of Whitby, though with no ambition to secure high office for himself, unlike the upstart Mayor and the majority of the Aldermen who were concerned only to secure and maintain their own privileged positions. Something would have to be done, he thought as he looked up the stair at his host, to secure some sort of title for Edgecombe.

It was no part of Gertrude's duty to serve the guests; she was interested only in supervising the activities of the girls as they came and went from the kitchen to the rooms in which the glittering crowd was congregated. Most of the people would not stay long; only a special core of them would be invited to take places at the table for the supper; the many invited to the mêlée would note the atmosphere and leave strictly on time, such was social protocol. That didn't prevent many of them casting envious glances through the rooms, hoping that one day they would attain the rank and station to be asked to sit with the Lord Lieutenant of the County. The jewellery, the hair styles, the elaborate and costly gowns and suits would provide conversation for many days to come; they'd have to make do with that, and with being able to say they'd been invited to the house.

'Come, stand beside me,' Mrs Edgecombe asked

341

Gertrude when finally all the guests had been received and she could flop into a chair with a gaggle of ladies around her. It was Mrs Edgecombe's custom to hold Gertrude by her side, attending to her wishes with a competence none of the girls had ever achieved. Mrs Edgecombe liked to take tea infusions on those occasions, though it was not altogether socially correct. Any form of alcohol – and more and more different kinds were being consumed on these social occasions from rum and brandy to elaborate liqueurs and distillations – made her damp, she'd once confided to Gertrude. A fat lady, she had problems with sweating and needed to use much powder on her underwear to keep down the odour. Gertrude had already noticed that Mrs Edgecombe was particularly pungent that evening – it must be to do with the excitement of such a grand occasion, she reasoned.

She was standing by Mrs Edgecombe when a portly figure passed by, stopped, and turned back. He held out a podgy hand to Mrs Edgecombe and she touched it briefly.

'Salutations, my dear Mistress Edgecombe,' he said. 'What a wonderful salon you have assembled for our delight. I quite vow you have outdone the splendours of London.'

Mrs Edgecombe flushed. 'Nay, Lord Barthwick,' she said, confused by the effusiveness of his compliment, 'we are but simple rural folk.'

Gertrude flushed when she heard the name, remembering the last time she'd seen his Lordship. Then he'd been a narrow-shouldered, thin-faced fellow with a mean expression that made him look incapable of a smile; now his fat face was wreathed in delight and his small eyes, set too close together for her taste, glittered as if he'd taken a touch of laudanum, which some people used in small amounts as a stimulating infusion. His bulk and weight must have increased three-fold since she'd last seen him; now the great hams of his legs were so fat he could hardly waddle along without swaying the lower part of his body to permit his thighs to pass each other on the stride.

342

'And this,' he said, offering his hand to Gertrude, 'must be your elegant daughter . . .?'

In truth the clothing Gertrude wore at the instigation of her mistress would have passed as elegant in any society, and simple. She'd protested when Mrs Edgecombe had specifically ordered the material for her; it was of the best quality, with a skirt that fell delicately over her hips, and two cross bands across her adequate bosom. Her hair was done in a style similar to that of her mistress and she wore a cap that had been made by the same seamstresses who'd confected Mrs Edgecombe's own, though the crotcheted flowers were not quite so numerous, nor so varied in their tints.

She saw Mrs Edgecombe looking up at her, bewildered by Lord Barthwick's remark.

'My daughter . . .?'

'I have the honour, Lord Barthwick,' Gertrude said distinctly, 'to occupy the position of *housekeeper* to Mrs Edgecombe.'

'Yes, Mrs Fossett is my housekeeper,' Mrs Edgecombe said.

'Dammit, one can hardly distinguish between mistress and maid these days,' Barthwick said, thoroughly ill-humoured at his error. 'I do declare you spoil your servant, ma'am, to trick her out so when humble stuffs would the more fit her station.'

He turned on his heels and waddled away. Mrs Edgecombe sighed as she watched him go, his petulance evidenced in every stride. 'Oh, my dear Mrs Fossett,' she said, 'I greatly fear we have offended his Lordship!'

'Perhaps I should retire below stairs, ma'am, and change my costume . . .?'

'You'll do no such thing! I'll not have my household upset by yon mountebank, even though he does strut in his uncle's ermine. I cannot think why he was ever invited here; the Captain must be quite bereft of his senses.'

She could not know that Lord Barthwick had not been invited, but had invited himself. He had come with two intentions in mind. Firstly and of vital concern, he wished to engage in the lucrative trade of taking shares, since his stewardship of the Barthwick Estates seemed to be yielding him but little income. After the enclosure he'd found it impossible to get men of character to work for him. Most of the former strip-holders had either left the land or had bought the strips of others, combining them and building stone dwellings to occupy their own land in their own way without the payment of tithe. Those he could employ were either itinerants who robbed him of his coin without working to provide profit for him, or inefficient Irishmen who knew little of the new husbandry. Many of his cattle had taken sick of the diseases of neglect and had died; his crops were not adequately weeded and stifled under the growths that had been provoked by the deeper tilling which disturbed long-dormant seeds. More and more he'd begun to realize that the ownership of land, the working of an estate, is a vocation bred in the blood; his branch of the Barthwick family had centred on London for many a year; he knew nothing of rural rhythms and methods and could not therefore check the inadequacies and inefficiencies of those he employed. Dammit, even his coach horses had been allowed to go lame for want, or so he'd been mockingly informed by an arrogant Sam Weighton, of a hot bread-and-mustard poultice and a bit of elbow grease. He further revealed his ignorance by asking from which beast he should procure elbow grease, only to be laughingly informed that elbow grease came from humans, and was the rural name for hard work!

His second reason for coming to the Edgecombes' had been his conversation with Percival D'Arcy, who'd passed on the intelligence he'd learned from Arthur Aysgill that one of Peter's relatives, Gertrude, was employed in a fine house here. He meant to make discreet enquiries in the morn to find out where, another fact in the dossier he was compiling against Peter Aysgill, to use in his revenge for the snub at the home of Lord Newsam.

He was walking along the reception gallery after dinner

when he almost collided with the housekeeper, who had emerged from a door in the gallery. He'd been stalking along with his head down listening to Maurice Edgecombe talking about the merchant trade from Whitby, whetting his appetite to invest in such a lucrative trade if only he could find an opening. Mrs Fossett stepped hurriedly back but couldn't prevent her hand brushing against his side. 'Dammit, wench,' he said, 'are you so impertinent as well as insolent ye must strike your mistress's guests as they pass you by? Give room to your betters, you trollop, or I'll take a birch to thee, I'll be bound.'

'Nay, my Lord, 'twas but an accident for which I apologise,' Gertrude said spontaneously.

He stopped still, quivering with rage. 'Ye dare to speak to me!' he demanded. 'Ye *dare* to *speak* to *me*? What is this man Fossett, that he permits his doxy tart to essay an argument with her superiors. Wert thou born and bred in a gutter, then?'

Once started, with her temper roused, Gertrude was not to be stopped. Service with the Edgecombes had taught her nothing of lick-spittling cowardice. She'd learned to carry out her duties with humility and obedience, but not to accept humiliation and insult. 'No sir,' she said. 'I was born in no gutter but in the village where your uncle, God rest his soul, maintained an orderly house. I fear the same cannot be said since his passing. I am an Aysgill, my Lord. An Aysgill of Barthwick born and bred. Would that you, sir, could say the same thing!'

He reached out his arm and held Maurice Edgecombe's. The small knot of guests had of necessity paused in the corridor and all had heard her words. 'Is that the tone of your rural entertainment, Edgecombe? Is that what a gentleman is to expect beneath your roof – to be insulted and berated by serving wenches. I'll warrant your Whitby styles are little to my taste, *Mister* Edgecombe. I'll be obliged if ye'll tell this chit to pack her bags and leave the house at once. I'll have an apology and satisfaction for this tart's insolence.'

'Go to your cottage at once, Mrs Fossett,' Maurice Edgecombe said with severity. 'I shall speak with your mistress immediately.'

Gertrude bobbed a curtsy to him and, ignoring Lord Barthwick, she returned through the corridor door from which she'd emerged. She fled down to the kitchen and already her anger had left her. In fear, and trembling throughout her body, she went into the kitchen and found Cook sitting at the large table with her assistant, eating a breast of pheasant. 'Oh Cook,' Gertrude said, the tears springing to her eyes, 'I fear I have ruined everything and will doubtless be sent away in disgrace this very night.'

Cook looked up. 'Nay, Gertrude, compose thyself,' she said. 'Come and sit down, and take a bite to eat while you tell me all about it. Sal, give your place to Mrs Fossett and take yourself out of here. You've already eaten enough to keep a horse flying from here to Scarborough!'

The tears ran unchecked down Gertrude's face as she told of the brief encounter, the terrible words that his Lordship had used on her, the way he'd insulted her beloved husband. 'It was when he mentioned dear Luke Fossett's name that I was obliged to speak out,' she said. 'I could have borne all he said of me, but to speak thus of my beloved Luke . . .'

Cook didn't know what to say and scratched her scalp beneath her thinning hair with the pheasant bone she'd picked clean while Gertrude had been speaking.

'You have seriously offended him,' she said. 'Of course, having mistaken you for Mrs Edgecombe's daughter and thus making a fool of himself will not have put him in good countenance,' she said wisely. 'Any further offence would be aggravated in his eyes. I greatly fear the Captain will be obliged to accede to his request and discharge you.'

'Where shall I go?' Gertrude wailed. 'Where shall I take my bairns?'

It was, in truth, the end of her world for Gertrude. She'd be obliged to take her sons from school; she and Luke would lose their home; she'd be disgraced and no-one

346

would employ her; she'd be obliged to go on the streets when her mites began to starve – these gloomy scenes passed through her mind like the scenes at the Whitby Playhouse in a dramatization that outshone even Mister Garrick and the best of his London company. She was still sitting at Cook's table when the door opened and the florid figure of Mrs Edgecombe herself stood panting there.

'Mrs Fossett!' she cried. 'Is this how you repay my years of kindness to you, by obliging me to descend these stairs in search of you? Where is my tea? My guests are gone and the girls are standing idly chattering in corners, while you sit here in the kitchen talking with Cook as if today were a holiday. I'll be obliged if you'd stir yourself *at once*, and bring my tea to me in my sitting room.'

Gertrude was speechless for a moment, while the door closed and Mrs Edgecombe went back up the steep stairs.

'That's the first time she's poked her nose in my kitchen this many a year,' Cook said. 'You must in truth have provoked her, Mistress Fossett!'

'She cannot have heard,' Gertrude said, finding her breath again. 'She cannot know what has happened, how disgracefully I have behaved, what dishonour I have brought on her house!'

Cook's eyes twinkled. 'She knows right well,' she said. 'Coming down here was her way of saying, take no notice of the foolish haverings of the so-called gentry, but kindly get on with the job. Take her tea, Gertrude Fossett, and don't speak of the incident unless Madam herself introduces it! Then tell her, as you've told me, how greatly you were provoked.'

Gertrude had dabbed her face with flour to take away the redness of her tear-stained cheeks when she knocked on the door of Mrs Edgecombe's sitting-room. On the way she'd brought the girls from corners, had ordered them to stop gossiping and get on with clearing everything to leave the house in order for the morning. They'd all looked at her most curiously and at the tray of tea she carried, but none had dared speak to her. She heard Mrs Edgecombe's voice call, 'Come in, Mrs Fossett,' and entered. Her mistress had removed her evening wear and was now sitting comfortably in her nightdress with a flowing robe over it tied with ribbons.

'Lady Malton was telling me of a tea being brought from China,' she said conversationally. 'We must try to acquire some of it.'

'To be sure, Ma'am,' Gertrude said quietly. 'I'll enquire of the provisioner tomorrow.' She realized what she'd said and brought her hand to her mouth. She had no expectation of being in employ tomorrow!

Mrs Edgecombe, watching Gertrude, smiled hugely at her. 'I would have thought, Mrs Fossett, that these years in my service would, at least, have given you maturity. That's if your three delightful children hadn't. You're still the fearful slip of a lass who came to me from the stage coach, I'll be bound. Let the men huff and puff, Mrs Fossett, but I am not going to sacrifice my housekeeper to satisfy the whims of an overbloated churl, even though he has the title of a Lord. Lordly *is*, Mrs Fossett, as Lordly *does*. After you descended to the kitchen in such a flurry, Theresa dropped a plate of trifle on Lord Malton's shoulder when she was tripped by another of the guests somewhat the worse for rum. His Lordship, a *true* gentleman, merely called for a cloth to brush the offence from his suit, and chucked the startled lass under her chin, telling her to dry her eyes. You'll be obliged to listen to a sermon from the Captain, I'll be bound, and my son will be snappy as a puppy for a day or two since he hasn't yet learned that a title is no more than a handle on a pot; it's what the pot holds that counts in this house, Mrs Fossett. And you'll do well to remember that. Now sit down by me, and take a cup of tea and a biscuit, for this day has been overlong for us both, especially as your man comes in tomorrow on the tide, God willing!'

The Newcomen Atmospheric Engine Jabez Broadley had installed before Matthew Aysgill first started to work in the mine was built into a brick tower near the top of the mine-shaft; its beam, thumping up and down every few seconds to draw water from the levels of the mine, had provided a continuous rhythm that symbolised the mine itself to all who worked there. Job Bentley had been re-employed when he was fit for work but couldn't descend to the lower level without spells of dizziness that threatened constantly to plunge him from the ladder, a danger to all the other men descending below him who would have been swept away in his fall. He worked now in the engine house, shovelling coal into the great maw of the furnace that fired the Newcomen boiler, and the heat seemed to agree with his damaged stomach and kidneys. His spirit had been broken and he could no longer bear to be with other people; in the intervals when he was not working he curled up on the coal heap with his knees drawn up to his chest; many evenings, they knew, he would stay there all night and not return to his home. Between firing the furnace he would laboriously climb to the trunnions of the beam to grease them, or check the workings of the valves on which the flow of steam and cold water to condense it depended. Though the cylinder had been worked with hand abrasives inside to try to achieve smoothness in the barrel it still permitted steam to escape with each downwards stroke past the leather ring of the piston head, fraying the leather all too frequently. Gradually the suction would fail, less water would be drawn from the mine and the coal-face workers would find it swirling round their ankles.

In desperation, Jabez would order the engine to work all night, and Job, reluctant to permit any other to handle his beloved engine, would live there, sleeping fitfully beside the fire bed on a palliasse of straw to keep the fire stoked.

The times came when the engine could no longer draw the water out even when worked all day and all night. Eventually, and most reluctantly, Jabez would order it to be stopped, the fire to be damped, and the leather ring changed. Each time he went into the cylinder, Job would examine the sides of the brass lining, seeing which parts

349

were scraped clean by the leather ring and which were permitting steam to pass by. Each time he'd abraid the lining with a cloth covered in fine chippings to try to make it more smooth and more circular so that the steam could not escape past it – if he could have spent a hundred years doing nothing but that he would ultimately have achieved his ambition of a straight smooth six-foot cylinder with perfectly parallel sides forty-two inches apart.

Job Bentley didn't have a hundred years to live; his injuries had left him only six lonely and painful months.

'Nay, Dad, they can't expect us to work knee-deep in water!' Matthew's oldest son Frank said. They had started on the lower level by the pillar-and-stall method, cutting the coal immediately before the mine shaft at right angles, leaving columns of uncut coal to hold the roof each four paces. Gradually they were advancing away from the shaft in a stall, cutting behind the prop at each four paces; other teams were advancing parallel with them. Though they had mutton fat lanthorns, most of the time they worked in semi-darkness, straining their eyes to separate the coal from the hard flint stones on which their hammers and chisels would ring, sending a shock up a man's arm that could numb his shoulder. Mostly the coal would drop away in lumps big enough to be carried away from the face – a task each did in turn, but when they'd encounter a stone they'd have to chase around it to remove it. Some of the stones were large boulders they couldn't break, extending deep into the pillar. To remove them would weaken the support of the roof, and could bring the mine crashing in on them. All they could do was to use some of the stone they'd brought out to build an emergency wall to take the place of the huge boulder, which must then be dragged out of the way of their digging. Sometimes if the boulder was too large they would be obliged to chip it where it stood, to crack it with wedges hammered in and wet to swell. All of this was time-consuming and reduced their output considerably, so that, even though Jabez Broadley was paying double the amount per ton, they were earning less since they had to do more work to get the coal. And that work was usually done in wet conditions, with their boots rotting on their feet.

'Aye, I reckon we had better ask Jabez to stop the pump again.'

Few of the men liked it when the pump was stopped. Even though it didn't work efficiently it was better than nothing and they could carry on earning.

Wilfred Oates heard what they said. 'Nay, Matthew,' he protested. 'Let him carry on a while wi' it.'

Matthew smacked the water with his shovel in frustration. 'If you lot would only listen to me,' he said, 'we could approach the Master again and get him to install a new barrel in that damned pump; then we'd be working in the dry instead of this slop.' From where he was working, Matthew could see into several other stalls. 'Let us approach Broadley again,' he said, 'and get a new barrel for the pump. They're making them now of cast iron, a lot smoother than the old brass ones.'

'Jabez will never thole the four hundred pounds for a new barrel,' Elias Brown protested, 'and we'll happen all lose our jobs this time. You've seen them standing at the mine gate hoping to be set on!'

It was true. Every day now a small knot of men, women and children gathered by the mine gate, hoping to catch the eye of the Master. Jabez encouraged them and would occasionally give one of them a job to do for a day or two at the higher wage the face men commanded; an astute man, he was completely aware of the effect of that knot of hungry folks at the gate on his existing workforce. There had been a flood of people into Leeds in the latter part of 1759, when many crops failed. In other rural communities the new methods of Jethro Tull were working so well that landowners could achieve much better crops using far fewer workmen; any they didn't need they threw out of their cottages and the general unemployment in the country districts was flooding the towns.

Jabez Broadley recently had set on a number of women

and children. He'd realized they were far more nimble than men at many of the necessary jobs and, since they were smaller, the tunnels along which they crawled could be cut smaller. Galleries leading to and from the productive coal faces could be considerably reduced if men didn't have to pass by them frequently – a man could crawl along to get to his work space at the coal face; when he'd picked out the coal, it could be loaded into skips and the journey back to the bottom of the mine shaft made by a woman crawling, dragging a wheeled trolley behind her. Children were more nimble, too, at climbing the ladder. In addition to the horse-driven engine that pulled the tubs of coal to the surface and dropped the empty tubs back, he now had a team of boys climbing the ladder with knapsacks on their backs in which the small coal was packed. He'd installed a double ladder, so that the amount of coal actually removed from the mine was greatly increased as the boys climbed up one ladder and back down the other in a continuous human moving cycle. These boys were paid by the number of knapsacks they carried, multiplied by the amount of coal in the knapsacks, since, in the early days, boys had been scampering up half empty. Now each of them was careful to take a full load each time.

The heat down the mine was terrible, and most people, even the women, stripped down to a chemise or vest to cover their chests; Matthew knew that the heat could be reduced enormously if only the down-draught and up-draught were improved. And that meant improving the quality and efficiency of the mine-top engines.

'We don't have to approach him *too* strongly,' Matthew said. 'Just talk sensibly to him so that he can understand our problems.'

'Tha's always rabbiting on, Matthew,' Elias Brown said in contempt. 'I' truth, I think tha'd be better in't pulpit than tha is down a mine, interrupting the work. Now, shut thy gob, and let's get on wi't work.'

'Tha shan't talk to my dad like that,' Matthew's second son, Richard, said hotly. 'He's only trying to do what's best for all of us.'

'I mean no offence, lad,' Elias said as he threw his arm round Richard's shoulder. 'I know thy dad's a good heart, but we mun get ahead and earn our coin, and we can't do that while we're standing around gabbing, can we?'

He took his hammer and chisel and went back to attacking the coal face in the centre of his stall. He'd seen Wilfred Oates listening avidly to what they were saying, and didn't want to be linked with Matthew in one of the reports he knew Wilfred had started making to Jabez Broadley in his new job of coal-face overseer.

Matthew looked about him, dispirited by everything he saw. He knew the conditions in the mine were abominable but none save he would speak out against them, and his words echoed back and mocked him. Man is not intended to live like a beast, he told himself. No man has a right to imprison the spirit of another, to buy him with coin and, as in the case of Wilfred Oates, with flattery and promotion. Half the men, he knew, including his own son Richard, were suffering the effects of standing constantly in dirty water and were developing sores on their feet which would never heal. Many of the women, crawling continually along the rough passages, were developing sores on their elbows and, presumably, on their knees.

Ellie Frost had fainted the other day and had been discovered five minutes later lying face down in the dirty water, drowned.

Young Michael Tenterer, nine years old, had fallen off the top of the ladder in his hurry to race up with more and more coal, and crashed to his death at the upper level, thirty feet below.

'Nay, Dad,' Frank his older son said, 'let's get on wi' it, else we'll have nowt to take home.'

He turned to the coal face, held his chisel and Frank hit it smartly with his hammer, splitting out a chunk of the black glistening coal almost a foot cubic. 'Us'll never change 'em, Dad,' Frank said softly. 'Tha might just as weel talk to yon coal face!' His dust- and sweat-covered face cracked in a smile revealing lighter coloured wrinkles. 'But I know tha mun go on trying since it's in thy nature.'

Elias Brown had had a stroke of fortune. For the past week they had run a soft seam that didn't carry a single stone and had been forging ahead. Now their stall extended twenty feet or more into the face. The workers on each side, the Aysgills to the left and the Barfords to the right, had been working the stone fault running either side of the soft seam and for every ton of coal they cleared, they'd had to dig a couple of tons of rock and stone.

Now the water was visibly rising during each day shift, clearing only a few inches each night while Job Bentley ran the Newcomen continuously. Each time a hammer hit a chisel there was increased pressure of water, since many of the stones blocked underground springs which welled with each new stroke. The stone into which Matthew was cutting was flecked with what a fool might think was gold; he knew only that it must have contained excessive sulphur, since it stank of bad food every time he hit it and broke the elements. For Matthew, that was the way Hell would smell!

'I'm going to have a word with Wilfred,' he said. He walked along the mouths of the stalls to where Wilfred was working at the far end in a four-man stall. Wilfred's earnings didn't depend on the amount of coal they sifted since he was free to walk away and see what the others were doing at any time.

'Aye, Matthew, what does tha' want? Tha'll make no coins strolling about like a wandering fiddler.'

'*You're* beginning to sound more and more like Jabez Broadley every day,' Matthew said, avoiding the familiar, comradely, *tha*. 'When are you going to tell him about the water down here? When are you going to ask him about getting a new barrel for that old engine? Aye, and a pair of bigger bellows; that lot were designed for one level, not two.'

'It's not my job to tell the Master what to do,' Wilfred

said primly. 'It's my job to see you all keep working. You'll earn no coin and beget no profit for the Master if you keep the men talking all the time about your dreams, your odd notions.'

Matthew turned back, knowing it was a hopeless task to try to rekindle a spark of understanding that had gone out when Wilfred took the advantage of his overseer's position and the money that went with it. He started back down the cross cut and was looking at Frank and Richard, hammering the face of the stall they were working, when suddenly it happened. Frank was holding the chisel. Richard was striking its head with the hammer, having swung it from behind his shoulder in a pounding arc. The chisel bit in; the rock cracked; a gout of water came rushing from the length of the crack, sweeping Frank off his feet, bringing Richard to his knees. The water, spring clear, gushed from the opened rock, carrying the force of an underground cavern under pressure with it. Matthew saw the pillar hit by it and swept away by its force. 'Run, lads,' he screamed, 'run for it!'

Everybody turned and looked at him and then saw the water pressure pounding and swirling about their lower legs. Frank and Richard had managed to get back to their feet and were staring in dismay, not believing the evidence of their own eyes as the water poured out in a cataract that, they knew, would fill the lower levels of the mine.

'Run for it,' Matthew yelled, and the men needed no second bidding as they streamed along the cut stalls between the standing pillars. One by one, the pillars began to snap as the water undermined them. The miners ran, yelling to the others to flee. Matthew heard a scream behind him and turned; the two pillars at the entrance to Elias's lucky seam had gone down, and the roof had crashed down at that place. Matthew turned but couldn't fight his way back against that swirling water. He knew, anyway, that his task would be hopeless; with the roof down the water would already have poured into the deep stall Elias had made. He knew he must go back; it seemed a

355

challenge to everything they'd ever said about him – that he was a dreamer, that he was unpractical, that he cared more for notions than he did for men. He fought against the rush of the water to try to reach the roof fall behind which Elias must already have been drowned, but his legs wouldn't move; he could make no progress. He hardly felt the hands on his arms as his sons grabbed him, turned him, and dragged him down to the gallery along which the people were scrabbling on their hands and knees, keeping their heads out of the water that swirled past them as best they could. Most of the lanthorns had been doused by the gushing stream; the one or two set high in the rock of the tunnel still gave a little light; all knew that gallery by instinct since it was their only way in and out.

Water swirled at the other end of the gallery where the coal was piled ready for transport to the upper level. They were scrambling up the ladder as fast as they could go, water from those above cascading down on the heads of those waiting to start.

'Must be some kind of underground lake?' Wilfred Oates was saying by way of explanation.

'Up you go,' Matthew said to Frank, but the two lads pushed him forward.

'We know thee, Dad,' Richard hastily said, fighting back the others trying to get to the ladder. 'Tha'll stand back and let everybody else go first. Get on and let's be away!'

Now the women and the children were shouting, and the colliers were handing the kids over the heads of the crowd. Matthew grabbed one of them and set his feet on the ladder, his face burying itself into the skirts of the woman already standing there waiting to climb.

'Get thee started, Dad,' Richard said, seeing the gap behind the boy.

Matthew couldn't. He slipped down and would have left his position as next on the rungs if Frank and Richard hadn't crowded him, pressing his body against the boy's legs as he started to climb.

'Get . . . thee . . . on!' Frank said, reaching down and grabbing the back of Matthew's breeches unceremoniously, hoiking him upwards without dignity.

Matthew gripped the ladder, sighed, then slowly began to climb to the safety and fresh air above. Behind him he could hear the panic screams of the women and children who were trapped in the other stalls and couldn't get out along the mean galleries, past the bodies of people who'd already been deluged by the onrush of water. He couldn't bear to look down and back; but the shouting and the panic, the frightful screams were suddenly cut off when the water flooded the mouths of the screamers, as slowly he climbed to the daylight of the mine shaft entrance above.

'You and your damned penny-pinching,' he shouted at Jabez Broadley when he emerged. He knew he was being irrational and unreasonable; no engine known to man could have coped with that sudden onrush of water; the lower level would have been flooded no matter how strong the pump had been.

The people had all assembled at the top of the shaft, watching anxiously as their sons and wives came out, their husbands and fathers. Elias' wife had recently started in the mine with his two young boys, trundling the tubs along the galleries of the low level. Matthew saw her standing with her arms round the lads, holding them in a tight group, looking as far down the shaft as they could see hoping for the sight of their father.

'He worked beside thee,' Margery asked fearfully. 'Tha mun have seen him, Matthew . . .?'

He put his arms round her shoulders. 'He's gone, Margery,' he said. 'Your Elias has gone!'

Margery gulped and stared sightlessly into his face. 'Gone?' one of the lads asked. 'What does tha mean, gone?'

'He's gone, lad. Thy dad's gone.'

Matthew stumbled through the crowd, Frank and Richard by his side watching over him. He went as if to speak to Jabez Broadley, but then, convinced of the hopelessness of his cause, he turned away and stumbled

357

out of the mine gate. The lads knew there was nothing to be done that day. It would take several days and nights to pump that deluge of water from the lower level; they had no hope of recovering any bodies before then.

Mildred saw the tragedy in their eyes when they arrived home. 'What has happened to bring you all home this early?' she asked Frank, seeing from Matthew's vacant stare she'd hear no sense from him. Frank told her exactly what had occurred in the lower level and how Elias had been blocked in and must have drowned.

'That poor Margery,' Mildred said instantly. 'I mun go to her to see what's to be done for her and the bairns.'

When Mildred had left, Matthew looked at his two lads. 'It's going to be up to the pair of you to keep the house going now,' he said.

'Nay, Dad,' Richard said. 'Tha'll be all right in a day or two. Tha's had a bit of a shock but tha'll get o'er it!'

'I'm not going down the mine again,' Matthew said with a quiet determination. 'I can't work wi' men who won't understand that if only they'd pull together, they could change things for themselves.'

'Don't talk like that any more, Dad,' Frank said. 'Tha'rt only rubbing folks on't wrong side talking like that all the time. A man's born to where he is, and where he is, he stays!'

'Jamie hasn't stayed,' Matthew said quickly. 'Your uncle Peter hasn't stayed.'

'Them's exceptions,' Frank said. 'Say what you like, Dad, we're going back down yon mine as soon as it's opened up again. Me and Richard. If tha doesn't want to come, well, that's thy choice. Any road, what will tha do, if tha doesn't go down the mine? Tha remembers what happened to Uncle Simon when he had nowt to do and brooded until he walked hisself into't pond. Tha'll go the same road, I'll be bound,' if tha doesn't have something to occupy thy mind.'

'I shall have something,' Matthew said, his eyes blazing passionately. 'You remember Jonas Sotherby . . .'

'The preacher?'

'Yes. The man who follows Wesley. He wants me to work for the Methodists in these parts, preaching.'

'Tha knows what's likely to happen,' Frank said, worried that the experience in the mine had unhinged him.

'I don't care!' Matthew said passionately. 'I remember the words of John Wesley himself when he said, "I always look a mob in the face." That's what I mean to do. I intend to look evil in the face. If I cannot convince them in the mine, then I'll take to the fields to do it. Men can't be influenced when all the time, Satan is by their elbow offering them a coin, like that devil incarnate, Jabez Broadley. I'll catch them away from the mine, away from the Jabez Broadleys and the Reverend John Shiptons of this evil world. There, in God's open air, I'll be able to convince them that evil must be fought. I'll be able to give them the message of God's goodness to carry with them all the hours of their days, all the days of their lives!'

'The Grace of the Lord be with thee, Dad,' Frank said. 'Tha mun do as tha mun, I reckon. Me and Richard, we'll look after Mam, have no fear. Aye, and thee too, when tha comes home again, beaten by the mob.'

Percival D'Arcy had advised Peter Aysgill to start humbly by aiming for a small elective office in the City Government of Leeds.

'It will give you experience, my dear fellow,' he'd said, 'which you so badly need. It will teach you to speak in public, to address a crowd, to answer questions in a *diplomatic* way. It will also enhance your stature. I've no wish to decry your achievements, but being a successful merchant and manufacturer is not sufficient, unless you're going to be blatant and buy your way into London, for which none would respect you. Take your time for a year or two. Become an Alderman, then a Sheriff; then you can aim higher, perhaps even buy one of the two parliamentary seats if one becomes available. I have heard there is a strong move afoot in London to change the parliamentary system now that George III has acceded to the throne. It could well be that there will be many opportunities in the future for men who have a record of public service to offer.'

Peter had heeded Percival's advice and had decided to put himself forward as a possible Alderman for the ward in which he lived.

He was nervous as he dressed himself for the evening meeting, which would take place in the exclusive Philosophical Club, of which he hoped, with Percival D'Arcy's sponsorship, to become a member. 'First we'll let them hear you speak politically,' Percival had said, 'and then we'll get you elected a club member. When the Alderman election comes thereafter, the club members will vote for you, since it is their policy to sponsor their own.'

He dressed himself conservatively but richly, trusting that, as Percival had said, understatement is the mark of a true gentleman. His man Dobbs, whom Percival had recommended to him, surveyed his master with approval.

'You'll be the equal of any man there, Mister Aysgill, if I might make so bold,' he said.

'Thank you, Dobbs,' Peter said. He was trying to learn in all things, even in the matter of being kind to servants and underlings, which had always come difficult to him. Though he hadn't regretted doing it, he knew he would no longer have exacted such a severe revenge on Willerby, Mrs Lakeham and Jenny, as to have them transported for life. However, it was too late to go back on that transaction, and no-one could despise him for what had seemed to be an act of justified severity. If he'd wished to press the charge of theft more vigorously, he could have had them executed, he told himself, salving his conscience and quite forgetting that they had not committed the crime with which he'd had them charged. The crime of permitting his wife to have an adulterous relationship, even conniving at his cuckolding, had seemed to him more heinous than theft would have been.

'May I wish you all success this evening, master?' Dobbs

360

enquired politely. 'It will be an even greater privilege to serve an Alderman.'

'We mustn't anticipate matters,' Peter said with mock severity. 'The gentlemen of the Philosophical Club do not readily open their arms to strangers.'

The conversation with his servant pleased him. It seemed to show how much he was improving under Percival's tutelage if he could maintain such an easy informal conversation.

D'Arcy was waiting in the entrance to the Club when Peter Aysgill arrived from his carriage; he seemed more nervous than Aysgill himself as he waited for the Club servant to divest Aysgill of his outer cloak. He glanced over him quickly. 'You'll do,' he said. 'You've brought your speech?'

Aysgill smiled proudly. 'I've committed it to memory,' he said. 'That way, I'll not be seen to read from notes.'

'You're certain you have it, in full?'

'Every bit of it. The need for strong government. The need to end the war by an honourable peace. The need to control the House of Hanover through the Whigs. The need to take strong lines on the new social reform movements that are costing so much time and money. The need for Parliamentary Reform to increase the representation of the County of Yorkshire in Parliament.'

'Aye, you seem to have it right enough. You've a narrow line to steer between the Whig Party line with its reforming zeal, and the entrenched position of some of the Tories hereabouts. Above all, suggest you're a supporter of the status quo, that you're not a man itching to change everything. You're prepared for the questions?'

'I think so. You prepared me well.'

'Then good luck to you!'

The members of the Club had taken their places in the comfortable armchairs with which the Club Room was littered. The chairs were arranged in no order and Peter Aysgill was dismayed to find himself standing on a lower platform than he'd hoped, looking at the backs of the members' heads. Only a third of the men there seemed to be taking notice of him as he crossed to the lectern at the centre of the platform. The air was thick with tobacco and reeked of snuff and brandy. At the far end of the room stood a barrel of the new port wine that was proving popular with members; the servants hurried back and forth through the genteel hubbub, fetching glasses of it, offering pipes and jars of tobacco.

'My Lords, Squires, and gentlemen,' Peter Aysgill said into the void of indifference. 'I have been invited by the Committee to come here this evening to give you my views on one or two matters I believe to be pertinent in this year of 1760.'

He paused, hoping that when they heard him start the members would, at least, turn their chairs to look at him, or to permit him to see their faces. Not one of them deigned to move, or to end their present conversations. Peter plunged desperately on. 'In this day and age, when change is in the air we breathe, it behoves us all to give consideration to the direction in which we, our fair city, and the country, are going.'

'I've a notion to go to the gaming room,' Sir Arthur Colefax said loudly, heaving himself grunting to his feet with the aid of a couple of servants. Though Percival had warned him that some members would certainly walk out, Peter was none the less dismayed. He was not to know that Sir Arthur, a staunch Tory, never listened to *any* political dissertation unless it was one he happened to be making himself. Peter felt a strong impulse to call after him. 'Wait, wait, listen to what I have to say, damn you!' but Percival had warned him that in no circumstance must he appear to be addressing any member directly. He should strongly avoid catching anyone's eye, or speaking pointedly towards any group of special interest.

'. . . to determine where we are going,' he said, aiming his remarks at the lofty chandelier which lit the room with its guttering candles. 'We must make certain we have strength of purpose, and that means, strength in

362

government, either in the home, the City, or in Parliament itself . . .'

'I'll join you for the gaming, Sir Arthur,' Lord Wenling said, calling across the room, seeming oblivious of the voice of the man addressing them. Peter was vastly encouraged when a couple of the members who had been looking at him, called 'Sssshhh' in voices as loud as those of Sir Arthur and Lord Wenling. *Strength of government.* What was the next point? He felt his mind go blank. Ah yes, *End the war by an honourable peace!*

'But, you may ask, how can we have strength of purpose if our resources and our strength are being sapped by fighting a war in Europe?'

The steward of the Club was flustered when Lord Barthwick arrived, shepherding his charges. 'I'm afraid you cannot bring them in by this door, my Lord,' he said severely. 'You can't bring them in here!'

'Are you out of your mind, Barker?' his Lordship thundered. 'Who are you, man, to tell the Chairman of the Committee whom he may or may not bring into the Club?'

The steward looked despairingly at the ragged band his Lordship had brought with him to the Club premises. A boy with a hole in his breeches, supporting a lady wearing working clothing. A man dressed in some sort of shabby clerical black, with his wife and two young men, probably his sons, on whom the grime of the coal mine could still be seen, despite their having washed. A working woman and her husband, with two boys wearing the costume of the Charity School. A man, obviously a sailor, with his wife and three children, all neatly but poorly dressed.

'Come along, come along,' Lord Barthwick said. 'We don't want to miss matters, do we?'

Each of the Aysgills had been astounded when Lord Barthwick had personally called upon them in his carriage.

'I realize I was responsible for dividing the Aysgill family,' he'd said humbly. 'Now it is my great desire to make amends by bringing you all together. The occasion will be your dear brother Peter's speech to the

363

Philosophical Club. He wants you all to be there to hear him. Like me, he wishes to make amends . . .'

Of course, they couldn't refuse, especially, in Gertrude's case, when his Lordship sent a coach all the way to Whitby to carry her, Luke Fossett and the three boys across the moors, and had interceded with the Captain for her to be granted a few days' respite.

Dodie had accepted instantly. 'I've oft been past that Philosophical Club,' she'd said to Mark Ottershaw. 'I'd dearly love to set my foot inside.'

'I mun go as I am,' Mark had said. 'I'll not thoil a groat on clothes for the one occasion.'

Matthew believed, of course, that the repentance of Lord Barthwick and of Peter, their brother, was due to Divine intervention. 'The dear Lord has heard our prayers,' he'd said to Mildred in near ecstasy. 'He can't have,' Mildred replied, 'else that churl of a brother of yourn would be dead. And Barthwick wi' him!'

Arthur was thrilled beyond measure at the thought that they would go into the Philosophical Club. 'I've heard, Mam, as they have marvellous food i' there,' he said. 'Sew us a bag neath my jerkin, and I'll see what I can bring away.'

The door into the Club Room where Peter spoke was behind the platform and covered by a screen to keep out draughts. Lord Barthwick stationed the family behind the screen, where, as yet, none of the members could see them.

'I believe,' Peter was saying, 'that it behoves each of us to be charitable while maintaining a sense of fitness.' He'd dealt with each of his points successfully, and now had come to his peroration, in which he was trying to establish a unity with the Club members, as a man who truly belonged among them, by fitness of wealth and position. This part of his speech had occasioned the most difficulty in the composition. He had to show that he saw unity between the liberal Whigs and the entrenched Tories. That he saw the need for capital to be used to increase production and therefore profit. That the poor, the common people, could be used in all of this as a labour force, a work force, to whom one had to show charity, leniency, forgiveness, but no weakness.

'We must realize that man in all his infinite variation,' he said, 'must preserve his station in life, must recognize the fitness of the privilege with which God has endowed him, and use it to the best advantage of all mankind.'

He heard the commotion behind him but thought it was merely the gamers returning now that he was reaching the end of his speech. He paused a brief moment, but then, noticing the looks of horror on the faces of those who could see past him, he paused. What the devil was all that shuffling behind him? Dare he turn round? Should he continue, regardless?

He glanced across at Percival for guidance, saw that he had let his head bend down into his hands, as if in despair.

'The best advantage to mankind, sithee?' he heard a familiar voice behind him say. 'Did you use your *privilege* to the best advantage to save your own brother, who drowned himself in a pond when you refused him the charity of a coin, leaving his wife and this bairn to live as best they might?'

He recognized the whiplash in Lord Barthwick's voice, turned round, and saw the Aysgill family lined up behind him with Lord Barthwick by their side.

'Did you help your brother escape from the coal mine, my dear Aysgill,' Lord Barthwick said, 'so that he could go round the district preaching the devil's Methodism? Or your sister, in service in Whitby? Or your ragamuffin nephew Arthur here, who has just stuffed the poacher's bag he carries beneath his jerkin with vittles from the kitchen? Or your own true sister, who has suborned our schoolmaster into accepting her sons for education by what means we can only guess? Nay, gentlemen,' he said, addressing the whole room. 'I think we want no more of *Mister* Peter Aysgill, bringing his hypocrisies into our Philosophical Club!'

The growl of assent was unmistakable.

Matthew reached forward his arms. 'Aye, Peter,' he

said. 'Together again at last. How our dear father, and our departed brother Simon, would have loved to see this day.'

Peter stumbled from the platform, and went from the room with his family clustered about him, hearing the jeers of the gentlemen he left behind.

'You've ruined me,' he said brokenly. 'All of you, have ruined me!'

'Nay, Uncle, doan't thee worry,' Arthur said as he trotted beside him. 'I've got a smashing pheasant pie in my bag. I'll gladly share it wi' thee.'

They all gathered about him on the pavement outside, none of them knowing what to say to their brother, who stood in the centre of them in utter dejection.

'I curse the day God made me an Aysgill,' he said brokenly as he stumbled from among them and set off to walk blindly down the street, pushing aside the packmen, the beggars, the pot-boys, the citizens of Leeds thronging the thoroughfare.

There seemed nothing to say, nothing anyone could do. Mildred gathered the two children about her and set off along the pavement. Matthew followed along behind them, his unopened Bible clutched in his two hands, his lips too closely shut for prayer. Gertrude touched Luke's arm. 'We must make for the coaching inn,' she said, 'if we're to find a bed for the night and a seat on tomorrow's Flyer.'

Mark Ottershaw held Dodie's waist. 'How are the mighty fallen,' he said quietly. 'Come away, lass, come away home. There'll be nowt but mischief from this night's vengeance, and I mun work i' the morn.'

Arthur clutched his mam's woollen coat. 'It were right what I said,' he told her confidently. 'I've a pheasant pie i' my pocket as'll do us nicely.'

The groups moved from the front of the Philosophical Club, out of the light of the brilliant scene around the doorway as men of wealth and privilege sought the seclusion of its interior, into the cold bleak streets of Leeds where the common man held sway as he bustled vigorously

366

along bent on earning his coin by any possible enterprise.

The moon had come out and it glanced along the streets, the clear clean reflections it made from the dirty water's surface rippling when pack-horse feet trod sturdily into them, when carriage wheels sent them splashing in rainbow hues which instantly vanished again. The moonlight reflected from the tops of slate covered roofs, the edges of gables, its rays unifying the ant-like throng below.

The clouds parted; the night air was clear as wine, and free.

The bell above the Parish Church began its chime, booming notes scattering birds who had scratched restless shelter in niches beneath it. The birds rose, screeching protest, over a townscape beautified by moon-wash which, for the moment, concealed all evil, all tawdriness, all vice and sin.

When the clouds closed again, it started to snow.

Thus, the year of 1760 surrendered to the new year of 1761, the year in which, everyone told himself, the promises of the last year must surely, finally, come true.